An Unexpected Attraction— to a Beautiful Young Woman

They'd met Meg while waiting in line to board. She was young, no more than twenty-six or -seven, with cream-colored skin that looked as though it never felt the touch of makeup. Her smile was warm, her eyes shy. More comfortable behind a camera, Shawn thought. She was loaded down with her backpack, the tripod, a cumbersome metal case and a sky blue camera case identical to David's. David offered to carry the metal case for her in spite of his own heavy load, but she shook her head.

"I'm fine," she smiled. "I'm used to it." She headed for the back of the plane.

"Pretty," David said as he buckled his seat belt.

"What?" Shawn asked.

"Meg. She's very pretty."

She thought of telling him he was old enough to be Meg's father. She did some quick arithmetic in her head and decided that would be stretching the truth, though not by much.

"Yes, very," she said. . . .

Also by Diane Chamberlain

PRIVATE RELATIONS

LOVERS AND STRANGERS

DIANE CHAMBERLAIN

J

JOVE BOOKS, NEW YORK

LOVERS AND STRANGERS

A Jove Book / published by arrangement with
the author

PRINTING HISTORY
Jove edition / June 1990

ISBN: 0-515-10331-4

Jove Books are published by The Berkley Publishing Group,
200 Madison Avenue, New York, New York 10016.
The name ''JOVE'' and the ''J'' logo
are trademarks belonging to Jove Publications, Inc.

PRINTED IN THE UNITED STATES OF AMERICA

10 9 8 7 6 5 4 3 2 1

for my parents,
John and Nan Lopresti

· One ·

SHAWN HADN'T SEEN another car since turning off the freeway. Not that she expected to. It wasn't yet six in the morning, and Blue Snake Road was often deserted even in the middle of the afternoon. Still, there was something eerie about it—this silent drive through shadowy golden hills that already had a heat-battered look to them, although it was only June.

The sun was a ragged finger of light edging over the scruffy chaparral of Elephant Ridge. Any other day she would stop to watch it lift into the sky. She would take the time to scan the hills around her for coyote, even though she'd been rewarded for that eye-straining search on only a handful of occasions. But today she had no time. She might already be too late. That fear had kept her awake most of the night and filled the little sleep she had with nightmares. Dreams about Heather. She would not think about that now, would not allow thoughts of her daughter to fill her waking hours, when she should be able to control them.

The sun poured a crimson pool of light onto the hood of the Jeep as she approached the small sign next to the iron gate. *San Diego Canyon Conservation Center.* The sign gave no clue to the activity behind the double row of fences running along Blue Snake Road. Its simplicity was intended to discourage the curiosity of tourists, though it would be a rare tourist who traveled this far from the city. Shawn turned into the drive and reached in her purse for her passcard. She slipped it into the machine and listened to the familiar *click-click* as it read her code and spit the card back out to her. The gate opened and she pulled onto the road that curled for a mile through the hills, past the acres of zebras and antelope, past the enclosure of the maned wolves, who, she imagined, wondered why she wasn't stopping to scratch their noses through the fence today. She was aware of the stickiness of her palms against the steering wheel. She was aware, too, that she wanted Evan to be waiting for her at the Tamarin Building, but she wasn't surprised to find the staff parking lot empty.

From the parking lot she could look down the hill to the Tamarin Building—the Pentagon, as they called it—an ingenious five-sided stucco building that housed five different families of the diminutive monkeys and that allowed observation from outside as well as inside. The shape of the building would make it difficult for a fire to consume. To Shawn and Evan, that was its most important feature.

Shawn picked up the pocket-sized tape recorder from the seat beside her and started down the path to the Pentagon. It was cool this morning. She should have worn something more than shorts and a T-shirt, but she hadn't given much thought to clothes.

She heard the calls of the tamarins before she reached the bottom of the hill. Incredible that animals that small could pierce the morning with their voices. Everything else was still, except for the muted cries from the exotic bird enclosure, a quarter mile away.

She could see Tika now, a furry little patch of copper and gold stretched out on a rock in Enclosure One, and she knew the vet had been wrong when he said she might last the week. Tika was dying. Her mate and their children leaped to the wire to greet Shawn with their long, ear-splitting calls, but Tika barely lifted her head from the flat rock.

Shawn knelt down so that her face was inches from Tika's. Tika's breathing was slow and choppy. Her eyes were half-closed and she mewed like a kitten. Flash sat next to her on the rock, gently grooming her coppery mane and looking at Shawn, in his eyes the question: *Why aren't you doing something?*

Shawn stood up and looked at the other tamarins in Enclosure One. Lucy, Flash and Tika's adolescent daughter, leaped from branch to branch while her twin brother, Lance, groomed himself on the nest box. A second set of twins, week-old infants, huddled together on the sawdust-covered floor near the rock where their parents sat. They were beautiful animals. She remembered the first time she'd seen a Copper Elf Tamarin. Four year earlier, one of those electrically charged days when the Center received a new shipment of exotics. Evan led her to the quarantine building, which was alive with the sounds of birds and primates nervous in their new surroundings. Shawn felt the excitement in Evan's hand on her arm. He stood her in front of a small wire cage and pointed inside. The animal, no bigger than the hand Evan pointed with, looked like some remarkably hued rodent, and Shawn thought it odd that Evan was showing her a rat when they worked exclusively with primates. But then the animal turned around. Instead of the pointy snout of a rat, it had delicately human features, complete with the wisest eyes she'd ever seen in an animal. Its face was white, its arms gold, its head and back a shimmery copper. Shawn sank to her knees to get a closer look.

"Is it an adult?" she asked.

Evan nodded. "Yes. A female."

They named the little monkey Annie, starting a long line of alphabetized Copper Elf Tamarins. She had been delivered to them from Meseta, one of the two isolated regions of the Amazon basin where the Copper Elves could be found. The Elves were a newly discovered species, highly endangered and doomed to extinction unless they could be bred in captivity.

That task fell to Shawn and Evan and no one could argue with their success, even though they'd lost more babies than they would have liked—ten out of thirty-two. Tika would have been one of those early casualties if Shawn hadn't rescued her from Annie, who seemed overwhelmed at having produced triplets. Shawn hand-reared Tika—no easy task. She stayed with Tika around the clock, letting her crawl on her, cling to her, carefully feeding her drops of formula from the tip of a syringe. It was no wonder she felt such emptiness now as she watched Tika die. A touch of something she'd felt three years ago, when Heather died. David at her side then, the dutiful husband and father, holding her hand, not speaking. He never did speak about Heather. He never spoke about anything of importance at all.

She was making the right decision, divorcing David. She needed only to work out the logistics now, beginning with how to tell him. He would probably respond as he did to everything else in his life—calmly, with a stoicism and tolerance that had once attracted her but now left her cold.

In all fairness, he should have the house. The divorce was entirely her doing; it would never be his. He could go on this way forever, never noticing the void. But the boys needed the house more than David, and certainly she would have the boys.

Shawn slipped the strap of the recorder over her wrist and walked inside the Pentagon to get a folding stool. When she returned to Enclosure One, she found Evan standing in front of the cage. He was dressed in his usual jeans and sandals. His hair, damp from a shower, was cut short in front but brushed the collar of his blue workshirt in back. His coloring was identical to hers—nearly black hair and pale blue eyes. His beard looked freshly trimmed, clipped close to his face. That was the way he liked it, the way she used to do it for him. She wondered if Robin had trimmed it for him this morning.

He stood with his hands on his hips, on his face a look of dismay. "She's going fast." He spoke quietly.

She nodded, handed him the stool, and went back to get one for herself.

"How long have you been here?" he asked when she'd settled down next to him.

"Twenty minutes or so. I couldn't sleep."

"Anything interesting?" He tapped the recorder on her knee.

"I haven't recorded," she said guiltily.

"You're one hell of a researcher." His voice was light, but she caught the serious undertone. He wished she would be as careful as he was. The breeding program was important to her, but it was not her obsession.

He held the recorder to his lips and spoke softly. "Six thirty-five. Flash and Tika huddle on the flat rock in quadrant B; Flash grooms Tika; the babies approach and Flash bats them away." He pressed the pause button on the machine. "Looks like we'll have to hand-rear those two . . . God, I hope they're females." They hadn't been able to sex the babies yet. He spoke into the machine again. "Lucy and Lance huddle in the branches of quadrant A; Lance sniffs Lucy's back . . . Uh oh, look at that." He pointed to Lucy who was rubbing her chest over the branches of the leafless tree in the enclosure, marking them with her scent.

"Somehow she knows Tika's dying and she's next in line to reproduce," Shawn said.

Evan recorded. "Six thirty-eight. Lucy's in quadrant A, scent-marking everything in sight."

Evan stood and walked over to the cage to come eye-to-eye with Lucy. It was the first clue Shawn had that he was truly upset. He never interacted with the tamarins during an observation. Whether he was stewing over the professional loss of one of his animals or over the fact that it was Tika, she didn't know. It used to be that she wouldn't have to guess at his feelings. He would tell her. But they didn't talk that way anymore. Not about feelings. Not about anything so dangerously deep.

For a long time they had been each other's confidants. Best friends and, for the year after Heather died, lovers. Evan made up for what she missed in David. She could have continued that arrangement forever, but when Evan met Robin, his conscience got the better of him. Shawn understood. She made a pact with him that their relationship would be strictly business from that point on. She thought it would get easier in time, that the longing she felt for him would gradually fade away, but it had not. Every day she found herself wishing he would touch her or talk with her about something he felt, something a little more charged than vitamins for the Elves. But he'd cut her off emotionally as well as physically. He spoke to her only of work, kept her locked outside his thoughts. The real Evan was lost to her now. It was like working with his shadow.

Lucy leaped to the wire in front of Evan and trilled at him.

"What are you up to, little girl?" he asked her. Lucy reached her thin golden arm out through the wire and stretched her long fingers toward him. Evan touched her palm and let her circle the tip of his finger with her hand, but he pulled his finger away before she had a chance to bring it to her mouth with its tiny, razor-sharp canines.

He took his seat again. "Damn," he said. "I hate like hell to lose a three-year-old female."

"She always was my favorite."

He nodded. "You raised her."

It was more than that, and Evan knew it. It was the timing. Tika was born right after Heather died. Evan was in South America and Shawn had no recourse but to take care of the infant tamarin herself or let her die. It had been the best thing for her, really, to lose herself in keeping Tika alive.

Evan lifted the recorder and started to speak but turned at the sound of footsteps on the path behind him.

"It must be Sam." Shawn turned to see the white-haired keeper pushing a cart of food down the path from the kitchen.

"Pinkies this morning!" he called.

Shawn walked over to the end of the path and put her finger to her lips to quiet him. "Tika's dying, Sam," she said.

"No!" He looked from her over to the Pentagon and back again. "I thought the vet said . . ."

Shawn shook her head. "She started looking bad last night."

Sam rubbed his chin with his hand, the silver whiskers scraping like sandpaper against his fingers. "She turned down a cricket yesterday. I thought she was just lettin' her kids have it like she does sometime." He put his hands on his hips and looked toward the Pentagon. "Pity. And you can't afford to lose your ladies, now, can you? You want me just to leave this cart here for you, so I don't disturb your observin'?''

She nodded, looking down at the five trays of primate chow and colorful fruit. She turned away from the little bowl of slithering pink baby mice—a delicacy for the Elves. Usually they wouldn't bother her, but her stomach wasn't right today.

''I'm really sorry about Tika, honey.'' Sam reached out with one arm to hug her, and she imagined the smell of crickets and dead mice on his navy blue uniform. She pried herself gently from his grasp to take in some fresh air.

Evan clicked off the recorder when she returned to her seat. ''Pinkies, huh?'' he asked. ''You should have brought them over. I haven't had breakfast yet.''

''Evan, *please*, not today.''

He leaned forward, rubbing his eyes with the palms of his hands. ''I didn't sleep well either,'' he said. ''We were already short on females. With Tika gone, we're really in trouble.''

She pictured him the night before, slipping quietly out of bed so he didn't wake Robin, sitting in their den to work out the breeding schedule for the Elves. She imagined him up with the stud book the same time she woke up in a sweat, crying out, while David rolled away from her in the dark.

''I called Peru last night, after we got the vet's report,'' Evan said. It was a confession. He called without consulting her. ''I told them we don't have enough females to breed without inbreeding now. They said we could take two females and a breeding pair from the Dacu region if we trap them ourselves.''

She listened to the cadence of his words, the way he carefully measured each one. She felt his eyes on her while she watched Tika. He didn't know if she would respond with enthusiasm or trepidation, and she wasn't certain herself.

She took a deep breath. ''You're saying you want the two of us to go to Peru to trap . . .''

''With Robin and David,'' he added, too quickly. ''Robin says it's a good time to go, since Melissa's ten months old. She said that from eighteen to twenty-four months a separation would be traumatic for her but that now it should be okay.''

She took the recorder from him and turned it on with fingers that felt suddenly cold. ''Seven-oh-two. The babies withdraw from Tika and Flash and approach Lance in quadrant A.'' She clicked off the recorder and looked at Evan. ''How nice that Tika's death coincides so neatly with Melissa's developmental needs.''

Evan let out a soft whistle. "Do you want to take that back?" he asked.

She looked down at the recorder, ashamed of herself. She was always careful to speak of Robin and Melissa with respect, reverence almost. "It's not the right time for *me* to go away."

"I know you want to go."

Did she? If she could just wake up in the rain forest with no memory of the last time she attempted that journey, no memory of the phone call in Iquitos that ended her trip even before she set foot in the jungle.

"I'm still your supervisor," Evan said, smiling. "I can order you to go." Usually the idea of Evan being her supervisor made Shawn laugh. He'd worked at the Center for three years before her arrival and in the beginning she learned from him. But after seven years of working together, the supervisory position was purely one of title, and a thousand dollars more each year. Right now she was irritated by the inequality the title forced on her.

"The twins will be starting high school in September," she said weakly.

"So?" He raised his left eyebrow, a gesture she always found provocative.

"So it's a big deal to them and I want to help them get ready." This was the truth. Her sons seemed confused. They were a couple of years younger than their classmates because they started school early and skipped a year as well. Sometimes they still played with GI Joe dolls. At other times, more ominous, they snickered together over the raunchy lyrics of a new record or carried the phone into another room so they could speak to a friend without being overheard. They were slipping away from her.

"Shawn, I'm talking about a couple of measly weeks. We can leave the last week in July. The boys can live without you for a while."

Perhaps, but could she live without them? "Maybe they could go with us?" she suggested.

"It's not going to be a picnic."

She sighed. "They already have plans for the summer, anyway." The boys intended to spend the summer on the beach, ogling pubescent girls. The last place they'd want to find themselves was in the jungle with their parents and no radio.

"David told me he has a load of vacation time built up," said Evan.

If they went to Peru, she would have to put off telling David about the divorce. How could she tolerate living in close quarters with him for two long, hot weeks when what she really wanted was to be free of him? She couldn't explain that to Evan. She couldn't talk to Evan about the divorce at all. It would be breaking the pact.

She put her face close to the wire of the enclosure. "I don't think she's breathing," she said.

Tika lay very still and Flash stared at her in confusion. The babies moved forward, one of them hunting for a nipple and jumping back when it encountered its mother's unresponsive body.

"We'd better start feeding the babies by hand," she said.

Lucy brazenly approached her father. She sat down on the rock and began grooming him, her clever eyes concentrating hard as her long fingers combed through his mane.

"God, that little hussy!" said Evan. "We have to get her out of there before she gives Flash any ideas."

Flash sat with his little gold hands limp on his thighs while Lucy chattered above him. He looked like a very old man, not certain of his next move.

Evan stood up and put his hands in the pockets of his jeans. "I understand why you're nervous about Peru, Shawn," he said, his voice soft now, the voice that used to tell her he loved her. "But I think you're being a little superstitious."

She said nothing. She could hardly deny it.

Evan continued. "I guess if I went some place, into a store let's say, and I received some terrible news while I was there . . . I guess I'd be hesitant to go back to that store again."

She smiled at his attempted analogy. "Could we avoid Iquitos this time? Indulge my superstitious nature to that extent?"

"We can probably arrange that. Does that mean you'll go?"

She shook her head. "It means I'll think about it."

• Two •

SHAWN SPOTTED DAVID'S plane in the gray sky above her as she drove home from the Center. She turned on the car radio.

". . . and there's clear sailing on Interstate Fifteen," David said. She heard the muffled sound of the engine in the background. She pictured him behind the controls of the plane, the bulky headset on his light brown hair, his neck craned to see the traffic. But the angle of his neck would be the only sign of exertion. In all other ways his body would be as comfortable and loose as if he were lying in a hammock in their backyard.

"Visibility's better down there than it is up here today," David continued.

Years ago, before Heather died, Shawn painted the words *I LOVE YOU* in red on a piece of sheet and tied it to the roof rack of the Bronco she drove back then. If David spotted her, he'd say "I love you, too, Shawn," right in the middle of his broadcast. He could get away with it. He was well loved by the classical radio station that employed him as well as by the commuters.

She took the sign off her roof one evening after a truck driver made obscene gestures to her from his cab. She was an avowed risk-taker, but that was not the type of risk she was after.

David's plane banked to the right. He was headed back to the airport, and she knew he'd be home within the hour. There was a time when she couldn't wait to see him in the evening, but she felt no pull now, no rush to get home to greet him at the door, rub his shoulders, tell him about her day. She no longer allowed herself to remember how fiercely she once loved him.

"Tika died this morning." She made the announcement at the dinner table, casually, between bites of stuffed zucchini.

David nodded. "I know. Evan told me when he called to set up the raquetball game for Saturday."

She could imagine the phone call, how little it had to do with racquetball. That game needed no arranging. David and Evan had played racquetball together nearly every Saturday for the last seven years. No, Evan called David to tell him about the trip to Peru. They'd be breaking her down both at work and home now.

"I don't get it," Jamie said, sucking on his empty fork. "Did Tika die because she had twins?"

Shawn smiled at her son, born thirteen years earlier, and just minutes after his brother. "No, of course not. Tamarins nearly always have twins, you know that. Tika had a cancerous tumor, and we didn't know about it until it was too late."

"Evan thinks that he and Mom should make a trip to the Amazon this summer to get some more Copper Elves." David kept his eyes on Shawn while he spoke to the boys. "If they do, Robin and I will probably go along."

"I haven't agreed to this trip yet, David," she said. "Why get the kids all riled up about it when it may not even happen?"

"I think it's a terrific idea." He spooned rice onto his plate. "We haven't had a vacation in years."

"Who'd stay with us if you go?" Keith asked, his face turned up to her, and she noticed again how his features were changing. The baby pink of his cheeks was ruddier, the nose longer and thinner. If she went away for two weeks, she might not know him when she returned. Only his brown velvet eyes with their feathery lashes would remain unchanged. David's eyes.

"You two would probably stay with Aunt Lynn," David said. Obviously he'd thought this through.

"*All right!*" said Keith. "We could use Matt's dirt bike."

"You broke it last time," said Jamie.

"It was already broken when I got on it."

"Eat your salad." Shawn pushed Jamie's salad plate closer to him, until she could see it reflected in the clear blue of his eyes. He looked nothing like his brother. He had her dark hair, less the unwelcome strands of gray, and her blue eyes. And he had a gentle soul like hers, so fragile he needed to wear spiked armor to protect it. Unfortunately, all anyone could see of Jamie these days was the spikes. On an impulse she reached over to touch his cheek and he snapped his head away.

"What are you *doing*?" he asked.

"An eyelash on your cheek," she lied, feeling exposed. She dropped her hand to her lap. She wished she could hold her sons close to her as she had when they were younger, but those days were lost. She could not even touch them now without reproach.

Keith swallowed his last bite of zucchini. "Where would we tell people you are?" he asked.

"It's not at all certain that we're going, honey," she said.

"But where would we say you *are*?"

"The Amazon Basin. The jungle. Tropical rain forest. Whatever you choose."

Jamie rolled his eyes. "We'll say you're in Paris."

Shawn laughed. "Why?"

" 'Cause it's embarrassing. Whose parents go to the jungle for a vacation?"

"All the kids already think you're weird, Mom," said Keith. "I get tired of hearing them say *your mother lives in the zoo*."

"It's not a zoo, it's a conservation center," she answered.

"You should be proud of your mother," David said. "How many of your friends' mothers have Ph.D.'s?"

Shawn stood up to clear the table, gesturing to David to stay seated. This conversation was nothing new, and the one thing she could count on David for was a good defense. She would miss that. What would it be like when it was just her and the boys living here in this house? Could the boys stand one more trauma in their lives? Would they blame themselves for the divorce? She had to be certain they understood it had nothing to do with them.

She carried the dishes into the kitchen and turned down the radio. David liked to listen to an opera during dinner—during *any* activity, actually—but the sopranos grated on her nerves after a while. She scraped the dishes onto a plate in the sink while Figaro and Carmen, the giant black Labs, watched her patiently, meaty pink tongues dangling from their mouths, waiting for leftovers. From the window above the sink she could see the blooming jacaranda trees in the backyard. Six of them, planted in a perfect ellipse. She and David bought the Spanish style house because of those trees, because of the oval of lavender blossoms and green lace. So rare to find that much true green out here, where growing things were gold or brown or at best a muted, military green. In a week or two the blossoms would be gone. She felt a sadness too great for the loss of a few flowers.

She turned the water off and set a plate of rice and carrots in front of the dogs, who looked at her in disappointment before they started eating. They were used to it, though, vegetables as leftovers. She never cooked meat or fowl or seafood. David took the boys out for a burger now and then, but the only meat she allowed in the kitchen was the processed stuff for the dogs.

"She's not *normal.*" Jamie whined from the next room. "Why can't she be more like other mothers?"

She took a bowl of cut fruit out of the refrigerator and turned the radio off so she could listen to the conversation.

"A normal mother wouldn't let you have snakes in your room." There was a smile in David's voice.

"The boas are more for her than for us," said Keith. "She plays with them more than we do."

That wasn't true. She'd forgotten about the snakes. She used to like to carry one around the house with her when she cleaned. She liked its power, the sensuous curling and uncurling of its heavy body against her breasts and back.

"And the ferrets were her idea completely," said Jamie. "Who wants a ferret? They're imbeciles. And they stink."

"No they don't," David said. "Mom had them descented and you know it."

Shawn began slicing a ripe peach into the rest of the fruit.

"Nobody else's mother lets ants crawl around the kitchen," Jamie said.

She looked at the kitchen counter defensively. It had been weeks since there were ants in the house. She hated to use chemicals on them and, besides, the ants had a cycle all their own. If you left them alone, they would eventually disappear.

"Plus she's got a shorter haircut than we do," said Keith.

Shawn scowled and ran a hand through her newly cut, undeniably short, hair. "Hey!" she called out. "Enough out there."

"I like it short, and I have more clout than you two," David said as she brought the bowl of fruit into the dining room.

Shawn sat down. "You know, guys, I haven't had a very good day."

"Sorry, Mom," said Keith.

"It's not like it's your fault or something that Tika died," Jamie said. He stood up so he could dig the biggest possible spoonful of fruit from the bowl, using his fingers to help him transfer it to his dessert bowl.

"I know that. But I still feel sad."

"You act like she was a real person instead of a monkey." He plopped into his seat again.

"She was important to me."

"But it's not like when Heather died." Jamie sounded impatient. "I mean you don't feel like *that*, do you?" The boys were ten when Heather died. It hit them hard; four-year-olds weren't supposed to die.

"No, of course not. But any death of someone—or something—you love makes you remember other deaths."

David stood up stiffly and headed for the kitchen, his bowl of fruit barely touched. He wanted out of this conversation.

Bastard, she thought. *You desert me now when I need you the most.*

"What time are we going out?" Keith asked Jamie, picking up David's cue. Some topics were off limits in this house.

"I think some time with Lynn would do those two good," David said to her from his side of the king-size bed. "A couple of weeks with her and they'd appreciate how good they have it."

Shawn sighed. "I'd like to go, but . . ."

"No buts. Our last real vacation was four years ago." David touched her shoulder, cautiously. "You haven't been happy for so long."

She grit her teeth to hold in the anger. "That has nothing to do with not having a vacation," she said. "And besides, David, it will only be a vacation for you. I'll be working."

"But you love that kind of work. And this is the perfect time to go. Louise is begging me to take some time off. And I'm almost done with the book I'm reading." He'd locked himself in the hall closet—his reading room—every night this week. Occasionally she could hear his creamy voice speaking into the tape recorder. He'd started taping books for the blind when they were first married. It was a labor of love for him. She used to admire him for it, but now she saw it as his escape.

"You make it sound so neat and simple," she said.

He raised himself up on one elbow to look at her. "You've been longing to go to South America since I first met you. What about your canopy dreams?"

Oh yes, the dreams. She'd had them ever since she first saw pictures of the jungle. She was ten then, sitting on the sofa in the house in Annandale with her veterinarian father, the *National Geographic* spread across her knees. Her father pointed out the howler monkeys, the jaguars, and the horned frogs. But the picture that most intrigued her was of the canopy—the ceiling formed by the treetops a hundred feet above the ground. There was something comforting about it. Protective.

The night after she saw that picture she dreamt she was flying, just under the canopy, her arms spread like the wings of a bird. She sailed for miles under the net of branches. She still had the dreams, every few months. If there was a pattern to them, it was that each one seemed to follow some stress in her life. They rejuvenated her. David said he could tell when she'd had a canopy dream because her mood was lighter in the morning.

"Can you give me one good reason, based on logic, why we shouldn't go?" David asked.

What could she say? He would never understand that she was afraid to leave her sons this summer, that they seemed needier to her now than they did the day they were born. He would never understand the dread she felt at trying to repeat a trip she equated with the death of her daughter. And he was ignoring the problems between them. The fabric of this marriage had deteriorated over the last three years until the tiniest stress threatened to tear it to shreds. Maybe that was what it needed—a good ripping apart. Then it would be obvious even to David that divorce was the only solution.

"It's going to be hard work there, David. And uncomfortable. Hot and buggy. Not really a vacation for either of us."

"Let's go."

She sighed. "All right," she said, thinking that if anything happened to the boys in their absence, it would be his fault.

She saw his smile in the darkness as he pulled her toward him for a kiss. "It'll be good for us, you'll see." He kept his lips on hers too long, ran one hand over her hip, up her side to her breast. She caught it and set it on the bed between them.

"I'm really tired," she said.

He leaned away to look at her and she dropped her eyes so he couldn't read the message in them: *I don't want you anymore.*

"I don't remember the last time we made love," he said.

Neither could she. She avoided memories that reminded her that this marriage had once meant something to her. She rolled away from him now, grateful for the space that opened up between them on the bed.

• Three •

DAVID RYDER WAS twenty years old and a junior when he transferred to Hollister University in West Virginia. He'd just received his AA in flight and navigation from a two-year school. "Not very useful," his father had said. "Suicide," said his mother. "Now that you know how to fly, they'll want you in Vietnam." He told her his number in the lottery was high, not to worry, but that didn't stop her from calling him a few times each week to ask if he'd heard from the draft board yet.

So now he would do what they had wanted him to do from the start: get into a serious major. His first thought was music. He would like nothing better than to spend the next two years at the opera. But if it was something useful he was after, music wouldn't do. His counselor suggested journalism. "With your voice and looks you could get into radio or television," she said.

He liked that idea. He was grateful for his voice. He learned early he could hide behind it. No one knew when he was scared or angry. He'd wrap the smooth circle of his voice around his emotions, until, at times, he lost track of them himself.

He hid behind his body as well. He'd been swimming competitively since he was eight years old, but he still thought the tall, muscular frame that had taken shape around him was an accident of nature. It made him look far more confident than he felt most of the time.

He wore his light brown hair short, unlike most of the guys on the Hollister campus. He got it trimmed the day after he arrived. Hollister was in a rural area. There wasn't much choice in barber shops, and he found himself in the hands of a woman barber who had long stringy hair the color of dead grass, and who cracked her gum in his ear.

"You should let it grow a little longer," she said, studying his face in the mirror. "You have a perfect face. A rectangle with tapered corners." She pulled a lipstick out of her purse and outlined his reflection on the mirror. "See? But your hair is too short for it. And you need to grow your sideburns."

He told her, politely, that he liked his hair the way it was. She shrugged her shoulders and started cutting.

The first week of the school year was student orientation and he was surrounded by freshmen, green and giddy. There were some upperclassmen around, enough so that he could categorize the student body. There was a stronghold of hippies and a tight, pretty group of fraternity-sorority types. There was a small group of blacks, political and well-organized, and tiny little factions of studious-looking kids with smarmy hair and thick glasses. He wasn't sure where he fit in. The only thing he knew for certain was that he was no hippie.

That's why he was surprised the first time he set eyes on Shawn McGarry and felt the earth slip out from under his feet.

It was the second day of orientation. She was in front of the science building, lying on her stomach in the grass, reading a thick textbook of some sort. She wore cut-off blue jeans, torn and frayed into very short shorts, the fabric of the seat worn thin over her perfect, round ass. But it was her hair that drew him closer. Was it real? It hung from a center part, thick and spike-straight, to a few inches below her shoulders and it shone like black satin in the sunlight. He sat on the wide steps of the science building, hiding behind his sunglasses, with his head facing the other direction so she wouldn't guess he was mesmerized by her.

He was late for one of the orientation meetings, but still he sat. Finally she stood up and stretched, the book held high above her head. Beads and feathers hung around her neck, the weight of them pressing her pale green T-shirt between her breasts. It was obvious she wore no bra, yet her breasts were high and full. She walked past him on her way into the science building and he saw the watered-down blue of her eyes, the lush black lashes. He caught a whiff of some searing fragrance, like incense burning, as she passed him, and he knew he was in the early throes of an obsession he would have no control over.

Orientation was forgotten. Instead he followed her around, carefully, at a distance. He didn't want to be caught at this. He'd never done anything like it before. He asked other students about her, trying to make his questions sound like casual conversation while his heart beat in his throat. She was well known, someone told him. Not popular, exactly, but everyone knew her name. A straight-A student on a full scholarship. She was a junior, on campus early because she was vice-president of a dissident student group—Students for Peace—that was gearing up for the school year. She was, someone else said, very peculiar.

It took him three days to work out a plan to get near her, to stay near her for the entire semester.

He lay in wait at a table in the student union, pretending to study the class schedule, glancing at the door every thirty seconds or so. He knew her routine now. She would come in any minute, and, unfortunately, she wouldn't be alone.

Four girls sat at the table next to him and he could tell from their stares and whispers that he was the topic of their conversation. All four of them were blond, their bra straps neatly visible beneath the thin flowered fabric of their summer blouses. There was some shape to their hair, curls and waves, something they'd worked at. A week ago he would have been interested. But now he thought they looked shallow, as if they were trying too hard to be something they were not.

Rod Stewart was singing "Maggie May" over the loudspeaker when Shawn walked in, laughing at whatever Jude Mandell whispered in her ear. David already hated Jude. Unreasonable he supposed, but Jude was an obstacle, a person so unlike David that he didn't know how to deal with him as a rival. Jude was president of Students for Peace. He wore his brown hair long, longer than Shawn's. Yesterday it had been in a pony tail, tied back with a leather band, but today it was loose, hanging down his back in a frizzy mop. He wore a full beard. He had to be at least twenty-five, an impossible age for a man of just twenty to compete with.

Shawn and Jude joined a couple of girls at one of the tables near the long string of windows. All those tables were full of their friends. The campus freaks.

David waited until Jude got up to enter the food line before making his move. He walked over to Shawn's table, his palms sweating. He'd worn his oldest pair of jeans for the occasion and he felt sloppy. He was accustomed to oxford shirts and chinos. "Excuse me." He smiled down at her, thankful for the smooth sound of his voice. She would never know he was nervous.

The two other girls at the table stopped talking, looked him up and down as if he were from another planet.

"I think we're signed up for the same biology class and I lost the book list," he said. "Could you tell me what I need?"

Her blue eyes were directly on him. "Which biology?" she asked. "I have three. Parker's ten o'clock?"

He hadn't counted on that, on her having more than one.

"Yes," he said. "Parker's ten o'clock."

"There's no book list. She'll tell us what we need the first day."

"Oh, thanks." He began to retreat but Shawn smiled at him. "You've never had Parker before?" She had *dimples*.

He felt himself grinning at her. "This is my first year here," he said. "I just transferred in."

"You'll like it. And you'll like Parker. She's dynamite."

Jude returned with a hot dog for himself and an orange for Shawn and took his seat again. He smoothed a napkin across Shawn's bare thighs as he looked up at David.

"Hey, man," he said, slowly. High on something, most likely. "Don't you belong on the other side?" Jude nodded toward the row of tables David had just vacated.

For a moment David didn't understand. He looked over at the tables and realized they were occupied only by very straight-looking students. He'd crossed over into alien territory.

Shawn laughed. "Give him a break, Jude." She looked up at David. "See you in class," she said.

He left to find the late registration line, hoping he was not too late to sign up for Parker's ten o'clock biology class.

The smell of the biology classroom was almost too much for him. A leaden smell, thick and heavy, emanated from the wide black slab tops of the lab tables. Years of gore embedded in the pores of these table tops, he thought. He didn't belong here.

He was one of the first to arrive, and he selected a seat that allowed him a clear view of the door. Professor Parker sat on the top of her big oak desk, smoothing her short, utilitarian gray hair with her fingers. She smiled and nodded at each student as they arrived. She seemed to know most of them.

Shawn swept into the room, black hair swinging like a shimmering veil. "Hi, Beth," she said to Professor Parker.

"Shawn!" Parker said. "We missed you this summer. Did you work with your father?"

Shawn nodded. "Yeah, it was far out, though my father was an asshole as usual. I'll tell you later what we did to this goat."

David winced, wondering if this was a woman with whom he could ever enjoy the sweet pleasure of an opera.

She took a seat, miracle of miracles, across the table from him and gave him a heart-stopping smile of recognition. She wore a gauzy white shirt, the pink disks of her nipples visible underneath. She raised her hand a lot, asked some questions, answered others. Her language was coarse; her wit sharp. She made the class laugh a few times. Everyone knew her well. So when Professor Parker directed them to choose lab partners, he knew he had to act quickly. He leaned across the broad tabletop.

"I don't know anyone here," he said. "Would you be my lab partner?"

"Sure," she smiled. "Why not?"

During the third class he asked her out. She said the only place she went on weeknights was the library. He told her he would meet her there that evening.

He found her studying in the science section and sat across the table from her. "Hi," he whispered.

"Hi." Her smile was warm, but it was obvious she didn't want to talk. He tried to concentrate on an article he was supposed to read for journalism. Every once in a while Shawn disappeared into the stacks for ten minutes or so, returning with an armload of books. She'd put her heels up on the seat of the chair and hug her knees as she leafed through them. He couldn't read. He was absorbed by the reflection of the library lights in her hair, and by her eyelashes. They were so black, so close together at the roots, that it looked as though she wore thick black eyeliner. But this close he could see she wore no makeup at all.

She agreed to let him walk her back to her dorm. "Can we go the long way?" she asked.

He smiled. The longer the better. But he soon realized it was not more time with him she was after. "The long way" consisted of a round trip across a narrow railroad bridge suspended over the Potomac River. The bridge was the width of one railroad track plus three foot-wide planks of rough and rotting wood. A steel pipe handrail was all that separated them from the pull of the water below, and the only lights were small bare bulbs hanging from the railing every thirty feet or so.

He began to doubt his sanity as well as hers as they started across. He felt the boards spring slightly beneath his feet and clutched the handrail to fight the vertigo.

"Have you ever walked across here before?" he asked. "Are you sure these boards will hold us?"

She was ahead of him and he had trouble keeping up with her. "I walk across here every night. It relaxes me." She stopped and pointed to the sky. "Look how close we are to the stars."

He could not look up, nor could he look down. "Let's keep going," he said.

"Are you afraid of heights? I thought you had a pilot's license?"

"This is different."

She smiled at him, with sympathy, he thought. "The first time is rough. At eleven in the morning and three in the afternoon, a train crosses it. You should be out here then."

He frowned. "You've done that?"

She nodded and stepped closer to him. When she spoke her voice was a whisper, as though the words frightened her as much as they did him. "Sometimes I lie down out here and read, just waiting for it to come. When it passes me, it's as though the earth is about to explode."

The cool September night air slipped up the sleeves of his shirt and he shivered. "Do you want to die?"

She laughed. "Shit, no." She started walking again and he followed her, feeling now as though he had no choice.

The following Friday each set of biology lab partners was presented with a fetal pig to dissect, and it was then David knew he'd made a mistake. There had to have been other ways to get to know Shawn McGarry.

She sat across from him, eyes wide with delight as she contemplated the pig in their dissecting pan.

"A little boy pig," she grinned at him. "Shall I set him up?"

David swallowed. "Be my guest," he said.

Shawn laid the pig on its back and tied a length of string around its right foreleg. She slipped the string under the pan and tied it to the left foreleg. Obviously she'd done this before. He tried to concentrate on her hands. She had long fingers and very short nails, not bitten short, but neatly cut, gently rounded at the tips. He thought they were beautiful, although a few days ago he wouldn't have given unpolished nails a second look. He forced his attention back to the pig. Shawn had tied the hindlegs as she had the forelegs, and the pig was spread-eagled, belly-up. David squirmed.

Shawn held out the scalpel to him. "Why don't you make the first incision."

He shook his head. There was no way in hell he could cut into this pig. "Go ahead," he said.

She shrugged. She lifted the skin near the umbilical cord and slipped the scalpel into it. "We just need to make enough room for the tips of the dissecting scissors," she said.

He watched the top of her head as she worked the scissors under the pig's skin and began to cut. In the edge of his vision he could see her fingers separate the skin from the flesh beneath it. Sweat broke out across his back. She leaned forward to study what she had done to the pig, and he caught her hair before it fell into the tray.

"Thanks," she laughed, swinging her hair behind her head. "I always get shit in my hair." She tapped the handle of the scissors on the back of his fingers. "Next incision's yours. I don't want to be a hog, so to speak."

"I can't do it." He figured he'd better admit it now before they got any deeper into this pig.

"What do you mean?"

"It makes me sick."

She frowned at him. "This pig's the smallest thing we'll be dissecting in here, David."

He shook his head.

"Why did you take this class?"

To be near you. "I needed another science."

"But this is an *advanced* class. You could've taken geology or something."

"I have to leave." His chest felt tight. He couldn't get any air into his lungs.

She put down the scissors and set her hand on his. "Slow down," she said. "You'll be okay. We don't even have this fat little bugger open yet."

He stared into her eyes, but saw the pig reflected there, in duplicate. He leaned away from the table.

"You're no bio major," she said.

"Journalism," he confessed.

She shook her head with a smile. "Look, I'll help you get through today. I'll do the whole dissection. It's a treat for me, anyhow. And then you transfer your ass out of here, okay? I mean, you're a fish out of water in here, Ryder."

She began to cut again while he stared at the perfectly straight part in her hair.

"I think it's sweet that you don't want to cut up this pig," she said as she worked. "It used to bother me, too, sacrificing these tiny little lives for our benefit. But it's necessary. It took me a long time to understand that. We could use models, but it wouldn't be the same." She chatted on, while he fell in love.

Finally she glanced up at him. "You're a good-looking guy, David," she said, her fingers still in motion.

"Thank you."

"I could see you with the homecoming queen on your arm. I can't see you with me, though."

"Why not?"

"We belong in different worlds. I don't mean biology versus journalism. I mean that I haven't dated anyone with hair as short as yours in . . . well, I never have. You know what I mean? And I'm a little freer than you. You're kind of tense."

"Not really." He felt defensive. "I'm very relaxed when I'm not cutting up pigs or crossing the river on a balance beam."

She smiled, the dimples little stars in her cheeks. "Have you ever gone out with a girl who wasn't a cheerleader?"

"Of course." He knew he was being insulted, and, to be honest, the girls he dated who were not cheerleaders were the type to lament that fact. "And I want to go out with you too. Not to the library either. Tomorrow night. There's a movie right here, in the theater of the science building."

"Okay."

He smiled triumphantly.

"On one condition. You look—really look—at what I've done here." She nodded toward the pig. "Let me explain it to you. It'll take the horror out of it."

He forced himself to look down and saw that she had snipped away every shred of skin that had made the pig decent, pulling bits and pieces of him out of the body cavity and pinning them to the floor of the pan.

"Okay," she said happily. "Let's start with the visceral organs. You know what *these* are, don't you?" She pointed the probe at the slimy wormlike intestines, and he shut his eyes.

He heard her slide the tray to the other end of the table.

"You really can't do it, can you?" she said.

He shook his head. "I'm good at other things, though."

She smiled. "I bet you are. Pick me up at seven tomorrow night?"

They sat together in the theater of the science building watching *The King of Hearts*, and for the first time he felt completely at ease with her. He laced his fingers between hers and she set her head on his shoulder. She had on long jeans tonight, frayed on the bottoms, and she curled her bare feet under her. Her blouse was a blue Indian print and she wore tiny scallop shells for earrings. She had a rich dusky smell, exotic, spiritual, like the inside of a church.

He had decided not to tell her about the conversation he had with Jude that afternoon. He'd been sitting in the student union when Jude sat down at his table, needless to say, without an invitation.

"You're out of your league, man," Jude said, gray eyes cool.

"I don't know what you mean." He stared at Jude, trying to see what Shawn saw in this man. He was probably not bad looking under the beard. He had an angular face with high, pointy cheekbones and eyes like the frozen surface of a pond. He wore a small gold hoop through his left earlobe. David felt very young.

Jude leaned forward and spoke slowly, as though he thought David might have trouble following him. "She needs more than you can give her," he said.

"What makes you so sure?"

Jude laughed. "She needs to live on the edge, you know what I mean?"

David nodded slowly. He pictured Shawn lying on the railroad bridge, engrossed in a biology book, waiting for the train.

"She likes only the finest Colombian weed." Jude pulled a lavender joint out of his pocket and set it on the table.

David glanced nervously around them.

"Take it," Jude said. "Come on, you'll need it."

David slipped the joint into his shirt pocket.

"She loves to drive on the backroads at night, the ones that go through the woods, and she turns off the car lights. It's black out there—can't see worth shit—and she drives that fucking car in the dark, slowly, 'til she can't take the tension any longer."

Lord. What was wrong with her? He was not good with darkness, blackness. Why would anyone play at being blind?

"So." Jude stood up. "Have you balled her yet?"

"No." He was so stunned by the question that he answered it without thinking.

Jude shook his head. "She's the best on campus, man. You better be worthy."

David was thinking about that now as Shawn sat next to him with her head on his shoulder, her hand in his. Was she expecting that, to make love tonight? He had no objection, he just didn't want to do anything that would hurt this relationship before it got off the ground. He planned to ask her back to his apartment after the movie. His roommates were out tonight; he and Shawn could have it to themselves.

But Shawn had other ideas. When the movie was over she took his arm and directed him to the end of the corridor and up the stairs to the third floor.

"Where are we going?" he asked.

"You'll see."

They walked quietly down the dimly lit hall, footsteps leaving pale echoes behind them. She stopped at the door to Parker's biology class and he groaned.

"Shawn, this is a *date*. I'm not interested in fetal pigs tonight."

"Neither am I." She produced a key from her pocket. "Shhh," she held her finger to her lips, giggled a little. Then she slipped the key in the lock and opened the door. "It's only fitting that we spend our date here, where we first got to know each other."

She left the lights off and the moonlight fell in soft gray squares on the black tabletops. She pulled him by the arm over to their table and boosted herself up.

"Join me," she said.

"Someone might come."

"Both of us, I hope." She giggled again and leaned down to kiss him, a quick, soft kiss that tasted like coconut. Her hair fell cool and slick across his cheek.

He had to smile. "Wouldn't you prefer my nice soft bed? Besides, I don't have any . . . protection here."

"I'm on the pill." She leaned forward for another kiss and this time he caught her breasts in his hands. They were warm beneath her blouse and filled his hands to overflowing. But he was moving too quickly. He took a step away from her and reached forward slowly to unbutton the single button at the neck of her blouse. His fingers rose and fell with her breathing. He took off his own shirt, folded it carefully and set it next to her.

"A pillow for you," he said. In the moonlight the pupils of her eyes were deep and black, barely rimmed with blue. He felt the heat of her body as she reached for his belt. He caught her hand and shook his head. "Not yet," he said. He was determined to take his time. He wanted this to be something she would remember. He wanted to be worthy.

After they made love he lay on his side next to her, watching the moonlight play on her body. She was not like other girls, embarrassed afterward, quick to cover themselves up. She was relaxed, her eyes closed, not minding that he stared at her.

"There's something on your ass," he said. In the darkness it looked like a bug and he tried to brush it away but his hand touched flesh, nothing more. She rolled onto her side to give him a better view. It was a tattoo, a peace sign the size of a quarter.

He touched it with the tip of his finger, frowning. "Is this permanent?"

"Uh huh."

He couldn't believe she would do something so irreversible to her body. "What about when the war's over? You'll still have this thing on your ass."

"I like the sentiment, Vietnam, or no Vietnam."

"I think you are very close to being crazy," he said.

"Shhh." She put her arms around his neck. "You're a wonderful lover," she said, changing the subject. "How'd a straight guy like you learn to fuck like that?"

He frowned at her again. "We made love, Shawn. Please don't talk about it that way."

She sat up abruptly and he braced himself for a defensive retort, but instead she put her arm through his. "I'm sorry," she said. "It bothers my father too."

"What does?"

"My language. It's a mess."

"It makes me feel as though what we just did doesn't matter to you." He picked up his shirt from the table and the joint fell out of his pocket onto her thigh. She looked at him.

"That's Jude's."

"How do you know that?"

"Who else uses lavender ZigZag? How did you get it?"

"He gave it to me. Wanted to be sure you enjoyed yourself tonight, I guess."

She looked depressed and he wished he'd left the joint at home. Jude Mandell was suddenly between them in the room. "Do you want to smoke it?" he asked.

She shook her head and he was relieved.

"How serious are you and Jude?" he asked, buttoning his shirt. He was afraid of her answer.

She lowered herself from the table and pulled her jeans on over her long bare legs. She'd worn no underwear at all. "I guess that depends on what you mean by serious."

"I'm asking if I stand a chance with you."

"You mean you want more than just to . . ." she caught herself ". . . to make love then?"

"Yes, of course. What did you think?"

He saw her blush in the moonlight. She finished dressing before she answered. "I've been with Jude a long time. He's got some kind of power over me." She shrugged. "But I like you, David. Please don't give up on me."

He hadn't told her about his parents. Now, as he waited for her in the cozy living room of her dorm, he wondered if that was fair. It was for her sake that he'd kept it from her, he told himself. His other girlfriends worked themselves into a sweat before they met them. He didn't want that to happen this time.

When she walked into the living room, he felt his heart twist in his chest. She was dressed in a blue skirt—to the knees—and white blouse, stockings on her legs, her hair pulled back with barrettes. After seeing her every day for a month, he knew very well that this getup was a major sacrifice for her.

He kissed her cheek and held her close. "You're sweet," he said into her hair.

"I had to borrow the skirt and pantyhose."

"Did you borrow the bra too?" He felt the strap under his hand on her back.

"I didn't know it was that obvious I was wearing one."

"It's just very obvious when you're not."

He waited until they were in his Volkswagen Bug. "There's something I haven't told you about my parents," he said. "They're blind."

She was quiet for a moment. "Completely?"

He nodded.

"How did they manage to raise two children?"

He shrugged and turned the key in the ignition. "They had a lot of help." He had aunts and uncles all over the state of West Virginia, but it was actually his sister who had taken the brunt of it. Lynn was five years older than him; she'd been forced into the role of second mother, which she played with a mixture of love and resentment. He never blamed her for leaving home the day she turned twenty-one. She eloped with her boyfriend, Stuart, and moved to California, as far from the family as she could get.

Shawn was quiet and the silence worried him because he read it as pity. It was the last thing his parents deserved. His hands tensed on the steering wheel.

"Were they always blind?"

He nodded. "They both had problems at birth."

"What was it like for you?"

A memory, not his favorite, elbowed its way into his mind. He was at a cub scout meeting, standing alone in the corner of a living room, pressed between the television and an end table. The other boys huddled in a group, laughing, taunting, pointing at the patch sewn upside down on the shoulder of his uniform.

"I don't think a day went by that I didn't admire them," he said.

His parents were waiting for them in the restaurant lobby. They sat on a low upholstered bench, close together, close enough to feel each other's presence. They had each turned fifty this year. To David, that seemed very old and gave him more reason to worry about them.

His father's hair was completely white, but thick and wavy. He had David's build, had been a swimmer once himself, but his body was rounder now, softened by the years. His mother's hair was still gold and she wore her usual warm smile, the smile that did all the communicating for her face, since her eyes were always masked by dark glasses.

Mandy was with them, the latest in a long line of Seeing Eye dogs, this one a pale blond golden retriever. She sat in front of David's father, alert and waiting.

Shawn didn't wait for him to introduce her.

"I'm Shawn McGarry," she said, touching their arms, letting them hold her hands. David began to relax.

Dinner was comfortable, more comfortable than any other he'd had with a girlfriend and his parents together. Shawn was fascinated by Mandy. She loved sharing a meal with a dog in a restaurant. She asked questions about her training—direct questions, the type most people would tiptoe around to avoid offense. She was polite without mincing words, and he saw the approval in his parents' faces.

She ordered a vegetable plate, which amazed his parents. When she explained her feelings about not eating animals, his father ordered the same. When it was time to leave, David's mother kissed his cheek and whispered to him, "She's a sensitive, gentle girl, David."

David smiled to himself, realizing maybe for the first time that she was exactly that.

Shawn was quiet again on the drive back to campus. She

kicked off her shoes and lifted her feet to the seat, set her cheek on her knees, and watched him. When he turned his head to look at her, he saw her lower lashes sparkled with tears.

"Don't feel sorry for them," he said. "Or for me."

"I don't," she said. "I'm just envious. The three of you are so close. It's as though you've conquered something together."

Yes, it was. He took her hand. "I love you," he said.

She lay down on the seat, her head in his lap. He stroked her black satin hair with his fingers as he drove.

She sat up when he pulled into the parking lot of her dorm. "I've been thinking about you a lot these past few weeks," she said. "About how weird it is that I'm going out with you. In the beginning I think it was because you were so good-looking that I was willing to put up with your conservatism."

"And now?"

There was a long pause before she spoke again. "There's something I haven't told you about my parents either."

"What's that?"

"I only have one. My mother died when I was five."

He was surprised. He always expected other people to have two intact parents. "I'm sorry," he said.

"I don't remember much about her." She looked down into her lap where she was locking and unlocking the catch on her borrowed silver bracelet. When she spoke again, her voice was thick. "I was carefully raised by my father who is an incredibly fine and gentle man—a lot like you. He would cut off his right arm for me." Her voice caught and tears slipped down her cheeks, surprising him. He wondered if she allowed Jude Mandell to see her tears. He put his arms around her and pulled her as close to him as the stick shift would allow.

"He worked so hard at being a parent, David. He really struggled to make me a good, responsible person. But for the last few years, I've been a disappointment to him."

"I think you're a good, responsible person. I've never known anyone who studies as hard as you do."

She shook her head. "Jude is a slap in my father's face. I'm so mixed up. I always figured I'd end up married to someone like Jude, someone rebellious, outside the norm. Then suddenly you appear and you feel so *comfortable* to me. My father raised me to end up with someone like you. But I'm not sure I can give up my radical side yet. I'm so afraid of getting *dull.*"

He tried to follow her. He hoped she was telling him in this convoluted fashion that she loved him.

"I want to try going straight for a while." She wrinkled her nose.

He laughed. "That doesn't mean you'll start wearing a bra all the time, does it?"

"No!" She pulled away from him, unbuttoned her white blouse, and took it off. "Let's get rid of this thing," she said, unfastening the bra.

She sat facing him, naked from the waist up, her breasts full and, by now, familiar. He shook his head at her. "You have a long way to go before anyone could consider you dull," he said.

· Four ·

THEY DATED FOR two years. For Shawn it was a time of change, of bending, giving up one part of herself for another. Still, she tested David over and over to see if he could put up with her, for she thought of herself as too strong in will and opinion to be very lovable. She spoke in language she knew irritated him, and while he chastised her, he never threatened to end the relationship. The words she used began to sound offensive even to her own ears, and she gradually discovered she could express herself as effectively without them.

There were a couple of things that pushed David's tolerance to the limit. She still slept with Jude during the first year she dated David. She couldn't give Jude up. He was showy and powerful and very sexy. Yet her relationship with him was not good that year. He was critical of the change in her, and he blamed her for the deterioration of Students for Peace.

"It's not my fault," she said. "It's the political apathy that's invading this campus."

"That's invading *you*, you mean," Jude said.

She couldn't argue with him. It was true that she was caught up in herself and her own happiness. The war seemed very distant. No one cared much anymore. It was not her fault that Jude couldn't let go of the sixties.

"You don't see what's happening to you," Jude said. "I mean look at yourself. You're going to *swim* meets, for Christ's sake."

She loved David's swim meets. She'd felt out of place the first time, but soon grew comfortable with the echoing cheers of the spectators and the steamy smell of chlorine. Swimming suddenly struck her as the most sensual sport imaginable, unsung and underrated. She loved to watch David cut through the water, his body muscular and slick, his stroke powerful, decisive, determined. She imagined him making love to her with that same unrelenting force, and by the end of a meet she was often in a frenzy to get to him.

Swim meets gave her time to think, time to compare the two men in her life, and she soon had no doubt that David was superior to Jude in almost every way. He was more accepting of the person she was, although clearly she was not the type of woman he'd expected to find himself with. He was also a better lover than Jude. She was stunned when she came to that realization. Jude went through sensitivity training in California, and she'd come to think of him as incomparable. But the Kama Sutra oil, the massages for the bottoms of her feet, began to feel mechanical and bookish, while David's lovemaking seemed as natural as a heartbeat, and equally as remarkable.

David never told her to stop seeing Jude—he wisely avoided issuing ultimatums, knowing the rebel in her would take over. But his happiness gradually became as important to her as her own, and the pleasure in being with Jude evaporated.

She broke up with Jude in May, and he left for Berkeley shortly after. "The only place left in the country where anyone gives a shit," he told her. She was relieved to see him go, to see that chapter in her life close behind him.

She gave up something else for David—those drives she loved to take through the woods with the car lights off. She tried to get him to go with her once. He flatly refused, got into something like a panic, ripping her hands from the steering wheel. He told her he hated the darkness. It was like being blind, he said. That was his greatest fear, to have his eyes open, yet see nothing. His vulnerability softened her, made her want to comfort him, to hold him for a long time.

Shawn was no longer certain who her friends were. The women she'd been close to at school thought David was extremely good-looking but terminally straight. *His* friends thought she was on something, but they were quite wrong. She drank very little, and stopped smoking marijuana as soon as Jude left for Berkeley. She and David tried to bring their friends together, but the blend was one of oil and water. Even at their wedding, held in a small church in Annandale, the people on the two sides of the church looked as though they must surely be attending different events. She and David worked out strategic seating plans for the reception, laughing over the vision of David's polished, dark-suited swim team members sharing tables with her friends, in their Mexican wedding shirts and denim.

As it turned out, she had no idea how anyone got along at the reception. She couldn't even have said who was there. She noticed no one except David. No one else mattered.

They moved into a small apartment in Washington, D.C., where they both attended George Washington University, David working on his Master's in communications, Shawn on her Ph.D. in primatology. David began reading books for the blind in his spare time. She often found his "reading" sign hanging from the doorknob of their bedroom closet when she got home from her classes.

After he received his Master's, David worked as a reporter for a Top Forty radio station. He wanted to work at a classical station, but couldn't wait for an opening. Shawn was pregnant with the twins, and either he or Shawn had to bring in some money.

She loved being pregnant and David seemed intrigued by the changes in her body. Aroused, actually. He wanted to make love as soon as he got home from work. He was a creative, earthy lover. David, whose stomach turned at the sight of scraped knuckles, was squeamish about nothing when it came to sex.

He failed her only once in those first few years of their marriage: he left her alone when the boys were born. Walked out on her in the delivery room without a word of explanation. She hadn't expected him to handle the delivery well, but he could have at least stayed to hold her hand. She was alone when the babies were placed in her arms, and she felt alarmed by her numbness. She'd grown so used to sharing everything with David that the twins seemed unreal to her without him there. But that evening she heard him announce the birth of his sons on his news report, his voice so full of pride that she wept for hours afterward, and her uneasiness slipped away.

The boys were good-natured babies, and she liked staying home with them. Yet there was this nagging little terror in the back of her mind that for every day she spent at home, a thousand of her brain cells died. She missed the academic world. She was afraid she'd forget everything she ever learned. She worried about gaining weight. She worried that her mind and body were deteriorating, that she was, in short, becoming dull.

David laughed at that, but he was sympathetic nevertheless. He paid for her scuba-diving lessons, which she took on Sunday mornings while he watched the twins. They hired sitters on a couple of weekends and went caving in West Virginia, hang gliding in North Carolina. She needed her quotient of risk. Motherhood seemed to have none, or so she thought at the time.

In spite of the fact that she missed school, she enjoyed domesticity. She baked bread, made her own baby food for the boys, experimented with new and exotic vegetables for her and David. That led to innumerable run-ins with the manager of the local supermarket who found her requests tiresome.

Once she asked him to stock jicama, a vegetable she'd read about and wanted to try. No one else would know what to do with it, he said. She struck a deal with him. She'd spend a Saturday morning in his store preparing jicama, giving away raw and cooked samples, educating his customers to its wonders, and he in return would stock it for a month or so to see how it went over. He reluctantly agreed.

She left David with the twins and set up her wok and a supply of the ugly brown vegetables on a table in the produce department. She looked like a typical housewife, she thought. Her hair was tied at the back of her neck, and she wore a green corduroy jumper covered by a flowered apron provided by the store manager. She chopped and cooked and gave samples and nutritional information to customers. She was coaxing a six-year-old to try a stick of the vegetable when she spotted a man across the aisle, in front of the potatoes, watching her. Jude Mandell. She felt her guard go up. What was he doing in Washington? He approached her and she saw the granola and yogurt cradled in his arms.

"Working for a supermarket?" He was smirking.

"This is on my own time." She explained about the jicama and he shook his head.

"How about some lunch when you're finished?" he asked.

She thought of David at home with the twins. "Just a bite," she said.

He was in town for a rally, he told her over lunch. "And what are you up to besides hawking vegetables?" he asked.

"I married David."

He frowned at her. "Shit, woman, where's your head?"

"I'm very happy with him. I'm working on my Ph.D. Primatology. But I took a year off to have a baby. Only I had two. Twins." She felt the smile spread across her face, thought of the picture of Keith and Jamie in her wallet but stopped herself from reaching for it.

"So, okay, that's cool, you have a couple of kids. But a year off? You put your life on hold for them. You used to demonstrate for peace and freedom. Now you're demonstrating this . . . hokima."

"*Hi*-ca-ma. And it's spelled with a *J*." She didn't like him. She studied the gold hoop in his ear, the strands of gray that were beginning to streak his beard. She used to sit across a table from him like a scrap of iron near a magnet. Incredible.

"Your values have warped, woman. You're stagnating."

"It was nice of you to ask me to lunch so you could insult me."

He grinned as if she'd complimented him. "There's a meeting tonight," he said. "Come with me. You'll meet some great people. Then maybe we could sleep together afterward."

"Jude, I'm *married*."

"So fucking what?"

She shook her head at him. "I'm not the one whose values are warped."

The twins were asleep when she got home and David was in the bedroom closet, his "reading" sign on the door. She wished he would come out so she could tell him about Jude. He would hold her and tell her she was far from dull, tell her that Jude's life sounded bitter and empty compared with hers. She set her ear against the door and listened. She couldn't quite make out the words. He was at a quiet, serious part. She shut her eyes and let the warmth of his voice fill her up.

• Five •

SHAWN WAS IN the Conservation Center nursery, alone with Tika's babies. She sat in the rocker, her feet propped up on the low table in front of her. Through the window she watched the sun ease its way over Elephant Ridge.

Twin B slept in the incubator while she cupped Twin A in her palm. She filled a syringe with formula and carefully forced a drop from the tip. She touched it to A's lips, and the little Elf obediently licked at the white liquid and waited for the next drop to appear. It was a slow business, but a nipple was out of the question. She and Evan learned long ago that this was the only way to feed the infants, the only way to keep them alive.

This baby was a charmer. There was not much difference in looks between one Copper Elf and another. Males and females both had the same coloring—the coppery manes and backs, white faces, golden arms and bellies. But every once in a while one stood out from the others by virtue of some quirk in personality. Tika had been like that. There'd been a cool sophistication about her. A strange way to describe an animal, perhaps, but even as an infant Tika held herself apart from the world with a calculated indifference. This new baby had his own style as well. Not reserved like his mother. No, he was a clown, all three and a half inches of him, tugging at Shawn's T-shirt, running up her bare thigh to perch on her knee. From there he watched her with his shiny black eyes and opened his mouth wide to trill. She laughed at the little toothless mouth—all flat pink tongue—and the feeble squeal he managed to push out. She knew she shouldn't interact with him too much, but he was irresistible. It was always a problem with the hand-reared infants. It was too easy to get attached. Too easy for them to start depending on humans for food and affection. Then the whole goal of the breeding program, the eventual return to the wild of self-sufficient Elves, was in jeopardy.

Evan appeared in the doorway. "What are they?" he asked, hope in his voice.

"You're going to be upset."

He scooped Twin B up from the incubator, lifted the lanky tail and made a face. "That one's a male too?" He pointed to the baby on her knee and she nodded. "Do you think it's something in the water?" he asked. "Killing off the X chromosomes?"

She looked up at him. He had on jeans, a tan shirt. There was tension in the muscles of his face, a tightness at the corners of his mouth. She wanted to see him smile. "Makes the trip to Dacu even more important, doesn't it?"

"You'll go?"

She had decided she would if he'd agree to a few conditions. "We avoid Iquitos." She handed him a second syringe.

He sat on a straight-backed chair next to her rocker. "Fine," he said, forcing the formula into a bubble at the tip of the syringe.

"We set an absolute limit of two weeks for the trip, even if we're short of our goal."

He gnawed at his lip. "Two weeks in the field, you mean. Not including getting there and back."

She nodded, although that was not what she'd meant. But he was right. She'd forgotten about the travel time, how long it could take to get anyplace in the jungle. "And we negotiate to be able to take out more tamarins. Four females in addition to the breeding pair. All of them juveniles. They're easier to trap, and we won't be breaking up already existing pairs."

He smiled now, broadly. She was letting him know exactly how invested she was in this trip.

"You're wonderful," he said, the tension out of his voice for the first time that morning.

She was not quite through. "And we use a decoy," she said.

Evan rolled his eyes. "Now you're getting pushy. A decoy is a hassle."

"It's a hassle to keep enough fruit on hand for trapping, too," she said. "How about a compromise. We try both types of traps and compare the two."

"You drive a hard bargain." Evan smiled at her.

Twin A slipped off Shawn's knee and landed in the lap of her khaki shorts. She held him there, letting him curl himself around her fingers. "We'll need a guide, won't we?"

Evan had been to Peru three years earlier, but that trip took him to the Meseta region. He didn't know Dacu at all. "There's a Peruvian woman who's led a number of expeditions into isolated areas of the Amazon," he said. "Tess Kirscher. She's a botany professor in San Francisco. Supposed to be excellent."

"Kirscher? *Peruvian?*"

"Of German extraction, I suppose." He touched the syringe to B's lips again. "Come on, baby," he coaxed. "Good boy. She lived in Peru as a child, then moved to California, but I guess she spends a lot of her time down there."

Shawn liked the idea of a woman guide. It gave the whole trip a softer, safer feeling.

Evan set down the syringe and lifted Twin B up to his face for a good look. "We've got to name these critters," he said. "What are we up to?"

"R. This one's Rascal."

Evan studied the tiny Elf in his hand. "Romeo," he said. "I think he has potential."

When they first started working with the Elves, she suggested naming them after their own relatives, working their way backward through their family trees. It was insensitive of her. If she'd given one second's thought to that suggestion she never would have made it. It hit a nerve in Evan as raw as an open wound.

Evan had been adopted at a few weeks of age by parents already in their forties. It was a private adoption, shrouded in mystery, and no amount of sleuthing on his part had provided any clues to his background. He knew nothing about his birth parents, and by the time he was old enough to ask questions, his adoptive father had died and his mother had developed psychiatric problems that left her swinging between a sharply lucid state and a consuming paranoia.

He had no siblings, no grandparents, no aunts or uncles. His parents had been socially reclusive, except for their involvement in the church. They were strict Catholics, and Evan found a solace in the church that was lacking at home. The priests and nuns were his true parents, he told Shawn once. It was a nun who took him shopping for school clothes, a priest who gave him advice when Evan first started dating. His parents seemed relieved to have someone else looking out for him.

His mother was still alive. He'd moved her from Portland to San Diego a few years ago. She was eighty years old now and in a nursing home, Alzheimer's compounding her other symptoms. He visited her regularly, sitting for hours at the bedside of a biting, caustic woman who rarely recognized him. Shawn

used to go with him sometimes, but on one visit last year she'd
chastised his mother for her rudeness to her son and Evan asked
her not to go with him again. She couldn't help herself. Family
was so important to Evan. He'd had so little of it that he ideal-
ized the concept. Sometimes just saying the word out loud made
his face light up. Watching him struggle to elicit some warmth,
some indication of caring, from this hurtful woman broke her
heart.

She willingly shared her own family with Evan. She shared
her children and her husband. Most of all, she shared herself.
But he no longer needed that. He'd created a family all his own.

"Hold Romeo a sec while I get the dye." Evan handed her
Twin B.

The two Elves grabbed for each other on her lap, and she kept
a careful eye on them so she wouldn't get them mixed up.

Evan sat down again and pried one of the squealing twins
from the arms of the other.

"That's Rascal," she said.

With a small brush, Evan painted a band of white dye around
the end of Rascal's tail. He painted the band on Romeo's tail a
little higher up, so they'd be able to tell them apart. In a few
weeks the tiny Elves would be tattooed on the inside of their
thighs with a code number. Until then the rings of dye were the
only way to tell the brothers apart.

"You want to see a *real* cute baby?" Evan stood up, Romeo
clinging to his fingers, and pulled a stack of pictures from the
back pocket of his jeans. He handed them to Shawn.

More pictures of Melissa. There she was, precariously balanced on Evan's willing shoulders or snuggled next to Robin in
the St. Johns' bed. Cute didn't begin to describe her. She was
an extraordinary-looking child. Huge blue eyes and a halo of
warm reddish blond curls. Melissa would always be handsome.
No gawky puberty with gangly limbs, no teeth crooked or too
large for her mouth. She would grow up to be, in short, just like
her mother.

She remembered seeing Melissa in the hospital, a few hours
after her birth, and seeing only Evan in her tiny features. Not a
trace of Robin at all, except for the dusting of strawberry blond
hair. Evan had never looked so full, so completely satisfied as
he did that day.

On the drive home from the hospital, she sat on the passenger
side of the car, hugging the door in the darkness, tears slipping
silently down her cheeks while David hummed along with some

opera on the radio. She told herself she was crying out of happiness for Evan. But she knew the real reason for her tears was less noble: Evan's joy had absolutely nothing to do with her.

He told her later that it had been the most exciting experience of his life, participating in the birth of his child. It made her angry at David all over again for leaving her alone in the delivery room when her children were born.

"There were fifty people in there, honey," he said the day after the twins were born. "I was hardly leaving you alone."

She didn't bother to tell him that fifty strangers didn't make up for the absence of one husband. She should have known right then that she would always be alone in this marriage, anytime something hurt. But it didn't take her long to learn that lesson, and by the time Heather was born she didn't bother to ask him to stay with her. He waited in the waiting room with her father, who seemed puzzled by the arrangement but who wisely never said a word.

She came to the last picture. Melissa laughing at the camera from her high chair, spoon held high in a sign of triumph, some glob of food blurring through the air. Shawn smiled.

Sometimes she wanted to share old pictures of Heather with Evan, but of course she never did. No point to it really. To the rest of the world, Heather was a closed book. Shawn looked at those pictures only when she was alone. She marveled at the little girl's blondness. Heather seemed to have been extracted from some gene pool that had nothing to do with Shawn or David. People sometimes asked, with a rudeness that bothered Shawn not at all, if Heather were adopted. Shawn always smiled and shook her head. Certainly she was Heather's mother, and David the only possibility as her father. Yet there were times now when she wondered if Heather had only been theirs to borrow. It seemed she never actually belonged to them at all.

Evan interrupted her thoughts. "You've lost that scared look you were carrying around with you yesterday."

"I feel better today." This could be a good trip, she told herself, if she could hold her internal demons at bay.

"You know," Evan stroked Romeo with practiced fingers, exploring him for any lump or bruise that could cause them problems. "Sometimes I like you better when you're scared, when I know I've got the upper hand." He laughed. "Sometimes I'm a little *afraid* of you."

She was surprised he gave words to the feelings. A year ago he told her she brought him nothing but trouble. She was dangerous, he said. She refused to take the responsibility for his feelings then, just as she would refuse to take it now.

"Afraid of me . . . or of your feelings about me?"

He looked at her sharply and she thought for a moment that perhaps she'd misunderstood him. Perhaps he was speaking in terms that were purely professional. But he smiled and stood up to set Romeo back in the incubator. "Definitely time to change the subject," he said. "Sorry. I blew the pact."

She didn't push him. Let him have his secrets, she thought. Maybe the pact was a good thing. If he spoke too freely to her, the words themselves might tempt her. No matter how lifeless her own marriage became, she would not allow herself to hurt his.

· Six ·

SHE HAD ASKED the boys three times to straighten the family room. Robin and Evan were coming over in less than an hour, along with the guide for their trip, Tess Kirscher, and the family room needed bulldozing. She waded through an ankle-deep sea of record albums, magazines, socks, and tennis shoes to get to the stereo and snap it off. The ferrets, knotted together on the top of one speaker, looked up at her in surprise before twisting themselves into a new formation and shutting their eyes again.

"Keith, Jamie, get in here!"

David appeared in the doorway, dish towel in hand. He frowned at the room. "Why didn't you tell them to clean this up earlier?" he asked.

She spotted a tennis shoe on the coffee table and had to stop herself from throwing it at him.

"What, Mom?" Keith sidled into the room, noisily eating a plum, total innocence in his eyes.

"I'm *angry* with you, Keith. Look at this mess. We have company coming and I want this room clean."

Keith stuck the rest of the plum in his mouth, inflating his cheek with its bulk, and started to pick up socks, slowly, straining, as if each sock were made of lead.

Jamie showed up in the doorway, next to David. He took in the scene. "Can't we do it tomorrow? We're supposed to be at Chris's in fifteen minutes."

"You had all day to do it, Jamie." Shawn lifted the ferrets to her shoulders.

"You can use the living room for your company," said Jamie.

"This is the only room where we can watch slides." David slung the dish towel over his shoulder and started stacking record albums.

"And that's not the point," Shawn said. "It doesn't matter

whether we're having company or not. I asked you to clean up after yourselves and you didn't do it."

"We're doing it; we're doing it." Jamie looked at her. There was not one speck of love or respect in his eyes.

"Hey, I've been looking for this!" Keith held up a scrap of molded plastic. "This goes to my headset. Now I can . . ."

"Keith," Jamie wailed. "We gotta get to Chris's. Just work."

"Fuck off," said Keith.

David rapped him on the arm with the back of his fingers. "Watch it," he warned.

Shawn watched the boys, trying to get it through her mind that these two nasty kids she barely knew were her sons. She sat down on the arm of the sofa. Maybe it was her fault. Not much warmth in the family these days. And she probably wasn't showing the kind of interest in them she had when they were younger.

"What are you doing at Chris's tonight?" Her tone was different now. Kinder, she hoped, more concerned.

Keith shrugged. "Nothing."

"Well, it must be something. Watch TV? Play games?"

"No, Mom," Jamie scoffed as he dropped a stack of magazines into the basket by the door. "His mother's taking us to Film City to get some movies."

"What movies do you think you'll get?"

Jamie looked disgusted. He stood up to his full, suddenly frightening height, hands on hips, and she looked into the mirror image of her own eyes. "Do you mind?" he asked. "We're cleaning up here, like you said. Do we have to talk to you too?"

"Yes, you *do* have to talk to me. I'm your mother, damn it." She shivered as if it were January instead of July. The ferrets wrapped around her neck were the only warmth in the room.

David stood up. "You know better than to use that tone of voice to your mother," he said.

She left the room before she could hear the boys' reply. She walked through the kitchen to her bedroom and lay down on the bed. The ferrets adjusted themselves to her new position with a few squirmy maneuvers and she stroked them with her fingers. Rodolfo and Mimi. Ridiculous names. Operatic names, provided by David of course. She never knew one ferret from the other, though David certainly seemed to. He'd manipulate them like puppets on his lap, have them take on the parts of whatever opera it was they were from. *La Bohème?* Yes, that must be it. Mimi with her tubercular cough. He'd dance that poor ferret around on his lap, raising his voice an octave or two to sing *Mi chiamano Mimi*, interrupted now and then by a gagging cough. Shawn smiled ruefully at the thought. *Ah, David, you are so offensively content with your life.*

She leaned on her elbow to look out through the big arched windows into the backyard. The jacaranda trees were completely green now; the lavender blossoms lay in a carpet on the ground.

David walked into the bedroom pulling off his T-shirt. He dropped it along with the dish towel into the laundry basket. "The family room's clean. The boys are gone, and the dishes are done."

She sat up slowly. "We've been too permissive with them," she said.

"This is just a phase." He walked into his closet, and she heard him sliding hangers along the rack.

"They worry me, David. They're changing and . . ."

"They're acting like teenage boys," David said. He stepped out of the closet, pulling on an ages-old white Mexican shirt, embroidered in blue, open at the neck. It used to make her skin tingle to see him in that shirt.

"Being a teenager is no excuse for rudeness." She could imagine what the next few years would be like if she stayed with David. The boys would grow more and more belligerent, with David's relaxed attitude forcing her to be the sole disciplinarian. She thought of the parent-teacher conferences of the last couple of years. David always went with her—appearances were important, and God, how he wowed those teachers. But she was the one who had to confront the boys with the bad news. "Those boys just don't *apply* themselves," one teacher after another would tell them. She was the one who had to enforce the restrictions, the "no TV," the "no phone." David pretended to help; he went through the motions, but he was ineffectual. The boys knew his heart wasn't in it. They waited out his directives and then went on their way. She would do just as well on her own.

"It'll pass, Shawn." David combed his hair in the mirror above the oak dresser.

"This isn't a good time to go away, while they're going through this metamorphosis."

"Listen, Shawn." He sat on the edge of the bed and put his arm around her. "You may want to stay here and supervise their transformation from butterflies to maggots, but *I'm* going to Peru."

She smiled. "It's a good thing you're a traffic reporter and not a biologist," she said.

* * *

Robin and Evan arrived first. Shawn was dressing when the doorbell rang. She heard the barking of the Labs and the scramble of their claws on the Mexican tiles of the foyer. *Damn*, she forgot to put them in the yard. She heard Robin's squeal of displeasure. The dogs were probably thumping their heavy tails around her legs in excitement. They wouldn't jump, and certainly wouldn't harm, but Robin wasn't much of a dog lover. She thought animals belonged in the zoo, not in the living room.

Shawn heard Robin's nervous laugh. "They've gotten bigger."

Shawn bit her lip. Had she really forgotten to lock the dogs out or was she subconsciously trying to make Robin uncomfortable? She always picked apart her feelings about Robin and was often ashamed of what she discovered about herself. She tried hard to treat Robin warmly to make up for the wicked thoughts lurking in her mind.

She finished dressing quickly and hurried to the foyer. She kissed Robin's cheek, squeezed Evan's arm. "Sorry about the dogs, Rob," she said.

"No problem," Robin smiled as she took a glass of club soda from David's hand. She looked terrific, as usual. And as usual, it looked as though it took no effort. She wore a soft, peach-colored dress belted at the waist in blue. Her throat was layered in gold, warm and rich against her tan. Shawn herself wore one necklace, which she thought was more beautiful than all of Robin's put together. From a distance the necklace looked like an intricately woven gold chain, but closer inspection revealed tiny gold tamarins, linked tail to tail, hand to hand. It was a gift from Evan. He'd had it made for her a couple of years ago.

They settled into the family room and talked about the weather—warm, very dry. David always spoke of how well-matched they were as a foursome, the St. Johns and the Ryders. Shawn didn't know what he meant. When the four of them were together, she thought they all wore masks, tiptoeing on the thin ice of a lake that would swallow them up if they risked a firmer tread.

The doorbell rang and Shawn answered it. A woman stood illuminated in the silver glow of the front porch light. She had to be Tess Kirscher, but she was not at all what Shawn expected. The gentle darkness she'd imagined in their guide was missing. Tess was tall and straight, as if a wire ran through her spine and held her taut. Her dark blond hair was cut just below her ears and swept away from her face. She was beautiful. But although she was dressed in long, soft beige linen pants and a blouse of green silk, there was nothing else soft about her.

"Dr. Kirscher?" Shawn asked, surprised at her inability to use the name *Tess.*

The woman nodded and offered her a cool hand. Shawn wanted to hold it for a few minutes to warm it up.

"I'm Shawn Ryder," she said. "Please come in."

The woman carried a projector in her hand and a purse made of some nubby fabric over her shoulder. She stepped inside and followed Shawn into the family room.

Shawn stumbled a little over the introductions and chided herself for being intimidated by this stranger in her own home.

David stood and shook the woman's hand. She was nearly as tall as he was. "Something to drink?" he asked.

"Do you have Jack Daniels?" She set the projector on the coffee table.

"Sure," David said easily, and he turned toward the kitchen.

Sure, thought Shawn. In the back of the cupboard somewhere. A very old bottle with dusty shoulders.

Evan cleared his throat and sat forward. "We're glad you can go with us," he said, his tone formal. "I've made an expedition to the Meseta region, but I don't know Dacu at all."

"Yes." Dr. Kirscher crossed her legs. The clothes didn't camouflage the long lines and sharp angles of her body. "Few people know Dacu, which is precisely why I am so fond of it."

Shawn could easily picture this woman lecturing to huge botany classes, with her clipped language and self-assurance.

David returned from the kitchen and handed Dr. Kirscher the glass of bourbon. Suddenly, Robin leaped from the sofa, club soda splashing on the cushions. She sat down again quickly, blushing.

"Sorry." She pointed to the wall near the fireplace where Rodolfo and Mimi were slinking toward the stereo speakers. "They startled me."

Evan put his arm around her. "I can imagine what life in the jungle will be like with you."

Dr. Kirscher took a swallow of her drink. "Perhaps this is not the best type of trip for you, Mrs. St. John."

Robin smiled. "I know what it will be like," she said. "I'm ready."

Dr. Kirscher didn't return the smile. She settled her carousel of slides onto the projector and played with the controls. "You might want to consider staying home. If it's a vacation you're after, wait until your husband returns from the *Amazonas* and then fly to Hawaii, perhaps. Or you might prefer meeting Dr. St. John in Rio de Janeiro when his work is completed."

Shawn tensed. The words had been spoken in a helpful fashion, but the condescension was clear. She placed her glass of wine on the coffee table. "First of all," she said, "let's use first names. After all, we're going to be *living* together in a few weeks. And secondly, if Robin is courageous enough to go, I think she deserves our support."

"There really isn't much to be afraid of, is there?" David asked.

Tess shook her head. She told them it was difficult to find the big cats or peccaries or bushmasters even when you were looking for them, and the only time she'd seen a vampire bat was while she was guiding a group of bat researchers. "But the trip could be miserable if you expect to find danger behind every tree." She looked at Robin.

"She'll be fine," Evan said, although it was obvious the mention of vampire bats had done nothing to increase Robin's confidence.

"We can pick up food and supplies in Iquitos before we head out to Dacu," Tess said.

Shawn and Evan exchanged looks. "We'd rather not go through Iquitos," Evan said.

Tess knit her brows. "Of course we'll go through Iquitos. It's the only logical starting point. My first slide here is a map . . . I'll show you." She turned on the machine, and a faint map of northeastern Peru appeared on the white wall of the family room. David switched off the lamp in the corner, and the map snapped sharply into focus. Iquitos had been circled in red, a line drawn from it south to the Rio Tavaco, then to a tributary that cut a path through Dacu.

Tess had their route going through Iquitos as though no other were possible. Shawn's heart sank as if someone told her her house had burned down. A totally ridiculous, completely out of proportion reaction to this map on the wall.

Evan sat forward. "We could start out in Pucallpa, couldn't we? There's an airport there."

Tess wore a full-blown frown now. "*Pucallpa?* That's much too far south. What's wrong with Iquitos?"

"It's because of me, Tess," Shawn said. "A few years ago Evan and I planned an expedition to Meseta, but I made it only

as far as Iquitos. I got word there of . . . a family emergency
and had to turn back. Evan went on alone. Going through Iquitos
would bring back memories and I . . .'' Her voice faltered. She
wanted to say that she was afraid something terrible would happen again but thought better of it. This woman with the cold
hands would never understand. Her reasons seemed suddenly
ludicrous even to herself.

Tess leaned back in her chair. "I have connections in Iquitos.
It will make it much easier to get the things we need.''

"Honey, this is a new trip," said David. "I'll be with you.
We'll all be together. We'll only have to be in Iquitos . . . what,
Tess, one day?''

"Just long enough to get our supplies.''

Shawn nodded, giving in. "You're right," she said. "It makes
better sense to . . .''

"No," said Evan. "I promised you we wouldn't go to Iquitos
and I don't care how inconvenient Pucallpa is, we can . . .''

"Evan, it's all right." At that rational moment she truly believed it. She would go to Iquitos. The three syllables alone were
enough to harden her stomach into a knot. Childish. She had
attached the loss of Heather to a place, made it tangible so she
could deal with it. It was a long time ago. She didn't need that
crutch any more. She looked at Robin who was keeping one eye
on the sleeping ferrets. The two of them—the two women—were
already proving to be difficult travelers, something of the hys-
teric in each of them. Shawn was embarrassed for them both.

Tess turned her attention back to the screen. "From Iquitos
we'll travel by road to the Rio Tavaco.''

A new slide was on the projector now. A river with water the
color of strong coffee, lush green vegetation on both banks.

"The Rio Tavaco is a black water river, a tributary of the
Amazonas that will take us to the smaller streams leading into
the Dacu region, where your tamarins live.''

For the first time, Shawn noticed Tess's accent. The foreign
names extracted it from her. It was very faint and hard to place.

"Dacu is one of my favorite areas because it's completely
uninhabited. That's why your Copper Elves have gone undiscov-
ered for so long." She sat back and chuckled. The sound was
unnatural coming from her. "I wonder if any of you realize what
an adjustment this will be for you. Obviously you're accustomed
to comfort.'' She swept her arm out to take in the room: the two
blue leather sofas, the stone fireplace, the wall of hi-tech ma-
chinery. This used to be Shawn's favorite room in the house.

When they first moved in, she decorated it with her collection
of folk art. But the primitive, handcrafted artistry seemed out of
place next to the computer, the VCR, the stereo, and all the
other machines the boys and David had gathered over the years.
Tess continued in a new voice, professorial. "Materialism is the
greatest threat to the South American jungle. They say, let's go
in, let's cut down the trees, let's develop the land. They're de-
stroying the most perfectly balanced ecosystem on earth."

Shawn stifled a yawn and let her mind wander. She could
make out Robin and Evan in the dim light, sitting so close together they might have been one person on the sofa. Melissa did
that for them. A powerful little baby, Melissa. She had power
even before she was born.

She looked at David, in the recliner on the other side of Tess.
When was the last time she sat comfortably entwined with him?
The light from the back of the projector glanced off his cheek
and lit the silver in his light brown hair. He had far more gray
than she did, although they were both thirty-eight. The gray only
added to his attractiveness. Classic good looks. Evan's features
by comparison lacked symmetry. His nose had been broken once,
the dark eyebrows arched at different angles. The beard was
never the slightest bit straggly, but it still lent him that earthy
quality that drew her to him from the start. He was slighter than
David. It startled her, early on, to feel the tightness of him, the
compact efficiency of his muscles. It startled her to know she
was not with David.

"Ugh," said Robin.

Shawn looked at the screen to see a long brown and yellow
snake curled around the trunk of a tree. She shuddered herself.
Her fondness for snakes was limited to the boas upstairs.

She remembered old nightmares, long ago, of a snake wrapping itself around her body, pinning her arms to her sides,
squeezing the breath from her throat. She would wake up clutching at David for comfort. She remembered his soft laughter, his
fingers on her throat, gently bringing the life back. She looked
over at him now and he winked at her.

Tess left early, as soon as she'd run through her set of slides.
She seemed to have no desire to turn this into a social occasion
and that was fine with Shawn. She was relieved to have Tess
Kirscher out of her house.

"How about a soak in the hot tub?" David suggested as he
closed the door behind Tess. "I thought of bringing it up while

she was here, but with all that talk about materialism I figured I'd better keep my mouth shut.''

Evan and Robin needed to borrow bathing suits. Shawn grabbed a plain black tank suit from her drawer for Robin. Robin would make it look as though it had been created for her. She found a pair of David's running shorts for Evan, then crossed the hall to the guest room where the St. Johns could change. She turned on the overhead light and ran a hand over the quilt on the bed to smooth it. It was Heather's old room, although most traces of her had long ago been cleaned out. There was the mobile of tiny stuffed penguins still hanging from the corner by the window—a gift to Heather from Shawn's father. And there was a picture of Heather on the wall, taken by David when Heather was about three. She was getting her face made up by a clown at a carnival, and her eyes were wide with delight at the miracle taking shape on her face. Her blond curls were pinned back with red barrettes shaped like butterflies.

''Mommy, I'm a clown!'' Heather took that responsibility very seriously, asking Shawn every five minutes if she was being funny enough to wear a clown face. ''Is this f-funny?'' she asked, blowing bubbles through a straw into her soda. ''Is this f-funny?'' she asked, putting her sneakers on her hands instead of her feet. The little stutter worried them. Heather saw a speech therapist at nursery school, and Shawn and David could see the improvement week by week. By the time Heather died, the stutter had nearly disappeared.

Shawn looked at the picture again. She had not been as patient with Heather as she should have been that day. She wished she could get inside her memories and change them. She would give Heather every speck of her attention. She would playfully tie her sneakers while they were on her hands, wouldn't scold her for blowing bubbles in her Sprite. Why did parents do that, yell at their kids for such stupid little things? A few months after Heather died, Shawn was leaving a restaurant when she saw a mother scolding her little boy for blowing bubbles in his milk. She stopped at the table before she had a chance to think through what she was doing.

She leaned down in front of the open-mouthed woman and said, ''If he died tomorrow, you would long for the sound of those bubbles.'' She left the restaurant knowing she was bordering on insanity, but not particularly caring.

Heather's twin bed with its white eyelet canopy had been replaced by a double brass bed. Six months after Heather died,

Shawn told David it was time to change the room. She could no longer tolerate the waiting-for-Heather-to-come-back look of it, as if Heather were simply away for a few days. David gave her one of those strange looks, blank and glazed over, as though he didn't understand what she said, and she knew she would get no help from him. She did it all herself, packing away the toys, the clothes, the pictures on the wall. The only thing she couldn't manage was the bed. Evan did that for her, keeping all the screws together in a little plastic bag, folding the white eyelet into a square, carrying the pieces of the wooden frame up into the attic.

"Is that for me?" Robin stood next to Evan in the doorway, pointing to the bathing suit in Shawn's hand.

Shawn nodded, shaking off the memories. "And these are for Evan," she murmured as she handed him David's shorts and walked past the St. Johns into the hall.

The water in the hot tub was warm and thick, and the bubbles formed hills and valleys of white foam on the surface. The air smelled of honeysuckle. Shawn felt the muscles in her back soften and unwind. She didn't use the hot tub often anymore, although David was in it nearly every night. She hoped he could find a place to live with a hot tub of his own.

"I hope," Evan looked up at the stars, "that Dr. Kirscher comes down off her pedestal eventually."

"She's pretty intolerable," Shawn agreed.

"She knows the jungle though," said David.

"We'll get our daily ecology lesson, I'm sure of that," Evan said dryly. He scooped up a handful of foam and crushed the bubbles in his palm. "She's a bitch. We should have pushed to go through Pucallpa. It's *our* expedition. She should accommodate us."

Shawn shrugged. "I'm sure it'll be fine."

"Of course it will be." David caught her hand under the water and held it on his thigh.

Evan looked unconvinced. "You settled too easily, Shawn. Kirscher thinks she can walk all over you now. Every decision we have to make she's going to think she can get her way."

David squeezed her hand. "It's better to save the arguing for things that really matter instead of nit-picking over every little detail."

"I think avoiding Iquitos really mattered to Shawn, David." There was a touch of surprising hostility in Evan's voice.

David looked at her. "Was it that important to you?"

She felt sorry for David, that he knew less of what mattered to her than Evan did. "I was upset about Iquitos at first, but now I'm just happy we're going. It doesn't matter what route we take." There. That should satisfy them both. She looked at Evan through the steam. *Let it drop, please.*

Evan turned his head away from her and put his arm around Robin. "This one is going to be our real problem. Vampire bats!" He made a dive for her neck with his mouth. Robin laughed, not bothering to put up a struggle.

Shawn leaned her head against the tiled edge of the tub and shut her eyes. She wished the longing inside her would die. She could not have Evan again.

David's fingers were woven through hers like the grasp of a creeping plant, tight enough to know he was there, yet not so tight she couldn't work her way free. That was the problem with David—he always left the choice in her hands.

· Seven ·

SEVEN YEARS EARLIER almost to the day, she was the mother of six-year-old twin boys and a four-week-old baby girl, brand new to the West Coast, and on her first day of work as a tamarin breeding specialist at the San Diego Canyon Conservation Center. Even now, the memory of that first day could be triggered by the smell of rich coffee. That was her strongest impression of that day, Evan's coffee. Or maybe the strongest impression was of Evan himself—the sharp contrast of his dark hair and light blue eyes, the provocatively arching eyebrow, the beard. What was it about a beard that made a man's lips look soft and defenseless?

Evan wore a welcoming smile with something held in reserve, as if she would have to win him over. She liked that.

"The shipment of Red-Ears is due in September," he said, instead of "hello." "We have a hell of a lot of work to do." He motioned her to sit on his office sofa. It would be a while before she learned it converted into a bed.

His office was small, twelve by twelve, she guessed. One wall was covered with the framed first pages of his articles, and she was touched and relieved by his pride. It made him a little less intimidating. A collection of primate posters lined the other walls. She was familiar with all of them except one—a capuchin monkey dangling upside down from the end of its tail, its hands peeling a banana. The caption read: "Happiness is a prehensile tail." It made her smile.

"Coffee?" he asked as she sat down on the sofa.

Later he told her the coffee had been a test. He brewed it dark and strong every morning from whole beans he kept in a wicker basket next to his grinder. If she paled at the first swallow, he planned to send her packing.

But she thought it was delicious and stood to examine the beans he made it from. "They're nearly black." She dug her hand deep into the basket and let the oily beans slip through her fingers. "Colombian?"

"Brazilian."

"Like the Red-Ears." She sat down again, thinking: *How is it that I'm sitting here with Evan St. John, about to become a partner in the only North American breeding program for Red-Eared Tamarins?*

He was wearing jeans and a T-shirt; she wore jeans and a sleeveless green blouse. She hadn't known how to dress. She didn't want to appear too casual, but this was hardly the type of job one dressed up for.

She'd had her hair cut just before the move. It barely reached her shoulders, and she wore it parted in the middle with deep straight bangs that were not in style, which pleased her. David called it the Cleopatra look, although she knew her blue eyes and Irish skin precluded anything so exotic.

Evan joined her on the sofa, sitting at the opposite end. "I admired the work you did at the National Zoo," he said.

"It's *your* work that inspired me." She hoped that didn't sound too pat. She had read every paper he'd written in the last five years. But the name Evan St. John was attached in her mind to an older man, someone graying and a little paunchy. She had imagined his speech would be touched with a British accent. She had certainly not expected to find him this young. And she had not expected to find herself attracted to him. That unnerved her. In nine years of marriage to David, she'd never felt this physically attracted to another man.

"Evan . . . may I ask how old you are?"

"Two years younger than you." He grinned maliciously.

"You're only *twenty-nine*?" She suddenly felt as if she'd accomplished nothing in her thirty-one years.

"Do I look that much older?" He looked worried now.

"It's just that you've done so much more than I have professionally."

"Well, I didn't need to take time off to get married and have babies," he said, and she thought she detected a wistful note in his voice.

She held out her mug. "May I have a second cup?"

He smiled and poured, and for the rest of that day as she toured the Center with him, she felt the rich liquid running in her veins.

The Center was different then. Much smaller. There were no Copper Elves. On that day seven years ago, neither Evan nor

Shawn had ever heard of a Copper Elf Tamarin, and the pentagon-shaped enclosures were still locked inside the head of some architect. Even then, Shawn was pleased with the tamarin facilities. There were two long concrete buildings, each with a central hall running between a row of tamarin enclosures and a row of bird enclosures. One building contained several families of Silver Tamarins, the species Evan had worked with for the last few years. The other building, which clung to the edge of the canyon, was new and stood empty, its ten enclosures waiting for the shipment of Red-Eared Tamarins.

Each morning began with the coffee on Evan's sofa while they worked on the schedule for the day. Shawn found herself looking forward to that half hour. She carried the memory of it with her for the rest of the day, sometimes into the night. She began to tell him more than her plans for the Red-Ears and her ideas for research. She told him about Jamie's skit at the breakfast table, about Heather smiling her first real smile. She spoke of her father, how he'd raised her by himself, how he could cure a sick animal with the touch of one rough hand. She told him how David had made a sacrifice for her by moving out here without a job, leaving his parents to fend for themselves back east. Lynn was here in San Diego as well, and Shawn knew David felt that both he and his sister had deserted his parents. He never complained, though. He knew this was best for Shawn's career, and he seemed to be enjoying the time at home with his new daughter.

Evan was slower to open up, but gradually he told her about his own family, or lack of family. He had no personal identity, he said, so he worked hard to make a name for himself professionally. That had cost him over the years. He didn't date much, mostly women he met through church. He had one serious relationship that ended a couple of years ago when the woman got fed up with his obsession with work.

"She told me, 'It's me or the monkeys, Evan,' " he laughed. "She should have known better than to hand me that kind of ultimatum."

In the afternoons of those early days at the Center, Shawn locked herself in her own square office with the rented breast pump to express her milk for Heather. She stored it in the small refrigerator Evan kept in his office and carried it home at night for David to give Heather the next day. Heather never balked at the bottle as long as it was offered by David.

When Heather was a couple of months old, David got the job

at the classical station as a traffic reporter. He had to convince the station he could handle both the reporting and the flying. It was the perfect job for him, being in and on the air at the same time.

For the three weeks before they found a sitter, she brought Heather to work with her. It was a treat, being with her baby. She kept Heather with her in a carrier strapped against her chest, or pushed her in a carriage as she went about her work in the Center. She took her time finding a sitter.

By the end of the first week, Evan was calling Heather his "favorite little primate." He begged to cart her around with him in the carrier, always with one hand supporting her as if the sack might break and he'd lose her. At times Shawn caught him having conversations with her baby, speaking quietly to Heather's wobbly little head. By the beginning of the second week, he asked Shawn not to lock him out of her office when she nursed. She could think of no good reason why she should, although she had to do battle with her feelings for him. Having him in the room while Heather nursed forced her to define him as a man she felt no attraction to, and that she found she couldn't do.

"Evan needs a baby," she said to David at the dinner table one night. "If there are any single women at the station, keep him in mind, okay?"

"Uh huh." David straightened Jamie's chair and brushed the little boy's hair off his forehead.

"He's really good with Heather. He rocked her to sleep after she nursed today." She was confessing as a child might to a parent, testing to see if she'd done something wrong. She had.

"Evan was there while you nursed?" David set his fork back on his plate.

"Yes."

"Kind of personal, don't you think? He's a stranger really."

"He's not a stranger."

David picked up his fork again and nodded. "Sorry. You're right. I guess I'm just jealous that he gets to spend time with Heather during the day and I don't. I miss her."

Shawn guiltily returned to her dinner. Sweet, trusting David. It would never occur to him that it was *her* relationship with Evan that merited his jealousy.

She couldn't pinpoint the moment she realized she was in love with Evan. It was a gradual thing, each day building on the day before, warm-colored threads in an intricate tapestry. Her dreams were full of him, and she found herself blushing into her bathroom mirror in the morning at the memory of them. David attributed her intensified sexual fervor to the relief of feeling settled in San Diego, to his working, to the kids being taken care of. She reached for him constantly during those nights, but behind her closed eyes it was Evan's face she saw, Evan's lips she kissed. The fantasy didn't please her. She was angry at herself for not being able to control it.

They worked hard readying the enclosures for the tamarins. They expected twelve breeding pairs of Red-Ears and twenty juveniles, but some were always lost during the tricky period of transport. They spent more and more time over coffee in the morning, planning every detail of the care of the rare animals.

They were both nervous as the day of shipment neared. The coffee didn't help, and sometimes Shawn wasn't certain of the source of her jitters. She couldn't sit still. She checked the enclosures two or three times a day, rearranging the slope of the branches, testing the heating system that had to be in perfect order for them to be able to acclimate the new animals.

Only five tamarins were lost during shipment. "They're the ugliest tamarins I've ever seen," Shawn laughed when they'd gotten them into the new enclosures. The animals were emaciated-looking, long and stringy, their fur a mottled gray black with crimson streaks across the sides of nearly furless heads.

Evan nodded. "People are going to wonder why there's such a fuss to save them."

The tamarins were flighty, too. Shawn was bitten three times on one hand within the first few days.

For the first week, Evan stayed at the Center each night while Shawn went home to her family. In the morning she'd find him in his sofa bed, groggy from sitting up with the tamarins. The Stud Book would be lying on the pillow next to him, a substitute for a lover. He couldn't stand to be apart from that book. It contained their carefully transcribed pairings of the Red-Ears, with plenty of room next to each pair for their potential offspring. The book was full of promise.

"You know, they're not so ugly once you get to know them," he yawned to her one morning. He sat up in the bed, barechested, to accept the mug of coffee she poured him. Then he grinned. "Did I have a dream about you last night, Shawn McGarry Ryder."

"Yes?" She sat on the arm of the sofa and tried to look at his eyes instead of the dark hair on his chest.

"In between two skinny-monkey dreams."

"I'm flattered."

He told her he met her in a forest, thick moss under their feet. "You'd been bitten again. Not on your hand, but here." He touched her side, just below the ribs. "You said it was a tamarin bite, but when you lifted your shirt, I knew it couldn't be. The marks were huge and very deep. They weren't bleeding, but I could see torn muscle inside, and somehow I knew that meant it was a fatal bite. But I tried to pretend for your sake that it wasn't serious." He took a swallow of coffee. "And then it came to me that if I made love to you, you'd be cured."

She laughed. "Quite an ego you have."

He looked defensive. "It was a great dream."

She cupped her mug in her hands, remembering her own dreams. "So, did you cure me?"

"I don't remember."

"You mean it wasn't memorable?"

He smiled. "You know, it's a good thing you have to go home to your family at night and can't spend the night here."

"Why?"

"Because I don't think I could stand it, knowing you were sleeping in the next office."

She set down her cup. The light in the room seemed concentrated in the blue of his eyes. "I don't think I could stand it either, Evan."

He leaned his head against the back of the sofa. "It's a good thing then, isn't it?"

The phone woke her at five-thirty in the morning on the day before Christmas. It was Evan. "They just called me from the Center." His voice was tight. "There was a brushfire in the canyon. They said we lost some Red-Ears."

"I'll meet you." She was already out of bed and pulling on a sweater. She leaned across the bed to give David a kiss before she left.

She pulled into the parking lot of the Center as a huge red sun rose out of the blackened chaparral. The air tasted of soot. The buildings reflected the sun with an unearthly red glow, and puffs of pale gray ash floated everywhere. It already layered the roof of Evan's car and began to settle on her own. She felt it disintegrate under her fingers when she touched her hair.

The earth around the Red-Ear enclosure was charred, but the building itself looked untouched. Evan met her at the entrance. "I already took the live ones to the vet," he said. The whites of his eyes reflected the red of the sun. "There weren't many."

"There weren't many *alive*?"

For an answer he took her arm and led her into the building. The first thing she noticed was the silence. Where were the trills and the long calls? Where were the ever-present sounds of the birds? "All the birds bought it," Evan said. She saw a couple of the bird keepers far down the row of enclosures, moving quietly among feathered corpses.

"I don't *hear* anything." She coughed. It was hard to breathe.

The first three enclosures were empty. "They were okay," said Evan. "They're over at the vet's. A couple in enclosure three had some smoke problems, but I think they'll be all right." He was silent as they came to the fourth enclosure, and Shawn gasped. Three dead tamarins were sprawled along the back wall. A fourth lay dead on the ground beneath the nest box.

They walked slowly past the remaining six enclosures without speaking. Most of the tamarins were against the back walls, near the closed sliding doors that led to the outside runs. They'd tried to escape. Shawn imagined their panic. She felt tears run over the hand she clasped to her mouth to keep from screaming.

At the end of the hallway she stepped back out into the red sun and chill air. Evan put his arms around her, and they stood that way for a long time.

"None was burned," he said after a while. "It was the smoke. It just poured from one end of the hall to the other."

"We've lost . . . what, Evan? Two-thirds of our population?"

He groaned. "Think what that means in terms of potential population. *Shit.*" He banged his fist into the concrete wall. "All I've thought about for the past two years was these god-damned Red-Ears. Can you picture the telegram to Brazil? 'Have fried twenty-five of your tamarins. Will resume breeding program when you ship a couple of dozen more.' "

"Shhh. Let's get this mess cleaned up."

It took them most of the day. They had no energy to work quickly. They checked the tattooed thighs of the dead tamarins and marked them off in the Stud Book. They wrote the word *died* and the date next to the neatly written numbers that only a few hours before had been a record of hope and optimism. In the last enclosure Evan lowered himself tiredly to the floor and leaned his back against the wall. Shawn let him sit. She read the tattoos and wrote in the Stud Book while he stared at the ceiling.

"Is that the female?" he asked as she checked off the last one.

She nodded and handed the limp body to him. He laid it across his knee and rubbed the little belly between his thumb and forefinger.

"Pregnant?" she asked.

He nodded and handed the tamarin to her. "Every single enclosure had a pregnant female."

"Well, at least we know we were on the right track."

They spent the rest of the day sweeping woodshavings and ashes from the floors of the enclosures. Shawn's sweater and jeans were covered with soot. She would never get the smell from her hair.

She called David from Evan's office as the sun was setting.

"I'll be home soon," she told him. She could hear Heather howling in the background and the boys singing "Jingle Bells." She was missing Christmas Eve with her children. And poor David. This was not how he'd anticipated spending a day off. "Thanks for covering for me, David."

"We're doing fine. We're peeling carrots for Santa's reindeer."

"I don't think the reindeer mind the peel."

"Tell that to your finicky sons."

She hung up and met Evan's eyes. He was slouched in his desk chair. He looked too tired to move, and she imagined him sitting there all through the night and into Christmas Day.

"Merry Fucking Christmas," he said.

She stood next to him and held his head against her hip. His hair felt woolly with ash under her fingers. "I'm glad you're having Christmas dinner with us tomorrow," she said. "I would hate to think of you alone after this." She had invited him months earlier. Evan was already very much a part of the family.

He shook his head against her hip. "I would be poor company."

"You can't be alone on Christmas, Evan."

"It won't be the first time. And there's work to do here."

"The kids are looking forward to seeing you. Your favorite little primate misses you."

"No," he said flatly. His hand tightened against the back of her thigh. She felt the pressure of each finger, like a warning of what would come next. He lifted his other hand to her hip and slowly rubbed her hip bone through the denim of her jeans.

She felt one single stab of alarm that quickened her heartbeat. She thought of moving away, of picking up her jacket and leaving. But instead she shut her eyes and waited. His fingers unfastened the button of her jeans, slid the zipper down its track, and smoothed the triangle of denim to the side so he could lay his cheek against her skin. She pressed his head against her and felt her pulse beating deep in her stomach, pounding clear through to her spine. She wondered if he could feel it under his cheek, through the soft down of his beard.

He looked up at her, and she made certain that whatever he saw in her eyes couldn't be interpreted as resistance. He stood up and kissed her, and for the first time that day she welcomed the taste of soot and fire. She leaned against him, her jeans already open, inviting him. He pulled her sweater over her head in a flurry of gray ashes and led her to the sofa. When she felt his lips on her breasts, she knew that this was what she'd been waiting for since the day she first met him, since the moment she ran her fingers through the slick dark beans in the basket on his shelf.

She lay in his arms afterward, the two of them tangled together along the length of the sofa they hadn't taken the time to open. But although she relished the warmth of him against her body, something was not right. She was fighting for air. One breath was too deep, the next few too shallow. And a tremor crept into her stomach. Within minutes it spread to her thighs, up into her arms.

"You're shivering," he said. He rose and brought her a blanket from his closet. She sat up while he wrapped it around her, but the trembling was almost convulsive now and she clutched the blanket to her with damp palms.

"I think I'm going to be sick." She stood up and walked woodenly past him to the tiny bathroom in the corner of his office, swallowing hard against the nausea. She shut the door behind her and knelt in front of the high, white toilet, tucking the blanket under her knees. She began to cry. There had never been a single time in her life that she'd gotten sick without crying. Reduced to a two-year-old by a little nausea. She reached up to turn on the fan in the room, hoping Evan couldn't hear her.

The nausea held her on the brink, and she dropped the blanket to the floor as sweat ran down her neck. She was dizzy with images of David, changing Heather's diaper, peeling carrots for reindeer. *"David,"* she whispered. *"I'm so sorry."*

She gagged. Again and again. Nothing came up, but she was helpless to stop the spasms.

Evan was dressed when she left the bathroom. His face was white. "Are you all right?"

Her legs carried her just as far as the sofa, and she sat down, wrapped once again in the blanket. "I'm okay," she whispered. "Embarrassed mostly." She began to cry again, and he sat behind her, rubbing her arms through the blanket.

"I'm sorry," he said in her ear. "Never again."

She shook her head. "No, never." She stood up and began to dress. She spotted Evan's rosary on his desk. It was made of carved wooden beads, dark with age. He told her once that he had felt so guilty the first time he touched a girl's breasts, he prayed the rosary for hours afterward. Was that what he would do when she left him now? Was that how he would spend his Christmas Day?

She pulled into her driveway. The newly decorated tree blinked its blue and white lights at her from the arched living room window. Inside, David already had the boys fed and scrubbed and Heather in bed. He frowned at the sight of her. "My God, you're a wreck." He reached for her, but she slipped past him.

"Let me soak in the tub a while to get rid of this soot," she said. She couldn't meet his eyes. Somehow he would know.

He followed her into the bathroom. "Give me your clothes and I'll put them in the laundry," he said.

He made her cocoa, and she sat in the rocking chair in the living room watching him stack the gifts under the tree. He was concerned with order, arranging presents so that Jamie would open the race car before he discovered the track, and Keith would find some toys interspersed with the new clothes.

"He's going to hate getting all these clothes, but maybe it'll teach him not to play in tar the next time," David chuckled and sat back on his heels. "I wish Heather were a little older. Remember the first Christmas the boys knew what was going on?"

She nodded. Oh, it had been fun.

He touched a little glass unicorn hanging from a low branch of the tree. "Jamie wanted this here, but it's really too low. Think I should move it?"

She nodded again. She watched him hang the unicorn a little

higher and thought what a treasure he was, this big handsome man who wanted no more than to see the joy in his children's faces on Christmas morning. She felt a lump form in her throat. What a foolish risk she'd taken.

"Are you crying?" He stood up and set his warm palm against her cheek.

She shrugged.

"The tamarins, huh? Will you be able to get more?"

She talked about the tamarins, as if they were the source of her tears. He wanted her to sit on his lap, but she stayed in the rocker, feeling unworthy of his comfort. She wished she could tell him what she'd done. She needed his forgiveness. If it had been any other man she'd made love to, she would have, but not Evan. Evan was too much a part of their lives.

This would fade, she told herself. She and Evan would ignore what had happened, and it would gradually fade away. She promised herself it wouldn't happen again.

And until Heather died, she was true to her word.

· Eight ·

DAVID SAT AT the controls of the plane waiting for Jillian Craig. She was late, and that bothered him. She'd be covering for him during the next two weeks while he was in Peru, and he didn't want her to botch the job. They had to get in the air soon if he wanted to get the first report in on time. He didn't want to miss the sunrise, either. The stringy purple clouds over the mountains promised a good one. You'd think that after seven years he'd be hardened to the view. But no, every morning he rose into the air with a smile on his face. And to endure this torture he was paid $80,000 a year. He couldn't imagine a better job.

He looked at his watch again. *Come on, Jill.* He'd have to pass on the sunrise this morning. It wouldn't be the same with her there anyway. It was a solitary activity, although years ago Shawn went up with him every once in a while. She loved it. She tried talking him into taking risks with the plane, pleading with him to fly low over the water. She talked about jumping out when they were over Mission Bay, and for a long time she seriously considered sky-diving, talked about it day and night.

When she grew bored with the flight, she'd tell him she wanted to make love to him, in the air, in the snips of time between his reports. And once she did. She unbuckled his belt, unzipped his pants, and he waited, saying nothing, curious to see how far she would take it. She lowered her head to his lap and put an end to his guessing. He should have known she would, this woman who never did anything halfway. Mother of three, president of the PTA, four thousand feet above San Diego at seven in the morning, breakfasting on her husband.

And now she wouldn't make love to him even in their own bedroom.

Shawn's spirit disappeared overnight. One day she was animated, intensely loving. The next day she was cold, detaching

herself from everything that once brought her pleasure. And he
could blame no one but himself for the change in her.

She never went up with him again after Heather died. Never
let the twins go either. He invited them earlier this year to celebrate their thirteenth birthday. They'd been begging, and he saw
no problem with taking them up. But when he told Shawn, she
sat down at the kitchen table and cried, gut-wrenching sobs that
shook her shoulders and cut cleanly through his heart. She
wouldn't let them go, she said. How could he think she'd agree
to that? He didn't bother to ask her why. He knew her reasons.
And anyway, she would just give him that look that told him he
could not be trusted to keep her children safe.

"Sorry I'm late, Dave." Jillian climbed into the plane, catching her spiky heel on the hem of her red and white print dress.
She had pearls around her neck and she looked as though she'd
been primping, her cheeks a vibrant pink, too much gloss on
her lips. She tossed her light brown hair over her shoulder and
looked at him as he readied the plane for takeoff. "Where to
first?" she asked. She held a pencil at the ready above a small
pad in her lap, like an eager cub reporter.

"Fifteen," he said. She should know that by now, after listening to him every morning for the past year as she claimed.
Plus he'd taken her up with him during last night's rush hour
and he told her then that the route would be the same in the
morning.

She made notes on her pad, her hands shaking. The traffic
report would be sloppy while he was away. Ben Asher would fly
her around next week. Ben was good and he knew the route
well. Still, David didn't like turning the plane over to someone
else.

The traffic was bumper to bumper on Interstate 15. "Do you
see the reason for the backup?" he asked Jillian.

She craned her neck and her face lit up, all pink and gloss.
"An accident!" she said, pleased with herself.

David nodded and studied the three cars angled across the
road. An ambulance was already at the scene. One lane was still
open, but traffic was beginning to clog as the cars plowed ahead
cramming themselves together like the pieces of a jigsaw puzzle.

He spoke into the mike at his throat. "Three-car accident on
fifteen by the Penasquitos exit. The number three lane's open
but traffic's crawling and you have no alternate route here. Just
sit tight and hum your favorite aria, and we'll get you through
before you know it."

Jillian smiled at him. "Your voice is so calm. I'll never be able to sound like that."

"Let's check out five now," he said.

"Could you buy me a drink when we're through?"

"At nine in the morning? Maybe coffee and a Danish."

She touched his arm. "I think I'll need a drink."

She'd wanted a drink last night too, and he bought her one. She looked as though she needed it, but he didn't like the way she used alcohol. As an excuse. She had just one drink before she started flattering him, looking at him with those moony brown eyes. He wished she would just come out with the proposition, so he could give her the speech about his happy marriage. He'd used that speech for sixteen years now, and he wondered if it was starting to sound as false as the words felt on his tongue.

Sometimes he found himself staring at Shawn, searching her face for the woman she used to be. He never found her. He wanted to breathe life back into her, to see her laugh again or do something a little wild, out of the ordinary. He hoped this trip to Peru would make the difference.

He got out of work at ten and drove to the health club, as he did every morning. He never felt quite whole until he had some time in the water. Articles written about him said he stayed in shape by swimming. But he would swim even if it had nothing to do with muscle and body tone. The water was his refuge.

For a few months after Heather died he couldn't go near the pool. There was irony in his powerful stroke, irony that it was water that had taken Heather from them. Then one day, two or three months after the accident, Evan bought him a waterproof Walkman. It wasn't his birthday; there was no special reason for the gift. Evan just knew what it would take to get him back in the water. He even included a tape of Bizet's *The Pearl Fishers*. Evan didn't know one opera from the next, probably thought *The Pearl Fishers* sounded appropriate for swimming. David was certain he had no idea the story was about two men in love with the same woman.

So he returned to the water. With the music, swimming took on a new, sensual quality, but he quickly discovered *The Pearl Fishers* made him weep. That was all right. His tears were always close to the surface back in those days, and he was tired of checking them, never letting them out. The pool was the best place for them. No one would know they were there.

A few years earlier, *San Diego Magazine* did an article on him, big and splashy, titled, "The Soothing Voice in the Sky." The article was written entirely from that angle—David Ryder as the tranquil host of San Diego's rush hour.

"Soothing the frayed nerves of harried commuters . . ." Shawn read to him. He was on his back in their bed, she was straddling him, trying to keep him inside her for as long as she could. She was losing the battle. He was spent, slipping out. The kids would be in any minute anyhow. It was Saturday morning, and they were in the midst of their ritual. He'd locked the bedroom door, they'd made love, and now the three kids would race in and jump on the bed, all warmth and cuddles and chatter about the weekend. He and Shawn finally got a king-size bed when Heather was born just for these Saturday mornings.

It was so easy to take kids for granted. Once they were born, he expected them to always be there. The only thing he worried about regarding their health, and he worried about this an inordinate amount, was their eyesight.

". . . healing headaches and knotted shoulders . . ." Shawn continued reading, "patching gaps in each commuter's journey with his innovative suggestions for alternate routes." She leaned forward to kiss him. "Oh, David, now the whole world knows how wonderful you are."

The article was, all in all, embarrassing in its idolatry. There were photographs with the story, including one of him here at the indoor pool, standing near the diving board in his bathing suit, talking with someone. He had to admit he looked very fit. Shawn frowned and turned the magazine over to look at the cover. "What *is* this," she asked, *"Playgirl?"*

The week after the article appeared, the health club sold nearly a hundred memberships. They thanked David, but he was uncomfortable. The pool was suddenly speckled with women, two here, three there, who splashed around, eyes on him while he swam. He felt distrustful of all of them. Had the woman who said she found his towel actually found it, or had she taken it to arrange a chance to talk with him? Was another woman actually an opera fan, or had she boned up the night before so she could strike up a conversation with him? He wore his wedding ring all the time and mentioned Shawn in conversation. The interest in him peaked and then started a gradual decline, but there were still women here at the club clearly interested in him.

It disturbed him that he was beginning to welcome their attention. He'd see one woman or another at the pool and hope she'd try to talk to him. On a couple of occasions he started the conversation himself. Later he'd stand in the shower and ask himself: *What the hell are you doing?* But he was hungry. His body, his mind, his heart. He was *starving*.

Evan was waiting for him when he got out of the pool. He had called the night before to see if David would have time for racquetball today. It was rare for them to play on a Friday, but Evan was taking the day off to run errands before the trip.

They played two games, Evan winning both, as usual. Even after all these years of weekly racquetball, Evan kept an edge over David. David didn't care—he never took racquet sports seriously. He found their games relaxing after the workweek. But he had watched Evan play others at the club and saw a fury and rage emerge in him that was startling.

"Evan has a temper," Shawn told him long ago. "You never see it because you're so difficult to get angry with—you won't fight back. You keep your feelings so well hidden that it leaves your enemy nothing to work with."

They talked about Shawn in the locker room as they dressed. She was a regular topic for them, a connecting thread between them, although surely after all these years their friendship could stand on its own.

"She's nervous about the trip," David said, pulling on his socks. "Agitated. Barely sleeping. She gets up a few times at night to check on the boys."

"She'll be okay once she's in Peru," said Evan. "She'll get excited about the work and being outdoors."

David sighed. "That's the old Shawn you're describing."

Evan had told him how depressing it was working with Shawn these past few years. She was always technically accurate in her work, but it was mechanical and dispirited. The old spark was gone. They never spoke of the reason for the change in Shawn, except in the very beginning, right after it happened. That was before David learned how to give those subtle signals that he couldn't talk about that topic. So he and Evan formed this quiet conspiracy to bring Shawn back, never with a formal game plan, but always with the same goal.

"This trip is just what she needs, David," said Evan. "I'm sure of it."

David suggested they stop for lunch, as they usually did after their Saturday games, but Evan wanted to visit his mother.

"I should let her know I'll be gone a few weeks," he said, "not that she'll have the vaguest idea what I'm talking about."

"I'll go with you," David said. He was surprised at the hesitation in Evan's eyes. He hadn't seen it there in a long time. When Evan first moved his mother to San Diego from a nursing home in Portland, he didn't want David or Shawn to meet her. David understood—Evan feared pity. And the truth was, David did feel sorry for him. He hoped he never had to face the responsibility of a parent with Alzheimer's. He talked with Evan about his own parents, letting him know he understood the embarrassment and frustration, and Evan eventually learned to welcome David's company on his visits to the nursing home.

But today he looked reluctant. "She's gotten a lot worse lately," he said. "A whole lot worse."

Mrs. St. John's room was small and bare except for the crucifix above her bed and a vase filled with flowers on her dresser. Evan sent the flowers every week, but they couldn't mask the stench of bleach and urine that permeated the nursing home.

Mrs. St. John sat up in her bed with her legs on top of the covers, her shapeless yellow dress hiked up to her waist. Her thin gray hair stuck up in tufts from her pink scalp. "You goddamned bastard," she said as David and Evan entered the room. "I *told* you the soup was full of poison."

"Mom, it's me, Evan." Evan leaned over to kiss her forehead. She pushed him away with a bony hand on his chest. Evan extracted the blanket from under her to cover her legs and sat on the edge of her bed. "You remember David?" he asked.

"Hello, Mrs. St. John." David sat down in the orange vinyl chair near the door. She did seem worse, although he couldn't put his finger on it. Angrier, he guessed. More hostile.

"You're the boy that's leading him to hell," she pointed a finger at David.

David smiled. "I'm Evan's friend. We play racquetball together." They had this conversation every time he came, though in the beginning she appeared to understand what he meant.

"And you'll go to hell together, too."

"Has Father Glenn visited you yet this week?" Evan asked.

"Who?"

"Father Glenn. Has he been in?"

"What's wrong with your hair?"

Evan sighed. "Listen, Mom, I want to tell you that I'm going to South America for a couple of weeks. I've got some work to do down . . .''

She leaned forward and spit in Evan's face. David winced. Perhaps he shouldn't have come after all.

Evan pulled a handkerchief from his pocket and wiped his cheek. ''I'll be back August eighth. The day before your birthday.''

''You've been a sinner since the first day I carried you. Used to kick at me, snarl up my insides.'' She started to hike up her dress again, but Evan caught her hands.

''You never carried me, Mom. You adopted me, remember?'' He stood up. ''I'll be back for your birthday.''

She wailed as they left. Evan shut his eyes against the sound. He was quiet until they got into David's car.

''I'm sorry, Evan,'' David said.

Evan leaned back against the seat. ''I wish she'd die.''

''You don't mean that.''

''Yes, I do. I'd like her to die while I still have one or two good memories left of her. As it is, they're fading fast.''

Perhaps Evan was right. His mother was suffering; her life only promised to get worse. If Evan wished she would die, then David would wish it too. Because next to Shawn, Evan was his closest friend.

• *Nine* •

THEY HAD TO split up in the waiting area of the airport. Their first flight would take them to Miami. In Miami they would board a plane to Lima. From Lima they would take a smaller plane to Iquitos. The stopping-starting itinerary overwhelmed Shawn. So much work to get to a place she didn't want to go.

Shawn sat cramped into a corner of the room, next to a gray-haired woman and a screaming toddler. The woman held her ticket in one hand as she moved the writhing child from one knee to the other, and Shawn tried in vain to get a look at her seat assignment, hoping she would end up nowhere near these two on the plane.

She stretched her legs out in front of her. Her muscles felt tight. She wore a gray warm-up suit over shorts and a T-shirt, since the flights would be long and she wanted to be comfortable. David sat across the aisle from her and down a few seats, in tan cotton pants and a blue chambray shirt, looking neat and pressed. No one would guess they were a couple, she thought. No one would guess they were going to the same place. David's new camera case, bought especially for this trip, was tucked under his chair. It was sky blue, waterproof, and padded with something that would keep it afloat if it fell into the river.

He was already absorbed in a paperback novel, *Murder in B Flat*, the title printed in bloodred letters on a white background. He was definitely on vacation. On the drive to the airport, she noticed how another line disappeared from his face with each passing mile, how he wore a smile in response to nothing. While every muscle in her body prepared to flee from danger, David sat free as a leaf in the wind.

The novel Shawn held on her lap was still open to page one, and although she'd read the first paragraph four times, she couldn't say what it was about. The last time she waited in this airport for a flight to Peru—three long years ago—she was armed with travel folders on Iquitos, maps of the Meseta region, charts of the rivers. She left all of that home this time. Intentionally. She was determined to make this trip as different from the last trip as possible. She rejoiced when Tess said they would not stay overnight in Iquitos. No hotel. No chance of getting a phone message with the power to destroy her.

This trip *was* different. Last time it had been just her and Evan. She remembered sitting next to him in this airport—at this gate? She hoped not—anticipating the adventure ahead of them. She remembered wishing David were going with them, but David couldn't take time off just then. He took her out to dinner the night before she left. Oh, she'd forgotten about that night, that incredible night. They went to dinner and then borrowed a friend's motorboat and took it out on the bay. They anchored the boat and lay on a blanket spread across the wooden bottom and watched the stars. And made love. The bottom of the boat was crisscrossed with wooden slats, and they knew they would be covered with bruises afterward. His back, her legs. Black bruises they could already see taking shape in the moonlight.

They talked about what it would be like to be apart from each other. In all the years they'd been married, they had never been apart for more than a few days. They were dependent on each other. She was afraid. Not of needing David—that was no sin—but of going off with Evan, afraid of living in close quarters with him when she had never lost her hunger for him. No matter how much a part of their family he had become, and no matter how close he was to David, she could not stop her body from reacting to his presence. She had come to grips with the fact that she loved two men—she simply was not allowed to have one of them.

She knew that trip would test her will. In her entire adult life she had never gone more than two or three days without making love, except after the births of her children. And here she was expecting herself to spend three weeks in the jungle with a man she'd wanted for years and not touch him. On some level David must have known, because he stroked her body and said they would think of each other each time they saw the bruises.

That was the last time she wanted David, sexually or otherwise. She looked over at him now. His eyes were lowered; he turned a page. He was unbothered, the unpleasant memories wiped away, his conscience somehow clear. She felt her breathing quicken, the muscles in her arms contract. God, she was sick of this feeling, this acidic hatred she felt toward him. The sooner she put an end to this marriage, the better.

Evan and Robin had found seats together a few rows behind
David. Evan leafed through a thick folder of articles. He pulled
one out and stroked his beard as he read a paragraph or two,
then tucked the article away again. She knew he was nervous.
He wanted perfection on this trip. No snags.

Robin had a stack of magazines on her lap. She was reading
a very fat *Vogue*, her last hold on civilization. She looked crisp
and freshly scrubbed in a short-sleeved yellow shirt and gold
drawstring pants. She'd reduced the gold around her neck to just
one chain and Shawn wondered why she chose that one. Did it
have some significance to her? Had Evan given it to her?

Shawn had not wanted to like Robin at first. She'd wondered
what Evan saw beneath the glossy facade. But there was a sweet-
ness, a childlike honesty, in Robin that was hard to discount.
She was the manager of a jewelry store, but she treated her
career as a hobby. What Robin really wanted was motherhood,
and the nested sort of existence Evan longed for.

Tess stood silhouetted at the window, looking out on their
plane. She stubbed out her fourth or fifth cigarette, one of those
long brown foreign-looking types, in the nearest ashtray and
glanced toward the hall again. This morning she told them she
was bringing a friend on the trip, one of her students who was
a professional photographer and who would record their journey
in pictures. The friend was late and there was an anxious quality
to Tess's vigil. Shawn couldn't make out her features against the
white backdrop of the window, but the cigarettes, the rigid
stance, the occasional fingers through her short, deep blond hair
gave her away.

A second silhouette appeared next to Tess, a young woman
weighed down by bags of various shapes and sizes and the unmistakable angles of a tripod. She was a head shorter than Tess
and had to stand on tiptoe to kiss her cheek. Tess made no
concession to the woman, didn't lean down to make her cheek
more accessible, didn't offer to relieve her of any of her bags.
Instead, she lit another cigarette and faced the window while the
photographer spoke to her, her arms moving in an animated
description Tess could not have seen. The woman was blond,
blonder than Tess. Her long straight hair, backlit by the window,
reminded Shawn of the silky mane of a palomino.

Despite the mob in the waiting area, the plane was not
crowded at all. She and David had a seat between them. So did
Evan and Robin, a few rows behind. Tess and her photographer
friend—Meg Solomon—sat back in the smoking section.

They'd met Meg while waiting in line to board. She was young, no more than twenty-six or -seven, with cream-colored skin that looked as though it never felt the touch of makeup. Her smile was warm, her eyes shy. More comfortable behind a camera, Shawn thought. She was loaded down with her backpack, the tripod, a cumbersome metal case and a sky blue camera case identical to David's. David offered to carry the metal case for her in spite of his own heavy load, but she shook her head.

"I'm fine," she smiled. "I'm used to it."

Was she used to Tess's long, fiery-smelling cigarettes too? Meg was no smoker. Shawn could tell by her skin, the sharp blue of her eyes, and the perfect white teeth. She would wilt in the smoking section.

But Meg seemed unconcerned. She followed Tess back to the bowels of the plane, puppylike.

"Pretty," David said, as he buckled his seat belt. He had the window seat for the flight to Miami.

"What?" Shawn asked.

"Meg. She's very pretty."

She thought of telling him he was old enough to be Meg's father. She did some quick arithmetic in her head and decided that would be stretching the truth, though not by much.

"Yes, very," she said.

"I picked out the same camera case as a professional." He looked pleased with himself.

It was five-thirty in the afternoon, San Diego time. She set her watch ahead three hours. Already it felt like eight-thirty. She was on Miami time. *Peruvian* time.

David fell asleep shortly after dinner, his head resting on a pillow between the window and his seatback. Shawn reached into the overhead compartment for two blankets. She draped one across his chest and arms and tucked it behind his shoulders. She moved to the seat next to him, covering her lap with her own blanket, and opened her novel again.

There was that same paragraph that had dogged her all afternoon in the airport. It read no more easily now. She looked past David out the window. The layer of clouds below them was gray, the bruised sky in shreds of pink and purple. It was darkening quickly. She watched black edging in, swallowing the colors and sinking down to cover the clouds. Then all she could see was the blinking light on the wing.

She rummaged in her purse for the list of things they needed to buy in Iquitos. Food. Pots and pans. Plates, bowls, and silverware. Machetes. Fishing line and hooks. Knives. She had wanted a fancy survival knife, one she saw in the back of a wilderness catalog at the Conservation Center. It looked sturdy and sharp and fit neatly into a leather sheath worn looped around a belt. Its most appealing feature, though, was the handle. It unscrewed and inside were a compass, long tweezers, a cable saw, needles, matches, and fishing line. Evan laughed at her. "You already have most of that stuff," he said.

He was right. But she regretted now not having sent for the knife. She liked the compactness of it, the knowledge that the knife at her side was more than just a knife. It could get her out of all kinds of dilemmas.

So she would have to buy a knife in Iquitos. *Iquitos.* God, she didn't want to go to that sour little town, where desperation hung in the thick air. She shivered under the blanket. In and out, Tess said. They'd go right from the airport to the market, get their supplies, and drive by truck to the Chala Zoo to pick up the decoy, then on to the Rio Tavaco. She would call Lynn from the airport, make certain Keith and Jamie were all right. She'd find a pay phone and . . . could she remember how to work the Peruvian phone system? Maybe Evan would know. She couldn't ask Tess.

She looked at her list again. Would they need more insect repellent? They had a couple of bottles, but Evan said he practically showered in the stuff the last time. They had antibiotics in huge quantities. "Every scratch, every bite, gets infected," Tess told them. They had toothpaste and sunscreen and shampoo. They remembered razor blades for David at the last minute. She couldn't picture him with a two-week growth of beard. She looked at him, reached over, and ran the back of one finger along his jaw. She knew how it would feel before she touched, the skin a little rough with a day's growth of hair. It was a beautiful face, asleep or awake.

"May I sit down?"

She looked up to see Evan standing next to her in the dim light of the plane. She picked up her novel from the spare seat to make room for him.

He sat down, holding one of the articles he was reading in the airport in his hand.

"Have you read this?" He handed her the article by Paul Nance, "Disadvantages of Primate Decoy Traps."

She nodded. She had the article memorized.

"Well, I haven't wanted to step on your toes about using a decoy, but after reading this I think we're going to have some major problems."

"Evan, I've thought it all through." She told him she'd packed dried fruit and eggs for the decoy to supplement the fresh fruit they could buy in Iquitos, and she drew a diagram of how she planned to put screening inside the cage to prevent injury to the decoy from another tamarin. His smile grew as she talked.

"You *have* thought it out, haven't you?" he said.

"Uh huh."

A silence fell between them. After a minute he reached up and turned out the light. "How are you doing?" he asked.

She looked at the back of the seat in front of her. The emergency card was dimly visible behind the air sickness bag. "Do you remember how to make an international phone call from Peru?"

"It's easy. You want to check on the twins?"

She nodded. "They have no way of getting hold of me for two and a half weeks."

Evan lifted the armrest between them and for the first time in a year, closed his hand around hers, palm to palm. "Are you going to be able to relax at all on this trip?"

"I'll be all right once I'm out of Iquitos." She shut her eyes to concentrate on the perfect fit of her hand in his.

After Evan returned to his seat, Shawn sat in the darkness listening to the steady drone of the engines. The novel lay unopened in her lap. She looked over at David. He was sound asleep, his chest slowly rising, slowly falling, beneath the thin blue blanket. He could fall asleep anywhere, his sleep never marred by dreams. He would probably sleep the entire way to Iquitos, waking just long enough to change planes. She wished she had that gift. How would she get through this night, with a novel that could not grasp her interest and a head full of memories?

· Ten ·

THREE YEARS EARLIER, the most noticeable feature of Iquitos was the smell. Smoke and sewage and the sweet smell of decay. She and Evan got off the plane and wrinkled their noses at each other.

They found a cab and gave the driver the name of their hotel. A guide from the local conservation center was to meet them there in the morning to take them into the jungle. Shawn already wanted to get out of this town and into the rain forest. She'd be glad when this leg of their journey was over.

They sat in the back of the cab, too tired to speak. Springs from the seat pressed against the bruises David left her. That sweet evening in the boat already seemed weeks ago. Evan suddenly took her hand and raised it to his lips. She knew it was a gesture of pure excitement at being here, but it sent a hot current through her body. She thought of how easy it would be to sleep with him tonight.

It had been four and a half years since the canyon fire that cost them their Red-Ears and changed the nature of their relationship, leaving them always wistful and cautious. Shawn never completely lost the guilt, but neither had she lost the longing. They never mentioned that Christmas Eve to each other, except occasionally to speak of "the fire," and in Shawn's mind those words took on a dual meaning. Sometimes she convinced herself their lovemaking that night had been no more than one of her dreams. But then she'd catch him looking at her, something raw, something unhealed in his eyes, and she knew he hadn't let go of the memory any more than she had.

"Evan," she said now.

"Mmm." He rested his bearded cheek against her open palm.

"I wish I had no conscience."

He understood immediately, let go of her hand as if it burned him. "But you do," he said. "We both do."

She nodded.

He smiled. "Every time I think of making love to you, I remember you getting sick in my office bathroom. That usually takes care of any romantic thoughts I might be having."

She laughed. "Aversive conditioning." She hesitated a moment before asking, "How often do you think of making love to me?"

He looked at her. "Do you want an answer you can live with, or do you want the truth?"

"Truth."

He leaned his head back against the stringy upholstery of the car seat. "I think of making love to you when I'm alone at night. I think of making love to you when I'm making love to someone else. And I think of making love to you when I see you at the Center . . . It doesn't matter what you're doing—observing, paperwork, drinking my coffee . . ." His voice trailed off and he looked out the window. "God, this is a shitty place."

"Oh, Evan."

They exchanged looks of dismay as they climbed out of the cab in front of the seedy little hotel. At one time, back in the days of the rubber boom, it had probably been a lovely building. The tiny balconies and front porch were decorated with tendrils of wrought iron, now thick with chipped white paint. Empty window boxes sagged on the walls, and from every direction came the cloying blanket of hot, wet air dripping with the overpowering smell of blossoms beyond their prime.

"I hope it smells better inside than out," she said as they climbed the crumbling steps to the front door. Her mouth felt dry and stale. She hoped there would be bottled water waiting for her in her room so that she could brush her teeth.

The woman behind the registration desk had skin like freshly risen bread dough. Globs of it clung to her cheeks, to the underside of her arms. She spoke to them in Spanish they couldn't understand, red blotches of frustration mottling the puffy skin of her neck. She grabbed Shawn by the wrist and held out a scrap of paper to her. A phone number was scrawled across it. *619-555-1555.* Shawn was struck by its symmetry.

"It's a San Diego number," she said to Evan. "Does it look familiar to you?"

He shook his head. "Whose number is this?" he asked the woman, his voice loud, as though volume could serve as an interpreter.

The woman rattled on in Spanish, one bloated finger poking Shawn's arm. Then she pointed down a dark hallway. *"Telefono,"* she said, giving Shawn a shove in the direction of the hall.

At the end of the hallway she and Evan laughed in the darkness as she tried to get through on the phone. They were both a little giddy. She felt light-headed from the scattered sleep on the plane. Evan's smile was tired-looking, but white and warm, and she thought again of how easy it would be to fall into bed with him. Would it be so wrong for them just to sleep together, to hold each other tonight?

There was a long series of clicks and scratches on the phone line that ended in the faraway voice of a woman.

"ICU," the woman said.

ICU? A business of some sort, Shawn thought. "Hello?"

"Yes?" the woman said.

"I'm in Peru and I'm not sure why I'm calling you . . ."

Evan chuckled and rubbed at his eyes while she continued.

"I'm checking into a hotel and the clerk gave me this . . ."

"Is this Mrs. Ryder?" the woman asked.

"Yes. Who is this?"

"Just a moment, Mrs. Ryder. Hold on."

"Who is it?" Evan asked.

Shawn shrugged. "Do you know someplace called ICU?"

Evan frowned. "You mean a hospital ICU? Intensive Care Unit?"

"No, it's some business or . . ." The words froze in her throat. She looked at Evan and saw that all trace of humor had left his face. *Intensive Care Unit.* Could it be her father? No, he wouldn't be in a San Diego hospital.

"Shawn?" It was David's voice, crackling through the phone line.

"David?"

"Are you at the hotel?" His voice was strong and sure now, despite the distance. Nothing much could be wrong.

"Yes. Are you calling from a hospital? What's going on?"

"Honey, listen. Heather's here. I . . ."

"Heather? Why?"

"Shh, listen to me. After you left yesterday I took the kids to the beach and Heather . . . took in too much water and she . . ."

"What do you mean, she took in too much water?" She felt Evan close his fingers around her arm.

"I mean she went under and they . . . had to rescue her and she's here now."

"My *God*, David. Is she all right?"

Silence, as if the phone had died, but it was only David's voice failing him.

"David?"

"She's pretty sick."

"Oh, God." The round dial of the phone blurred in front of her, and Evan slipped his arm around her waist.

"You have to get the next flight back, honey."

"What do the doctors say? Will she be okay?"

A long pause. "They don't know."

"David, *please* tell me everything will be all right."

"I called the airline. There's a flight out of Iquitos at two your time. Can you make it?"

Her watch said twelve-ten. "Yes." She thought of David having to deal with this alone. "Are you okay, David?"

"I'm all right. Get some sleep on the plane, honey. Don't worry; it won't do any good to worry. It'll be better if you can arrive here with some sleep behind you."

It was torture to be back on a plane so soon after getting off. Sleep was impossible. She told herself she would make the difference for her daughter. She pictured Heather, pale and limp in a bed much too big for her, coughing a little, crying because her lungs hurt. Scared because her mother wasn't there. Shawn couldn't wait to hold her, to feel the softness of Heather's hair against her lips, her little arms around her neck.

But her images of Heather in the hospital room were naive. That was David's fault. He'd handed her a pack of lies. While he was talking to her on the phone, about "taking in too much water," about "being rescued," Heather lay unconscious in the ICU, tethered to a machine that breathed for her but that couldn't return the life to her brain. David had asked the doctor to keep her hooked up to the machine until Shawn had a chance to see her one last time, to touch her while her skin was still warm. But Shawn's presence would not make a difference. It would mean nothing to Heather to have her mother with her.

David picked her up at the airport. He was not the same man she'd left a day ago, not the man who made love to her in the bottom of the boat on the bay. She couldn't connect to him. He didn't touch her, not on the ride from the airport, when he was as aloof as a chauffeur, not at the hospital where he stood dry-eyed while a woman doctor told her that for all intents and purposes, Heather died in the water. It was the doctor who held her while she cried, while David stood rigid as a statue on the other side of the room, his eyes on the floor. Why was he over there when she needed his arms around her?

"I know this is difficult to think about now," the doctor said, "but we need to know if you'd like to donate her organs."

She looked at David. His eyes brushed over hers and returned to the floor. He shook his head.

The ridiculous image of the fetal pig slipped into her mind. No, of course not. David would not be able to tolerate the thought of Heather being picked apart that way.

"I'm sorry," she said to the doctor.

After the respirator was turned off, she sat with David at Heather's bedside, waiting. She couldn't get it out of her mind that while Heather lay here dying, she'd been thinking of sleeping with Evan. It was her fault then somehow, wasn't it? This was her punishment. Did God work that way? No, there had to be a more earthbound explanation for what had happened here.

For all intents and purposes she died in the water. How could it be? What possible excuse was there for a four-year-old child to drown when she had a parent with her? And that parent was David, a one-time competitive swimmer. Where had he been? And where was he now, her husband? Surely he wasn't this stranger sitting next to her, limply holding her hand in his lap.

For a year or so after her mother died, Shawn imagined her father was not actually her father but a stranger who had somehow gotten inside her father's body. She was five then, and confused about her mother's sudden disappearance. One day her father came to pick her up from school, and she refused to get in the car with him. Her teacher finally coaxed her into the back seat, but both Shawn and her father were in tears by then. He took her to a psychiatrist who said she was reacting to the loss of her mother, that she was afraid now that she would lose her father as well, and that in time her odd behavior would pass.

She had that same feeling now as she sat by Heather's bed. Someone she didn't know was in David's body, sitting next to her, pretending to be her husband.

"I don't know you," she said out loud.

"What?"

"Who are you?"

"Shawn . . ."

"Do you have any bruises on your back?"

He looked away from her, shutting his eyes, and she may as
well have been alone as she watched her daughter fade away.

David drove her to Lynn's where the boys were waiting for
them to take them home and pretend they were still a family.
She cried in the car, softly, knowing the tears weren't real because there was no part of her that believed Heather was dead.
These were merely the tears of a close call, confused and uncertain.

David sat stoically in the driver's seat, watching the traffic,
his knuckles white on the steering wheel.

"Tell me how it happened," she said after a while.

He drew in a breath and she knew he'd been waiting for that
question. "I took Heather and the boys to the beach and . . ."

"Which beach?"

"La Jolla."

"The Cove?" She knew as she said it that he had not taken
them to the Cove. A child couldn't drown in those protected
waters. That was the reason she always insisted they swim there,
and only there.

"No," he said. "I took them to Windansea Beach."

She pictured the craggy rocks and foamy surf of Windansea,
and if she had not already pinned Heather's death on David, she
did now.

"She went in the water with me, and she really had a good
time. She was so proud of herself for going in—you know how
afraid she was of the water . . ." He looked over at her and she
turned her face to the window.

"Then we lay down on the blanket and when I opened my
eyes, she was gone."

"How long were your eyes closed?"

"A few minutes. I fell asleep, but it was only for a few minutes. I thought she was asleep too."

She pictured Heather lying on the blanket next to David, in
her yellow bikini, blond curls on her cheek. Probably squirming
around. "You should have known she wouldn't sleep there."

David let go of the steering wheel for a few seconds to rub
his palms together. "I thought she was fine," he said.

How could he not cry? "Then what happened?"

"The lifeguards found her within seconds. She was close to
shore, but there was a little seaweed tangled around her . . ."
He touched his calf. ". . . around her legs. They tried to resus-
citate her but couldn't. They kept trying until they brought her

to the hospital, then they worked on her in the emergency room for a couple of hours, but . . .''

"Why didn't you tell me she was brain-dead when I spoke to you on the phone? You misled me. You made me think she had a chance."

David sighed. "I didn't know what to say to you. The doctor suggested I tell you that things weren't good, you know, prepare you without telling you yet just how bad they were."

They were a block from Lynn's house, and her pulse pounded in her temples. In another minute they would have to tell the boys that Heather was dead.

"Please pull over," she said.

David obediently pulled the Bronco to the side of the road and turned off the ignition. He switched on the emergency lights although there were no other cars on this side street.

She found a tissue in her purse and blew her nose. "I don't know how to face the twins," she said.

"They know everything. They know that as soon as you got here we'd take her off the respirator and that she . . . it'd be over."

"She's really dead."

David nodded and she was frightened by the hatred she felt toward him. She looked at him squarely. "It's a good thing I didn't stay away the full three weeks or you might have lost them all," she said.

He dropped his eyes too quickly for her to see if there was pain in them. She could say worse things if that didn't work. She wanted to say worse things. She faced forward in the car. "I want to see my sons."

He started the Bronco and they drove the block to Lynn's in silence.

The boys had lost their ten-year-old cockiness overnight. They called her "Mommy" when they saw her. They didn't cry, but they may as well have because their pale, pinched features gave them away.

Lynn took her aside before they left. "Shawn, I'm so worried about David," she said. Her hair, the same light brown as David's, was up in a pony tail and she wore a leotard, shorts, and running shoes. "He's shut down. He's taking it so hard. He blames himself . . . he thinks what happened was his fault."

"Who else's fault was it?"

Lynn looked at her in alarm. "It was an *accident*, Shawn, for heaven's sake."

Shawn turned to go. "I want to get Keith and Jamie home."

Lynn grabbed her arm. "You're not thinking straight. I'd feel the same way, I know. But honey, David would have done anything in the world for Heather. You know that. Deep down, you know that, Shawn, don't you?"

A couple of social workers from the child protection agency came to the house that afternoon to speak to David. He took them into the study, closing the door behind them. She wanted them to find him guilty, to take him away for his punishment. But they had pained looks on their faces as they left. They offered her their condolences.

She tucked the boys in that night while David escaped to the station. At least she assumed that's where he went. He wasn't speaking to her. That was all right. She had nothing to say to him either.

She sat on the edge of Keith's bed, stroking his arm through the sheet. "Do you two understand what happened?" she asked. "Do you have any questions?"

They were quiet for a moment. Then Jamie asked, "Where is she now?"

"She's at the hospital. They'll keep her there until the funeral." This was not quite the truth, not the truth at all. Heather was at the coroner's office, but Shawn didn't want to say that to the boys.

"No, I don't mean her body," said Jamie. "I mean her *soul*."

She didn't have an answer for that. She'd never decided this question for herself, and now she wished she had. Heather had to be *somewhere*. Evan would have an answer, some comforting stuff about heaven. She wouldn't believe it, but it would still feel good to hear it. She needed Evan right now. It would be more than two weeks before she could talk to him. "I don't know, Jamie," she shook her head. "I just don't know."

She looked down at Keith. In the light from the street lamp she could make out a bruise on his cheek. "How did you get this, honey?" She touched it lightly with her fingertips.

"Daddy hit me," he said.

"What?"

Keith began to cry. He was suddenly very small and very young, crawling out from under the sheet into her lap. He struggled to fit his entire body in her arms as he sobbed against her neck. His ribs were slender and delicate under her fingers, and she felt overwhelmed with the need to protect him.

Jamie sat up in his bed. "Daddy hit him for crying," he said.

Shawn covered her mouth with her hand. What was happening here? She'd turned her back for a second, and the family she'd known had disappeared, had left this shredded group of people in its place.

Jamie woke up around midnight, screaming, gasping for breath, on the waking-up end of a nightmare. Just as she got him settled down, Keith threw up. He tried to make it to the bathroom, but got only as far as the throw rug in the hallway. She managed to get him into the bathroom before he started again. She sat on the edge of the tub, watching him. His striped pajama bottoms were too big for him; his shoulder blades looked like sharp cleavers under the bare skin of his back. She studied the round blue bruise high on his cheekbone, wondering what part of David's big hand had caught him there.

She had them both in bed and the rug in the washing machine by the time David came home.

"Why are you up?" he asked. "Are the boys okay?"

"They're just fine," she said, walking past him toward the bedroom. "Never better."

It was another hour before he came to bed, but she was still awake. She said nothing as he undressed and climbed into his side of the bed.

He lay on his back. "Shawn, I'm sorry," he said quietly. "I know I made an error in judgment. I don't know how to make it right. All last night I thought that when you got here everything would be okay. But it's not okay. It's not okay at all."

She stared at the ceiling. "Keith said you hit him."

"Yes, I . . . It was a mistake."

"You made more than your share of them yesterday, didn't you?"

He said nothing more. He got out of bed, pulled on his robe and left the room. She heard the door to the room next door—Heather's room—open and close; she heard the familiar squeak of the bed springs as he settled down there for the night.

He withdrew from her further after that night. In the mornings his voice woke her from the radio, telling her where the worst traffic was, what routes to avoid. She lay there, exhausted from being up with the boys, and listened to hear if his voice sounded any different than it had a week earlier. It was the same. He still had that lilt, that I'll-help-you-get-there, you-can-count-on-me, quality the commuters loved.

He sounded that way even on the morning of the funeral, as well as the evening after. Maybe that was because he insulated himself so well from the pain. She and the boys stood at Heather's grave site, sweating in a hot Santa Ana wind, surrounded by neighbors and friends, Lynn and her husband and son, and Heather's weepy nursery-school teacher. David said he felt sick. He waited in the car with the air conditioning on while the little coffin was lowered into the ground. Shawn avoided Lynn's eyes, kept one hand locked on each of her son's shoulders as if she feared they might try to flee, or that she might herself.

She had to do everything alone. She was the one who called family and friends to tell them about Heather; she was the one who made the arrangements for the funeral. She was the one with the boys night and day. People talked about how strong she was. She wasn't strong; she was numb. Just doing what had to be done. What choice did she have? David was simply not there, on any level, although she was not certain if he was pulling away from her or if she was pushing him out. She didn't care so long as the end result was distance.

She started wishing there was a gun in the house. The thought bordered on obsession and gave her the only pleasure she had. If she owned a gun—and if it were not for the boys—she would kill both David and herself. There was satisfaction in the thought of driving a bullet into David's heart, although she wondered if that would be too quick a death, not allow for the full measure of suffering that was due him.

Two weeks after the funeral, Tika was born. Sam, the primate keeper at the Center, called Shawn. "Annie had triplets this morning," he said, "and she's cast one off."

She called Lynn to take the boys—she wouldn't leave them with David—packed her toothbrush and a few changes of clothes and moved into Evan's office. He was still in Peru. She could sleep in his sofa bed, be at the baby's beck and call.

She and Evan were up to the letter *H* in the alphabetical christening of the Copper Elves, but Shawn couldn't bring herself to think about names beginning with *H*. She was relieved when the name *Tika* popped into her mind. She would let Evan name Tika's two brothers.

In the middle of her second night at the Center she woke to

find Evan sitting barefoot and cross-legged next to her on the bed.

"I'm so sorry," he said.

She sat up and he put his arms around her, the first time she'd been held in weeks.

"I called your house as soon as I got in tonight, and David told me what happened. I said I'd come see you in the morning, but then I was lying there in bed, thinking about you, and I had to see you. I had to see how you're doing."

She let the tears come, knowing she'd been saving them for this moment when it was safe, when there was someone with her stronger than she was, someone who wouldn't collapse under the weight of her grief. He held her for a long time without speaking, rubbing her back through her T-shirt, stroking her hair.

"How did it happen?" he asked.

She told him the details, watching the creases deepen in his forehead as she spoke.

"David must feel like shit," he said.

She pushed him away from her. "How come everyone's so goddamn ready to feel sorry for David? The man had one teeny tiny little task to do, watch a four-year-old at the beach, and he blew it. He blew it in a big way."

"Shh, okay." He put his arm around her again and leaned against the back of the couch. "It didn't sound that serious when you were talking to him on the phone from Iquitos."

"He lied to me."

"To protect you."

"You give him too much credit."

"You two need each other right now."

"God, I despise him."

Evan sucked in his breath. "Shawn, come on, you and David have the best marriage I know. Don't let this destroy it."

She said nothing, and after a while he spoke again. "You know what I was remembering while I was driving over here?"

"What?"

"That time you went onstage at the zoological awards dinner, in front of the TV cameras and everyone, and Heather called out from the audience, 'Mommy, please get *back* here. I gotta go *potty, now.*' "

Shawn smiled into his shoulder. No one had spoken to her about Heather. No one else seemed to remember her.

"It's so hard to believe she's gone," Evan continued. "She

was such a lively little thing." He tightened his arm around her shoulder. "My favorite little primate."

"Evan . . . I want her back."

"I know."

"I keep imagining what it must have been like for her to die like that. How scared she must have been."

He hesitated a moment. "I've heard that drowning is not as terrible to go through as it sounds," he said. "There's a moment of panic, but it's quick and then . . . the dying is gentle."

"If it weren't for the boys, I would do it myself."

"Do what?"

"Die."

She felt his whole body stiffen. "Don't even think that," he said.

"It's all I think about."

"Does David know how this is affecting you?"

"David's like ice. He hasn't talked to me. He hasn't touched me. It's just as well, because I can't stand the sight of him. I feel less alone here with the Elves than I did at home."

Evan let go of her shoulder and stood up. He began to unbutton his shirt and she looked up at him, wondering if he could see the relief in her eyes, if he knew that this time she would feel no remorse. She leaned back against the sofa and shut her eyes, waiting for him.

He made love to her, and she felt treasured and safe again. But later, when she felt his tears in the hollow of her shoulder, she wondered if they were tears for Heather or tears of regret.

· Eleven ·

SHAWN FOUND A phone in the Iquitos airport but there was
no answer at Lynn's. She tried twice, but by that time Tess had
produced the papers and the Spanish they needed to get their
bizarre luggage, with Shawn and Evan's collapsed traps and
blowguns, Tess's shotgun and machete, past the authorities. Outside, several men tried to persuade them to ride in the rickshaw-
like carts attached to the backs of their motorcycles. Tess led
them past the men and packed them into a taxi, an old station
wagon that smelled like stale beer.

Shawn covered her eyes against the sunlight reflecting off the
whitewashed walls of crumbling buildings. She would try to call
again from the Chala Zoo when they picked up the decoy.

"It's lovely," Robin said, her head close to the grimy window. "Look at the hibiscus."

"*Malvaceae,*" Meg said.

Tess looked surprised. "You've been studying," she said to
her friend.

"I had an inspirational teacher." Meg smiled out the window.

"The jacarandas are still in bloom here, Shawn." David
turned to speak to her from the front seat.

Shawn nodded without looking. She didn't want to see the
rotting garbage in the streets or the ragged children on the corners. *The boys are all right. Lynn won't let them get hurt.* But
they were so hard to handle these days. Would Lynn be able to
see how fragile they were? Just little boys, really.

"We'll have lunch at the Plaza de Armas." Tess looked at
her watch. "Manuel, my friend with the truck, will meet us
there and watch our things while we eat and buy supplies."

The heat seemed different this time, a little drier, but there
was that same acrid smell in the air. Herbicides and burning
trees—the stench of a city trying to hold back the jungle. They

got out of the taxi in front of a church. Across the street, a man waved to them from a rusting truck with missing fenders and doors tied shut with rope. Tess called to him in Spanish and he smiled, displaying a set of perfect, white teeth in a gaunt brown face. In a moment he was helping them load their gear into the back of his truck.

Tess led them to a door in the side of one of the buildings skirting the square. "Best restaurant on the Plaza," she said, as they made their way down a dark stairwell to a cellar. The room was packed with burly, dark bodies. The smell of sweat clashed with the smell of grilled fish. "A lot of drug trade here," Tess said, as if that were the sign of a good restaurant.

She ushered them to a corner of the room where they pulled two small tables together and sat down.

"There are lizards on the floor!" Robin said.

"Roach control," said Tess.

Robin hugged her arms and tried to focus on the menu. "We should eat lightly for the first few days, shouldn't we?" she asked.

"*You* may eat as you like," said Tess. "But this is our last meal before we're on jungle rations, so I plan to eat heartily."

"What do you recommend?" David asked her.

"*Pisco*, to start," said Tess. "It's very potent grape brandy. And something—anything actually—with *aji* and *ajo*. Peppers and garlic. It puts hair on the chests of young girls."

Shawn looked at Evan. *Wonderful guide you found us,* she said with her eyes.

Evan gave her a resigned smile and turned to Tess. "Could you tell us what on this menu a gringo stomach can tolerate?"

Tess gave in. She described the selections, mostly fish. They listened carefully. No one wanted to have to ask Tess to go through the menu a second time. Shawn ordered shrimp, bottled water, and coffee. She didn't usually eat seafood, but knew she would have to on this trip. It would be their primary source of nourishment in the jungle.

"Let me get a picture of all of us around the table." David stood up with his camera as their drinks were served. He wormed his way backward through the crowd.

"Watch your light meter, David," Meg said.

They smiled into his camera, all except Tess, who drew with relish at her *Pisco*.

"Tess said nature photography is new for you." David moved his chair a few inches closer to Meg as he sat down again. Tess had told them Meg took her botany class solely to learn more about plant life for her photography.

Meg nodded. "I've been doing portrait work mostly, or compositions with people and architecture. And I do weddings nearly every weekend for the money. It's a very depressing way to spend your weekends, at strangers' weddings."

"Why is that?" Shawn asked, thinking that Meg was probably most interested in attending a wedding of her own.

"It depresses me because I look at the couples and think about what lies down the road for them. They get married thinking it's forever. Every time I do a wedding I wonder if the bride and groom will be together in five years, or even next month."

Shawn watched her as she spoke. Meg wore a white shirt, olive pants. The palomino hair hung loose around her shoulders. Her beauty had a strange effect on Shawn, gave her a twisting pain in her chest as if she was watching a sad movie. It was the eyes, perhaps. Clear, yet looking as if they might well up at any moment. Only the steel line of her jaw, the determination in her mouth, would keep the tears from spilling over.

"Sometimes," Meg took a swallow of bottled water, "I feel as though I can predict who will make it and who won't from the way they act at the wedding."

"Isn't it hard to do a good job with the photography when you have the feeling the marriage is doomed?" Robin asked.

Meg shook her head. "I always do my best with the pictures. I figure, if they're off to a bad start and then they get these great shots of themselves laughing together, looking like they're in love, they'll try harder to make it work."

"You're quite a romantic," said David.

"Too much so," Tess said coolly. "I think it's way past time for you to turn your attention to plants and animals and away from human subjects."

Meg reddened, immediately subdued.

Shawn was irritated by Tess's power over them. "It must be hard to switch to nature when you're used to doing weddings," she said. She wanted to take the crimson out of Meg's cheeks.

"I'll find out on this trip, I guess. Tess's class helped me see plant life in a new way." She looked to Tess for some form of validation, but Tess lit another one of her long brown cigarettes and dropped the match into her drained glass.

"There are some tricks to jungle photography though," Meg continued. She turned to David and began questioning him about the speed of his film, the make of his camera, the lenses he had with him. They spoke in technical terms and Shawn had little idea what they were talking about. She'd brought her own camera with her, a nice 35mm that did all the work for her.

The outdoor market took in all the senses. The smoke-and-chemical smell of the city seared the nostrils. The rapid-fire Spanish of the bargaining buyers and sellers and the wails of children trapped among the knees of the shoppers muted the sounds of the jungle behind them. People pressed against them from all sides, dark women in synthetic prints and plastic thongs, men with sweat rings under the arms of their cotton shirts.

They clung to each other as they worked their way from one stall to the next, laughing, taking in the carved wooden furniture, the weavings, and the jewelry.

"How about this for the boys?" David pointed to a stuffed piranha, its mouth a jagged circle of pointed teeth.

She nodded. The boys would love it. But it would be cumbersome to carry with them now. "On our way back," she said.

They bought five dozen oranges at the first fruit stand.

"They'll keep," said Tess. "Buy a lot of what will keep."

The old woman behind the stand beamed and held out a bunch of ripe bananas.

"We want the greenest," said Tess.

They bought four huge bunches, along with a dozen rock-hard papayas and mangoes and two kinds of melons.

"We need to buy a little more than we think we need," Tess said, "in case we're delayed for some reason."

"We can't be delayed," Shawn said. "We have to go back right on time."

"That's not always possible." Tess began loading potatoes into a bag. "We're not going to an American city with bus service you can set your watch by."

"We'll be back on time, Shawn," Evan said.

"Onions and carrots." Tess pointed to the vegetables. "And garlic. You all like garlic, I hope?"

Shawn was certain it wouldn't matter to Tess if they were all allergic to garlic.

At another stand they bought a sack of rice and bags of lentils and beans. At yet another they bought a wheel of cheese, a foot in diameter, which the seller wrapped in newspaper.

"Cheese?" Robin looked doubtful. "Without refrigeration?"

"It'll keep." Tess pointed to a little shop on the corner near the church. "Canned food in there. And we need to get cooking supplies and machetes and lanterns. We'd better split up if we hope to make it to the Chala Zoo before five.''

Robin chose to go with Tess, shadowing her as if she didn't want to lose sight of the one person who knew what she was doing. Meg and David went off together to get the canned food, and Shawn felt a dark cloud above her as she watched them push their way through the crowd. She tried to give the cloud a name. Jealousy? That hardly fit. It was more a sudden sense of losing control over David. Well, that was what she wanted, wasn't it?

She and Evan found the shop that sold lanterns and fishing gear.

''And cutlery,'' said Evan as they examined the machetes on the countertop. He laughed. ''I can't picture Robin with one of these things. I'll have to get David to take a few shots of her with it.'' He fingered one of the long wide blades and nodded his approval to the shopkeeper. ''Five.'' He held up five fingers and then grinned at Shawn as he pulled a buck knife from its sheath. ''Finally,'' he said. ''Shawn gets her knife.''

She held it up for a close inspection. ''It's beautiful.'' Her breath fogged the shiny blade. She balanced the handle in her palm. ''Perfect.''

''Two,'' Evan said while she slipped the knife back into its sheath and looped it around her belt.

''I feel dangerous,'' she said.

''An understatement.'' His hand was suddenly on the back of her neck, his face so close that she felt her hair catch in his beard. But he let go of her quickly, and she felt a brief, almost tangible, tension pass between them.

He's worried about you, she told herself. He feels responsible for bringing you to Iquitos. His touch is no more than a gesture of comfort.

They bought fishing tackle, not at all certain they'd made the right choices for the fish in Dacu. They bought three kerosene lanterns and four dozen mosquito repellent coils. Back at the truck, they found Manuel batting children away from their baggage. They piled their purchases in the back. In addition to the cooking utensils, Tess had bought a few bottles of rum and more *Pisco*, along with what looked like beef jerky.

''It's not beef,'' she said. ''It's *chancho de monte*.''

''Peccary?'' Evan asked, but Tess turned away without replying.

Maybe she's hard of hearing, Shawn thought. There had to be some excuse for her rudeness.

Tess pulled a ream of black plastic bags from her duffel bag. "Let's get the food in these bags," she said. "Everything we take with us in the canoe will get wet."

They stuffed the bags and secured the open ends with wire, then stood back to look at the truck, laden with food and luggage, traps and machetes. Meg took a picture.

Tess spoke to Manuel and then turned to the others. "Meg and I will ride in the cab with Manuel. You four ride in back."

They climbed obediently into the back of the truck, arranging their duffel bags so they could sit on them. Shawn sat next to David and looked around her at their supplies. "We have enough to last two months instead of two weeks," she said with a sense of security that had been evading her most of the day. She touched the handle of the knife at her side and settled down for the ride.

It took them forty-five minutes to reach the Chala Zoo.

The decoy was hardly recognizable as a Copper Elf. Her colors were deeper from the tropical sun, the copper very red, the gold bordering on orange.

"Does she need to be anesthetized for me to handle her?" she asked the keeper.

He shook his head. "She's tame," he said, his English heavily accented. He was black-haired and thin; the bones of his elbows stuck out in knobs. His dark skin was stretched tight across his cheekbones like the tanned hide of an animal. "She was a family pet before we got her. Her name is CoCo."

Shawn reached into the cage, and the tamarin climbed into her hand and let her draw her out. The tiny monkey sat on her palm, holding onto Shawn's thumb with one hand, her little finger with the other. She looked Shawn in the eye and trilled.

"Evan," she bit her lip. "Maybe you're right about not using a decoy. I don't want anything to happen to her."

The keeper shrugged. "She's at least nine years old. That's why we're letting you take her. She won't be so great a loss."

Shawn shook her head. When she'd thought about using a decoy, she'd forgotten about the little life involved. How could she confuse this beautiful creature by taking her out in the wild, confining her to a tiny cage and feeding her dried egg? CoCo sat patiently on her palm while they decided her fate. Her wise old-woman eyes never left Shawn's face.

Shawn looked at Evan, waiting for him to tell her to forget the idea, to leave this poor animal here.

"She'll be okay," Evan said. "Let's take her."

Outside the building Evan took the cage from her. "If the keeper views her as no great loss, I'm sure she'll be better off with us," he said.

CoCo rode in her cage in the back of the truck, between the St. Johns and the Ryders. She trilled her annoyance at the rutted road as she clung to her perch. Evan cut a length of twine with his new knife and reached into the cage to tie it to CoCo's slender leather collar. He lifted her out and handed her to Shawn. The Elf climbed up to Shawn's shoulder, wrapped one little arm around her neck, and stretched out for a nap.

Robin laughed and snuggled against Evan. "She's so cute," she said. "She makes me miss Melissa."

The twins. "I forgot to call Jamie and Keith," Shawn said.

"I'm sure they're all right," said Robin.

"No, I've got to call. We have to go back to the zoo."

They'd only been riding fifteen minutes since leaving the zoo. It wouldn't be that far out of their way to turn around now.

David took her hand. "Honey, forget it. They're fine."

"How can you be so sure?" she asked. "Because you're not with them?"

No one said a word, and she felt her face go hot. She hadn't said anything like that to David in a couple of years, hadn't hit him below the belt that way. She didn't look at him as she got to her knees and leaned out of the truck toward the cab window. "Tess!" she called. "We have to go back!"

Manuel stopped the truck, and Tess got out to talk with her. She stood at the side of the road, hands on hips, a look of disgust on her face. "We're not going back," she said.

"We have to. Just to the zoo. Just to call my sons."

Tess shook her head. "You're the one who wants everything to be on time, aren't you? We're behind schedule as it is."

Shawn handed CoCo to Evan and stood up. She boosted herself over the side of the truck to the road. "Go on without me then," she said. "I'm going back."

"Oh, shit," said Tess. "Get in the goddamn truck."

No one helped her back into the truck and she felt their annoyance as she took her seat again. She stared into space as Manuel maneuvered the truck through a miserable series of K-turns that took them sloshing into the mud on both sides of the road, tires spinning. She hoped they didn't get stuck. No one would forgive her. No one was speaking to her as it was. They were probably thinking she'd be a thorn in their sides for the entire trip. She didn't care if she was making a scene. She needed to know Jamie and Keith were okay.

The Chala Zoo was closed for the night, but the keeper was still in and he led Shawn and Evan to the phone in his cluttered office. Evan sat on the edge of the desk and placed the call for her. She spoke with both boys. They sounded anxious to get off the phone and back to whatever it was they were doing.

Her entire body was trembling by the time she hung up. "I shouldn't have agreed to come," she said.

"Take it easy."

"I feel trapped, and we're not even in the jungle yet."

"The boys are okay and you're okay." Evan stood up. "Let's get back to the truck."

She turned for the door, but he caught her arm.

"One more thing," he said.

She waited expectantly.

"You owe David an apology."

· Twelve ·

DAVID WAITED IN the back of the truck with Robin and CoCo
while Shawn called the boys. He held the Elf on his shoulder,
her little body a patch of warmth against his neck. He heard
Tess and Manuel speaking in Spanish from the cab, saw blue
smoke from Tess's cigarette snake out the window into the thick
dusky air. He still felt shaken by Shawn's words. She'd caught
him off guard. He used to be prepared for her anger, had built
a shield around himself for protection. He had to back then because, Christ, she could be cruel. But she never spoke to him
that way anymore. It had to be the stress of the day, too many
reminders of the last time she made this trip.

Robin was watching him and it made him uncomfortable. She
hadn't been around that miserable year after Heather died, so
this was probably the first time she'd seen this side of Shawn.
He felt embarrassed for Shawn, more so than for himself.

Robin leaned toward him. "I don't think Shawn meant that
comment about the twins to come out the way it sounded," she
said.

He nodded, although he didn't agree. Shawn meant exactly
what she said. But he didn't want to talk about it with Robin.
There was no way she could understand.

He felt neutral toward Robin. Nothing about her elicited strong
feelings in him one way or another. He was surprised the first
time he met her. He expected Evan to seek out a woman like
Shawn—down to earth, pretty in the rawest sense. But Robin
was a classic beauty, with thick, strawberry blond hair, ever-
perfect makeup. Even now he could see the green shadow above
her brown eyes, the fine dark line along her lower lid. She was
polite, gentle, always trying to smooth things over, just as she
was doing now. But she was not particularly good at it. She
didn't read subtleties well, and she lacked Shawn's wit, Shawn's
ability to see through the murk to the core of things.

Since the first time he laid eyes on Shawn, he compared other women with her. There was never any contest, although he wondered if it might be the old Shawn he was holding up for comparison. Maybe he'd been wrong about this trip bringing her back. The panic he just witnessed here in this truck, the nasty regression that caught him in its flow, worried him. He hadn't considered the possibility that this trip could make her worse.

Shawn and Evan climbed back into the truck, and she took her seat again next to David. "They're okay," she said. She looked sheepish, avoided his eyes. He knew by the mottled color in her cheeks that she'd been crying, or close to it.

"Good," he said as he set CoCo in her lap.

"I'm sorry, David," she said quietly. Her fingers shook as she lifted a hand to smooth her hair. Her trembling always gave her away. He felt a surge of love and sympathy.

He put his arm around her. "It's all right, Shawn. I know it's been a hard day."

Manuel drove the truck back into the forest. As the darkness fell around them, David was reminded of the time he and Shawn camped in Sequoia National Park, four or five years ago. He wasn't certain what triggered that memory. The tall, spindly trees lining the sides of the road here were nothing like the giant redwoods at Sequoia. But he had the same feeling now as he did then, of the forest closing in around him, dwarfing him, reminding him of his insignificance.

That had been a wonderful trip, one of many. They were constantly on the go back then, sometimes taking the kids with them but more often leaving them with Lynn. The trips were never boring. Shawn saw to that. Everything had to be an adventure. Hang gliding, canoeing white water, scuba diving. Jude Mandell was right when he said Shawn needed to live on the edge. David was careful never to stand in her way—with the one exception of the skydiving lessons—and he gradually discovered that he had a respectable sense of adventure himself.

They drove the 250 miles to Sequoia in a morning, the Bronco packed with their camping gear. Shawn had made arrangements to watch the rangers trap and tag bears. He found that experience a little disconcerting, seeing those huge, powerful creatures up close as they were taken from the traps, realizing that there were others just like them roaming loose in the forest. Shawn was so excited by that idea that she purposely left their food out at night to attract bears to their campsite. There were warnings posted all over park about keeping food locked up at night, but he said nothing. Shawn stayed up the first couple of nights, her camera around her neck, but they had no visitors. It wasn't until the fourth night that a bear tore through their provisions, leaving nothing in its wake but huge muddy footprints and scratches on the Bronco where it tried to claw its way to the bag of potato chips on the front seat. Both he and Shawn slept through it all, much to David's relief.

Whenever they visited someplace new, he could see Shawn casing the turf for a place to make love. The tent wasn't good enough—risky enough?—for her, although she never turned down an invitation to join him inside. He remembered one night in Sequoia, making love on a bench outside the visitors' center while other campers watched a movie on animals of the high country, and one afternoon in the midst of a cluster of redwoods, so tall that when he and Shawn lay on their backs and looked up it made them light-headed and they had to hold onto each other to ground themselves against the dizziness.

The truck hit a deep pothole in the road, and he tightened his arm around Shawn's shoulders. He leaned toward her ear. "Remember Sequoia?" he asked.

She nodded. "A previous life."

Shawn's sexuality had been a bonus. He would have loved her if her interest in sex had been merely in the neighborhood of the norm, and in the beginning he wondered if he could keep up with her. But his own sexual hunger surprised him. It was as if the more they made love, the more they needed to. One afternoon a long time ago, she left work in the middle of the day, drove home, flung open the door of the closet where he was in the middle of reading *Madame Bovary* into the tape recorder, and said: "David, I've got to have it, *now.*" After they made love, she told him they were addicts. Their tolerance kept increasing, and they would never be able to get enough.

So she had built up his tolerance and then cut him off cold turkey. How had he managed these past three years, with Shawn freezing him out? He simply had. There was no choice. And he deserved it, really, being cut off. He would never have considered going outside their marriage, not for moral reasons as much as for lack of interest in any other woman. That was changing though. The women at the pool, and now, the woman in the cab of this truck. Meg. God, what was that all about? All afternoon he'd wanted to get close to her and push her away from him at the same time. In the little shop at the Plaza de Armas she picked out cans of food and set them in his arms, and each time her fingers brushed his skin he felt a rush. A delicious feeling, a curious, dangerous yearning. Perhaps the feeling would pass. He hoped it would. Maybe as he got to know her better he'd see a catty side to her, some ugly quality that lay hidden beneath the surface, and the feeling would die a natural death.

But right now he was drawn to her warmth like a man left out in the cold too long.

· Thirteen ·

AFTER ABOUT AN hour the pavement turned into a mud road, and the walls of the jungle slipped closer to the truck. The vegetation changed from tall, slender trees to heavy brush and thick vines that took on a shadowy, stifling appearance in the darkness. This was it, Shawn thought. For two weeks they would not be without these walls, this feeling of being inside instead of outside. High above them, invisible in the darkness, stretched the protection of the canopy.

A sense of calm fell over her now that she'd spoken to Keith and Jamie. She was sorry she behaved like a lunatic, and sorry for lashing out at David. She didn't want to revert to her old way of relating to him. She wanted a civil end to this marriage, nothing ugly. She could sense from his arm around her, the gentle tone when he spoke to her, that she was forgiven. David was easy.

Robin looked over her shoulder into the woods. "It's so dark. How can Manuel see where he's going?" She had to speak loudly to be heard over the buzz of insects.

Manuel had only one good headlight. Shawn peered around the cab to see it illuminate the narrow rutted road and the overhanging curtain of foliage. It *was* eerie out here.

They could barely see each other, and as the ruts grew deeper they lowered themselves from their duffel bags to the cool metal floor of the truck to keep from being tossed out. Shawn moved CoCo to her lap.

"Can I hold her again?" David asked.

CoCo went to him easily, as all animals did, and David cupped her in his palm.

After four long and uncomfortable hours the truck made a sudden turn into the trees where there seemed to be no road at all. Branches scraped against their shoulders and leaves caressed their cheeks. They bounced their way for a mile or two, none of them speaking. Shawn tensed her muscles against the jostling.

"We better put CoCo back in her cage," she said, taking the Elf from David's fingers. The little tamarin gave her a dejected look as Shawn locked the cage door on her.

"There's a light." Evan pointed into the trees.

The light began to form into the four square windows of a small building, or so it seemed, but as they got closer Shawn saw that the windows were in the cabin of a boat. The canopy of trees parted above them and a sliver of moon appeared in the sky. She saw water in front of them, shimmering in the soft light of the moon. "It must be the Rio Tavaco," she said.

They could see the boat clearly now. A woman with long dark hair stepped out of the cabin, the screen door slamming shut behind her. She carried a kerosene lantern. "Tess?" she called.

Tess climbed out of the cab and walked toward the woman, who hugged her with a laugh.

Tess must have another life, Shawn thought. One in which she softens her edges. How else could she elicit a hug and a laugh from a friend?

"I'm Charlie," the woman said, ignoring Tess's lack of an introduction. She kissed each of them on the cheek as if they were old friends and helped them carry their bags and supplies from Manuel's truck to her boat.

The boat was about thirty yards long, and in the darkness it looked as though it had not aged well. The deck that surrounded the cabin on all sides was crooked, and Shawn felt the edges of the swollen boards beneath her feet. Still, it was good to be on a surface with a little give to it after sitting for hours on the unyielding metal floor of Manuel's truck.

"You've been alone on this boat all evening?" Robin asked.

"I've been alone on this boat for a month." Charlie laughed and brushed a strand of thick hair away from her cheek. She was slender, but her large breasts and the mass of black hair gave her substance. She wore a loose white blouse, the yoke embroidered with orange and blue birds. Her skin was dark; her huge eyes black. She turned to Manuel. "Stay for dinner, Manny?"

Manuel made excuses, but before he left he pulled Charlie against him and kissed her hard on the lips. She laughed. "Remember your wife," she said. *"Recuerdate Maria."*

Shawn wished he would stay for dinner. He would have to drive all the way back to Iquitos tonight. She felt frustrated that she didn't know the Spanish to thank him properly. They watched him drive off, the truck bouncing back over the rutted terrain with its one headlight glancing off the trees. Then Charlie turned to them with a gleam in her eyes.

"I have turtle!" she said, opening the rickety screen door. A kerosene lantern illuminated four narrow beds topped with thin bare mattresses, two on each side of the cabin. A small stove stood in one corner, and a huge battered pot sat on one of its burners. The room was filled with a warm, savory smell.

"You've stayed here *alone*?" Robin asked again.

Charlie shrugged. "Safer than the city. I have protection if I need it." She nodded toward a shotgun in the corner. "I like the solitude." She pulled a hinged table down from the wall, and it fell between the beds. "Sit," she said.

Shawn sank down gratefully onto one of the soft mattresses.

"What are you smiling about?" Evan grinned at her from across the table. Everyone turned to look at her.

Was she smiling? "I didn't know I was," she said, and felt the smile grow broader. "Feeling content, I guess." The word surprised her. Maybe she was just too tired to worry. Or maybe it had something to do with Charlie's earthy welcome, and the hominess of this decrepit boat. Maybe it was the smell of turtle cooking that made her feel like she was ten years old again, sitting in the kitchen while her father fixed her corned beef hash and told her about the animals he treated that day.

Charlie set soup bowls heaped with fleshy chunks of turtle in front of them. Shawn felt Robin's eyes on her, waiting to see if she would eat it. It was not exactly seafood, but then it was not a mammal either. She hesitated only a moment before digging in. It was delicious.

"Tastes like pork," Evan said encouragingly to Robin.

Was this what pork tasted like? Shawn couldn't remember.

"Where did you get the turtle?" Tess asked.

"Friends. Remember Pacita and Marco? They bartered for a few up the river and brought him to me along with some fruit."

Meg barely spoke during the meal. She's afraid of Tess, Shawn thought, afraid of saying the wrong thing. Tess sat next to Charlie, speaking to her in an esoteric shorthand that left the rest of them out of much of their conversation.

It was hard to imagine the two of them as friends, Tess with her cold hands, Charlie full of ready laughter.

"How do you two know each other?" she asked.

Charlie and Tess exchanged looks and Charlie laughed. "You don't want to know," she said.

"Through an organization," Tess said.

"Botanical?" Shawn asked.

"Political," said Tess.

"You could call it that," Charlie nodded.

"Charlie and I belong to an organization that fights for women's rights, which are sorely overlooked in Peru."

Robin lifted her spoon from the soup she'd barely touched. "But it seems as though Peru hasn't held you back, Charlie. You're out here, a woman alone in the jungle with a boat and a gun."

"Owning a boat and a gun hardly constitutes equality," Tess snapped at her.

Evan leaned toward Tess. "There's no need to bite her head off."

"Leave her alone, Tess." Charlie reached over to touch Robin's arm. "It might look as if I've got all the freedom I want. But I don't. I don't have my kids. I'm not even allowed to see them. I was divorced three years ago, and my husband was given custody of my children."

"You can't even visit them?" Shawn asked.

Charlie shook her head.

"I thought that custody would always be awarded to the mother in a South American country," said Evan.

Charlie nodded. "Well, you can just imagine what a monstrous mother they thought I was."

There was a long silence. Shawn saw the pain in Charlie's eyes and thought it made no sense. Charlie was a nurturer. Shawn felt cared about for the first time all day. What could she have done to her children? Beaten them? She hardly seemed the type.

"Did you have a good lawyer?" David asked finally.

"Several."

"How old are your children?" Shawn asked.

"They'd be six and seven now. Both girls."

There was another lengthy silence.

"You have no accent at all." Evan changed the subject. "Are you Peruvian?"

Charlie told them she became a Peruvian citizen when she married her Peruvian husband, but she was actually of Greek descent, having been born in Athens to Greek parents. Her family moved to New York when she was ten.

"If I have any accent at all," she said, "it's from the Bronx." She laughed and they joined her. Her dark looks suddenly lost some of their exotic quality.

She stood up. "*Pisco* sours?" she offered.

"Of course," said Tess.

Perhaps Charlie was an alcoholic? Would that be enough to prevent a mother from even visiting her children?

Shawn risked sipping at the *Pisco* now. They all did, except for Meg, who stuck to her bottled water. She didn't look happy.

"I have a mango," Charlie said. "Would your little tamarin like some?"

CoCo had sat patiently in her little cage watching them eat dinner. Now she looked up expectantly as though she knew there was a treat in store for her. Shawn took her out and set her on the edge of the table and fed her slivers of yellow mango. The Elf took the slices daintily from Shawn's fingers and slipped them into her mouth, chewing politely. Everyone watched her, hypnotized by her delicate movements.

"I don't think CoCo is the right name for her," David said.

Shawn groaned. "No, David, *please*."

"Cho-Cho San is close."

Meg lifted her head. "Cho-Cho San? Madame Butterfly?"

David nodded. "We once had a canary named Madame Butterfly, remember, Shawn? Our cat ate her though."

Meg laughed. She had suddenly come to life. "What was the cat's name?"

"Mefistofele."

"Fitting," she said. "Did you have a Faust?"

David nodded. "Our older cat. He was ten years old when we got Mefistofele."

"And you figured Mephistopheles would make him young again."

"Yes." David leaned forward, excited now. "But the cat's name was *Mefistofele*, not Mephistopheles." He was testing Meg, and Shawn had the feeling she was about to pass.

"Ah," Meg said. "Boito rather than Gounod."

"Exactly." David sat back against the cabin wall, eyes smiling. "You're an opera buff."

"An opera *fanatic*," Meg corrected him.

Shawn had gotten lost somewhere in the middle of their conversation. She remembered embarrassing herself by falling asleep during the opera *Faust*. Even the usually unflustered David had been upset with her. "Couldn't you at least have made it through the first act?" he'd asked.

"Do we stay tied up here all night?" Robin asked. "Can't a jaguar smell the food and burst through that screen door?"

Charlie laughed. "A jaguar has better things to do with his

time than waste it on us,'' she said. ''But don't worry. We'll
take off shortly and I'll pilot the boat while you sleep.''

Four of them could sleep on the beds, Charlie said, the other
two outside in hammocks. That appealed to Shawn. She pictured
sleeping under the stars as the boat sailed lazily down the river.

Charlie helped her string a hammock from the overhanging
roof of the cabin and rigged the mosquito netting over it, while
Tess hung her hammock on the other side. ''You have to sleep
on the diagonal,'' Charlie said. ''It takes a little practice.''

''How far do we travel tonight?''

''We measure in time out here, not distance,'' Charlie said.
''We'll spend half the night on the Rio Tavaco, then a few hours
on a smaller river. That'll put us at the mouth of the stream that
will take you into Dacu. I'll drop you off there and you'll go the
rest of the distance in the dugout, another eight hours or so.''
She pointed to a huge, motorized canoe on the side of the boat
deck. In the darkness, Shawn could barely make it out as something separate from Charlie's boat. It was at least ten or twelve
yards long. She stroked her hand over the wood and felt the
irregular planed surface of the tree it had been made from.

''I wish you were coming with us, Charlie.'' She was worried
that her new-found sense of calm would leave her when they
waved good-bye to this self-assured woman.

''Tess is the best,'' Charlie said. ''She knows everything there
is to know about living in the jungle. You'll see.''

The boat had no bathroom. Before going to bed they carried
their flashlights and rolls of toilet paper into the forest, walking
along the rutted path Manuel's truck had followed. David
hummed a song, something familiar, something she'd heard him
sing around the house. In Italian, or perhaps it had been French.

''I don't think I'll be able to go out here,'' Robin said as she
followed Evan into the trees, twisting her hands together. Shawn
heard Evan respond, but she couldn't make out his words.

She and David headed in the opposite direction, fighting off
the branches and vines that snapped at them as they walked.

''How about here?'' David pointed his flashlight into the dark
tangle of undergrowth.

''As good as any place,'' she said, taking a few tentative steps
forward. ''God, it's spooky out here.''

She heard David unzip his pants in the darkness.

''I don't think I really have to go,'' she said.

"Better go now. You don't want to have to come out here in the middle of the night, do you?"

No, she didn't. She pulled her shorts down to her knees and squatted in the darkness. "Nothing's happening," she said. Her bladder was rock solid, and her concentration was absorbed by what might be lurking inches from her bare flesh. "Do you realize the animal life that's around us right now?" She felt her voice quiver, and with some surprise, realized she was afraid. "Can you imagine that Charlie comes out here alone all the time?" she said in an attempt to reassure herself.

David zipped his pants without answering her. "Ready?" He pointed his flashlight in the direction of the path, and she followed him back to the boat.

In the cabin, she brushed her teeth with Charlie's filtered water. She watched Robin climb into her sleeping bag, set head to head with Evan's on the other bed. And then she noticed the other pair of beds. David was spreading out his sleeping bag so that he would be lying head to head with Meg. Shawn felt the dark cloud again, settling heavily around her shoulders. It was her own fault. She had set it up this way herself by saying she'd sleep outside. She'd only been thinking of how good it would be to sleep in a hammock under the stars. She'd forgotten she had a husband to sleep with. She could say she changed her mind. She could move her sleeping bag inside, put it on the floor next to David's bed. But that would look pretty obvious. *Fine,* she thought, slipping her toothbrush back in her toiletries case. *Let them talk* Faust *all night.*

The hammock was more comfortable than she'd imagined, every inch of her suspended. It made her feel drugged, floating that way, and for the moment she was glad she'd made the choice to sleep outside.

She had to get used to this anyway, being without David. This is what it would be like after the divorce. She would no longer know what he was doing at night, whether he was sleeping with another woman or not. David with another woman. Hard to imagine. He had never shown an interest in anyone but her.

She heard laughter coming from the cabin. David's, followed by the soft voice of a woman. Then all four of them laughed together. She strained her ears to listen, to join in the joke, but it was no use.

What if David wanted custody of the boys? She thought of

Charlie and her children. How horrible. But it wouldn't be a problem in her case. She could make David look negligent based on the incident with Heather. Certainly that would be enough.

He could get an apartment closer to the airport. Or on his salary, he could buy a second house, something big enough to accommodate the boys when they visited. That was a terrifying thought, handing Jamie and Keith over to him for a weekend.

The divorce would be hard on the boys. They were not stupid kids; surely they knew this marriage was no longer the best, but it would still be a shock. She wasn't certain they could handle another trauma in their lives. She'd thought of waiting until they were out of school, but four more years? She'd be so filled with bile by then she'd be worthless as a mother.

And how would David react? He hadn't a clue this was going on in her head. He would hear her out, nodding occasionally, avoiding her eyes as he did when she talked about something serious. He would get all the facts from her, say something like, "I see," and then walk away. Perhaps that was best. He wouldn't make it difficult for her.

He wouldn't like being without the kids. He loved Jamie and Keith, and he'd loved Heather too. Not like she did, though. He was able to turn off his love when she died, so he felt no pain. She resented that part of him. He would do the same with the divorce. *Click!* Tune out the hurt, get on with his life. He could easily find someone new. He had the opportunities. He had the sack load of fan mail dumped on his desk each week. As soon as the news of the divorce hit the papers, he'd be inundated. She hated the way her private life became public knowledge. When Heather's death hit the news, she felt as though people on the street scrutinized her grief and judged its degree of correctness. Sympathy letters poured in from strangers all over San Diego County, nearly all of them addressed to David alone.

So he'd be first to find someone new. That was all right. She didn't need a man. In many ways she didn't want to share her life with a man again, and she certainly didn't want to share her children. She'd proven to herself that she could exist without sex. Not happily, but it was possible. Still, she would have to find a man to fill her time or she wouldn't be able to keep her mind off Evan, and that wouldn't be fair to him. This divorce would be hard enough on Evan as it was. He loved them both.

The boat sailed smoothly with the hum of the engine. Shawn felt the hint of a breeze off the water, but the thick air still weighed heavily on her chest. The lights from the boat shimmered on black water, and above her hung thousands of stars and one thin moon. *There is no one else out here,* she thought. *Just us.*

She heard sounds from the bow of the boat where Tess sat with Charlie. They were just out of Shawn's sight in front of the cabin, but she could see occasional puffs of smoke from Tess's cigarettes and hear the bottle of rum clink against the rims of their glasses.

They spoke in low tones. From time to time she heard Charlie's laughter, and as the night grew quieter, and the rum was consumed, she made out more of their words. They were speaking of mutual friends; it seemed they had many. This one was returning to Bogota in the fall, that one opening a restaurant in San Francisco.

"And Meg?" Charlie asked.

"Very young," said Tess. A 'ong pause, another puff of smoke. "She thinks she knows what she wants but . . ."

"*I* know what she wants," said Charlie. "That look was in my own eyes once."

"She'll have to learn she can't have it. Not to the extent she'd like it, at any rate." That malicious chuckle of Tess's again. It gave Shawn gooseflesh.

"I have to say I was disappointed to see her. I was hoping that . . . It's been so long since you and I . . ." Charlie seemed at a loss for words.

"Not with this group I wouldn't have, Meg or no Meg. Fucking uptight. I don't know how I'll last two weeks with them."

Shawn clenched her fists at her sides. *Bitch.* Maybe they didn't have Tess's grip on the jungle, and maybe she'd acted a little crazy on the truck out of Iquitos, but when it came to being uptight, Tess had them all beat.

"Can I see you before you go back to California?" Charlie asked. Pleaded, actually. Her voice had a new, little-girl quality to it. "Can you spend a few days here?"

Shawn held her breath, waiting for Tess's reply, but when it came it was in Spanish, and so low, so whispered, that it sounded like little more than the lapping of the river along its banks. And then it was quiet. There was no smoke, no sound of glass tapping glass.

She thought then that she understood why Charlie, even with the best of lawyers, had lost her children.

The soft hum of the motor lulled her to sleep. She dreamt of the canopy and the black water, and of Evan making love to her on the taut linen cords of the hammock.

· *Fourteen* ·

THE AFFAIR WITH Evan lasted a little over a year. She didn't like that word: *affair*. It rang of something illicit and dirty, and she would never have described their relationship in those terms. She felt no guilt, not even over the lies she told David about where she was going, who she was with. They grew easier to deliver as the months wore on, rolled off her tongue as simply as the truth. David never suspected anything. He took on more books to read and when she came home, his "reading" sign was on the closet door more often than not. David was only a presence in the house, sometimes intrusive but usually reliable in his distance from her. If he ever accused her of having an affair, she would have felt insulted. She'd convinced herself of her innocence. She was only trying to survive.

She wished it had been that easy for Evan. One afternoon he told her he no longer received communion when he went to mass.

"Why not?" she asked.

He looked at her as if she should have known. "I'm hardly deserving these days," he said.

She was struck by what she cost him, what he was willing to pay. She resented Catholicism for the pain it caused him. It was hard for her to understand his attachment to the church and his acquiescence to its rules.

"What about confession?" she asked. "Isn't that supposed to cleanse you of your . . ." she hesitated, she refused to use the word *sins* here, ". . . of the things you feel bad about?"

He smiled at the euphemism. "You can't confess to things you intend to continue doing," he said.

When she pressed him, he told her he hated the deception, that her lack of guilt amazed him. He said he loved David. How odd it was that he loved David when she did not. In the beginning Evan tried to talk her into straightening things out with

David, forgiving him. She let him know with her silence she didn't want to talk about David. Meanwhile, Evan and David continued to play racquetball together every Saturday as though nothing had changed, while she took the boys shopping, or skating, or to the mountains. She knew she put Evan in an impossible position. If she felt any guilt, it was over that.

There was another part to Evan's suffering that was far more evident to her. She saw it every time she looked in his eyes—he wanted more of her than he could have. She couldn't consider divorce back then. The boys could never handle it, right on top of losing their sister. But her reasons for not divorcing David went deeper than concern for her sons. She had a haunting feeling that if she ended the union that created Heather, she would be denying Heather's existence, wiping out her memory altogether. She knew that was illogical, as much of her thinking was during that year; still she wouldn't consider ending her marriage.

In March, Evan gave her the gold necklace with the delicate tail-linked tamarins. "It's a way of keeping me with you when I can't be there myself," he said. She hardly needed that. He was always there for her, even in the middle of the night. That was the hardest time. The year after Heather died she was perpetually awake. Had a night gone by that entire year that she didn't cry in bed? David was oblivious to her tears. Occasionally he got up and slept in Heather's room to get away from her. She called Evan on those nights, talked to him from her bed— 2:00 A.M., 3:00 A.M. He never complained about the hour.

"I shouldn't have gone back to work right away," she would say into the phone. "She was only four weeks old. What kind of mother would do that?" or, "I should have given her swimming lessons," or, "I can't believe she went in the water alone."

She was obsessive. Everyone except Evan tuned her out. She heard the weary impatience in her friends' voices when she talked about Heather, but she couldn't stop herself. After a while, no one called her. Even her father was tired of listening to her.

"You have to get on with your life, Shawn," he said. "You have a family to take care of."

If Evan felt impatient with her, she never knew it. He listened to her for hours on the phone. He told her what a terrific mother she'd been to Heather. "You took every Friday morning off to be with her," he reminded her. "To bake cookies or hunt tarantulas. What more could you have done?" She pictured him lying naked under his covers, eyes closed, the receiver wedged between his ear and the pillow. Sometimes she felt like screaming because the need to be lying next to him was unbearable.

That summer, almost a year after Heather's death, things started to change. David demanded more of her, and Evan less. But nothing changed inside her. She still clung to her sanity by a thread, and as the overcast weather of June gave way to the dry heat of July, she began to feel panicky. August twenty-sixth would be a year. That day crept toward her, a palpable reminder of Heather's death, much more than a date on next month's calendar. It could not be avoided or skipped over. When she was able to sleep at all, she had nightmares. She'd wake up disoriented in the middle of the night, reach out for Evan, and recoil when her hand touched David's bare skin.

Sometime in the middle of July she had the first serious inkling she was losing Evan. The day started poorly. She woke up very early, her nightgown damp and twisted around her legs, and struggled to get her bearings. David was still home; she saw the light under their bathroom door. From her bed she could make out the shapes of the full jacaranda trees outside her bedroom window.

The boys. She sat up. She'd had some kind of dream.

"David!"

He came into the room dressed only in his pants, belt buckle undone, face half-covered with shaving cream. He had a towel around his neck and his razor in his hand.

"What's the matter?"

She started to get out of the bed. "I had a dream . . . I have to check on Keith and Jamie."

David caught her arms. "They're not here, honey, remember? They're at Disneyland with Kevin Jensen." He leaned toward her to look into her eyes. "Do you remember?"

She sat back on the edge of the bed. She should never have agreed to let them go. "I have to call them," she said.

David wiped the shaving cream from his face with the towel and sat next to her. "It's five in the morning. I doubt the Jensens would appreciate a call right now."

She lay down again and looked at David. "You think I'm nuts."

He shook his head. "Listen. Since you're wide awake, why don't you get dressed and go up with me this morning?"

"No."

"You haven't been up with me in such a long time."

What he meant was she hadn't been up with him since Heather's death, but he would never come out and say those words. You wouldn't know he'd ever had a daughter.

"I don't want to go," she said.

"Well, how about dinner after work? Some place really nice."

He wasn't going to leave her alone today. She felt trapped. "I have a meeting tonight." She slipped her fingers under the gold chain. Her meeting was with Evan, at his apartment.

"Skip it."

"I can't."

He sighed. "I just thought that with the boys gone for a couple of days we could enjoy some time together."

That made her angry. They'd argued about letting the boys go, and for the first time in a long time she let David win. He said she was suffocating them, they'd lose their friends, they needed to get out and have fun. She bought it all, and now she realized that he'd gotten rid of them to try to force her into spending time with him, doing things she didn't want to do.

She rolled over and pulled the covers to her chin. "You thought wrong," she said.

Evan lived in the upper story of an old, pink stucco house in the dusty outskirts of Escondido. The house stood alone on a hill, surrounded by scruffy, red-barked manzanita trees. The owners of the house lived on the first floor. They thought of themselves as farmers, and Shawn walked past a crumbling chicken coop and five thin goats on her way to the front door.

She let herself in with her key. Evan was stopping off at the grocery store; they were going to make dinner together. She poured a glass of wine for each of them. There were two juice glasses in the sink, one with a smear of lipstick on it. It wasn't the first time she found a sign—a tangle of bedsheets, earrings on the coffee table—that let her know he hadn't slept alone the night before. He was always apologetic. "Sorry," he'd say, his cheeks red. "I should have made the bed," or "I should have done the dishes." He was pretty when he blushed. She liked to think he was loaded with Irish ancestry.

She'd tell him it was all right. After all, she slept with David every night of the week, although they both knew that was hardly the same thing. Anyway, it was hard to feel threatened by Evan's other women. None ever lasted long or seemed to mean much to him.

But there had been a lot of signs lately, and she had a feeling it was the same woman each time.

"Hi." He walked into the kitchen with a bag of groceries and a smile. He had on baggy gray shorts and an old, soft green shirt he must have picked up in a thrift store. Evan had his own sense of style.

She held the wineglass to his lips and he sipped, eyes closed. "Wonderful," he said. "Thank you."

She watched him unload the milk and yogurt, a couple of frozen dinners, and the fresh pasta they'd be eating that evening. He handed her a head of lettuce to wash.

"Let me call the boys in Los Angeles first," she said, setting the lettuce on the counter.

She spoke to each of them. They sounded happier than she'd heard them in a long time. She got off the phone, and Evan put his arms around her waist and pulled her toward him.

"So," he said. "Are they enjoying Disneyland?"

"They sound so happy."

"Good."

She shook her head. "Something's wrong with me. I mean, I'm not a good mother, not to mention that I'm a terrible wife." She laughed a little at that.

"Well, I know why you're a terrible wife," he kissed her lightly. "But you seem like a pretty good mom to me."

She shook her head. "It bothers me that my kids sound so happy."

He leaned back and narrowed his eyes at her, and she thought he looked enormously sexy. "Why, babe?"

She shrugged. "Because it's too soon."

"It's been nearly a year."

"And David's just forgotten her too. If I acted happy and content, he'd never give her another thought."

He stroked her cheek with his thumb. "Nearly a year, Shawn."

"When they're happy, I feel left out. Deserted."

"You were her mother. The feeling's stronger for you."

"Sometimes I want to make them miserable. It scares me. I fight that urge with Keith and Jamie—I really try to keep it under control. But not with David." She bit her lip. "I *like* hurting him. I want to see him suffer."

Evan let go of her and reached for his wine. "Is that why you're with me? To hurt David?"

She shook her head. "I'm not using you, if that's what you mean. At least not to hurt David. If I'm using you at all, it's because you make me feel good."

He put his arm around her shoulders and pointed her toward the bedroom. "Come on," he said. "The fettuccine can wait."

"Are you seeing a lot of a particular woman?" They'd made love and now she was sitting up in his bed, holding the sheet to her chest while he traced the gold necklace with his finger.

"What makes you ask that?"

"A feeling. Same pair of earrings a few times. Same lipstick color on the juice glasses."

"You're a sleuth," he said.

"Well?"

"Yes. I am."

"Oh."

"Do you want to know more?"

She nodded. "I think so."

He sat up and put his arms around her. "Not in bed. Not tonight. We'll talk about it tomorrow."

"It's serious."

He hesitated. "I don't know. It's different. But I'm *not* going to talk about it now. Not with you in my bed."

"I've wanted to tell you about her," he said over coffee in his office the next morning, "but I was afraid you'd feel hurt."

"Try me," she said bravely.

Once he started he couldn't stop. Her name was Robin. She was beautiful and the whole thing made him nervous, because she was so much his opposite. She had an MBA. He shuddered just to say that out loud. To him a business degree meant materialism and a lack of social conscience. "She's not like that, though," he said. "She still has a sense of her own values."

"How did you meet her?"

He was slow to answer. "She manages a jewelry store. I met her when I ordered your necklace."

Her fingers flew to her throat, and she tried to keep the disappointment from showing on her face. She was no longer the sole owner of this necklace. Evan must think of Robin each time he looked at it.

"I feel guilty," he said. "As if I'm betraying you."

"It had to happen someday, Evan."

"I want you to like her."

"I'm sure I will." She didn't even want to meet her.

"She's not an animal lover." His tone was apologetic. "But she's Catholic. She goes to church. And she wants kids."

She studied his face. There were long, deep lines at the corners of his eyes that she'd never noticed before. He was not quite thirty-three. He'd spent his life working hard, and he deserved better than she was giving him. She set her mug on the floor and leaned over to kiss him softly on the mouth.

"She's a lucky woman," she said.

As July gave way to August, she grew more apprehensive. She stopped sleeping again. She walked around the house at night in her bare feet, sitting in one room after another, staring at the shadows on the wall. She couldn't eat. She threw away the little she put on her plate. David didn't seem to notice.

But Evan did. One day, after watching her toss her sandwich into her office wastebasket, he leaned toward her and rested his hand on her flat stomach.

"Starving yourself isn't going to bring her back," he said.

"One year exactly on Saturday," she said.

"I know."

"I wish it fell on a workday so I could be with you."

"It's David you should be with then. He's probably going to be feeling pretty miserable himself."

"I don't even think he knows."

"Then tell him."

"No. Evan, could you back out of the racquetball game with him on Saturday? It would bother me if he played, as if it was any other Saturday."

"*Tell* him that. Tell him it would bother you."

She shook her head.

"Jesus, Shawn, you've got to start talking to him. We let this go on way too long. *I've* let it . . . I feel responsible for how screwed up your marriage is."

She turned her head to the window so she wouldn't have to see the desperation in his face. She had to stop draining him. She had to let him get on with his life.

"Kevin's mom asked us to go with them to the beach Saturday," Keith said at the dinner table that evening. His brown hair was too long in the back; it curled down over the collar of his shirt. He looked like a child who was not well cared for. No wonder Kevin's family seemed to have adopted her sons. Probably took pity on these two little boys whose parents were too preoccupied to get their kids' hair cut.

"Can we go?" Keith looked at David. He knew David was an easier mark than Shawn.

David looked at her across the table and she shook her head. "I thought we might do something together as a family on Saturday," she said.

Jamie made a face. "Like what?"

"Something . . . quiet and . . . just with all of us together." She felt David's eyes on her.

"We'd rather just go to Kevin's," Keith said.

"Well, you can't."

"Maybe we could have a picnic somewhere," David said.

Jamie curled his mouth in disgust. "Oh, great," he said.

Shawn leaned forward and grabbed Jamie's arm. She felt her fingers tighten, pinch the skin. "You little brat," she said. "One year ago Saturday your sister died. You're not going anywhere that day." She stood up and threw her napkin on the table. "And the very last place I'd let you go is the *beach*."

David followed her into the bedroom. He put his arms around her and she cried against his chest, realizing it was the first time she'd let him comfort her, and allowing it now only because she had no strength to back away from him.

"I think we should let them go," David said.

"I don't."

"Think about it. If they feel coerced into staying home, they'll start resenting Heather."

He said her name. She looked up at him. She hadn't heard him use Heather's name since she died.

"But the beach?" she asked.

"They'll be okay."

She made it through Saturday, and the rest of August as well. Her visits to Evan's apartment became less frequent, and each time there were more traces of Robin. Boxes of herbal tea in his cupboard, a second toothbrush in the bathroom. Worst of all, the scent of her perfume laced his sheets. Robin was scent-marking her territory.

Evan no longer apologized for the stockings hung over the curtain rod in the shower or the camisole on his dresser. Still, he was careful of Shawn's feelings, careful never to speak of Robin when he and Shawn were together in the evening. Robin was a topic saved for morning coffee and the light of day.

But one night he stood across the bed from her, hands in his pockets, making no move to pull down the spread, and she knew.

"Let's just talk tonight," he said. He walked around the bed and put his arm around her waist. "I'll make us some coffee."

She had tears in her eyes by the time they reached the kitchen, and she switched off the light so he couldn't see them.

He looked at her. "How am I going to see what I'm doing?"

"I'm so selfish."

"No you're not." He put his arms around her.

"I don't want to lose you."

"You know that if you said you'd divorce David, I would forget about Robin."

She shook her head. "I can't do that right now."

He was quiet for a moment before he spoke. "I want to marry her. And I can't marry her and continue to . . ."

"I know," she said. She tried to imagine never kissing him again. "I won't make it hard for you."

· Fifteen ·

CHARLIE'S BOAT WAS anchored next to the shore in the morning. Shawn could see the heavy rope leading from the bow to a thick vine on the bank. She could make out the canopy of trees high above her, slivers of sunlight piercing it here and there in long narrow columns of white light. She lay still, sorting out the early morning sounds: bird song on every side and behind her the steady rush of the Rio Tavaco as it swept along its banks. Someone was up in the cabin. She heard footsteps, teeth being brushed, a zipper sliding up its track. The screen door creaked, and Evan stepped from the cabin to the deck.

"Wow." He walked to the railing and looked over at her. "Paradise."

She climbed out of the hammock and stood next to him in her bare feet. She was still wearing the shorts and shirt she'd worn the day before. "Thanks for talking me into this," she said.

He reached over to touch her hair. "This is a great haircut," he said. "You don't even have to comb it when you get up in the morning, and it still looks good."

She wondered if there was something behind the casual stroke of his fingers over her hair, or the way he'd touched her neck in the shop the day before. She had to be careful. She'd been away from the security of the Center for only two days, and already she was allowing herself to feel things that could only hurt her.

"How about a walk?" he asked.

They pushed their way through the thick brush near the banks, and the vines threw tendrils around their necks and caught in their hair. They'd forgotten their machetes. It would be an adjustment, learning to carry those knives with them all the time.

There was mist in the jungle. It swirled softly around them, concealing a tree one moment, exposing it to clear view the next. They walked carefully, trying not to break the perfect, dew-studded spider webs that stretched from tree to tree; and they scanned the shrouded canopy for Copper Elves, although they knew they were still a day's journey from Dacu. She felt peaceful. Iquitos was far behind her, and the boys were safe.

"I think Charlie and Tess are lovers," she said when they were far enough from the boat that she could not be overheard.

He looked at her quizzically. "You're kidding."

"I heard them talking last night."

Evan frowned. "I can't picture Tess making love to anyone, regardless of sex. She looks like all take and no give to me."

She ducked under a spider web. "I bet that's why Charlie doesn't have her children."

"Mm," he nodded. "God, that's cruel. What about Meg? Do you think . . . ?"

"Not sure."

"That would break David's heart."

"What do you mean?"

"He seems a little smitten."

"David doesn't get smitten."

"The man still has blood in his veins, Shawn."

Yes, he did. She became aware of that later in the morning as they loaded the enormous dugout canoe. She watched David study every inch of Meg's body as though he would be tested later on the shape of her hips under her khaki pants, the long line of her thighs, the way her pale blond hair curved over her breasts.

Robin was last to get into the canoe. "It might tip over," she said, although the dugout was as big and solid as a house.

"Five of us have already gotten in, and it hasn't tipped over yet," Tess said impatiently.

They'd set a small yellow paddle canoe upside down in the center of the dugout and packed their gear around and under it. Evan sat in the bow where he could watch for obstacles in the stream. Shawn and Meg sat on one side of the yellow canoe; David, on the other. He patted the space next to him, encouraging Robin to take a seat.

"It's not going to tip over." Charlie took Robin's arm. "And even if it did, you're only in two feet of water here."

Robin finally got in and everyone applauded. Except for Tess, who rolled her eyes and pulled the cord on the outboard motor. It started with a great, peace-shattering sputter.

"Meet you here in two weeks!" Charlie called as they sailed onto the thin black water of the stream.

Within a few hours, the inside of the canoe felt like a sauna. The sun was absorbed by the black plastic bags that held their food and supplies. It steamed the half-inch of water in the bottom of the boat so that they were all bathed in a damp, thick heat.

The current was against them, but it was mild, and Tess said they were making good time. The banks above the stream were choked with heavy green bushes and knotted vines. It felt as though they were moving from one small lake to another, as each hairpin turn propelled the canoe into a new circle of water, and the green surrounded them again on all sides. Once they came head to head with a gigantic turtle sitting on a rock in the middle of the stream, and Shawn regretted her meal of the night before. She wouldn't eat turtle again on this trip.

Most of the wildlife hid from the noisy intrusion of the dug-out, and there was little to see other than the black water and green forest. Shawn found herself hoping they'd hit a patch of white water—something to challenge them a little. As she watched the water in the bottom of the canoe lapping at the soles of her tennis shoes, she willed it to rise a little higher. Not too high, not a real threat, but enough to let them know they were not alone out here, that nature would be their constant companion, both friend and enemy.

ChoCho, as everyone was calling the Elf now, was in her cage at Shawn's feet. She looked bored. Occasionally she reached one arm through the wire mesh of the cage to touch the water in the bottom of the boat and lick it from her fingers. But most of the time she sat on her perch, studying her tiny pointed claws, a look of weary resignation on her round white face.

Meg had taken a dozen pictures of ChoCho during the first hour or so of the trip upstream, but now her lens was aimed at Tess. Tess didn't seem to notice. She sat in the stern, one hand on the engine so she could steer the canoe around the rocks and branches littering the stream, the other hand holding one of her long brown cigarettes. Meg snapped a picture, then lowered the camera to her lap, and unscrewed the lens. She pulled a long, fat lens from her camera case. She seemed very attached to that case, unzipping it slowly and carefully, closing it tightly again before tending to her camera. She had the strap from the case wrapped around her ankle. She wore a small, anticipatory smile on her lips as she fit the lens onto the face of the camera. Shawn watched her, remembering Tess and Charlie's conversation from the night before. She remembered Charlie talking about the look in Meg's eyes, the look she recognized as once having been in her own. What could she have been talking about if not desire? Wasn't that what Shawn saw in Meg's eyes right now?

Meg lifted the camera with its heavy-looking lens and pointed it at Tess. Shawn winced when she heard the snap of the shutter. She wondered how Meg would feel a few weeks from now, when she looked at this picture of her cold and unyielding friend and remembered the raw longing that inspired it.

"I'm getting burned right through my shirt," Robin said, touching her hand to her shoulder.

Tess had managed to keep the dugout in the shade along the banks most of the time, shifting it from one side of the wide stream to the other as they came around each turn. But when the sun found them, it burned their skin like hot metal. The tops of Shawn's thighs were pink. She was the only one wearing shorts. She'd ignored Evan's warnings about scratches and stinging insects and sunburn. It was just too hot to wear long pants.

"Tree ahead," Evan called out. A fallen tree blocked most of the stream, and Shawn thought they might have to carry the canoe around it. But Tess expertly navigated the boat through the small space left for them near the bank, while Evan dipped a paddle into the water to keep them on course. The back of Evan's T-shirt was dark with sweat. Shawn felt her own shirt sticking to her chest and back. It reminded her of another time in a canoe, years ago, on another excruciatingly hot day. She and David took a canoe out on the canal in Georgetown. They had headaches from the heat, and after a while they stopped paddling and let themselves drift. When she could no longer tolerate the sun beating on her, she shifted her weight ever so slightly, just enough to make the canoe tip over. David watched her, incredulous, as if he couldn't quite believe she would do it. He should have known better.

"You're out of your mind!" he said when they surfaced in the warm, buggy water. But he was laughing. He caught her hand and pulled her under, and when he let her up, their heads were in the pocket of air under the overturned canoe. He kissed her in the darkness while they tread water. Then he started singing "Memory" from *Cats*. It was one of the few songs she knew the words to. Their voices echoed furiously inside the canoe as they drifted down the canal. When they finished the song, they emerged to applause from passersby on the bank.

She watched David now from her side of the boat and thought of asking him if he remembered that day as well, but she couldn't do that. There was no point to reminding him of the good times between them, and no point to remembering them herself.

They stopped for a break at noon. The forest was oddly quiet as they climbed onto the bank. They ate the smoked fish Charlie sent with them. It was full of bones, but delicious. Then they spread out to "use the woods," as Tess called it.

As Shawn was returning to the boat, she spotted Robin and Evan through the brush. Their backs were to her. Robin had taken her shirt off and was holding up her hair while Evan smoothed sunscreen on the nape of her neck. Shawn leaned against a tree, the skin on the back of her own neck stinging. Her short hair left that part of her completely exposed. She could ask to borrow some sunscreen—she could step between the two of them right now. But of course she wouldn't. She dug her nails into the soft bark of the tree as she watched Evan unfasten Robin's bra. He slipped the sunscreen tube into his pants pocket so he could use both hands to smooth the cream over her back and shoulders. His head was close to hers, his cheek touching her hair. He was whispering to her. Shawn turned away. Evan always sheltered her from the intimate side of his marriage. He allowed her to pretend that he and Robin were cardboard figures who never really touched one another. This would be unbearable, watching them for two weeks, the reality of their closeness detailed for her each day.

She walked back to the stream and let David help her down the bank to the dugout. He squeezed her hand as she stepped over the gunwale. *"Memory,"* he sang softly, so that only she could hear him. *"All alone in the moonlight . . ."*

And she smiled at him before she had a chance to catch herself.

They reached Dacu shortly before three. At least Tess told them it was Dacu. How could she possibly know? One patch of jungle along the stream looked exactly like the next.

"I guarantee you," Tess said as she helped them unload the dugout. "This is it. See how narrow the stream is here?"

The stream had indeed narrowed, the banks so close together that the trees met overhead and formed a leafy green tunnel above the water, hiding the sky.

"About a hundred yards in that direction there's a bathing pool." Tess pointed upstream, and then nodded toward the forest on her left. "And right here is where we set up camp."

"A bathing pool." Robin brushed her damp hair off her face with the back of her arm. "I would love a bath right now."

"No time now," said Tess. "Tomorrow you may bathe. It's a good pool. Not too many piranhas."

"Piranhas!" Robin said.

Tess lifted one of the black bags of food out of the boat and heaved it onto the bank. "They won't attack unless there's blood in the water." She went on to describe tiny toothpick-sized fish that would lodge in any body openings they could find. She was taking sadistic pleasure in Robin's squeamishness.

"I'm not going to bathe at all while I'm here," Robin said.

"Whose tent do you plan to sleep in?" Evan handed her a bag and stood up straight. He eyed the trees skeptically and looked at Shawn. "This better be it," he said under his breath. "We don't have time to waste in the wrong area."

As they climbed up the bank and into the forest, they could see that this patch of ground had been cleared before. That was encouraging. The brush was low and thin; the trees, saplings. When the Copper Elves were first discovered, a team of primatologists came to Dacu to make a survey of the Elf population. Shawn hoped this area was the remnants of the primatologists' camp.

"Let's purify some drinking water," Evan said. His lips had a dusty look to them.

"You can drink straight from the stream," Tess said.

"That sounds pretty risky," David said.

"Bullshit," Tess scoffed. She marched off toward the stream with a bucket over her arm while Shawn hunted through the bags for the plastic mugs. Tess returned with the water and poured some for herself. She held it to her lips and swallowed, leaning back to get every drop, as if to prove her point that it was palatable. Shawn dipped her mug into the bucket. The water was clear, but it was impossible to miss the tiny invertebrates squirming across the surface. She looked hesitantly at Evan who shrugged and tapped her mug with his own.

"Cheers," he said as he lifted the mug to his lips. She did the same, eyes closed, swallowing quickly.

Tess coached them in the use of their machetes and Shawn struggled to keep up with her easy, swinging rhythm. They cut the low brush and small trees that had taken root in the clearing, and their hands were quickly blistered.

Every few minutes, Shawn stopped cutting to scrutinize the trees around them, hunting for the tiny Copper Elves. Her eyes hurt from the search. This would not be easy. The only wildlife they could see were huge rats with bristly brown fur. Hundreds of them scurried around in the undergrowth as their homes were disturbed. Spiny Rats, Tess called them.

The clearing began to take shape. Tess dug a firepit in the center and went into the forest to gather dried wood. They covered their food and supplies with a tarp at the back of the clearing. Shawn hung ChoCho's cage from a branch of a tree near the stream. She stood back to look at it. The tree had two low, horizontal branches and she could imagine how it would look a couple of weeks from now, laden with filled traps.

"We won't bother with a latrine since we'll only be here two weeks," Tess said. "Walk away from camp when you have to use the woods, and bury whatever you create with your machetes." She looked up at the sky through the trees. "We'd better get the tents up. We can finish working on the clearing tomorrow."

They paired off and walked in three different directions from the clearing, like spokes on a wheel. Shawn and David cut a crude path with their machetes as they walked parallel to the stream. Shawn wanted to be far from the others.

"This looks good," she said finally. There was a patch of ground big enough for their tent and no menacing dead tree limbs above it.

"Hold this." David handed her the nylon tent and began digging holes for the posts with his machete. A feeling of foreboding came over her as she watched him. No matter how isolated she made herself from the others, she would not be able to get away from David. Every night she would be completely alone with him in this tent. There were no other rooms to go to, no escape at all.

"You can't eat lentils the second day because they go bad," Tess said as she ladeled out their dinner of rice and lentils from the huge black pot on the fire. "So we have to eat all of this tonight. I have beans soaking for tomorrow."

They were sitting on camp stools in a circle around the fire. The lentils were seasoned with chili powder and garlic, and Tess had also made stickbread, coiling dough laced with cheese around sticks and baking it over the fire. Both Shawn's appetite and thirst were sharpened from the work of the afternoon, and the meal tasted as good as anything she'd ever eaten. Tess gave them a powder to mix with the water that made it taste like unsweetened grape Kool-Aid. It made it harder to see the invertebrates, and even Robin was able to get down a mug or two.

From somewhere in the darkening forest came a roar, deep-throated and mournful. The sound grew, echoing beneath the canopy until Robin put her hands over her ears.

"Howler monkeys!" Shawn said. She recognized the sound from the Conservation Center.

"They must be close to be this loud." Tess had to yell to be heard. "You'll hear them at both dusk and dawn."

"Monkeys are making that noise?" Robin shivered. The calls of the Howlers sounded as though they were created by something not quite alive.

"Spirits that haunt the forest," Tess said, as the sound slipped out of the clearing and into the distance. "The natives in the inhabited regions of the Amazon eat them."

"Are there any plants out here we can eat?" Shawn asked.

Tess balanced her bowl on her knee. "Not many, and you have to know what you're doing. The natives eat the insects, though. Termites, ants, grasshoppers. These caterpillars." She pointed to a fat, lime green caterpillar inching its way across the tabletop. "They're everywhere. A good source of protein."

"Repulsive," said Robin.

"They're not bad," Tess said. She went on to tell them about other foods the natives ate—the Spiny Rats, for example, and the piranhas—and Shawn felt her mind drift away from the circle as the evening song of the cicadas grew louder. Then suddenly, from somewhere far behind her in the shadows, came the unmistakable long call of a Copper Elf. Plaintive and pale in the distance. She looked across the circle at Evan. He'd stopped his fork halfway to his mouth, his eyes on hers. No one else had noticed; the talking went on around them.

Evan set his bowl on the ground and nodded in the direction of the forest. Shawn reached into her day pack for a roll of surveyor's tape and her fieldbook, then stood up to follow him.

Robin looked up. "Where are you going?"

Evan turned around, his finger to his lips. "An Elf," he said quietly.

The trees enveloped them almost immediately. She could no longer hear voices or see the light from the fire. But she heard the long call again, closer now, cutting like a slim blade through the trees. And this time there was an answering call, quite close, from the trees on their left. She saw the excitement in Evan's face as he tied a length of the pink surveyor's tape to a tree to mark their trail and took a compass reading.

"On line eighty degrees," he said, and she wrote the reading in her fieldbook. They walked thirty-five paces—twenty-five meters—and tied another piece of tape around a tree, but they needed to go no further.

They both saw the Elf at the same moment, a tiny patch of red in the shadows of the tree above them. They held up their binoculars, and Shawn smiled as she brought the pale human features of the little monkey's face into focus. The Elf watched them as well, studying them with her own curious eyes.

"I wish we could pluck her right out of the tree," Shawn said quietly.

"That would take the fun out of it. And for all we know *she* may be a *he*." Evan lowered his binoculars and took her arm, his hand warm against her skin. "We'd better get back while there's still enough light to see by," he said. "We'll start work right here in the morning."

· Sixteen ·

THE SOFT LIGHT of early morning sifted through the mosquito netting of the tent and Shawn lay still, listening. The drone of the cicadas rose and fell in waves against the steady hum of some other insect or, perhaps, frogs. There was an occasional low-pitched cooing, and once in a while a scream, chilling, soul-piercing. That's what woke her up, that scream. What animal could make a sound like that? How far was it from their tent?

She listened to David's breathing and felt his hip against hers, his feet touching her calf. She shifted a little on the double sleeping bag to move away from him. She had slept well. The air mattress and the exhausting work of the day before made her first night in the heart of the jungle quick and dreamless.

The front and back walls of the tent were made of mosquito netting. It was a four-man tent, but the air mattress took up nearly all the floor space. They'd set their sleeping bag unopened on top of the mattress and used a light sheet as a cover, pillow-cases stuffed with sweatshirts as pillows.

She switched on her flashlight to check her watch. Nearly five-thirty. It would be light soon, and they could begin their work here in Dacu. *Dacu.* For years she'd heard of it, slipped the word off her tongue at speaking engagements, typed it into print in professional articles. It was hard to believe she was finally here. She shut her eyes again but knew she wouldn't sleep. Her mind was too full. She and Evan would just observe today. They'd see what was out there and determine the best places to set the traps. She loved that part of her work with Evan—the problem solving, the focus on tasks that made her feel justified in being with him.

She sat up. Through the mosquito netting she could see the early morning stillness of the forest. Fog shifted and turned through the trees, like something alive, absolutely silent.

Even this far from the clearing, she could smell coffee. Tess, despite her unpleasantness, was going to be invaluable to them. She had a way of making the jungle feel like home.

David sat up and peered through the netting. "Pretty out," he said.

She nodded without speaking. She didn't want to encourage his intrusion on her solitude. The air around him was thick with his scent, a heavy, male scent she was not accustomed to. David took two showers a day. If he smelled of anything other than aftershave, it was chlorine that left its trace on his skin. But his scent this morning was not offensive, actually not unpleasant at all, and she sat a few minutes longer with him, watching the fog lift out of the forest.

She and Evan set off toward the area where they'd spotted the Elf the night before. They took careful compass readings, counted paces, tied the pink tape to the trees. The entire process felt complicated and artificial, but there was no doubt in Shawn's mind it was necessary. The undergrowth slipped back over the path she and Evan just cut in what seemed a deliberate attempt to confuse them. A warning, perhaps, that the jungle would settle for nothing less than their total respect.

"Did you hear that screaming animal this morning?" she asked.

"No, but Robin told me all about it, that and every other sound. I don't think she slept at all."

"She's worried about Melissa." That would certainly be her own worry if she were in Robin's place. She realized guiltily that she'd barely given Keith and Jamie a thought since calling them yesterday.

"She's not worried about Melissa," Evan said with a laugh. "She's worried about Robin. Robin and the jaguar, Robin and vampire bats, Robin and fire ants. She thinks she was set down here as manna for the wildlife. I think she . . ."

He suddenly caught her elbow and pointed above them. It took her a moment, but finally she spotted the tiny red monkey sitting motionless in the branches above them, its white mask peering down at them. Then she saw the second Elf, and the third, this one with two tiny babies clinging to its back. She remembered a puzzle book her father had given her when she was a child. *How many monkeys can you find hidden in this tree?*

The Elves didn't move, as if they were waiting to be counted. Shawn found eight, including the babies. Then one of the Elves gave a piercing alarm call, the same high-pitched *shree, shree* that the tamarins at the Conservation Center made when they were disturbed or nervous. The others joined him as they leaped from branch to branch, their eyes never leaving Shawn and Evan. But as suddenly as the frenzy started, it stopped. The Elves' hearts were not in it. They had decided Shawn and Evan were not their enemies. They turned their attention back to the work of the morning—hunting for insects on the underside of leaves.

Evan still had one hand on her arm. "Up there." He pointed to the right. She spotted a second baby-carrying adult.

"It must be two troops," she said. All the studies had found that each troop of Elves would have only one reproducing female, along with two males who cooperated in taking care of the infants. The female might mate with both males, but seemed attached to only one of them.

"I count thirteen," Evan said.

She nodded as she unfolded the campstool she'd been carrying on her back. She pulled her pen and fieldbook from her pack and sat down, ready to observe for as long as the Elves were willing to let them.

After an hour or so, the Elves suddenly jumped from their branches and began racing through the trees, leaping, flying, swinging from vines, like tiny fireballs shooting through the jungle. Evan and Shawn ran behind them, clearly the underdogs in this race.

The tamarins pulled them deeper into the forest. There was less undergrowth, less need for the machetes. Still, Shawn slapped at the branches they passed to leave a trail of a sort. There was no time for the careful tying of surveyor's tape and the counting of paces. The idea seemed ludicrous now.

"They're splitting up!" Evan said.

The Elves had come to a fork in their path, visible only to them, and several of them leaped north, the rest east.

"See you later," Shawn called to Evan as she ran after the group racing east.

She was flying, as close to flying under the canopy as she was likely to come outside her dreams. She came to a creek, a ribbon of water slipping between two brush-tangled banks, and she stepped into it before she could stop herself. The momentum carried her across in four wide strides, the water up to her ankles, but she didn't care. She would not lose sight of this troop.

She fought her way through the undergrowth on the other side of the creek until her foot caught on a root and she fell to the ground. She looked up slowly. The only sound she heard was her own breathing, heavy and fast. The tamarins had stopped running as well. She spotted them a few trees ahead of her, watching her with great curiosity. Or maybe it was concern. She liked that idea, that they were a little worried about their partner in the game they were playing. She got to her knees and lifted her binoculars to her eyes. She counted five adult-size Elves. Probably a couple of them were juveniles.

The Elves chatted to each other, trying to decide what to do about her. She leaned back to sit on her heels. After a few minutes, the Elves passed through the branches above her head and settled into the tree behind her.

Little devils. They'd gone past their nesting tree in an attempt to trick her. Now that she stopped running, they'd decided she was of little concern.

She spotted a pair of babies clinging to the back of one of the adults. She stood up quietly and lifted the binoculars to her eyes again. She moved under the tree, trying to sex the Elves, to look for signs that would separate the adults from the juveniles, but it was hopeless. They were so *tiny.* It was much easier to observe them at the Center. After a while, the Elf with the babies handed them to another Elf to nurse. Well, finally. She'd found the adult female, the alpha female, the one who pulled the strings in this group.

Her back was stiff and her arms shook from holding up the binoculars. How long had she been out here? She'd better get back before the others sent a search party. She had no tape with her, so she cut branches to mark the nesting tree of this troop and took a compass reading. Tomorrow they'd set a trap here.

She glanced down at her feet and had to stop herself from screaming. At least one hundred tiny ticks were making their way up her legs. Her sneakers and socks were speckled with them. Some were already imbedded in her calves, others had set their sights higher, marching in narrow black trails up her thighs. There were a few on her shorts.

She forced herself to walk calmly over to a fallen tree. She set one foot on the trunk and brushed off the ticks that had not yet attached themselves to her skin. They were seed ticks, no bigger than a pinhead. She shuddered to think some were under her shorts. She would check later, when she got back to camp.

At first she could find none of her machete markings, and she felt a moment's panic, followed by an odd, almost forgotten, thrill of being in danger. What if she were lost out here? She was starting to enjoy the fantasy when she heard the sound of rippling water. The creek. It was right in front of her. She felt an undeniable twinge of disappointment. She took the time to drag a couple of stout branches over the water so she could cross it without getting her feet wet this time.

There was no sign of Evan at the tree where they'd first seen the Elves, and both their campstools were gone. She spotted the last pink marker they'd set and followed the trail to the clearing.

• *Seventeen* •

"PHOTOGRAPHY WILL BE a challenge out here," Meg said as David tied a length of surveyor's tape to a tree. "The wildlife wants nothing to do with us."

It was true. He and Meg had walked for nearly an hour, and except for plants and insects they had not seen a single living thing. He felt as if he had on sunglasses, the type that intensified colors, deepened the greens, and made them richer. There were no sounds at all, except for their footsteps through the leaves and the occasional *whack!* of their machetes. There were places where the growing things were so close together that vines slipped over their shoulders and long green leaves swept across their faces. It reminded him of swimming, of being immersed in something that could lull you to complacency or turn on you without warning. There was that small niggling edge of fear that lay just beneath his awe, that kept him vigilant in leaving the surveyor's tape tied to the trees they passed.

He wondered if Meg's eyes saw the forest the same way his did. She did not seem like other people to him, not typical in her perceptions. He watched her now as she walked ahead of him. Her shirt was pink, her pants dark green and tucked into white socks. She wore a little white hat with a blue and pink parrot painted on its short, floppy brim. Her tripod jutted out of the top of the camera bag slung over her shoulder. She was glued to that bag. In the canoe yesterday she clutched it to her chest like a life preserver.

"Could we sit for a while?" Meg pointed to one of the fallen trees that criss-crossed the forest floor.

"Sure." He thought she looked tired. He took the poncho out of his day pack and set it, rubber side down, on the fallen tree.

She sat down slowly, a crease across her forehead.

"Are you all right?" he asked.

"A little stomachache."

He sat next to her. "I think we should be boiling our water."

"I'm sure this is nothing."

He could see she was not well. Shards of sunlight pierced the canopy and caught in her pale hair, and her pulse beat against the smooth skin of her throat. The camera hung between her breasts, and she had one hand flat across the lap of her pants. He didn't like to see her in pain, uncomfortable in any way. There was a delicacy to her that unearthed some protective instinct in him he hadn't known was there. Shawn had certainly never required it of him.

"Maybe we should head back," he said.

She shook her head. "It's just a twinge. Talk to me to get my mind off it."

"Well." He looked down at his hands. There was a tick resting on the knee of his pants, and he snapped it off with his fingers. "How do you like living in San Francisco?"

"Ah," she said as if he had selected the right topic. "I love it. Especially the fog."

He thought she was joking. Golden Gate Park, maybe, the hills, or the food. But the fog?

"It's so ethereal," she said. "So thick, so full of substance, yet when you try to catch it in your fingers, there's nothing there."

"Is there anything you don't romanticize?" he asked.

She smiled. "Very little." She told him the fog was important to her photography. She'd had a show in San Francisco a few months ago. "Portraits in the Mist," it was called, pictures of people veiled by San Francisco fog. She was fascinated by mist because of what it hid. It was different from one second to the next, she said, changing the portrait, changing the person being photographed.

He listened to her, a wistful feeling working its way into his chest. How was it that he'd ended up with a woman like Shawn, pragmatic and matter-of-fact, when it was the fanciful, sentimental part of life that enticed him?

They sat an hour longer, and then slowly made their way back to camp. The clearing looked like home, a fire burning at its center. Tess had made a long table and benches out of the saplings they'd uprooted the day before. She'd stripped the bark from them and strapped them side by side with heavy cord. Then she set them on top of forked branches stuck in the ground.

Plastic plates, one of them filled with thick, white chunks of catfish, covered the top of the table. This was roughing it?

Evan took David aside. "Shawn's not back yet," he said. "We split up because the troop divided in two. I'm not sure how far in she had to go."

David tried to decipher the expression on Evan's face. Was he worried? Should David be worried? But before he had a chance to decide, Shawn appeared at the edge of the clearing.

"Hi." She was grinning.

Evan wore an unmistakable look of relief. "Where have you been? I've been back for more than an hour."

"Your troop must not have been as interesting as mine." She poured herself some of the grape-flavored water and described the Copper Elves she'd seen and her thoughts on trapping. David sat down on one of the rough, knobby benches and watched her face. It had color in it from yesterday's sun on the stream; the bridge of her nose was a little burned. Her smile was quick, and her hands worked the air furiously as she described the Elves. He hadn't seen this face in a long time. For the first time in years she looked youthful and alive, and it suddenly hit him how much she had aged over the last few years, how she had come to carry herself weighed down as though a sack of stones rested on her shoulders. The stones were gone now. He'd been right about this trip after all.

"Did you feed ChoCho, Ev?" she asked as she bounded toward the tree that housed ChoCho's cage.

"Yes." Evan sat down across from David at the table. "Just what the doctor ordered," he said with a smile.

David nodded. "I thought this Shawn was gone for good."

Shawn returned from ChoCho's cage and stood at the end of the table. "It's *wonderful* out there," she said. "Except for the ticks."

She had ticks on her shorts and T-shirt, and stuck in the laces of her shoes. Tess disappeared into her tent and returned with a roll of masking tape. They watched as she tore off eight inches or so, wrapped it around her hand, sticky side out, and ran it over Shawn's clothing. The ticks stuck to the tape like flies to flypaper.

"Your shoes are wet," Tess said.

"I had to run through a creek to follow the Elves."

"Change them and put powder on your feet," Tess ordered. Her face was flushed from working with the fire. "If you leave your feet damp out here, you'll end up with fungus between your toes.''

Shawn made a face at Tess behind her back and sat down at the table. She gave David a conspiratorial smile that felt like an embrace to him.

Tess took the plate of catfish from the table. ''And you'd better have your husband check the parts of your body you can't see for ticks,'' she said to Shawn.

Shawn dropped her eyes then. He'd lost her.

''That goes for all of you,'' Tess continued. ''Check each other every night. The quicker you get them out, the better.''

''I'm allergic to them,'' said Meg.

''What do you mean, allergic?'' asked Tess.

Meg cowered beneath her white hat. ''The spot gets a little swollen and itchy, that's all.''

Tess sat down on the bench with a sigh. ''And what else are you allergic to?''

''Bee stings. But I've got a kit.''

''Carry it with you at all times, you understand?'' Tess sounded like a mother whose anger camouflaged her concern. At least David hoped it was concern, that Tess was not as annoyed with Meg as she appeared.

The catfish was excellent, but he could hardly enjoy it. He watched Meg. She still wore that crease across her forehead. She moved pieces of fish around on her plate as though she wished they would disappear without her having to eat them. Her face was white, the skin an iridescent mother-of-pearl around her eyes. The soft bangs on her forehead were damp with perspiration.

Tess finally noticed. ''What's wrong with your food?''

Meg swallowed. ''I'm not feeling well.'' She stood up and without a word left the table and walked toward the woods.

Tess watched her for a few seconds and then shook her head and continued eating.

''Maybe you should go with her,'' David said.

''She'll be fine,'' Tess said without looking up.

He noticed how Tess's hair stayed in place, back from her face, as though it was made of metal filaments.

They were nearly through eating by the time Meg returned. She smiled gamely and sat down again. ''I'm all right now,'' she said. ''Just a touch of the runs.''

''Maybe you should take something,'' Robin suggested.

"Better to let it take care of itself," Tess said. She pushed the bowl of rice in front of Meg. "Eat your rice. It's binding."

After dinner, they worked and read at the table by the light of a kerosene lantern. They burned mosquito repellent coils that gave off acrid streams of smoke. Evan and Shawn attached screening to the bottom of a trap, while Tess pored over a botany book, trying to match the leaves she'd collected that day to pictures in the book. David and Robin and Meg read. At least the three of them made a show of reading. David's eyes were on Meg, who hadn't turned a page since opening her book. And Robin looked up from her thick paperback every time a new sound joined the discordant evening chorus.

Meg glanced up at him. She looked surprised to find him watching her, but she didn't shift her eyes. There was a question in them, as though she was asking him what she should do. But before he could respond, she decided for herself.

"Tess," she said. "I'm really in pain."

Tess looked up from her leaves with a sigh. "You managed to hide your weak constitution well in San Francisco, didn't you?"

Meg stood up and he was surprised at the ready tears in her eyes. "You make it sound as though I intentionally deceived you." She turned and ran into the forest. He heard the rustle of her footsteps. She had no flashlight. Worse, she had no toilet paper.

He took his flashlight and a roll of toilet paper from his day pack and followed her into the woods. He spotted her, squatting at the base of a tree. He switched off his light and held out the toilet paper to her.

"Please go back, David," she said. "Don't embarrass me."

"I'll stay over there." He pointed a distance away with the flashlight. He set the toilet paper on the ground within her reach. "I'll wait to be sure you're okay."

He walked north from her until he could barely hear her. She was vomiting now, and he was glad he was no closer.

The boys had the stomach flu this past winter, and he and Shawn spent an entire night in the bathroom with them. He'd never seen anyone so sick. Just as he and Shawn climbed back into bed after tucking one of them in, they'd hear the other one scrambling toward the bathroom. He wasn't good at that part of parenting. He'd had to force himself to stay. Every once in a while he went into the other bathroom to vomit himself. Shawn would shake her head at him in disbelief, but he couldn't help it. Hearing another person get sick triggered a gag reflex in him. It was happening to him now as he listened to Meg. He swallowed hard and concentrated on the sound of the cicadas and the rustle of the undergrowth near his feet.

"David, are you still there?"

"Yes." He shined his flashlight at the ground so she could follow the beam. The leaves scattered as she walked toward him.

"I'm so weak. There's nothing in my middle to hold me up."

"You'll feel better once you're lying down."

"I can't go back like this . . . this weak."

"What do you mean?"

"Tess thinks I'm too soft as it is."

"Let that be her problem."

"She expects me to be strong and . . . Could we sit down?"

They sat directly on the ground. Probably a mistake.

"Why do you care what Tess thinks?" he asked.

It was a few seconds before Meg answered. "She's the reason I'm here," she said.

"You mean you feel obligated to her for bringing you on this trip?"

"You don't understand." Her hand was on his arm, her eyes were large, trying to get something across to him. "I'm in love with her."

"Oh." He let it sink in. Christ, he had not been expecting that. "Does she know?"

Meg smiled. "It's a mutual thing, or it was. After the past few days I'm not so sure. When we met in her botany class, there was an immediate attraction between us. And we spent a lot of time together and got close very quickly. I thought things were good. But now . . . She's beautiful, don't you think?"

He hesitated. He felt strangely deflated, on the edge of a world he had no entrée to. "She's striking," he said. "But I think you deserve someone better."

"Someone with a penis, you mean."

He was insulted. "No, that's not what I mean at all."

"Sorry. That's what I'm used to hearing. I thought . . ." She shrugged.

He could tell even in the dim light that her cheeks were flushed. "What I mean is she doesn't treat you very well," he said. "She doesn't treat anyone well. You deserve better."

"You're not seeing the real Tess out here. I think she's tense because of the responsibility. When she's with me alone, she's different. She's well known in San Francisco, David. She's *sought* after. A few hundred women would love to be in my shoes. I don't want to give her any reason to regret being with me.''

David stared at the beam of his flashlight where it cut through the trees. ''Did you ever make love to . . . someone who wasn't a female?''

''I take it you mean a male?''

He smiled. ''Yes.''

''In high school. It wasn't good, but I knew it wouldn't be. I never felt anything for guys. I pretended to be interested in them, to fit in with my friends. I hung pictures of rock stars on the walls of my room, but it was all an act. It was a relief when I went to college and could finally let the real Meg out.''

He tried to picture her as a teenager, frightened by the secret she knew about herself.

''Maybe if those early experiences with boys in high school had been better . . .''

''It goes beyond sex, David. I'm more at ease with women. I'm not even sure why I'm telling you all this, why I feel able to talk to you. You're an exception, I guess.''

He felt enormous pleasure at her words. ''Why?''

''You're open. You don't play games.'' She stood up, a little unsteadily. ''I think I'm ready to go back now.''

Meg headed straight for her tent when they reached the clearing. Tess looked up at David from her book. The light from the lantern cut sharp black wedges in her cheeks. ''If you treat her like an infant, she'll behave like an infant,'' she said.

He swallowed the caustic response that came to mind. They needed Tess too much to risk alienating her.

Shawn was lying on the bed in her underwear, reading by the light of the kerosene lantern set outside the mosquito netting. David liked the glow it cast into the tent, the soft shadows it painted on the tent walls as he moved inside.

''Could you check me for ticks?'' she asked him.

He felt as happy as if she'd asked him to make love to her. ''If you'll reciprocate,'' he said. ''I was sitting on the ground.''

She shifted position until her head was in his lap. He set the flashlight on his duffel bag and combed through her short hair with his fingers. He loved the thick, silky feel of it. This was the first chance he'd had to run his hands through her hair since she cut it. The ticks were a blessing in disguise.

"You had a good day." He scraped a tick from her temple.

She nodded. "How's Meg doing?"

"All right now. She was pretty sick out there."

"I think she's a lesbian."

"Yes, she is." ·

"How do you know?" She opened her eyes to look up at him.

"She told me." He waited, prepared to defend Meg against an attack. Though that would not be Shawn's style. She always had a live-and-let-live attitude about that sort of thing.

"She's far too nice a person for Tess," she said.

"I think so too. Roll over."

He checked her back, then lifted the elastic top of her underpants. "Take these off."

"No." She sat up and turned her back to him as she took off her bra. Then she pulled on a T-shirt—one of his undershirts, actually—that she liked to sleep in. She looked sexier in them than in the sheerest negligee.

"Come on," he said.

"I'm sure I don't have any there. Let me check your hair."

She gave him a quick once-over, letting him know not to expect anything more from her. He'd already figured that out. He had to be careful not to rush her. They'd made gains today that he couldn't risk losing.

But when he took off his pants, he found three ticks high on his thigh, and there was only so much of his body he could see. She was already under the sheet, eyes closed. He couldn't ask her to help him. He couldn't make himself that vulnerable.

He turned out the lantern and lay down next to her. Lord, it was dark. And in the days to come it would only get darker as the moon shrank in the sky.

Please God, don't let me go blind.

It was an old litany. For over thirty years he'd been saying it to himself, ever since he realized that people could *become* blind. His mother always told him not to worry about blindness, that she and his father were *born* blind—not the truth exactly, but it was years before he figured that out. He was greatly comforted by her words because he could imagine nothing worse than fumbling around in darkness as his parents did.

But when he was five years old, a boy in his kindergarten class was hit with a baseball bat and knocked unconscious. When the boy woke up, he couldn't see, and for weeks David was afraid. He wouldn't play baseball, wouldn't ride a bike. He feared anything that could even remotely harm his eyes or render him unconscious. He lied to his mother about not seeing well because he wanted to get glasses. They would shield his eyes from injury, he thought. But the eye doctor said there was nothing wrong with his eyes, and he had to do without that protection.

It was the dark that frightened him most. He still slept with a nightlight, although early on, Shawn labeled it a ''nocturnal vision enhancer.'' She didn't want him to feel like an idiot. She never teased him about it. Fearless though she was for herself, she never scoffed at anyone else's insecurities. He was afraid sometimes that he'd forgotten how good a person she was deep inside, how loving a wife she had been.

He thought he felt something crawl across his thigh and slipped his hand under the sheet to feel for ticks, but it was no use. They were too small, and all he could feel was the erection beneath his wrist. He moved closer to Shawn and touched her arm.

''Shawn?'' he whispered, not certain what he would say if she answered. But she was too soundly asleep to hear him, and he rolled onto his back with a sigh. He'd spent more nights than he could count alone with this erection. Tonight would be nothing new.

· Eighteen ·

SHAWN AND EVAN sat on their campstools, observing the troop she'd followed the day before. She thought of it as *her* troop; she'd worked hard to track it down, and she already felt an attachment to the members. The Creek Troop, she dubbed it. Evan called the troop he'd followed the Inland Troop.

Eventually, they would use ChoCho as a decoy for the Creek Troop, but this morning the little Elf had other duties. They'd set her cage in the nesting tree of the Inland Troop, hoping she would attract one of the Elves to the trap attached to her cage. Then Shawn and Evan would feed the captured Elf bananas and release it to teach its troopmates about this new gastronomical pleasure. Then they'd be able to trap from the Inland Troop with fruit alone.

They had a good feel for the makeup of the Creek Troop now. There were definitely two adult males and one adult female, as Shawn had thought. The two other large Elves appeared to be juveniles of undetermined sex. The adult males passed the twin babies back and forth to one another while the female foraged in another tree. When she wasn't eating, she contemplated the end of her tail while the males took care of the babies. When the time came, of course, she would repay both of them with her sexual favors.

Shawn had thought long and hard about this arrangement, with one burning and impossible to research question: Did the female view the arrangement as a cost to her or a benefit? She was emotionally attached—if that was the right phrase to use— to just one of the males. That was obvious to Shawn as she watched the Creek Troop. The female gave one of the males a quick grooming each time she left the tree—love taps, Evan called them—and the other she ignored. Yet the males seemed to share equally in the handling of the infants.

During the affair with Evan she'd pointed to the tamarins' behavior to justify her own life-style.

"The correlation's weak," Evan told her. "You've glossed over the fact that the male tamarins are all aware of and in agreement with the arrangement. No one is being deceived."

After spending a few hours with the Creek Troop, they moved their campstools closer to the creek to eat their lunch of fruit and rice crackers.

Evan bit into his banana. "David was good with Meg yesterday," he said. "I like the way he stood up to the Ice Queen."

She dug her nails into the peel of her orange and felt the juice spray her hand. "I'm divorcing him, Evan." So much for the pact. She had to tell him. It was a relief. The only other person she'd told was her lawyer, and that didn't count. She didn't care what her lawyer thought of her decision.

Evan stopped the banana halfway to his mouth and stared at her. "That's a mistake," he said.

"What was a mistake was not divorcing him three years ago. All we've done is make each other miserable."

"What's David's reaction?"

"He doesn't know yet. I'm waiting until we get back to tell him."

Evan pounded his fist into his knee and she jumped. "Damn it, Shawn. You always put me in the middle."

She dropped her eyes. His anger unsettled her, as it always did. It was extreme, like all his emotions, not too predictable or easy to assuage.

He put the cap on his canteen and stood up. She sat stiffly as he folded his campstool. "Let's check the trap at the Inland Troop," he said.

"Evan . . ." she said, but he was already across the creek and storming down the trail.

"We've got one," he said when she caught up with him at the Inland Troop. She saw a Copper Elf in the trap. It was tormenting ChoCho with its groping and shrieking. Shawn felt relief, but no elation. She was still shaken by Evan's reaction to her news.

They approached the trap quietly, making sure the door was down so the new Elf couldn't escape. Shawn thought ChoCho looked relieved to see them. The little decoy darted back and forth in her cage to escape the probing arms of the intruder.

Shawn reached in her day pack for her blowgun and an anesthetic dart.

"What are you doing?" Evan asked.

"I'll dart her and . . ."

"Shawn, she's right in front of us. You don't need a god-damned blowgun."

She felt herself blush. What was she thinking? They could use a syringe this close. She watched Evan pull one out of its wrapping and fill it with anesthetic.

"Grab its tail," he said.

She pulled the Elf to the side of the trap by its tail, but she lost her grip and the Elf ran squawking to the other side of the trap. Evan lowered the syringe with an impatient sigh. She caught the tail again and held it tight while Evan injected the anesthetic into the tamarin's thigh.

"You're being a real bastard, Evan," she said.

"Let's concentrate on this tamarin right now and save the conversation for some other time, all right?"

After a few minutes, he took the Elf out of the trap and sat down on his campstool. He held the Elf on his thigh while Shawn pulled her fieldbook and pen from her pack.

"Sex?" she asked.

"Female."

"Age?" she asked, writing.

"Juvenile." Evan lifted the Elf's lips to check her teeth. "Seven, eight months."

Shawn pulled the little scale and tape measure from her pack. Evan stretched the Elf out on his knee for her to measure.

"Six inches." She set the Elf on the scale. "Eight ounces."

Evan buckled a small leather collar wrapped with yellow tape around the Elf's neck. Then he set her back in the trap with a banana. They would keep her until early evening, then free her to return to her troop to tell them about her delicious adventure.

"I want to keep ChoCho in camp at night," Shawn said.

"That's crazy. Night would be a perfect time for an Elf to stumble into her trap."

"The decoy was my idea to begin with, and I don't want to leave her in the jungle at night."

"And it was your idea that we spend only two weeks out here. If you keep ChoCho in camp at night, it will make it that much harder to get our work done in time."

She felt a knot in her throat. "Evan, please. Let's not fight."

He slung his pack to his shoulder and looked her straight in the eye. "You need to think through this divorce idea."

"I have thought it through."

He folded up his campstool, then set it down again, and turned to face her. "I can't give you any more of myself than I already have, Shawn. I've got a wife and a baby and I . . ."

She frowned at him. "I'm not *asking* you for anything."

"Bullshit! A month after you two split up, you'll come crying to me that you're lonely, please Evan, just this once?"

She felt as if he'd punched her in the stomach. "That's totally unfair." She picked up her campstool and walked ahead of him. Her eyes stung. *Damn him.* She knew what he was talking about. It wasn't the affair; it was that one time last year that left him feeling like a victim. She wished it had never happened either, but it had. And he had been a willing partner.

It was the second anniversary of Heather's death. If Shawn lived to be one hundred years old, that date on the calendar would always leave her numb. The boys were at soccer camp, something she was not happy about, and David watched her the whole goddamned day. He was busy making suggestions for things they could do. Nervous, she thought. Ingratiating. Like a child who's done something wrong and tries with subtle maneuvers to be absolved, never directly addressing the wrongdoing itself.

It was unbearably hot and dry. The air burned the back of her throat with each breath. She spent the day grooming the dogs, battling with herself to keep from calling the boys at camp. David barbecued chicken for dinner, wearing an apron Evan and Robin had given him for his birthday the month before. It was red with his name in blue block letters across the front. What had she given him for that birthday? Tickets to *La Traviata* in Los Angeles and dinner reservations someplace, she didn't remember where. A generous but impersonal gift, like the card she picked out for him. She used to buy David cards that were deeply sentimental, a little flowery. She'd add a note of her own about how much she loved him, appreciated him. Stuff that used to make the boys gag dramatically when David read it out loud at the dinner table. Now she bought him funny cards, the kind she could just as easily send her secretary.

While he barbecued the chicken, she fabricated a way to avoid spending the evening with him. It was not that she had other plans. And it was not that, on any conscious level, she was thinking of Evan. Evan was home with Robin, who was eight months pregnant and not having the easiest time. It was simply that she couldn't face four or five more hours alone with David.

She walked onto the patio. "I forgot to tell you," she said. "I have a meeting tonight."

He looked up, the long barbecue fork in his hand dripping sauce onto the concrete floor of the patio. "Tonight? A Sunday night in August?"

He didn't believe her. Ironic. Last year she'd invented dozens of meetings so she could be with Evan, and David swallowed them all. Tonight, when she had no idea what she would do when she pulled out of their driveway, he wasn't buying it.

"The board's trying to get things squared away for September," she said. Why couldn't she just tell him the truth, that she needed to be alone for a while? Lying had become too easy for her.

David poked at the chicken. "Can I come with you? I didn't want to be alone tonight." His voice was a soft and hesitant plea, and for one terrible moment, she felt sorry for him.

She touched his shoulder. "It'd be boring for you."

She drove to a bar. She wasn't much of a drinker, but where else could she go? Her office would be depressing. Here she could sit in a cool, dark corner and lose herself watching other people. But it was a staid Sunday night crowd, not much to focus on except the drinks, and by nine o'clock when she stood up to go, she knew she was drunk, as drunk as she'd ever been in her life. She made her way to the front door. A man there caught her arm.

"Ma'am?"

She turned to look at him. He had the face of a coyote above his three-piece suit. "Yes?" she said.

"Are you driving yourself?"

Yes, she thought, nodding, *I'm driving myself crazy.* She laughed out loud.

"Let me call you a cab," he said.

Her cheeks burned. He thought she was too drunk to drive. She glanced around her. People stared at her, whispered about her. She lowered her head.

"I'll call my husband," she said quietly.

The coyote led her to a pay phone and left her alone. She dialed Evan's number and was relieved when he answered. She didn't know what she would say if she had gotten Robin.

She explained her situation to Evan, her voice echoing inside her head. It hurt her ears, and she had to whisper as she told him where she was.

"Don't drive," he said. "I'll be right there."

Then she called the boys' camp. The twins were already in bed, the counselor told her; they couldn't come to the phone.

"You mean they're alive?" she asked.

The counselor hesitated a minute. "Yes, Mrs. Ryder. They're fine."

She hung up. God, she hoped she didn't sound like an alcoholic. There would be rumors spread about her at the camp in the morning. She didn't want the boys to have to put up with that sort of thing.

She felt sober by the time Evan arrived, but he shook his head at her suggestion that she drive herself home. He took her back to his office and made her coffee. The office was hot after being closed up for the weekend, and the posters on the walls looked parched and faded. Evan turned on the air conditioner and opened the sofa bed for her. "We'd better call David to tell him where you are, that you're safe."

"No. I told him I might be late," she said, curling up on top of the blanket.

He sat on the edge of the bed. "I was glad you called."

"You were?"

He nodded. "I don't like the weekends. Sometimes I feel as though it's too long for me to go without seeing you, Friday night to Monday morning."

Dangerous talk, Evan, she thought. She wondered if he had been drinking as well. She doubted it. His eyes were a clear blue; the arch in his left eyebrow looked as it always did, invitational. She would give anything if he would put that invitation into words.

He took his handkerchief from the back pocket of his jeans and wiped his forehead. "I'm nervous about this baby," he continued. "I can't tell Robin that. I have to pretend everything's fine, and by the end of the weekend I'm ready to explode from holding it all in."

"What are you afraid of?"

He shrugged. "That Robin and I aren't right for each other, I guess. That when this baby comes, we'll be locked into this marriage for life."

"Nothing has to be for life."

He nodded. "Oh, yes it does. My kids are going to have a solid family."

"Well, everybody gets scared about their marriage before they have a baby. It's normal." Everyone except her and David. Once they were married, she never doubted it was right. That seemed incredible now. There should have been a warning that things could disintegrate with such dizzying speed.

Evan circled her wrist with his hand, stroking his thumb along the line of her pulse. "Robin is my substitute for you, you know that, don't you? I couldn't have you, so I had to find someone else or face up to having a lifelong affair with you."

She shut her eyes and felt dizzy from the alcohol and the heat. "Evan . . ." She opened her eyes and looked directly at him. "Couldn't we make love? Just this once . . . What would it hurt?"

"No." He shook his head and stood up. "I'm not starting down that road again." He headed for the door. "I told Robin there was some kind of emergency out here with the tamarins, so I might as well check on them while I'm here."

It had been a long time since she'd been in this bed. Evan's scent was on the striped pillowcases, and she turned her head to breathe it in. God, she missed being with him. What possible damage could it do if they made love tonight? He was teasing her, although she knew that was not his intention. He wanted what he thought he mustn't want, and his heart and words and actions were at war with one another. She was caught in the crossfire.

The phone on his desk rang and she jumped. It had to be the wrong number this time of night. It never occurred to her that it might be Robin. She ignored it, and the caller gave up after only three rings.

In a few minutes Evan was back. He opened the door, and she felt the fiery Santa Ana heat sweep across the room. He leaned against the doorjamb, his eyes on her, his shirt damp down the front of his chest. He walked toward her and moved the coffee cup from her hand to the table. He sat on the bed and pulled her against him, and she felt his lips on her eyes, then her chin, her throat. His hands pulled her shirt from her jeans.

"Just this once, Evan," she whispered, her body melting under the heat of his fingers. "It'll just be this once."

She was home by eleven-thirty and took a shower before she got into bed.

"This Santa Ana," she told David. "It's so hot." She needn't have bothered with an explanation because David seemed to know better than to come near her. He clung to his side of the bed as if it were a guardrail at the edge of a cliff.

* * *

The next morning she learned how much damage their love-making could do. Evan sat in front of his littered desk, hands folded limply in his lap. His face was drained of color; his hair, uncombed. He spoke quietly while she sat on the sofa, sinking deeper into a guilt that threatened to devour her.

He told her that when he arrived home the night before, he found Robin in their driveway, fumbling in her purse for the keys to her car. She was dressed only in a silver nightgown, her belly a huge pearly globe in the light from the street lamp. When she saw him, she fell against him, sobbing. She was carrying laundry downstairs, she told him. She tripped and fell a few steps before she caught herself on the railing. She thought she was all right, just shaken up a little. But then the pains started, and the bleeding. The doctor said to get to the hospital. She tried to reach Evan, even called the Conservation Center switchboard, but no one knew anything about the emergency with the tamarins.

Shawn's heart went out to Robin. She wished she could erase the night before. She was so selfish. She had no right to Evan.

"Is she okay?" she asked quietly.

He nodded. "They want to keep her at the hospital for a few days, though, to make sure there's no problem with the baby." He looked up at her. "If anything happens to that baby, Shawn, I'll . . . I don't know what I'll do."

She covered his icy hand with hers. "Evan, I'm sorry."

He pulled his hand away and locked it under his arm. "If we have to keep working together, you and I," he said, looking out his office window instead of at her, "we have to find a way . . . make a rule . . ." He stumbled around, trying to find the words ". . . make a *pact* that there is nothing more between us. Work, that's it. I mean it, Shawn. I'm dead serious. I don't want to hear about your problems, and I'm not going to tell you mine."

Something in his eyes told her he really did mean it. He didn't touch her as he spoke, and she knew he meant never to touch her again. But that was not to be the worst price she would pay for the night before.

By the time Melissa was born, Shawn knew that she herself was pregnant. She hadn't given birth control a thought that night. How could she have been so stupid?

She put off the abortion for weeks because she cherished the feeling of life inside her. She had felt dead and empty for so long. She lay in bed at night trying to think of a way she could have this baby. There *had* to be a way. It could not be passed off as David's—his vasectomy was five years old, and besides, they hadn't made love in months. She would have to admit it was Evan's. She would turn Evan's life upside down. And what would it do to Robin? Robin's world revolved around her husband and daughter. Shawn couldn't take Evan's love and attention away from the circle of his family. She had to have an abortion. She wept quietly into her pillow night after night, angry at herself and at Evan. She wanted to feel she had a choice, and she had none.

She waited until the last minute. The doctor at the clinic frowned when he examined her. "You just about missed the deadline, sweetheart," he said. "Another couple of days and you'd be too late for a clinic abortion."

But they didn't do the abortion that day after all.

"You're too distraught, Mrs. Ryder," the counselor said, shaking her head. "You need to give this more thought."

"I don't have *time* to give it more thought." Shawn couldn't stop crying. The tears were always with her. Her face was swollen, her eyes rimmed with red. She didn't blame this young woman for being concerned.

"I couldn't live with myself if I let you go in there feeling like you do right now," the counselor said. "If you had someone with you, it would be different. Could you come back tomorrow with a support person?"

A support person? Shawn shook her head. She had told no one. Not even Evan. *I don't want to hear about your problems, and I'm not going to tell you mine.* She would never tell Evan. Besides, if she told him she was carrying his child, he would never let her go through with an abortion.

The next day she went to another clinic. She was prepared this time. She dressed in a suit, carried a briefcase. Her eyes were hidden behind dark glasses. When they put her feet up in the stirrups, she concentrated on the paper she was writing for next month's primatology conference.

"You look like you're a thousand miles away," the young doctor said to her.

She smiled at the ceiling. "I've got a lot on my mind today."

It was more painful than she expected.

"Because you're so far along," the nurse said as she offered Shawn a hand to hold. Shawn rejected it. She'd never felt so alone. If she touched the warm skin of another human being, she was afraid she would fall apart.

• *Nineteen* •

DAVID WANTED TO talk, and that was fine with Shawn because she didn't want to lie awake in the darkness and think about Evan's ire or the memories it triggered in her.

But it was Meg he wanted to talk about. He'd spent the day with her, taking pictures, paddling the small canoe around in the stream, and talking. It sounded as though they did quite a bit of that. There was an eagerness to David that disturbed Shawn, a new light in his eyes she felt he had no right to possess.

"Her grandfather sang at the Met," he said as he slipped under the sheet. He sounded awestruck, as proud and crowing as if he were describing his own grandfather. He folded his arms behind his head. "She even toured with him a couple of times when she was a kid. She grew up surrounded by opera."

He told her about Meg's photography; how she was making a name for herself with her pictures taken in the fog. Shawn listened with an eerie fascination, thinking of the jungle mist in the morning. Everything that was clear and in focus by nine o'clock had been shrouded and mysterious at six.

She fell asleep listening to David's voice, not wanting him to stop, not wanting him to leave her alone with her own thoughts for even a second.

At breakfast the next morning, Evan told them that Robin had gotten lost in the forest during the night. She'd gone out to use the woods and her flashlight batteries died. It took him twenty minutes to find her.

Robin sat next to him as he spoke, and it was obvious the night had taken a toll on her. Shawn watched her turn away from her oatmeal and stare into space, her brown eyes hollowed out. She looked drugged, her movements slow, muscles heavy.

"Eat your oatmeal," Evan said to her.

"I can't. It was made from that water with bugs in it."

"Doesn't matter," said Tess. "The oatmeal already had bugs in it."

Everyone laughed except Robin, who set down her spoon and hung her head.

"Are you going to eat nothing for the rest of the trip?" Evan asked her.

She lifted her head to look at Evan, tears welling up in her eyes. "I want to go *home*," she said.

"Robin," Meg said brightly. "Come with David and me to take pictures today. You brought a camera, right?"

Robin shook her head. "No, thank you."

Shawn stared at Meg. She looked different this morning. She looked *sexy*. She sat at one end of the table, hair uncombed and hanging straight and loose and very blond over her shoulders. The sun lightened her blue eyes to the color of Caribbean water. It was an odd sexiness, as though Meg were completely unaware of it. Or maybe Shawn imagined the sensuality here, as she struggled to see Meg through the eyes of a man. Through David's eyes.

Earlier this morning, before David was awake, Shawn reached outside the tent for her shoes. Her hand accidently picked up one of David's tennis shoes instead and she felt a piece of paper crinkle under her thumb. She drew it out of the shoe and carefully unfolded it. It was a single sheet of lined paper torn from a small spiral-bound notebook. *David,* it read, *Thanks for making the last few days such a pleasure.* Meg's note of course. The handwriting was sweet and girlish, rounded letters slightly slanted. A flourish at the end of each word. She folded the note back into its neat square and returned it to David's shoe.

Now as she watched Meg, she wondered when she had delivered that note. It must have been early this morning. Very early, when the mist rose out of the woods. She felt uneasy, thinking of Meg making her way through the fog to the patch of forest Shawn had selected for its privacy. She pictured her moving on cat's feet, or wings perhaps, to approach the tent noiselessly and plant her message.

"David told me about your mist pictures," she said to Meg.

Meg shot David a look, admonishment, though gentle. *What else have you told her?*, Shawn read into it.

"They're fun to make," Meg replied.

"*Fun.*" Tess shook her head as she lit a cigarette. "You consistently downplay your talent. Meg's an artist. I'll show you." She rose and headed for the path to her tent.

"Oh, Tess, don't," Meg protested.

"You didn't tell me you had any of your photographs with you," David said.

"It's a gift I brought for Tess."

Tess returned with a cardboard tube and pulled a large photograph from it, perhaps twelve by sixteen, and laid it flat on the table. It was extraordinary. The picture was dominated by a thick, silver white fog. In the lower right corner, a woman dressed in a blue sweatshirt and jeans sat on a bench. She looked off the paper to the left. It was Tess. Shawn would have known even if the features of the woman were less distinct, because the camera captured her cool, regal beauty. From the upper left corner of the picture to the center top ran the tips of the Golden Gate Bridge.

Tess stood behind Meg at the table, resting a hand on her shoulder. So that's the reason for this new look to Meg today, Shawn thought, the reason for this rich sensuality. Things were good between these two this morning.

"The most promising new talent in photography today, the *San Francisco Chronicle* said." Tess took her place again next to Meg.

Meg looked at her. "Shall I come with you today?" she asked.

Tess shook her head. "You know I have to be alone when I'm working."

Meg dropped a cheerful mask over her disappointment and looked at David. "Are you ready?"

David nodded and stood up. He turned to Robin. "You sure you don't want to come with us?"

Robin shook her head. David didn't look too disappointed, Shawn thought. She watched him and Meg gather up their camera equipment and head into the forest.

"We better go too, Shawn," Evan said, rolling up the sleeves of his blue striped shirt. He was being curt to her today. Still angry. They would have to have this out at some point, but not this morning. If he lashed into her again today, she was sure to say things better left unsaid. She often wondered how he would react if she told him about the abortion. Evan mourned the loss of a pregnancy even in an animal; she could imagine the depth of his anguish if he knew what she'd done. He would have allowed his world to be turned upside down for his own child. He would be angry with her for not allowing him that chance.

He stood up now, but Robin grabbed his arm. "Please don't leave me here."

"You can come with us if you eat your oatmeal," he said. "I don't want you toppling over out there."

Robin was close to tears. "I can't eat this."

"Have some fruit," Shawn suggested.

"We need the fruit for lunch." Evan looked directly at Shawn for the first time that morning, and she cringed and looked away. "Besides, we'll run out of it for the tamarins if we eat too much of it ourselves."

He was being stubborn and irrational. And so cool to Robin. Shawn had never seen that before. She had the feeling Robin was getting the anger actually meant for her.

Robin folded her hands on the sapling table and stared at the pale pink of her nails. "I have to get out of here," she said quietly, not looking up. "You don't seem to understand that, Evan. I can't survive here. I can't eat or sleep."

Tess lit another cigarette. "And *you* don't seem to understand you have no choice."

Robin looked over at Evan. "I did this for you, and now that I'm having second thoughts you don't even care."

"There isn't a damn thing I can do about it, Robin." Evan walked over to the side of the clearing and began working with the traps.

"Come with Evan and me," Shawn said. What Robin needed was to get out in the woods, shift her focus from the horrors of this place to something that could capture her interest—the tamarins, the traps, the beauty of the canopy. And besides, Shawn didn't want to be alone with Evan this morning.

"I had enough of the forest last night," Robin said, her eyes filling.

Tess leaned toward her. "Don't you cry," she hissed. "Don't you dare cry. You're going to lose your husband if you keep this up. It's no skin off my teeth. I've seen it happen a dozen times on these trips. One partner relishes it; the other loathes it. You move apart overnight. Yes, it was a mistake for you to come here. I knew it from the first. You should have stayed home. When he came home, you could have welcomed him, listened to his tales, and he never would have guessed at your cowardice. But you're here now, and you better make the best of it."

Shawn finally persuaded Robin to join them. The closer the moment came for her to go into the forest alone with Evan and his anger, the more desperate she became for the insulation Robin would offer.

They carried ChoCho in her cage to the Creek Troop. The going was slow with Robin along. She checked every patch of earth before setting her foot on it, and once she'd accomplished that, her eyes darted to the trees, scouring the jungle for danger. How sad to be trapped by all that fear, Shawn thought.

"How much farther?" Robin asked, when they came to the creek. Shawn walked through the water to help Robin across the crude sapling bridge. She would get the foot-fungus lecture from Tess again for sure.

"Shh," Evan said. "You have to be quiet."

"We're almost there," Shawn whispered.

They were nearly to the nesting tree of the Creek Troop when Robin screamed and leaped into the air. She ran back down the trail a few yards, then turned to point. "A snake!" she cried.

Shawn had to look twice to see it. The long thick fer-de-lance blended beautifully into the leaves. Evan had walked past it, but it was right ahead of Shawn on the trail. She lifted her camera slowly to her eyes.

The tamarins, frightened by Robin's scream, screeched and dove through the trees above them. Evan rolled his eyes, and when he spoke, his voice was a growl. "Christ, Robin, you can't scream like that. You scattered the Elves everywhere."

"What was I supposed to do, walk right on top of a snake?" Robin backed up another step or two. "Is it poisonous?"

"Very," said Shawn as she pressed the button on her camera.

"Oh, God, kill it."

"It's more afraid of you than you are of it," said Evan.

"*Kill* it."

"I'm not going to kill it," he said.

The fer-de-lance had lifted its head and was studying Shawn. She stomped her feet and it took off into the undergrowth. They watched the leaf litter rise and fall in a long wave as the snake passed beneath it. Shawn put the lens cover back on her camera, her hands shaking. She'd put on a brave front, but she wondered what would have happened if Robin hadn't seen it, if one of them had stepped on it. Surely then it would have struck. She and Evan had quickly grown cavalier out here. They would have to be more careful.

"Why didn't you kill it?" Robin asked. "Now it could be anywhere."

"Robin, look." Shawn pointed into the tree above them where a Copper Elf sat watching them, two babies clinging to its back.

It looked as though it took all Robin's strength to raise her eyes from the ground to the tree. "A mother?" she asked.

"More likely a father." Shawn made conversation with Robin about the Elves while she helped Evan set up the trap, but soon her concentration was absorbed by the work. They adjusted the screen on the cage to protect ChoCho from the arms and teeth of her visitors. They attached the trap to her cage carefully and checked the door to make certain it would fall shut easily at the right moment. With each task, Shawn felt Evan's mood lifting. His fingers touched hers as they adjusted the trapdoor. He gave her quick smiles, spoke to her in primatology jargon that cut Robin out. He set ChoCho's cage in Shawn's arms and made sweet clucking sounds at the Elf, told her to do a good job as she had the day before, and called her a little seductress. Then he locked his fingers together to make a step for Shawn and lifted her up so she could attach the cage to a branch high off the ground. She felt his beard against her thigh, and her fingers shook as she wrapped the wire hanger around the branch. Now she wished Robin were not with them so that she and Evan could clear the air.

Robin refused to return to the forest with them after lunch. Shawn and Evan were quiet as they walked along the trail leading back to the Creek Troop. They doubted they had anything in the trap yet, but they planned to stay at a distance and observe.

They were halfway to the creek when they heard a sudden trill above them. Their ears were so sensitized to that sound that they both stopped without speaking and looked up. A Copper Elf was perched on a branch, not two yards above their heads.

"It's so far from the troops we've found," Evan whispered. "Do you think it could be one of ours?"

She smiled at his choice of words: *one of ours.* Already they had assumed possession of these wild creatures.

The Elf suddenly turned and dove for the branch of a neighboring tree.

"I'll follow him." Shawn handed her day pack and campstool to Evan and took off after the Elf, remembering their first day here, how she'd flown through the forest after the Creek Troop. But this was just one Elf, a minuscule copper blur in the trees, and she had to struggle to keep him in sight. She came to a fallen tree that blocked her path and quickly assessed that it would be faster to go over it than around it. She climbed up, the rough bark scraping the skin on her calf, and stood up. Directly beneath her was a broad patch of tall grass and beyond that a damp-looking swamp. Her feet were already wet from helping Robin across the creek that morning. A little swamp water wouldn't hurt. She spotted the Elf diving from branch to branch above the swamp, teasing her. She leaped forward in the air, landed in the waist-high grass, and took a step toward the swamp. There were sudden sharp pains in her legs. She cried out, reaching her hand down to touch her thigh, and watched in horror as the grass sliced through the skin of her forearm. She pulled her arm out. It took some effort. The grass held her fast like glue, left long red cuts from her elbow to her wrist.

"Evan!" she called. "I'm in razor grass!"

In a moment he was standing on the fallen tree behind her.

"Jesus!" he said. "You just jumped into that stuff?"

She swallowed her annoyance. "I'm an idiot, I admit it. Now help me out."

He lowered himself to his haunches on the tree. "You're not an idiot," he said quietly. He reached out and touched her shoulder with such affection that she had to turn away to hide the confusion in her eyes. "You had just one thing on your mind, and that was the Elf." He stood up again. "You'll have to take a step closer to me so I can pull you up."

She grit her teeth and forced herself to take a step toward the log, feeling the grass slice through the skin on her legs.

Evan leaned over, and she wrapped her arms around his neck as he lifted her straight up, the grass licking at her legs with its razor tongue for the last time. He sat her on the tree, and she stretched out her legs in front of her to look at the damage. The skin was crisscrossed with thin red streaks of blood.

Evan touched one. "They're shallow," he said. "They'll heal quickly. How do they feel?"

"Not too bad. They sting a little."

"You'd better not swim until they're healed. The piranhas would be delighted." He stood up straight. "I hate to say I told you so about the long pants, but . . ."

"Then don't."

He smiled at her, then sat down on the log. "I'm sorry about yesterday, Shawn. I'm sorry for the things I said to you."

"All I want is to get out of my marriage. It has nothing to do with you."

He nodded. "It's just that I'm afraid of you . . . of your being unattached."

"I'm not going to hurt you or Robin. That's not my intention."

"It doesn't matter what your intention is. I'm going to be thinking about you constantly. It's already happening. I couldn't get you out of my mind all last night."

"If you have problems in your marriage, Evan, they're not my fault."

"I'm so *angry* with you."

"*Why?* You have no right to be."

"Why didn't you do this before I married Robin? Then you and I could have been together. Legitimately. Or would that have taken the fun out of it for you? To legitimize it?"

He knew how to hurt her. "That's another low blow, Evan," she said.

He took her hand, traced one of the long red cuts on the back of it with his finger. "It's been a long time since we were . . . close. I mean, we did a good job with that pact, didn't we? I think we're superhuman. But I don't know how I can keep that up if you won't be going home to David every night."

"We'll keep everything business, just as we've been doing." It was hard for her to say that with him holding her hand. His finger touched only the back of it, only the slivered skin, but she felt as if he'd found a direct line to her breasts, the skin on the inside of her thighs.

"I'm scared, Shawn. I love you. And right now I feel nothing for Robin. Less than nothing."

She lowered her eyes. *Don't do this to me, Evan.* "I think the pact was a very wise idea," she said quietly. "I'll stick to it myself, whether you will or not."

· Twenty ·

IT WAS ONE in the morning, and David had not slept in more than an hour. He could no longer deny the existence of the pain low in his gut. Half-dreaming, he imagined a phantom hand, muscular and greased, tying his intestines into knots, resting only long enough to lull him to the edge of sleep before beginning its twisting, wrenching work again.

He finally sat up and peered out at the forest through the mosquito netting. The moon could not be much more than a sliver tonight, and the darkness taunted him. He lit his flashlight and faced it toward the back of the tent. He remembered Robin's ordeal of the night before; he could imagine nothing worse than being stranded in the jungle at night without a light. With relief he noticed the pain in his stomach had eased. Maybe he would be all right for the rest of the night.

Shawn lay on her side, facing him. Her eyes were closed, the long black lashes flat against her cheeks. She'd come to the clearing this afternoon, her legs and arms covered with long red scratches, a thousand nasty paper cuts that she bathed in alcohol. She said they didn't hurt much, but he wondered. She was a champion at pain. He remembered the time, six or seven years ago, when she was bitten by a maned wolf at the Conservation Center. Evan called him from the emergency room of the hospital.

"Thirty-two stitches," Evan said. "She climbed into the goddamned enclosure, David."

By the time David got to the hospital, Shawn was entertaining the kid in the next bed with animal stories. "It's a scratch," she said to David when she saw the worry in his face.

The sober-looking doctor unwrapped the bandage so David could see the "scratch." "She's not taking this as seriously as she should," the doctor said. He flattened the gauze to the side, and David quickly looked away. Even stitched closed, the bite was hideous, a huge ugly **W**—for *Wolf*, Shawn said. It would heal into a scar she would carry with her for the rest of her life, a white **W** on the smooth tanned sphere of her shoulder.

She left the emergency room, chiding the staff and Evan for overreacting. It was a front. There was that tiny telltale indentation in the muscle between her eyebrows that didn't disappear even when she laughed. She kept up the jovial act when they got home, although he saw her frustration when she couldn't pick up two-year-old Heather for a kiss. She spent some time with the boys, warning them against strange animals.

"The wolves and I were great friends through the fence," she told them. They listened raptly. It would certainly make good show-and-tell news at school the next day. *Our mother was bitten by a wolf!* "My mistake was entering their territory," Shawn continued. "Then I became their enemy. It was dumb. I should have been more careful." There. Lecture delivered, her duty as a mother. He wondered if in a month or two she would be tempted to try again. She didn't like to fail.

She was upset that the bite would prevent her from taking her first skydiving lesson, planned for that Saturday. He had been thinking about that and finally spoke to her about it in bed that night.

"I have a favor to ask," he said. "I'd like you to put off skydiving. Just until the kids are out of school and able to survive without a mother. I'll even take lessons with you then."

She looked as if he had suggested she cut off her right hand. "Out of school? But Heather's only two."

He said nothing, just stroked her cheek, waiting. She had shown her human frailty today. She had little to argue with.

"How about when they're in high school?" she negotiated.

He knew what a concession that was for her. She had talked incessantly about skydiving for months. "High school would be fine," he said.

Sometime during that night she let the pain of the wolf bite take over. He held her while she moaned and dug her nails into the flesh above his ribs. He was grateful she allowed him to see this side of her. He wouldn't give away her secret, he told her. He would tell no one that she was not so strong as she pretended to be.

The pain in his stomach teased him again, a subtle threat. With a sigh, he pulled on his clothes, picked up his diminishing roll of toilet paper and his flashlight and stepped outside the tent. He couldn't see the moon above the canopy. His hand was sweaty around the flashlight. He switched off the light to test himself. It was not bad. Dim and spooky, but there was still enough light to see by. He turned the light on again and walked north from the tent. In the beam of his flashlight the trees were a brilliant green, but outside its reach the forest was thick with shadows. A woody vine snapped at his face and he jumped. The pain gripped him again, and he lowered his pants and squatted above the leaf-covered earth.

He felt remarkably better when he had finished, rid of the poison. He turned to walk back to the tent but stopped when he heard voices. He took a few steps in their direction. Ahead of him he saw a tent, light green, camouflaged by the surrounding brush. Tess and Meg's? It had to be. He must have walked at an angle. God, it was easy to get turned around out here.

He listened. They were not talking; they were making love. He stood still, ashamed of himself for not turning around and walking back to his own tent. It was Tess who was being plea- sured, whose voice was reaching, straining. He felt a suggestion of nausea, a bitter taste on the back of his tongue, but it faded quickly. He knew other lesbian couples; this didn't upset him. Still he didn't like to think of what Meg was doing to Tess's body. And would Tess reciprocate? Or was their lovemaking as one-sided as the rest of their relationship? He wanted to stay where he was and listen. He wanted to hear Meg get her turn. But perhaps she'd already had it. Or maybe closeness was all she was after. Not all women were as hungry for sex as Shawn.

As Shawn used to be.

There was laughter, bell-like, ringing through the forest and getting caught in the canopy. It surprised him. That relationship struck him as deadly serious. They were talking, words outside his hearing. A rustle from inside the tent. They were coming outside! *Christ.*

He turned off his flashlight and pressed against a tree, barely breathing. He felt the bark through his shirt. Tess stepped out of the tent first and reached in to pull Meg out by the arm. They giggled and fell against each other, and he imagined they had both gotten into Tess's *Pisco.* Meg's legs were bare; her blue and white plaid shirt, open. The pale moonlight held one small round breast in its glow, and David lowered his eyes. He had no right to be here. Meg was a private person. She didn't open up easily and yet she was talking to him, sharing more each day. She would be hurt by this, his voyeurism, his betrayal. If there were any way he could escape at that moment, he would.

He was relieved when they started walking into the woods, away from where he stood. But suddenly Tess turned Meg to face her. She kissed her, slipping her hands inside Meg's open shirt. He stared at the dark ground, willing them to stop, to continue their walk. He wanted them to move away from each other. He wanted to see once again the uneasy tension between them.

All right, he admitted to himself, he couldn't stomach this, seeing them kiss, touch this intimately. Did that make him a homophobic male chauvinist? Or was he just a man who wished he were the one holding Meg in his arms?

• Twenty-One •

SHE HEARD THE rustle outside the tent early in the morning, heard it come closer, stop in front, and move on. So Meg's human, she thought. She makes noise passing through the forest just like the rest of us.

She sat up quietly and unzipped the mosquito netting. The forest was thick with mist. Shawn watched its silent dance through the trees as she tried to decide if she should reach into David's shoe or not. The first time had been an accident. She was not responsible. But this would be a deliberate invasion of his privacy.

She had to see that note. She stared at his shoes, at the soiled canvas, the laces curling on the ground, trying to reason in her mind what possible purpose it would serve her. For the first time she did not know David's every thought. In the last couple of days he had become mysterious to her. The note held the key, she thought. She would have a clue to his feelings.

She slipped the folded paper out of his shoe and opened it.

Do you remember Calaf's aria in Act III of Turandot? Meg had written. A question of fact, a clue to nothing. Perhaps their days were spent doing nothing more than quizzing each other on opera. That alone would be enough to keep David happy. Shawn put the note back in his shoe and lay down again. She felt drained. She didn't care if she stayed in this tent the entire day. The cuts on her legs burned under the thin salty screen of perspiration that covered her body. In the distance she heard the eerie dawn calls of the Howlers, and a chill ran up her spine.

Was she jealous? Incredible, but that had to be it. Meg was communicating with David on a level Shawn did not even understand. But why should she care? In sixteen years of marriage she had never once felt this way. Now when she'd decided to get a divorce, she was suddenly jealous of David's relationship with a woman who was not even interested in men. That made no sense at all.

There had been plenty of opportunities over the years for her to be jealous. David worked with a lot of women who never hid their admiration for him, who called him late at night with thinly veiled excuses, and who David always dealt with politely, careful of office politics. Then there were his fans. The week David started at KZFT, the local gossip columnist reported that she had gotten a glimpse of the new traffic reporter, and "his satin voice is matched by his silken good looks." Women started congregating in KZFT's parking lot, waiting for a glimpse of their own. David became hot copy in the San Diego press. Although his "attractive zoologist wife" was frequently mentioned in the articles, that didn't stop his female fans from sending him letters. Some enclosed their pictures. A few were pretty; others enormously overweight or heavily made up. Every once in a while he received a nude photo. He would hold the picture by the edges as if he didn't want to be contaminated. "What kind of woman would do something like this?" he would ask. He read all the letters, threw out the propositions and adulations, and kept the ones that asked something of him—talking to a high school class or volunteering at a charity event.

He was so open about it that Shawn never thought to be jealous. Besides, he had told her often enough that she was one of a kind, completely irreplaceable. How irreplaceable had she been these past few years when all she offered him were her wrath and accusations?

David rolled onto his back and opened his eyes. "Look," he said, pointing to the roof of the tent.

She looked up and saw the silhouettes of two lizards, poised at right angles to each other, noses touching. "They must be between the tent roof and the rain fly," she said.

"Alfredo and Violetta." He sat up, stretched, and let out a sigh. "I was sick last night. Montezuma's Revenge."

"Really?" She hadn't heard him. He looked fine this morning. Did all men look this good when they first woke up? Skin dusky, hair disheveled just enough to make him look younger than thirty-eight. Sleepy gentle eyes. "How do you feel now?"

"Okay." He reached for his shirt. "How about your legs?"

"I'd rather tangle with razor grass than Montezuma any day." She watched him pull the shirt across his swimmer's shoulders, button it over his chest. The hair on his chest was smooth and light brown, dusted with silver. His fingers were long and nicely shaped. She once loved those hands, longed to feel them against her skin. Watching him now she remembered the ways he used to touch her, the ways he could make her body open up to him.

She looked away, back to the lizards, still frozen nose to nose. She was losing sight of who he truly was; the mistake he made she could never forgive him for. It was being out here. You saw things differently, saw people differently. That was the real danger in the jungle, not the snakes or the jaguars. You could do things, feel things, that would make no sense back home. Once home, you would spend months undoing the mistakes you'd made. In their house in San Diego she would never look at him this way, with these alien stirrings in her body.

He pulled on his pants and turned to give her a quick, distracted smile. "You'd better get up or you'll miss breakfast," he said, reaching outside the tent for his shoes and his latest fan mail.

Shawn spent the morning setting traps with Evan, then joined Robin on a walk to the bathing pool. Robin did her snake-walk down the trail that ran next to the stream, eyes glued to the earth, each step taken only after a thorough scouring of the ground below. Shawn did her best to point out the few plant species she recognized, but it was a wasted effort. Robin could not take her eyes off the ground.

There was a sudden full-throated cacophony to their left. Robin grabbed Shawn's arm.

"The Howlers!" Shawn laughed. "We've found them." She pulled her machete from its sheath and began hacking through the thick green curtain that blocked their path to the interior.

Robin held fast to her left arm. "No! We can't go in there. They sound angry."

The air shook with the Howlers' roars. "You can wait here," Shawn said. She had to raise her voice to be heard above the din. "I'll just . . ."

"Don't leave me here, Shawn. Please."

She was beginning to understand Evan's frustration with Robin. "Let me just get a look at them," she said, pulling free.

She cut through the foliage and found herself in another world. It was a circular clearing, formed by the shade of an enormous fig tree, by far the largest she had ever seen. Fifty feet or so above the tree, the canopy supported the sky. Sunlight broke through the embroidery of trees in long narrow columns of light. Scattered throughout the fig tree were the rust-colored Howlers.

Their voices echoed from the canopy and filled the air around her.

"Robin, come here!" she ordered. Robin had to see this.

Robin whimpered as she made her way through the undergrowth and tangled vines, but once inside the clearing she was quiet, mouth open, eyes wide.

"It's like a church," she said. Then she smiled. "A very noisy cathedral."

Shawn grinned to herself. Something had finally struck Robin with enough force to make her forget her fear. The Howlers shook the branches of the tree and hooted at them. Shawn ducked as a wad of dung whipped past her head. "They're not too pleased with our visit," she said.

She knew that was the worst the Howlers would do, pelt them with waste and assault their eardrums. She began slowly circling the tree. Aerial roots hung from the boughs like thick woody curtains. The branches were heavy with ripe, purple figs clustered high off the ground.

She heard Robin scream and turned to look at her. A piece of dung had caught her on the side of her head and dropped out of her hair to the ground.

Shawn laughed. "At least we're on our way to a bath," she said, leading Robin out of the clearing.

The bathing pool was a circle of water carved into the bank at the side of the stream. The current pulled in fresh water and flushed out old, but the water in the pool itself had the still, dark look of a cup of strong tea.

Shawn took off her brown-and-white-striped shirt and khaki shorts and sat on one of the flat rocks surrounding the pool to examine the cuts on her legs. The blood had formed into fine beaded chains crisscrossing her calves and thighs. The cuts looked good, no infection. She set her soap and shampoo on a ledge of the rocky bank, took off her bra and underpants, and stepped into the warm water.

Robin followed her lead, but left on her ankle socks and pink bikini underpants. She had obviously taken Tess's warning about the tiny, orifice-seeking toothpick fish to heart. She made a face. "I hate the way the bottom feels here, like it's going to suck you into the earth."

Good description, Shawn thought. In most places the bottom was solid and firm, but every once in a while a patch gave way under her, wrapping around her foot like heavy wet velvet.

Shawn sank back into the warm soft water and watched Robin soap her hair. Robin was very thin. The top of her bikini underpants rode from hip to hip without ever touching the concave line of her stomach. The toothpick fish would have no trouble at all zipping through that gap.

She had seen Robin in bathing suits before, but somehow it had never struck her how different they were from one another physically. Robin was at least five-nine, long-waisted, with smooth bronzed skin that sculpted itself around the curves of her body. Shawn was five-six and certainly not overweight, but she knew it would take more than a visual inspection to locate her hip bones. Her breasts were fuller than Robin's, though Robin's were quite lovely, high and round. More resilient than Shawn's, the skin tighter, sleeker. Too many years of going braless, perhaps. Or three children.

"You have beautiful breasts," she said to Robin.

Robin's face registered surprise, then amusement. "I hope you're not gay, too," she said.

Shawn floated on her back, weightless. "Hardly."

The sky slipped through the canopy here and there, a sharp, crisp blue. She'd forgotten about the sky. She wished she could see more of it. There was something claustrophobic about the jungle.

Robin lowered herself into the water to rinse her hair. "They're not really mine," she said.

Shawn stood up, the water to her shoulders. "Your breasts? You had them . . . ?"

"Implants," Robin answered. "I was tired of looking preadolescent up top." She picked up a tube of hair conditioner from the rock and squeezed some into her hand. "I did it a few months before Evan and I got married. You never noticed?"

Shawn shook her head. She lay back into the water again, let it lift her up. She wouldn't have noticed if the sky turned yellow back then. She was still stinging from the reality that she had lost Evan. And he never mentioned Robin's surgery to her. She respected him for that, for allowing Robin that privacy.

"Evan thought I was nuts for doing it. He said he couldn't care less about the size of my breasts, but that it was my body and I could do whatever I wanted with it."

Yes, he would say something like that.

"He never complained afterward, though," Robin laughed.

Oh, please. Let's not talk about Evan and your breasts.

The water filled Shawn's ears. She could hear things move

underwater: the swish of catfish tails, the gnashing of piranha teeth.

Robin sighed. "He's really annoyed with me right now."

"He'll get over it."

"I think I'm a little touchy. My period's late."

Shawn stood up again and saw Robin's smile. "You're pregnant?" she asked.

"I'm ninety-nine percent certain. I feel exactly like I did last time, but I haven't had it confirmed yet, and I don't want to tell Evan until I do. I hate to get his hopes up."

A few responses ran through Shawn's mind, unbidden, all with the aim of hurting Robin, of wiping that smug gloating smile from her face. *It's so soon after Melissa,* she could say, or *You won't have time to breathe,* or *You'll never be able to go back to work now.* Or how about, *Evan certainly has no fertility problem.* Robin wouldn't get the full meaning of that.

"That's wonderful, Robin." She forced the words off her tongue. "How far along do you think you are?"

Robin shrugged. "Four weeks, maybe six."

Shawn turned toward the bank, feigning preoccupation with uncapping her shampoo. She had carried Evan's baby for thirteen weeks. She'd dreamt about that baby, a little girl, of course, with dark hair and blue eyes. She took prenatal vitamins, drank milk she despised, did everything she had done with her other pregnancies, all the while knowing the child she nourished was not a child she would ever hold in her arms.

"I hope it's a boy," Robin said. "I'm so glad it didn't take me long to get pregnant again. We want four kids and since I'm already thirty-four, we don't have that much time to play with. I should have hung onto my maternity . . . Shawn? Are you okay?"

Shawn pressed herself against the rocky bank, trying to keep from crying, but it was no use. Robin came toward her, braving the spongy bottom of the pool to get to her. She put her arms around her, pulled Shawn's head onto her shoulder.

"I'm sorry, Shawn," she said. "It must make you think about Heather. I shouldn't have said anything."

The baited trap near the Inland Troop had a Copper Elf in it. It darted from one side of the trap to the other while Evan tried to get a peek under its tail. "Female, I think," he said.

Shawn anesthetized the Elf and took it from the cage. She and

Evan exchanged looks of disappointment. This tamarin was too old to be useful for their breeding program.

Evan sighed. "Let's collar her and let her go," he said. He pulled a leather collar, this one wrapped in red tape, from his pack and handed it to Shawn. As she lifted the tamarin's little head, her thumb touched a lump on the side of its neck. She knew what it was immediately and instinctively drew her hand away.

"Look." She pointed to the Elf's neck. Evan had brought a similar lump back with him after his trip to the jungle three years ago. It had been on his chest, near his shoulder.

Evan lifted the tamarin and examined the lump. "It's a botfly larva all right. You can see the spiracle."

Now that her initial disgust was over, she was curious. She took the Elf from Evan and held it under a sliver of sunlight. A tiny spiracle protruded from the lump like a little snorkel. She remembered the lump on Evan's chest, how it had grown so large he could see the fat white larva inside. He killed it by taping wet tobacco over the hole and squeezing the larva out after it suffocated. She didn't watch. She had lost her daughter just three weeks earlier. She needed time away from the grotesque.

"I don't care what else happens to me out here," she said now, "so long as I don't get one of these things in my body."

They were on the trail leading to the Creek Troop when they spotted another Copper Elf leaping through the branches above them, heading south. Shawn looked around them. They were in the same spot where they'd seen the Elf the day before. There was the fallen tree, the innocent-looking razor grass and swamp area behind it.

"Maybe it's the same Elf," she said.

"I'll go this time." Evan slipped his pack off his shoulders and set it on the trail. He unsheathed his machete and set out around the fallen tree to avoid the razor grass.

"I'm coming too," she said, dropping her pack next to his.

She tried to follow close on his heels, but the undergrowth was thick. Evan hacked at the branches blocking his path, cursing, the back of his blue workshirt soaked with sweat. She had nearly caught up with him when he stopped short. A tangle of liana blocked the path, the thick ropy vines braided and netted together.

"The Elf's in that tree." Evan pointed through the vines.

"We're going to lose him again, damn it." He gave a frustrated chop at the liana with his machete. The vines caught the blow of the machete like a trampoline catching a gymnast, flinging the knife back at him, into his left arm.

"*Shit*," he hissed, dropping the machete. He shut his eyes and clutched at his upper arm.

"Let me see, Evan." Shawn tried to pry his hand away from his arm, but he wouldn't let go. Blood seeped into the cloth around his fingers.

"I think it went clear to the bone," he said.

She unbuttoned his shirt and tugged gently at his sleeve. He let go of his arm and leaned against a tree, shutting his eyes.

"Tell me how it looks," he said.

There was a lot of blood, too much for her to tell how deep the cut went. It was a jagged, J-shaped wound that would definitely need stitches, but she wouldn't tell him that now.

"I don't think it's too deep," she said. "Just a little bloody." She folded the shirt into a square and pressed it to his arm. "Can you hold it while we walk back to camp?"

They walked quietly, Shawn asking him every few minutes if he was all right and Evan grunting his reply. She was going to have to stitch that cut herself. She had sewn wounds on dogs and cats in her father's veterinary office, but a human being was another matter. Maybe Tess would know how.

But Tess was not in camp. Shawn thought of trying to find her, but one look at Evan told her he couldn't wait. She didn't want him to think she was afraid of treating the wound. She wanted to do nothing that would disturb his confidence in her or add to his fear. His face was lined with pain. The shirt he pressed to the wound was soaked with blood that pooled across his fingers where they held it in place.

She put everyone to work. "Bring something he can lie down on," she ordered David. She looked over at the fire. The embers still glowed. "Get the fire going and boil some water," she told Robin. "Meg, get Tess's first aid kit. And some of her *Pisco*."

David spread a tarp on the ground, and Evan lowered himself onto it without any encouragement. He lay back and shut his eyes.

Robin sat down on the tarp. The headset of a Walkman was around her neck, a cassette player attached to her belt. "The water's heating." She twisted her hands in her lap and looked at Shawn. "There's so much blood. Is he all right?"

"I'm fine," Evan said without opening his eyes.

"Please don't go out there again, Evan," Robin pleaded.

"I did this to myself, Robin." Evan looked up at his wife. "Nothing attacked me. I was bitten by my own machete." He turned to Shawn with a weak smile. "That doesn't make a very good story, does it? Could we make something up?"

David sat down next to Shawn. "How can I help?" he asked.

She shook her head. "Nothing yet." She was surprised he was here. This was the kind of situation that usually sent David flying off in another direction.

Meg brought the first aid kit and the *Pisco*. Evan reached hungrily for the bottle. He drank more than he should have, wincing as it burned his throat. Shawn gently pried the bottle from his hand. "It hurts, huh?" she said.

"It's all right."

She cleaned her hands with alcohol and then gingerly pulled the shirt away from the wound. The bleeding had slowed and now she could clearly see the jagged J carved deep into his arm.

Robin's hand flew to her mouth. "God, it looks terrible!"

Shawn bristled. "Hold this," she said to David, pressing the shirt back to the wound. She stood up, grabbed Robin by the arm, and pulled her to the side of the clearing.

"Look, Robin, he's scared enough as it is," she said. "He knows it's not some little scratch from razor grass. If you can't get a better grip on yourself, then stay away from him."

She returned to Evan who smiled up at her as she took her seat again. "You've got quite a temper," he said. "Kindly calm down before you touch my arm again."

David handed her the blood-soaked shirt. His fingers were stained red. He stood up and walked away, and she thought it had finally become too much for him. But he returned a moment later with the boiling water. She looked up at him. She couldn't believe he was doing this. She would have to thank him later.

She rummaged through the first aid kit and found black nylon thread and a needle. She dropped them into the pot of water David held out to her and looked up at her husband. "Let them boil a few minutes," she said.

There was no anesthetic. She hunted through the contents of the first aid kit twice, her hands starting to shake. Evan watched her, his eyes already a little glazed from the *Pisco*.

She slipped her fingers into his hand. "I have to stitch it," she said. It sounded like an apology.

He nodded. "I figured."

"But there's no lidocaine in here." She felt her eyes well up. You would even put a dog to sleep for stitches.

"Well don't cry, for Christ's sake. You won't be able to see what you're doing. And pass the *Pisco*."

Meg sat on the dirt next to the tarp, holding the bottle of *Pisco*. She handed it to Evan, and he took another long draw. Then he looked up at Shawn again.

"How many stitches?" he asked.

She studied the cut. The top and bottom were fairly neat, it was only the curve of the J where the edges refused to come together. "Ten?" She sounded as if she were asking his permission. He nodded.

David returned with the needle and thread. "What can I do?" he asked, sitting next to her again.

"Just let him squeeze your hand." Her fingers shook as she threaded the needle, and she held them low so Evan couldn't see.

Meg passed Evan the bottle again, and he looked up at her. "You're a beautiful woman, Meg," he said. "But there's one thing about you I don't understand."

Shawn smiled to herself. "Not now, Evan."

"I'm drunk," Evan said.

He was not quite drunk enough. He tensed and shut his eyes when she slid the needle into the skin near the middle of the wound and up through the other side. The muscles in his arm contracted defensively under her fingers. She clipped the thread and tied the ends together in a tight knot. It looked good, very neat, the skin meeting with precision beneath the thread.

"Nine more like that?" Evan looked at her unhappily.

"Maybe just eight. Four on either side of that first one should do it. It's better than thirty-two, Evan."

"Oh yeah," he grinned, letting go of David's hand to lift her shirt sleeve. He traced the W-shaped scar with his fingertip, and she felt that familiar bolt of electricity shoot through her. He was lying below her, bare-chested, his guard down, letting her pierce his skin over and over. "This is ironic," he said, slurring. "We'll have scars in the same places."

She had been nuts back then, jumping into the wolf enclosure. She thought those wolves loved her. Every day she stopped to pet them through the fence or feed them a treat or two. They greeted her happily, as though they'd been waiting for her arrival. It never occurred to her that crossing the boundary between them put her in danger. She had nightmares for weeks afterward, remembering that stilt-legged animal lunging at her, catching the skin of her shoulder with its canines.

"Your scar will be in the shape of a J, Ev," she said, closing off the fourth stitch. "We can say you were attacked by a jaguar."

"I was attacked by a jaguar," Evan repeated. He was grinning, dopey looking. He no longer tensed when she planted the needle. "I love you guys," he said solemnly, looking from her to David and back again.

"Don't get maudlin," she said. "I'm just stitching a cut, not amputating your leg."

"We love you too," David said, and something inside Shawn shriveled in defeat. This triangle. There was no way to break out of it. She was trying, but these two seemed conspired to hold her with them. Two males, cooperating, with the same goal in mind.

· Twenty-Two ·

SHAWN WALKED TO the Creek Troop as the early morning sun worked its way through the canopy. She was alone, and she took the time to notice the quiet beauty of the forest, thinking that this must be what David and Meg enjoyed on their leisurely walks through the jungle each day.

Do you know we spent four hours in the forest yesterday afternoon and didn't take a single picture? Meg wrote in that morning's note, damp with mist. *You are wonderful to talk with, David.*

David talking for four hours? What would he talk about? Or maybe talking was not all that occurred. Could they be lovers? She hugged her arms against her body. She couldn't imagine it. *The man still has blood in his veins,* Evan had said.

David *had* been wonderful to talk with, once upon a time. A good listener. He liked to touch her when he listened, the back of her hand, her hair, her pregnant belly, stroking with the tips of his fingers, the warm flat of his palm. Meg wouldn't want that, would she? Being touched by a man? Her little notes to David had a tenderness to them. Yet they were cryptic, as though she was leaving something out, asking David to read between the lines. Cryptic, in case Shawn was first to find them.

She smelled the scat before she saw it, and the muscles in her legs contracted. She'd heard about the foul smell of jaguar scat; this could be nothing else. She stood rigidly in the center of the trail, not breathing. She turned her head slowly, searching the ground, the undergrowth. She started walking again, slowly rounding the corner of the trail. There it was, the mound of scat, in the center of the trail in front of her.

She raised her eyes to see the jaguar himself. He stood on the trail, no more than ten yards ahead of her. His head was turned toward her, eyes riveted on her own. He was half in shadow, but a column of sunlight fell on his head, and she saw the gold of his eyes, the white of his whiskers. The rest of the forest fell out of focus. She lifted her camera slowly to her eyes, but before she could press the button, the jaguar shot off into the jungle, the undergrowth camouflaging him instantly.

She stood still another few minutes, as winded as if she'd run a mile. Evan would be sorry he missed this, although the smell of the scat would have finished him. He stayed behind this morning, not so much because of his wounded arm as from the aftermath of the *Pisco*. Robin said he was sick much of the night.

There was a tamarin in the trap at the Creek Troop, this one a female who was antagonizing ChoCho. Shawn anesthetized her and wrote down her weight and length. The Elf was no more than three or four years old. Probably the mother of the infant pair. They would have to try to trap her mate and the babies by using her as a decoy. She rigged another trap to this one and headed back to the clearing.

They caught the male and the babies after lunch. Evan was with her. He was pale and not too steady on his feet, but he was so excited by the news of the captured female that he refused to stay in the clearing.

The male was aggressive, plunging his arms through the bars and trying to gnaw the wire with his teeth. The babies screeched with hunger. Shawn had to anesthetize the male before she could get to the babies to turn them over to their mother. It was a happy reunion, the babies—both females!—leaping, clinging, sucking, while their mother groomed them and chatted with them. Evan weighed and measured the male. Two years old, they judged. This would be a good breeding pair.

"But what if he's the wrong male?" Shawn asked. She hadn't thought of that. What if this were not the male Copper Elf the female was attached to?

"You're going to worry about *that*?" Evan said.

She shrugged. She guessed there was not much they could do about it now.

"We can't trap from this troop any longer," Evan said. "The other Elves would be too closely related to these four."

"We'll have to find another troop," she said. They looked at each other, and she knew they were both remembering the nasty little Elf that had caused her slivered legs and his wounded arm.

He shook his head. "Not today, okay?"

* * *

David and Meg found the scat but not the jaguar. Shawn had told them the jaguar left the trail and headed toward the stream, so he and Meg did the same. They had their cameras ready, and they tried to keep the use of their machetes to a quiet minimum, but the vegetation was heavy. Dozens of trees had been uprooted in this part of the forest, leaving obstacles and undergrowth.

David stopped walking and wiped the sweat from his forehead with the back of his arm. His enthusiasm for this outing was gone. He frowned at the trees around them. Were they walking in circles? Which way was the stream?

It was getting late. There were no beams of sunlight shooting through the trees, and he was tired of concentrating on marking the branches with his machete. They had left in a hurry when Shawn told them about the jaguar. They left their day packs behind, with their compasses and surveyor's tape.

"Isn't that a Copper Elf?" Meg pointed at one of the trees.

David looked up and saw not one but several tiny white faces peering down at him from the shadows. He smiled. Another troop. Evan and Shawn would be pleased.

He tied his handkerchief to one of the lower branches to mark the tree. He wished he had a compass so he could take a reading. It would be difficult to tell Evan and Shawn exactly where to find this tree when he didn't know where he was to begin with.

He could not get the image of Shawn working on Evan's arm out of his mind. Evan had finally passed out, and Shawn finished the stitches in silence. She turned to David when she was through. "Thanks for helping," she said, formally, as if it were the proper thing to do. She knew, she had to know, what it took for him to sit there with that bloody shirt, the open wound, the needle slipping in and out of Evan's skin. He felt every one of those stitches as if it were his own arm beneath Shawn's fingers.

Tess had looked at the stitches in amazement. "As good as I could do," she said. "Better." But then she told Shawn quietly, apologetically, that she did have lidocaine. "It's in another pack," she said, and he thought he saw sympathy in Tess's eyes. Perhaps she was not an inhuman, unfeeling woman after all.

"We'd better go back," Meg said now. "It must be nearly time for dinner, and it's too dark now to get a decent picture anyway."

He looked up. The patches of sky behind the canopy were a forbidding pre-dusk color. He looked at his watch. Five-thirty. The forest would be black in less than an hour.

"Come on," he said, walking back the way they came. He

studied the trees for the marks of his machete but could find none. Nothing looked familiar. They were in a maze, and the path they followed grew narrower with every step. The forest was denser than it had been an hour ago, full of shadows.

They walked a while in silence. They heard the Howlers' dusk calls and tried to determine which direction the roaring came from, but the sound pummeled their ears from all sides at once.

A mosquito bit David's elbow, and he rolled down his sleeves, buttoned them at the wrists. He blinked to try to clear away the veil of darkness falling quickly over them.

"We'd better stop," Meg said. "We're getting more tangled up in this maze."

"We can't stop. We'll be stranded out here for the night."

"But we might be walking in the wrong direction from the clearing."

There would be no moon tonight. His hands shook as he checked the pockets of his pants for matches. "Do you have any matches in your camera case?" he asked.

"No. Let's try calling. Maybe we're close enough for them to hear us. Tess!"

He joined her. They pooled their voices, trying to make themselves heard over the mounting night sounds of the jungle, straining their ears to listen for a response. And all the while, the darkness closed in around them.

"Let's sit," she said, pointing to a fallen tree.

He hesitated. If he sat down, he'd be giving in. They would have to stay here. He looked up and could no longer separate the canopy from the black sky above it. He watched helplessly as the forest lost its pattern of light and shadow and surrendered to a black velvet darkness that sucked the breath from him. He sat next to Meg, feeling the bark of the tree beneath his hands. He held his hand in front of his face and saw nothing. His pulse raced in his ears and hammered against his throat.

He stood up abruptly. "I can't stand this." He heard the panic in his voice. "I can't breathe."

"What's wrong?" Meg reached into the darkness and her hand grazed his wrist. He grabbed her arm as if it were a lifeline. He clung to her, to the fabric of her sleeve, his knees like water. "Here's the log," Meg said. "You're okay. Sit back down."

He lowered himself onto the log again. "I can't see," he said.

"No. Neither can I." She crouched in front of him, and he held onto both her arms.

"Don't let go of me," he said.

"I won't."

He couldn't slow his breathing. God, he needed to *see* something. *Anything.*

"I'm sorry," he said. "This is my worst fear. Being blind."

Meg pulled away from him, and he batted the air in a panic to find her again. Then he felt her body slip next to him on the fallen tree, felt her arms wrap around him in a tight, calming circle. "You're not blind," she said.

How could she know that? He felt as though the light of morning would make no difference. Once his eyes had experienced this total darkness, there could be nothing else. He held his hand in front of his eyes again, blinked hard to be sure they were open. Nothing there. He had no hand. He had no eyes.

He felt Meg's head rest against his shoulder. Her hands stroked his arm, and slowly his breathing settled down. Within a few minutes, he was calm enough to feel embarrassed.

"My parents are blind," he said.

"Ah."

"You'd think that growing up around it would make me less afraid of the possibility."

"There are worse fears you could have. I mean, how often do you find yourself stranded in total darkness?"

He shook his head. "It goes beyond that," he said, wondering how much to tell her. But the night stretched in front of him, long and black, and he began to talk. He told her about avoiding the births of his children. He hadn't intended to do that. He was as excited as Shawn about the pregnancies. He loved watching her body change. He went through the childbirth classes with her, steeling himself for the physical side of it, for the blood and Shawn's pain. He was determined to be with her, and if blood and pain had been the only considerations, he would have made it.

But in the delivery room a terror mounted inside him. He couldn't breathe. He must have looked bad, because the doctor whispered something to a nurse who took David by the arm and escorted him to the waiting area. She told him to put his head between his knees, and he obeyed, feeling like a fool. It was not the blood he feared. It was that something might be wrong with the babies' eyes. That sometimes happened at birth—not enough oxygen, twisted cord. It had happened to both his parents, and in his mind, that made the odds too high. And *twins.* What possible chance did they have?

When he finally saw his sons, he didn't count fingers and toes.

He stared into their eyes, and only when he was certain they were gazing back at him did he begin to relax.

He never tried to explain his escape to Shawn. If he spoke the fear out loud, it would give it credibility. He let Shawn think whatever she wanted about his cowardice.

"Births?" Meg said.

"What?"

"It sounded as though you were talking about two different occasions. I thought you just had twin boys."

"Oh." He thought for a moment. He could say he'd had a daughter, but then he would have to explain. He was amazed he even considered mentioning Heather to Meg. But no, not tonight when he was already this vulnerable. "I was only talking about one time," he said, uncomfortable with the lie. "Just the twins."

For a few minutes neither of them spoke. "I have to get up," Meg said finally. "I have to . . . use the woods."

"I'll come with you."

"No. Stay here so we don't lose our place."

He didn't want to stay alone. "We'll find the log again. We'll walk from it in a straight line."

"No, David. I need some privacy."

She took a long time. He heard her not far from where he sat, fumbling in her camera case. When she came back, her voice was different, thick and uncertain. She had been crying.

"What's wrong?" he asked. He'd been moaning about his irrational terror while she kept her fears to herself.

"Nothing's wrong. I'm fine."

They tried sitting back to back, their legs stretched in opposite directions along the fallen tree. It was better, but the tree was not quite wide enough to allow them to relax completely. They had to stay vigilant or risk rolling off.

"David," Meg said quietly. "Can I tell you something personal?" she asked.

"I wish you would. I just told you that I'm thirty-eight years old and still afraid of the dark."

"Well, I wasn't completely honest with you when I told you I had a male lover in high school."

"No?"

"I went out with a guy for a while, but we never . . . went all the way. I was afraid to because . . ." her voice trailed off and except for the press of her back against his, he would have thought he had lost her in the darkness.

"Meg?"

"I'm trying to think of a way to say this. My father had a friend who came over our house a lot. He always touched me when no one was looking. A few times my parents left me alone with him. They went out . . . they had no idea. He said things, like the way I walked made him crazy, made him want to do things to me. He said that the way I said hello to him drove him nuts. So I stopped saying hello to him, and then he said it was the way I ignored him. He said I was teasing him. So I felt it was my fault somehow. I did something that made him lose control. He'd tell me to hold very still and let him do whatever he wanted to me."

"How old were you?"

"Thirteen when it started."

He tried to picture her at thirteen, a fragile little flower. "How far did it go?" he asked.

"Usually he just touched me. But twice he had intercourse with me."

He reached across his chest to wrap his hand around her arm. He felt the back of her head against his neck.

Meg sighed. "I walked around my house in tears, but my parents never suspected. Then one day he died. A heart attack. I thought maybe I caused that to happen too, somehow."

"No wonder you're not interested in men."

She snapped her head away from him. "That has nothing to do with it. It doesn't work that way. I was *born* a lesbian, not made into one. I knew long before that incident that I was different."

"Okay," he said. "I'm sorry."

"I can't sit like this anymore," Meg grumbled. "Maybe we could take turns lying down? Use each other's laps as pillows?"

She lay on her back, her head in his lap, and he sought out a neutral place for his hand, finally resting it along the line of her belt. His arm rose and fell with her breathing. He imagined what she would look like if he could see her: blond hair loose on his thighs, long legs and narrow hips balanced on the log. He pictured her body stretched out beneath his arm, tempting him to play it like a musical instrument. Was it wrong to think about making love to her? Thinking about it was no crime. He would never actually do it. She had just made it very clear that she was not interested in sex with a man. Maybe that was why he tried to discount her gayness. He wanted her to feel as tempted by him as he did by her. But that would be risky.

He couldn't help the fantasy. Three years had passed since he and Shawn were lovers. Oh, they had sex a few times, when for one reason or another he felt encouraged to try. But Shawn, when she agreed at all, acted as though she were performing a service for him. She never seemed to enjoy it, no matter what he did. Most of the time, he was left feeling as though he'd used her.

He stroked the top of Meg's head with his fingers. She wriggled against him, childlike, seeking comfort, and covered his forearm with hers. "Let me know when you want to trade places," she said.

Sometime during the night, Meg woke with a start and struggled to sit up. David felt her body shaking under his arm.

"Are you cold?" he asked, although the night was sticky with heat.

"Where's my camera case?"

David felt along the rough bark of the tree, as far as he could reach. "It must have fallen on the ground," he said.

"I *need* it." She slid off the log and rooted through the leaves. "It's not here." She stood up, her hands on his knees. "Oh, God, David, listen to me, please. Are you listening?"

Her panic was contagious. He felt adrenaline rush through his arms. "What's the matter?"

"I'm having an insulin reaction. I'm diabetic. I need . . ."

"*Diabetic?* What are you doing on this trip?"

"Stop it! I'm not a cripple. And I don't have time to argue with you about it. I'm slipping. I have to find my case. It has glucose tablets in it. They're big square tablets, three to a package. I need to take all three. If I start acting strange, give them to me. If I lose consciousness, there's a syringe with some liquid in it and a vial with powder. They need to be mixed together, and then you'll have to inject me."

He dropped to the ground himself, hunting for the camera case. He was terrified of her instructions. He couldn't possibly give her a shot. And mix things in the dark? His hands felt the smooth bulk of the case. "Here it is!"

There was no response.

"Meg?"

He heard her walking away from him.

"Meg! Stay here!"

"I have to go back."

Was this what she meant by acting strange? He unzipped the case and reached inside. He found the tablets almost immediately, a strip of square wafers sealed in plastic. He followed the rustling sound and caught her arm. "Take this." He unwrapped one of the pills and held it to her mouth. She chewed and swallowed, and he gave her the second and third in the same way. He put his arm around her and felt his way back to the fallen tree. He helped her up and sat next to her, pulling her close to him.

"You take insulin?" he asked, as her trembling subsided.

"Yes. I keep it in the stream to keep it cool. That's why I get up early, to get that taken care of before anyone else is up. I carry what I need for the day in my camera case. But it's confusing when I'm not eating regular meals. I base how much insulin I need on the amount of food and exercise I get. I missed dinner last night, and I got a lot of exercise walking around, so I knew I should take very little insulin. But I couldn't see to adjust the syringe in the dark. I must have taken too much."

"Is that what you were doing when you wouldn't let me come with you to use the woods?"

"Yes."

"Do you have the insulin you need for the morning with you?"

"No. I'll have to get it from the stream."

"What if it takes us a while to get back?"

"It's hard to predict. I've always been so careful to control it. My doctor thought this trip would be okay since it was only two weeks, and I could eat regularly and carry my insulin with me. Without the insulin I'd eventually die, but it would take a while to get to that point." She shrugged as if she were saying she could get a headache. He remembered his behavior last night, the idiotic way he'd acted when darkness fell around them.

"We'll get you back," he said. "As soon as it's light enough to see where we're going."

They gave up the search an hour after nightfall. Shawn thought that was too soon, and she continued on her own for another hour, shining her flashlight into the haunted darkness of the forest, calling David's name. She had that old familiar feeling that something precious was being stolen from her.

"We'll look again early in the morning," Tess told her before they went to bed. "There's nothing we can do now."

She lay in her tent, surrounded by the thick, moonless night and imagined the worst scenario. David and Meg found the jaguar—or the jaguar found them—and it was not as harmless as she made it out to be. Maybe David and Meg trusted too much, grew incautious when they found him.

She heard footsteps outside her tent and saw the beam of a flashlight. "David?" She sat up.

Evan knelt outside the mosquito netting, shining the light at the ground. "You okay?" He unzipped the netting and sat down on David's side of the bed. She struggled to see his face, half in shadow, one wide blue eye, one arched eyebrow, questioning. "Do you understand why we had to give up looking tonight?"

"Because it was pointless."

"It's too dark, and they're in too deep. We have no idea what direction to look in. We'll do it methodically in the morning."

"I'm afraid he's dead."

"He's not dead."

"He's such an innocent; he never anticipates harm." She looked at the white circle of light Evan's flashlight formed on the wall of the tent. "And he's afraid of the dark. He's afraid of feeling blind." That was the worst of it, imagining him lost in this inescapable darkness. She felt his fear. At least Meg was with him, and he was not totally alone.

Evan moved next to her and put his arms around her. She smelled the heat of the day on him, the alcohol from his bandaged arm, the warm earth smell of his neck. His closeness was old and familiar, like a quilt from her childhood she thought she would never curl up with again. The thin cloth of her T-shirt brushed her skin like a feather under his hands.

"It's been so long since I've touched you," he said.

His hand softly cupped her left breast, and he lowered his head to press his lips to hers, but she turned her head away from him. "Please, Evan, no."

He stopped abruptly, his forehead touching hers. His eyes were closed; the sound of his breathing filled the tent. At that moment she loved him very much, too much to make love to him.

"It's no good, Evan. I'd feel guilty. You'd feel guilty. You'd blame me . . ."

He shook his head, his eyes still closed.

"Yes, you would. You'd blame me tomorrow when the guilt set in. I need your help to resist you. Don't make me do it alone."

He smiled slightly and sat back, lowering his hands to his lap, folding them like a schoolboy. "Did I ever tell you I once wanted to be a priest?"

"No," she smiled. "Why are you telling me now?"

"I thought you could use a good laugh."

She touched the white gauze on his arm. "Seriously?"

"When I was in high school."

"You were an altar boy then." She went to a mass with him once, a high mass, and felt transported to another world. The service was long; it seemed to her that they were in that church for hours. The words were mystical; the singing, disquieting. She watched Evan's face and didn't recognize him as the man who had made love to her the night before, all fire and passion. She studied the devoted faces of the altar boys, tried to picture Evan in their place, and found that she could not. He was too much of the flesh.

"Well," he said to her now, "maybe we could say a prayer together. You know, that David and Meg get back safely."

She started to laugh, but caught herself. He was serious. "I can't do that," she said.

He shrugged. "Okay."

"One minute you want to commit adultery, the next minute you want to pray."

He half-smiled. "I'm fucked up, what can I say?"

"How do you pray? I mean, what do you say?"

He lay on his side, propped up on his elbow. "I thank God for whatever it is I'm thankful for that day. Then I pray for what I'd like to see happen. Tonight I prayed that David and Meg are safe. Then I God-Bless everyone."

"Everyone?"

"Everyone I care about. Robin and Melissa. You and David."

"Really?" She'd never known that Evan prayed for her, much less for David.

"And Jamie and Keith," Evan said.

She lowered her voice. "Did you used to God-Bless Heather?"

"I still do."

She felt the tears threaten and shook her head to clear them away. She lay down next to him, close, letting him wrap his arms around her again. "You should be with Robin," she said.

"She suggested I check on you."

Shawn wondered if she herself would ever be capable of that kind of unselfish concern for another human being. It couldn't be easy for Robin to be alone in their tent on a night as black as this. "She's so trusting, Evan. Don't abuse it."

"You're still in love with David," he said.

"No."

"You can't stand thinking of him out there, hurt or afraid."

"I don't love him."

"It's not a crime, you know. He's your husband."

"If it weren't for him, Heather would be alive."

"An accident, babe."

She shook her head but said nothing. She'd thought about this many times. An accident was something you had no control over. David was guilty of negligence.

She sat up. "You'd better get back," she said. "And please thank Robin for sharing you."

He opened his eyes to the welcome light pouring through the canopy above him, burning off the mist. His head was in Meg's lap, and she scratched his forehead with her fingernail.

"Hold still," she said. "You have a few ticks."

He looked up and saw a red welt across the creamy skin of her jaw. There was a black pinhead in its center and reality sank in. The fallen tree was infested, and now they were as well.

He sat up and scraped the tick from her jaw, and another from her cheek, near the hairline.

"I know I have them too," she said. "I felt the welts forming during the night, from being allergic." She unzipped her pants and slipped them off. Her calves were covered with welts and the tiny black bloodsuckers. He took her pants from her and turned them inside out to pluck out the ticks that had not yet made their home in her skin. He knew they were crawling under his own clothes, but his discomfort was nothing compared with Meg's.

"Give me your shoes and socks," he said.

She did so without speaking, and he rousted the ticks from the fabric. He crouched behind her and scraped five ticks from the backs of her legs. Her legs were covered with a pale blond down. She didn't shave.

She put her pants on again while he checked her hair.

"Better have Tess check the rest of you when we get back," he said.

"Get back?" Tears slipped from her eyes, liquid diamonds on her cheeks. "We're still lost, David. I need to test my blood sugar and get my insulin. And I need something to eat."

David looked up. The sun was brightest to their left. That had to be east, so the clearing should be in the opposite direction. "This way," he said, scraping a tick from his wrist.

"David," she held back. "Please don't tell anyone about the diabetes. I don't want them to know."

He frowned at her. "Tess knows, doesn't she?"

She shook her head. "Especially not Tess. She wouldn't have let me come if she knew. She only likes strong women."

"It's not as though it's your fault you're diabetic."

"That wouldn't matter to her. Please, David. Not even Shawn, okay? I don't want everyone watching me like I'm an invalid."

He nodded, accepting her request to keep her secret and the burden of responsibility that came with it. He would have to watch out for Meg.

In less than an hour they heard Tess's voice call to them. Meg started running, and when she reached Tess, she flung her arms around her. Tess stood rigid, and David turned his head because he didn't want to see the disappointment in Meg's eyes.

"Where were your compasses?" Tess asked.

"We forgot them," Meg said.

"You can't afford to be forgetful in the jungle. You cost all of us valuable time and a good night's sleep."

He walked past the two women. "Thanks," he said to Tess. "We're happy we're safe too."

Shawn met him in the clearing. She closed him up in her arms, her head buried in his neck, and he held her tight until she pulled away from him, averting her eyes, trying to compose herself. He watched with fascination how quickly she put up the cool facade again. A facade, yes, that's all it was. She had given him a glimpse of the old Shawn, the real Shawn.

"Would you help me with the ticks?" he asked, and she nodded. She turned and walked ahead of him down the trail to their tent.

He lay on his stomach, eyes closed, feeling her fingers move lightly over his bare skin, occasionally stopping to scratch out a tick, then moving on again until she'd covered every inch of him with her touch. He curved his hand around her calf, and she made no attempt to move her leg away.

"There was no moon last night," she said.

He still felt embarrassed about last night, how he panicked in the darkness while Meg kept her own fear to herself. "It was hard," he said.

"We can sleep with the lantern outside the tent tonight if you like."

He smiled to himself. He wished he could tell her he loved her, but it had been too long. It used to be so easy. Not a day went by without those words being spoken. Not half a day. But it was too chancy now. She might pull herself up short; she might remember why she'd cooled toward him. He didn't want that. He would have to take it very slowly with her.

Thank God Meg didn't like men. He might have made love to her if that were not the case. It would have been easy. He felt so unattached to Shawn and out of touch with reality, lost in the forest. Now as he felt his heart fill with love for Shawn, he was glad he'd done nothing more foolish than panicking in the dark.

That afternoon, he managed to lead Shawn and Evan back to the troop of Copper Elves he and Meg discovered the night before. The troop was embarrassingly close to the stream and only fifty yards from the cathedral where the Howlers made their home. The forest seemed open and unthreatening in the light of day, and he felt ridiculous for his panic last night, ridiculous for getting lost at all.

Shawn was asleep when he slipped into their bed that night. He couldn't remember a day when he'd felt this close to her since before Heather died. He sat up for a while, watching her in the soft light of the kerosene lantern outside the mosquito netting. Few women could get away with a haircut so short. On another woman it might look mannish, but Shawn's big blue eyes and slender throat turned that cut into something utterly feminine. He loved her high cheekbones and her chin. Something about her chin reminded him of Heather. They spoke often of how Heather looked nothing like either of them, but sometimes when he looked at Shawn, he felt a jolt. Heather was there, in the indignant point of Shawn's chin.

She made a sound, half-sigh, half-moan, a contented sound, and rolled onto her side away from him. He lay down next to her, his arm around her and his mouth against her neck. He gently pulled her body close to his. There was no resistance. She rolled toward him and wrapped her arms around his neck, and he kissed her, dizzy from his lack of sleep and the taste of that evening's rum on her tongue. Her body was hot, almost feverish, beneath his hands. He slipped his thigh between hers, and she pressed against him hungrily.

"Shawn," he whispered, lifting her T-shirt. "Help me take this off."

She darted up, hand to her mouth, as if she had committed

some grave social error. Her eyes were frightened. She looked as if she'd awakened to find a stranger in her bed.

He touched her shoulder and felt the tremor under his hand. "Honey, what is it?"

"I don't want to make love," she said, lowering her eyes.

"A minute ago you wanted to. You really wanted to, Shawn." That had been no act this time, no mere placation.

"It was just a physical reaction."

He smiled. "Well, of course."

"No, I mean it meant nothing. I . . ."

"Listen, I think I woke you up too suddenly. You don't know what you're talking about."

"*No*, I'm thinking clearly." Her eyes filled. Shit, she was going to cry. The helpless feeling hit him, the marbles were out of the bag and rolling in all directions. He didn't know which to go after first.

She looked him straight in the eye, lips quivering but working at control. "David," she said quietly, deadly calm. "I've decided I want a divorce."

He shook his head. "You can't mean that."

"I was going to wait until we got back to tell you, but I can't continue to pretend things are okay between us when they're not."

He barely heard her. She was talking to him from faraway, a great canyon spread out between them. No matter how sour things became between them, he had never anticipated this. Divorce wasn't in their vocabulary. This marriage was a commitment for life.

"Are you listening to me, David?"

He looked at her. She no longer trembled. She had said the scary part. The free fall was over; now she could ride the parachute to safety while he crumbled under the weight of her news.

"I think that's an extreme solution to our problems."

"It's the only solution."

"What about a marriage counselor?" He was terrified of counseling, but he would do it if that's what it took. Would a therapist let him get away without talking about Heather?

"I want out."

He stared at a spot on the tent wall, trying to imagine what his life would be like without her. He would be alone, in some repulsive, glassy apartment. Eat his meals alone, spend his evenings alone, wake up alone. Shawn would have the house. That was always the way it went—the wife got the house. And the kids.

Oh God, no. He would lose them. He saw it happen all the time, fathers living apart from their teenage children, seeing them on the weekend when the kids wanted to be anyplace but with a parent. You needed to be with kids that age every day, needed to be the central core in their lives, the person they bounced the events of the day off of. He was that for the boys, more than Shawn.

"What if I said I wanted Keith and Jamie?" he asked.

"Don't put yourself through that, David. My lawyer says you don't have a chance."

He swallowed hard. "I haven't been a bad parent to them."

"We'll work out visitation that will be fair to . . ."

He grabbed her arms. "You're going to cost me my sons!"

She struggled to free herself, and he let go of her.

"Please, Shawn," he begged. "I can't lose them too." His voice broke, and he turned to unzip the netting. He stepped outside, picked up the lantern, and walked away from the tent.

There was no place to go in this goddamned jungle. He walked down the trail to the clearing and sat at the table in the miserable darkness. The pain he felt was physical—intermittent pain down his arms to his wrists, across his chest, in his gut.

He had nothing left. He'd built his life around Shawn and his children, and he was about to lose it all.

• Twenty-Three •

DAVID DIDN'T SPEAK to her the next morning. Shawn watched him sit up in bed to read the note from Meg—this one covering two sides of the paper—without changing expression. She was certain he knew she was awake—they were both completely aware of one another. She thought of breaking the silence, of saying she was sorry, but she was afraid of what he might say in return. She was most afraid he would say nothing at all.

Had she really expected him to accept the end of their marriage stoically? She should never have blurted it out that way. She didn't mean to hurt him, but she panicked, startled by her feelings. She had wanted him close to her last night, and she couldn't allow that to happen. Telling him about the divorce seemed the only way to put some distance between them.

Well, it had worked, she thought, as she watched him dress and leave the tent. She was tempted to stay behind until she was certain he had left the clearing, and she wouldn't have to face him. But there was too much work to do today to procrastinate.

Everyone was at the table. She walked past them to the tamarin tree and stood in front of the cage that held the new male and female and their babies. It was the wrong male, she was certain of it. The female ignored him, turning to him only when she wanted him to take the babies.

"Oatmeal's getting cold, Shawn," Tess said.

Shawn walked woodenly to the table and sat down at the only empty seat, directly across from David. He didn't look up. He stared into his empty cereal bowl, and she could almost see the weight on his shoulders that made him slump like a tired old man.

"We'll go creek-drifting tonight," Tess said, lighting a cigarette. They would travel upstream in the canoe, she explained, then extinguish their lights and drift back with the current while trying to spot animals lured to the water's edge by the dark and quiet. It reminded Shawn of the drives she made long ago in the dark woods, the drives that terrified David.

"I'll stay here," he said now.

"Oh, come with us, David," said Meg. "We might get some pictures we'd have no chance to take otherwise."

He shook his head. "I'd rather not."

"I did it the last time I was in the jungle," Evan said to David. "You really don't want to miss it."

Shawn wanted to get the heat off David. "I'm certain we have the wrong male," she said suddenly. Everyone looked at her. "The female is only interested in him for child care."

Evan set his spoon in his empty bowl. "So what are you suggesting? That we release him and try for the other male?"

She knew that would be insane. This pair would mate when the time was right, and they were obviously good parents, so why should she care if the female was attached to the male?

"I think she feels a loss," she said. "I think she's grieving."

Evan smiled at her patiently. "That female's brain is the size of an acorn. The only thing she feels is hungry and itchy."

After breakfast, she and Evan carried ChoCho to the troop David and Meg had found. Evan named it the Lost Troop, and it looked very good. There were at least four or five juveniles in the nesting tree. Probably one of them was the little Elf they had tried to chase across the swamp.

They left ChoCho with the Lost Troop and walked through the forest to the Inland Troop. There were two tamarins in the trap, both year-old females.

"Two at once!" Evan said, as they carried the newly captured Elves back to the clearing. "We should celebrate. Let's get Robin and David and go for a swim."

Shawn shook her head. "I don't think David would want to. I told him about the divorce last night."

Evan turned to look at her. "Your timing's really splendid. He spends the night fighting for survival in the jungle, and you welcome him back with the news you want a divorce."

"I had to," she said wearily. "He was trying to get too close."

"Is he okay?"

She stopped on the trail and set down the cage. She needed a break. She needed to look at the canopy above her, to see the comforting lacework of sunlight above the trees. "I don't know," she said quietly. "I don't know if either one of us is okay."

* * *

They settled into the dugout after dinner. David agreed to go, and it was obvious he was in better spirits after spending the afternoon with Meg. He and Meg had quizzed each other on the opera over dessert, a treat of melons and bananas. There was fruit to spare now that Shawn and Evan needed to trap only from the Lost Troop. David didn't look at Shawn once during dinner, as though he was saying, *See, Shawn, you thought my world revolved around you, but you're wrong.*

The mood in the boat was almost festive, although there was an undeniable undercurrent of nervous anticipation. They kept a lantern burning as they chugged steadily against the current. Shawn sat in the bow, shining her flashlight ahead of them to keep the boat on course. They hit just one rough spot, where the stream forked and the water flowed toward them in white-tipped ripples from the left.

"There's a waterfall up there," Tess said, as she turned the outboard motor to take them onto the right fork.

Even with their lights, the stream was eerie at night. Robin cuddled against Evan, and he put his arm around her. Shawn wished Robin would tell him about the pregnancy. That would put an end to any longing he felt for Shawn. He would no longer tempt her.

The beam from her flashlight picked up a group of boulders along the side of the stream, and she was surprised to see a sleek metal canoe resting upside down on the bank behind them.

"There's a group of ornithologists back in there, about a mile," Tess said. "They came in by helicopter."

So they had neighbors. It felt strange to realize they were not completely isolated after all.

After another mile, they turned the boat around. The stream here was only as wide as the length of the canoe, and it took them several minutes to untangle themselves from the vines that clutched at their shoulders. Then Tess turned out the lantern, and Shawn switched off her flashlight, and they were quickly engulfed by a thick, inescapable blackness.

"Oh my God," said Robin.

"Shhh," whispered Tess, as the boat began to drift with the slow, easy current. "We have to be absolutely silent."

Shawn set her oar across her knees and felt the cool water trickle from it onto her calf. The air was full of smells she hadn't noticed before, earth smells of soil and damp wood. The trees were no longer trees but enormous, expanding shadows moving slowly, smoothly past them on both sides.

Shawn turned to look into the darkness where David sat. How

could he tolerate this? She leaned forward to touch his arm with her unlit flashlight. "Take this," she whispered, the first words she dared speak to him the entire day.

"I have my own, thanks."

Shawn sat back in the bow again and tried to relax. Tess suddenly turned on her flashlight, pointing it toward the left bank. A tapir stood at the water's edge, illuminated and surprised. Its short, hippopotamus-like body looked like a boulder. It lifted its head and let out an undignified squeal before fleeing into the shadows of the forest.

Tess turned off her flashlight again. "That's only the second tapir I've seen while creek-drifting," she said.

"I don't like this," Robin said. "That animal was too close."

"Yeah," Evan teased. "We had a narrow escape there."

Shawn felt the sticky filaments of a cobweb on her face and smoothed them away with her fingers. She heard the gasps behind her as the web surprised the others in the darkness. Then it was still once more, so still that she could hear twigs breaking ahead of them, an animal lapping at the water. She aimed her flashlight toward the sound and turned it on. *The jaguar.* Its eyes were caught in the beam of her light and shone like hot red embers. It was so close that one easy leap would put it in the center of the dugout, yet it stood calmly, its huge head turning smoothly to follow their progress. Only when they were well past the jaguar did a collective breath of relief fill the boat.

They were not far from camp now, and in the distance they heard the gentle rumble of thunder. Rain! She would have to get ChoCho from the Lost Troop as soon as they got back.

David whispered a few words to Meg over the dark center of the boat, and Meg laughed. Suddenly, David began singing. The song was in French, a haunting melody Shawn recognized as one he frequently sang around the house. His voice filled the darkness as they drifted through the black tunnel of water and trees.

After a few minutes, Meg joined him, her voice soft and unpolished, the harmony achingly sweet. Shawn felt intrusive listening to them. It was like listening in on lovers. Surely they were not lovers.

There was silence when they finished, broken by the low growl of thunder again, getting closer.

"That was beautiful," said Robin. "What is it from?"

"The Pearl Fishers," David said. "A duet meant to be sung by two men, but Meg makes a fascinating baritone."

Meg laughed softly, shyly. No, they were not lovers. Not yet.

* * *

The rain started as they climbed out of the dugout, and within seconds they were soaked. Water gushed at them from all directions, as though they had capsized in the stream and were being buffeted by waves.

ChoCho. Shawn grabbed a lantern and started for the trail to the Lost Troop, but Evan caught her arm. "You can't go in this storm," he said. His dark hair was plastered to his head, and water streamed from his beard.

"I can't let her stay out there all night, either." She pictured ChoCho, delicate and unprotected in her cage. She tried to wrench her arm free, but Evan held tight.

"You can't go, Shawn," he said.

She dropped her arms to her sides. In the light from the lantern she saw that her feet stood in an inch of mud. Water sheeted over her eyes. The stream would be flooding, the trail underwater. She couldn't go.

She stripped off her clothes outside the tent and laid them next to David's on the rain fly. David was already in bed, reading by the light of his flashlight. He didn't look up when she entered.

She wiped the rain from her face and neck with a towel and dug in her duffel bag for a clean T-shirt. Everything was damp— her clothes, the towels, the sweatshirt she stuffed into her pillowcase. She longed for the dry heat of a San Diego summer.

She got into bed, the sheet catching on the damp skin of her legs. She was careful not to let her body touch David's. The rain pounded on the roof of the tent, and the walls shook under the weight of the water.

"Do you think the tent might collapse?" she asked.

"No." David turned a page.

Somewhere in the distance a tree was falling. Shawn listened to the cracking of the trunk, the roots pulling free of the earth. The ground shook as the tree landed hard in the brush. Then it was quiet again except for the sound of the rain.

"David," she said, "we'll work something out about the boys."

"Fine."

She sighed and stared at the shadows on the roof of the tent. Why did she feel so wistful? David was no longer in her control. All the cards had been in her hand before. If she wanted to talk to him, or touch him, she could do it and know he would welcome her. Now he was free to say, "I don't want to talk to *you*, Shawn." She had only herself to blame for this change. She had made him off limits to herself.

• *Twenty-Four* •

THE BOYS BURST through Shawn and David's bedroom door.

"You blew it," David said. He had his arms around her, his head on her shoulder. "It was your turn to lock the door."

It was a Saturday morning, and it *had* been her turn to lock the door before they made love, but she hadn't wanted to leave David's warm body to do it. "It's early enough," she told him. "They won't be in for a while yet." And she and David had managed to complete their lovemaking. Just.

Keith carried Heather in his arms, his wiry eight-year-old body staggering under her weight. He dumped her on Shawn's side of the bed and climbed up himself. David handed Shawn the T-shirt he had taken off the night before, and she put it on under the covers. It smelled of aftershave. It was hot in the bed, a good heat, her body sticky with David's dampness and her own. The boys had that musty sweet smell they took on after a heavy sleep, and Heather smelled of powder, maybe a hint of a diaper in need of changing. The children wormed their way between Shawn and David, snuggling, begging for closeness. David tickled Heather under her arm each time she lifted it, which she did repeatedly, her loving, trusting blue eyes on her daddy, giggling before the tips of his fingers had even found their mark.

Shawn opened her eyes and saw Alfredo and Violetta silhouetted on the tent roof. She sat up quickly. *Goddamn it.* She hated those memories of Heather, the ones that came in her sleep and tricked her into thinking nothing bad had happened, nothing bad could ever happen. When she woke up, reality hit her like a whip, and she felt the sting of losing Heather all over again.

"Are you all right?" David put his hand against the small of her back. She didn't budge, just nodded, afraid that if she moved, he would take his hand away. She needed that touch right now.

"Nightmare?"

She shook her head. "Memory," she said. If she said to him,

I remembered a Saturday morning, back when Heather was alive,
he would understand immediately. He would picture the scene,
the smells, the feel of five bodies interconnected. But she
couldn't say it. She stared at the seams in the closed flaps of the
tent until David took his hand from her back.

The trail leading to the Lost Troop was flooded, and Shawn
and Evan had to travel deeper into the forest to avoid the water.
It took them a long time to cut through the undergrowth. Evan
was cautious with his machete, and though his arm was healing
well, it was still stiff, and he held it close to his side.

Shawn was apprehensive as they neared the nesting tree of the
Lost Troop. They had hung ChoCho's cage and the accompa-
nying trap in a nearby tree, but all she could see now were the
tree's lush green branches, rainwater dripping from the leaves.

"ChoCho's gone." Evan spoke her fear out loud.

She looked down at the mud. She could see an indentation in
the ground where the trap had fallen from the tree, along with
the nearly illegible tracks of a small animal.

Evan lowered himself to the ground to examine the tracks.
"Looks like a paca," he said.

"There's the trap!" Shawn spotted the cage about ten yards
in front of them and began sloshing through the mud to get to
it. It was empty, one side caved in. She looked up at the trees.
"ChoCho's probably watching us. We have to find her."

"She's probably inside the paca."

"Evan."

"Let's go back. We need to get some bait to use here now."

"We can't go back without ChoCho," she said. "She's tame.
She won't be able to survive on her own."

"If I thought there was any chance she survived whatever
happened with that paca, I'd spend the rest of the day helping
you look. But I don't. Let's go."

She pressed her fingers to her eyes. She should have come out
here last night to get ChoCho. She couldn't believe she let a little
rain stand in her way. What kind of scientist was she? What kind
of *person*? She opened her eyes and touched Evan's shoulder. "I'd
like to pretend she's all right, okay? That maybe she'll appear in
our traps tomorrow or the next day. Let me have that fantasy."

"We have to save our fruit," Evan announced at dinner that
evening. "We need it to bait the trap at the Lost Troop now, as
well as to feed the tamarins."

"Fruit isn't the only thing we're going to run out of," said Tess, ladeling more water from the bucket. "We're low on toilet paper. You must be using it for things other than it was intended. We need to divide the remainder among us."

"Is that really necessary?" asked Evan. "Some of us might need it more than others."

"Yes, it's necessary." Tess turned to Meg. "And you won't have enough film for the trip back if you spend every hour of the day out there." She nodded her head toward the forest.

"It's not as though we're taking pictures nonstop," said David.

Tess balanced her mug on the table, in the crack between the saplings, and looked at David. "No, I'm certain it's not. Just what do the two of you do out there all day?"

Shawn tensed. There was a threat in Tess's voice.

"Talk," Meg said quietly. "It's nice to have someone to talk with."

"What are you insinuating, Meg?" Tess asked. "Am I depriving you?"

"No, I . . ."

"Leave her alone," said David.

"You!" Tess pointed her finger across the table at David. "You should be the last to cast stones. Why don't you pay some attention to your wife? You ignore her, while you chase after Meg like a dog with his tongue hanging out. She's a lesbian, you fool. Or is that what intrigues you? You think that maybe she'll begin to see things your way if you woo her just right?"

"Mind your own business," said David, his cheeks dark.

"I can't," Tess replied. "Not when your business crosses over into mine."

"Tess, there's nothing between David and me other than friendship." Meg looked desperate to be believed.

Tess stood up. "To be honest, Meg, I don't care what you do. Your body is your business. If you want to let a man have his way with you, fine." She leaned forward until her face was close to Meg's. "But do it on your own time. Not while you're my guest."

Tess grabbed her flashlight from the ground and stalked across the clearing to the stream. She disappeared into the darkness, and in a moment the engine on the dugout coughed to life. No one spoke as they listened to the sound of the motor fade downstream.

"Where is she going?" Robin asked.

"She probably just needs some time alone," said Meg.

"She scares me," said Robin. "I think she's crazy."

"She's not crazy," said Evan. "She knows exactly what she's doing. She's a calculating bitch."

"I'm sorry," Meg said. "I shouldn't have gotten her angry."

"You're not responsible for her," said David.

Meg looked at Shawn. "David and I are only friends," she said. "I hope you know that."

Shawn nodded uncertainly. She should have rescued David, said something about the divorce. David was only turning to Meg's company in self-defense.

Or was he?

It was very late when David came to bed. Shawn was still awake, listening, waiting. She knew he was with Meg. Comforting Meg. Was Tess justified in being jealous? And what if they *were* lovers? She was divorcing him. Then why did the thought of him making love to Meg cut a gash through her heart?

"Where do you think she went?" she asked him as he slipped under the sheet next to her.

He shrugged. "I don't know."

"The fishing tackle was in the boat. Maybe she'll just do some fishing."

"Maybe." He rolled onto his side, away from her.

She wanted to feel the length of his body next to hers.

"David?"

"Mm?"

"Are you going to spend our last few days here not talking to me?"

"I'm talking to you."

"Monosyllables."

He was quiet for a moment, and when he spoke, his words were heavy with frustration. "Nothing I do pleases you. I try to get close, and you push me away. I move away, and you want me closer."

She swallowed. "I know." What did she want from him? She was no longer certain.

"You're going to criticize me no matter what I do," he continued. "I can't win. You don't want to relate like husband and wife, and I can't make small talk with you as though we're no more than acquaintances. I'm doing the best I can, Shawn. I wish you'd just leave me alone.''

David found Meg sitting on a log by the stream the next morning, twisting a long blade of grass in her fingers, watching the water for a sign of the dugout. She'd written in that morning's note that Tess hadn't returned, and he knew she blamed herself.

He sat next to her. ''Let's go for a walk.''

She shook her head. ''I can't. If she comes back and finds I've gone off with you . . .''

''Meg, you're not guilty of anything.'' Last night he watched her inject herself with insulin, and he realized that the thought of being stranded had a different meaning for her than for the rest of them.

''My blood sugar's off,'' she had said to him as she drove the needle into the flesh below her ribs. ''I'm confused about what I should eat and how much insulin to take. The food's different than what I'm used to.''

''Come on,'' he said to her now. ''Maybe when we get back, she'll be here.'' Meg was his escape, and he wasn't about to give her up.

They walked along the stream, far past the Lost Troop. It felt good, the purposeless walking, although he knew Meg selected the route along the stream in the hope she would spot Tess.

When they were about to turn back, Meg caught his arm. ''Shh,'' she said.

He listened. There was a steady whisper coming from the trees ahead of them. They walked toward it and soon made out the sound of rushing water. They turned a bend in the stream, and there it was, a narrow blue-and-white cascade of water tumbling into the stream from a plateau high above their heads.

''This must be the waterfall Tess told us about when we were creek-drifting!'' Meg pushed her way through the tangled vines to the bank. She wore the first smile he'd seen on her face in a while. He opened a path in the vines with his arms, and stepped onto the bank next to her. The waterfall emptied into a pool similar to their bathing pool, but this water had a foamy, fresh look to it. There were flat rocks below them, and Meg stepped onto one, lifted her camera to her eyes, and snapped the shutter.

There was a hole in the canopy, and the sun poured through it, concentrating its rays on Meg's hair where it spilled from her hat. She changed her lens, then shot a few more pictures. She moved around on the rocks, stepped back on the bank, then back to the rocks again, and he could tell she was creating something magical inside her camera.

"I'll have to come here in the mist some morning," she said.

"It's too far to walk before the sun comes up. You'd have to camp here the night before." He sat down on a rock and looked into the water. He watched a school of long translucent fish as they nipped at the green algae that covered the rock just below the water's surface. "Maybe I could come with you."

She looked at him. "I've been thinking about what Tess said, about how you should pay more attention to Shawn. I think she's right."

He stared at the translucent fish. They had long pointed noses, like needles.

Meg continued. "Don't you worry about all the time she and Evan spend together?"

"No." He stretched out his legs and leaned back on his arms, feeling the sun on his face for the first time in days. "I'm grateful to Evan. He's been there for Shawn when I haven't been, for one reason or another."

"The past few days you've been awfully cool to her. I hope you don't mind my saying that. Interfering, I mean."

He took a deep breath. There was no reason not to tell her. Still, he had to force himself to say the words out loud, because then he could no longer pretend he had heard Shawn incorrectly. "Shawn wants a divorce," he said.

Meg sat up straight, back arched like a dancer's. "A *divorce*? Why? It's not because of me, is it?"

"It has nothing to do with you." The reason was clear in his own mind. Shawn didn't need to spell it out for him. "It has to do with something that happened a long time ago. Something I did."

"I can't imagine you doing anything that terrible."

He was going to tell her. He rubbed his palms together, and his heart galloped against the walls of his chest. He would get through it, every detail. Everything he'd hidden from himself for the last three years.

"I'd like to tell you about my daughter," he said.

• Twenty-Five •

HE TOOK THE day off to drive Shawn and Evan to the airport for their trip to Peru. Shawn was excited. David had no idea it would be the last time he would see that familiar, anticipatory glow in her eyes, that devilish grin, and the dimples that made her look girlish despite the fact that she was thirty-five. She sat between the front seats of the Bronco, ignoring the seat belt warning sign, clutching David's arm and gnawing on his shoulder. She told him she loved him, that she would think of him when she was alone and horny in her tent at night.

In the rearview mirror, he caught Evan's smile.

"You should be coming with us, David," Evan said. "I can't be responsible for her behavior if we meet up with any native men, with their loincloths and fertility drugs."

He had not considered going. He would miss her terribly, but the thought of a few weeks alone with his kids was seductive. They could go to Disneyland, Universal Studios. The kids were as excited as he was. As soon as he got back from the airport, he would take them to the beach.

There was more to getting ready for the beach than he'd anticipated, and it was eleven by the time the four of them climbed into the car for the ride. He was certain he'd thought of everything. He had plenty of sunscreen, a blanket for the boys, another for himself and Heather. Towels, shovel and pail, a cooler with juice, a little straw hat for Heather because she was so fair. He worried her nose would burn even with the sunscreen. It had happened before. He would keep an eye on her; they could leave early if she was getting too pink.

"We don't have to go to La Jolla Cove again, do we?" Keith whined as he climbed into the backseat next to his brother.

"No." David buckled Heather into her seat.

"Don't pinch my tummy, D-daddy." Heather cringed, her

hand across her stomach, above the ruffled yellow bikini bottoms.

"I won't, honey." He did that once; it must have been two years ago, but she never forgot. He accidentally caught her skin in the seatbelt buckle, and it left a tiny purple mark on her stomach for a week. He thought then how vulnerable she was, how dependent she was on him not to make a mistake.

"So what *beach*, Dad?" Keith asked impatiently.

"Windansea?" David started the car and smiled to himself as the boys whooped happily in the backseat.

Heather made up songs as they drove. He tried to join in the singing, which made her giggle, and he thought there was no finer sound in the world. But suddenly her face clouded over. "When's Mommy coming home?"

"Heather, you're so dumb," said Jamie. "She hasn't even gotten where she's going yet."

Heather's lower lip started to quiver, and David turned around to give Jamie a warning look. He parked the car a block from the beach and took the boys to one side while Heather unbuckled herself from her seat.

"She's only four, guys, come on," he said. "She's not used to being without Mom, and it doesn't help when you tease her like that. She's a little scared right now."

"She's always scared," said Jamie. "She's such a baby."

Jamie was right. Heather was more fearful than other four-year-olds. Her nursery-school teacher called them in to talk about it a couple of months ago, and David and Shawn lay awake the night after that meeting, trying to puzzle it out. Shawn had a theory.

"She does the worrying for the rest of us," she said. "She probably figures someone's got to do it in this family."

That made as much sense as anything else. After all, Heather had a father who spent morning and evening in a small plane, and a mother who walked around the house with a snake draped over her shoulders and who spoke incessantly about skydiving. Her brothers landed in the emergency room monthly with one battle wound or another. Someone had to do the worrying. But it made him sad to think of his little girl carrying that burden around with her.

They spread their blankets close to the water, and he slathered lotion over every exposed inch of her and on the boys' shoulders and cheeks.

It was hot. Heather played by the blanket, dragging buckets

of water up from the ocean to wet the sand. She dug holes and
built mountains and made up more songs while he lay on the
blanket, opening his eyes from time to time to see the dusting
of sand on her busy little arms and legs.

After a while he sat up. The ocean was nearly as calm as the
bay today. He had given the boys money to rent rafts, and he
spotted them in the water, trying in vain to find a decent wave
to carry them to shore.

"Let's go for a swim, Heather," he said.

Heather squinted toward the water. "Those waves look way
too b-big."

He laughed. "They're pretty puny today," he said, but then
he remembered that she was used to the sheltered water of the
Cove. "Come on," he said. "Piggyback."

That she couldn't resist, and he carried her on his shoulders
to the water's edge. He set her on her feet, and she began jumping up and down in excitement.

"Let the waves try to catch you," he coaxed.

She hesitated a moment, but then suddenly she was running
through the water, laughing and yelping. He was pleased. Maybe
something happened at age four. Maybe old fears fell away, a
new security set in. He sat down where the waves washed up on
the beach and watched his brave four-year-old daughter taunt the
ocean.

How many times then did he say the words "See? There's
nothing to be afraid of"? If only he said, just once, *Be careful*,
or, *Only go in with me*.

He took her back to the blanket and dried her off. She giggled,
giddy with her achievement. "Now I can go out where Jamie
and Keith are," she said.

"That's too far for you." He rubbed sunscreen on her nose.

"I c-could float on a raft."

"I'll go out with you again later." He stretched out on his
back, and she lay next to him on her stomach. There was a ridge
of sand above her upper lip that made him smile.

"I love you," he said. He watched her shut her eyes, and then
he shut his own.

"Where's Heather?"

David opened his eyes to see Jamie above him, rubbing himself with a towel. He sat up and looked to his side. Keith sat
where Heather had been. For a moment, he felt nothing in the
way of alarm. She was all right, probably within a few feet of

the blanket. He looked around them, sectioning off the beach with his eyes, hunting for the yellow bikini, the straw hat.

"I don't see her," he said. He felt the boys looking at each other. "Let's spread out and look . . ." Then he saw the straw hat. The waves were larger now, white and swollen, and they tossed the hat into the air. He ran into the water and grabbed it.

"Heather!" he called, but all he heard was the crashing of the waves.

The lifeguards found her so quickly that he thought surely she would be all right. She *looked* all right, except for the seaweed that wrapped around her legs like some insidious sea creature. The lifeguards laid her on the beach and pumped the water out of her while he watched. He felt a horrible paralysis work its way into his limbs. He couldn't move. Then one of the lifeguards, a very young blond boy, began breathing into her mouth. *That's right,* David thought, *that's the way to do it.* Any minute she would begin breathing on her own.

A crowd gathered around them, but he barely noticed. Jamie and Keith clung to him, suddenly little boys again. Keith was crying, pressing his head against David's rib cage.

"She'll be okay." He put his arm around his son. "She'll be fine."

They followed the ambulance to the hospital, and he told the boys that by now she was probably breathing on her own. They'd gotten to her quickly, he said, and the ambulance had special equipment. She was probably waking up right now as he spoke. She would be pretty scared, waking up with a bunch of strangers around her, but that would be the worst of it: She'd be scared.

The boys said nothing. Keith would not stop crying, and David was annoyed that his son wasn't listening to his words of comfort, that he didn't believe him. When he pulled into the emergency room parking lot, he thought he would explode if he had to listen to another second of Keith's sniveling. He turned the boy toward him and smacked him across the face with the back of his hand. "Stop it, goddamn it! I said she'll be all right!"

Keith stared at him, openmouthed. The tears left wide, wet bands down his cheeks, and his soft brown eyes were still full. David took his son's face in his hands. He never hit his kids, rarely even raised his voice to them. "I'm sorry," he said. "I'm upset. Let's go inside."

Someone in the emergency room found shirts for them to put on over their bathing suits, and someone else called Lynn. She arrived and took the boys back to her house, then she returned

to the hospital and sat with David in a tiny, private room next
to the central waiting area. They sat on wooden chairs on opposite sides of the little room for over an hour. David stared at
his hands. He wished he could take back hitting Keith.

"Mr. Ryder?"

He looked up into the eyes of a very young woman. No, not
so young. There was gray in her reddish hair and something in
her eyes that looked like her own personal failure.

"Yes." He didn't get up.

The woman lowered herself to one knee in front of him, as if
she were about to propose. She wrapped a cool hard hand around
his where it rested useless on his knee.

"I'm sorry," she said. "She's on a respirator, but there are
no brain waves. We tried everything."

Lynn began to cry, but David was mesmerized by this woman's eyes. There were tears along the lower lids, reflecting the
fluorescent light above them. She had no right to those tears.

He stood up abruptly, knocking her off balance. "I want to
see her," he said. Obviously, they had done it wrong. He had
to get to her quickly, before it was too late.

They left him alone with her. She was lying on a long table.
She was so small, smaller than his memory of her. There was a
thick tube in her mouth attached to a machine behind the table.
He stood next to her and took her hand. "Heather?"

They had told him she couldn't hear him, that her brain waves
were flat. How flat was flat? How carefully had they checked the
monitor? They could have missed a little hill or two, couldn't they?

"Heather, honey, it's Daddy." He began to cry. Oh, God, he
hoped she hadn't suffered; he hoped she had no idea what was
happening to her. How quickly had she lost consciousness? *God,
don't let her have been scared.* He remembered the seaweed
knotted around her legs. He hoped that happened after she lost
consciousness. She would have been terrified. He could picture
that frightened look on her face. He wondered if she tried to call
out for him, while he lay asleep on the blanket.

He needed Shawn. She was in a plane right now, putting thousands of miles between them. How could he tell her? What words
could he use? He would give anything to have her here, to feel her
arms around him, to lay his head on her shoulder and cry.

He felt Lynn's hand on his arm. How long had she been standing next to him?

"Let's go back to my house, David."

"It was my fault."

"Oh David, no. Don't even think that. She was an inquisitive little girl. How could you know she'd go back in the water?"

David sighed. "Heather was not inquisitive," he said. "She played it safe every step of the way. She was four. She needed to be watched at the beach. I fell asleep. I screwed up, Lynn."

When he opened his eyes, he was alone on the rock, stretched out on his back. Through the opening in the tunnel of trees above him, he saw the liquid blue of the sky. The sound of the waterfall filled his ears. He shut his eyes again. His head felt heavy; his throat tight from the strain of holding back tears.

"You're awake." Meg sat next to him on the rock. "You slept a long time. How do you feel?" She touched her palm to his cheek as if testing for fever. That was how he felt, as though he had just endured a brief but brutal illness, an attack of something he fully expected to die from. But he was alive. Surgery, that's what it was. The cancer had been successfully removed, cut out. Still, his surgeon looked concerned as she leaned over him.

He rolled toward her, set his head against her thigh, and wrapped an arm around her waist. "I'm all right," he said. He was not a monster. He had told her the worst about himself, and she was still here, her hand stroking his hair. He had been braced for her to pull away from him as he drove home the point that he was responsible for Heather's death.

"When are you going to forgive yourself?" she'd said to him. "Never."

"What good will that do?" She pointed out his good intention, wanting to take his children to a different beach as a special treat. Others had said this to him. Many others. Everyone except Shawn. But the words never rang true until now. Maybe enough time had passed. Yes, he should have kept a better eye on Heather, but that in no way diminished his love for her. Shawn kept his guilt alive. He felt a flood of anger toward Shawn, a feeling terrifying and new. *Damn her.*

He sat up now and took in a deep breath, full of the fresh scent of the waterfall. His left arm still circled Meg's waist, and with the fingertips of his right hand he traced the line of her cheek. He leaned over to kiss her, gently, gratefully, and she left her lips on his for a moment before turning her head away.

"You're just beginning to forgive yourself for one mistake, David," she said softly. "Don't put another in its place."

· Twenty-Six ·

DAVID WAS CHANGING. It had been gradual over the last week or so, but now there was a sudden leap, an iciness, a wall Shawn couldn't dent. Something pulled him away from her. When he returned from the forest with Meg the day before, he was different. He actually *looked* different, although she couldn't put her finger on it. Maybe it was the way he stared at her at dinner. He looked hard into her eyes until she had to look away. And that was what he wanted, she thought, to make her look away. For the first time *he* wanted the distance between them, and for the first time he had the power to create it.

He was still asleep next to her when she unzipped the mosquito netting to reach for Meg's note. She unfolded it quietly and held it into the early morning light. Just one line: *Thanks for trusting me.*

"I think that's mine."

She started at the sound of his voice, her cheeks burning. "I'm sorry," she said. "I reached for my shoes and got yours by mistake."

He held out his hand, and she set the note on his palm. His expression remained impassive as he read it.

"From Meg?" she asked, innocently.

He nodded as he reached into his duffel bag for a shirt.

"You've gotten close."

"She's easy to talk to."

"You used to say that about me," she said, as though she were the injured party in this relationship.

"You haven't been easy to talk to for quite a while."

He left the tent without saying anything more. She watched him walk down the trail to the clearing, his machete slung low on one hip. What did she expect? She was the one who started this roller coaster. Now that she wanted to get off, it was too late. David was enjoying the ride.

* * *

"Hey, wake up, we've got problems!"

She opened her eyes as Evan reached inside the tent to shake her foot. She groaned, checked her watch. It was after seven. She must have fallen asleep again after David left.

"What's wrong?" She sat up.

"We lost most of our food. Something got into it, not sure what. Something big. A tapir, maybe."

She knelt forward. "Come in," she said.

"I'll stay out here, thanks. I don't trust myself in there with you." He pulled the mosquito netting to the side with his fingers and looked at her. "We never got to wake up together in the morning. I wish we had . . . You look so good. Your eyes have this half-sleepy, half-sexy look to them and that T-shirt . . ."

"Are you trying to drive me crazy?"

"Probably." He dropped the netting, and it fell between them. She pulled on her shorts. "Is Tess back?"

He shook his head. "I don't know whether to be worried or angry. She could be hurt. We should take the little canoe out and look for her."

"Tess is invulnerable," Shawn said as she buttoned her blue workshirt over the T-shirt she'd worn to bed. "She's probably staying away to make us squirm. But she'll be back. She has her professional reputation to protect."

The blue tarp over the food supply was shredded and torn. Pieces of it adorned the bushes around the clearing. The plastic bags containing rice and beans had been chewed through, and flour dusted the ground and nearby shrubs. The mangoes and bananas that had been under the tarp were gone, but there were still a couple of bunches of bananas hanging from the tamarin tree.

David and Meg gathered the cans of food that were scattered in the brush, while Robin sat on the ground staring at a handful of dried beans in her palm. "What are we going to do *now*?" she wailed. "We don't even have enough food to last until Tuesday."

"Yes, we do," Evan reassured her. "Tess will get back with the fishing tackle, and she knows which plants are edible. We'll be fine."

Today was Friday. Tuesday they were to leave, travel in the dugout back to the Rio Tavaco where they'd meet up again with Charlie's boat. The trip would be longer this time, going upriver.

Manuel wouldn't pick them up until late Wednesday, and they wouldn't reach San Diego until Thursday night. *San Diego.* It sounded good to Shawn. She was ready to go home.

Later that morning, one of the baby Elves cut herself on a piece of wire jutting from the side of the cage. Shawn and Evan peered into the cage from opposite sides. The gash ran the length of her tiny back, and blood glistened against her fur.

"It's our fault," said Shawn. They should have been more careful with the wire.

"Let's see what we can do for her," said Evan.

David, Robin, and Meg watched as Shawn set the trap on the table. The Elf's eyes were closed and she mewed, as Tika had done just before her death. She flinched when Evan injected her with the anesthetic.

Shawn gently lifted the tamarin out of the trap and set her on the table.

"Ugh," said Robin. "Its back's a mess."

Evan secured the little monkey between the saplings of the table top and poured alcohol over the wound. He handed Shawn a needle and thread. "You're the seamstress," he said. "I want to watch this time."

She tied the stitches while Evan held the edges of the wound together. The top of his head touched hers as they worked, and she sewed more slowly than she might have otherwise. Her fingers brushed his each time she moved the needle.

"God, that's nice, the way you do that," he said quietly, as if he were commenting on how she touched him instead of the work she was doing on the Elf.

If no one else were around and Evan suggested they make love right now, she would say yes. She felt so needy, and his gentleness was a lure. No one could make her forget her pain the way Evan could. She would have to watch herself today. Her will was very weak.

David stood up suddenly. "I found some fishing line down by the stream," he said. "Maybe I can catch something for dinner."

"That'd be great," said Evan, without looking up. Then he said to Shawn in a quiet voice, "I think this will heal nicely." He ran his thumb over the back of Shawn's hand, and she met his eyes. What she saw in them had nothing to do with tamarins. She lowered her eyes back to the Elf. Whatever she felt, Evan felt as well, and that made it twice as dangerous.

* * *

David was not much of a fisherman, and his equipment was limited. He found a fairly decent length of line with a hook miraculously attached to one end. Tess must have left it behind on one of her outings. He tied the line to a long branch and impaled a fat roachlike bug on the hook. He sat on the small yellow canoe that rested upside down on the bank and set his line into the water. The roach floated on the water's surface, looking dead and unappetizing. He watched it for a few minutes, then fashioned a sinker out of a small stone, and tried again.

He had taken the boys fishing a few times. They rented a little boat and took it out on Lake Wholford. They never caught a thing, but he remembered the outings warmly. Time with the boys alone, the men in the family. Each of those days followed a pattern. The morning was given to quiet anticipation, a discussion of the fish in the lake, the possibility of bringing home supper. The afternoon took a different turn as the boys talked to him, about school, about friends. They talked to him easily, better than they did to Shawn. Didn't that count for something? Wouldn't a judge say the boys should be with the parent who knew how to draw them out? Shawn used to be good at it, but the last few years she frightened them with her unpredictable moods. He saw it in the boys' faces, in the ugly bravado they showed her to protect themselves from being hurt. Either she lashed out at them for no apparent reason—not apparent to them, at any rate—or she drew them so close to her that they panicked under her overprotective wing.

She was not a bad mother. He had to admit that. But he needed justification for the anger he felt toward her today. He couldn't shake it. That was why he went off alone, without Meg. He wasn't certain he could control what was festering inside him. Talking about Heather yesterday freed him, unleashed something in him he'd been holding tight for the last three years.

Shawn had punished him. God, how she punished him! He welcomed it at first because he thought he earned it, but now he knew better.

He'd watched Shawn and Evan working together on that tamarin, putting the little Elf back together again. He saw the precision in their work, the way they read each other's intent. Their heads touching, their hands. He watched until he could watch no longer. Not today, with the anger bubbling to the surface. He didn't know if he could be civil to Shawn for the rest of this trip.

* * *

In the first few weeks after Heather died, David spent most of his time either working or alone in the house. Shawn was at the Center taking care of the abandoned infant tamarin, Tika. He knew she was glad to have an escape from him. Before she left, she took Keith and Jamie to Lynn's. She didn't trust David with them. He should have put up an argument, but the truth was he didn't trust himself. He felt his life slipping through his fingers; everything he touched seemed liquid. Being left alone in a house scattered with memories of Heather magnified that feeling. The only place he felt in control was in the plane.

He had killed his daughter. As surely as if he'd taken a knife to her heart, he killed her. The Child Protection people let him off too easily. He told them he had fallen asleep; he even told them that he *intended* to fall asleep, that it never occurred to him it would be a problem. He waited for them to say he was negligent and in need of punishment. But they looked at him with sympathy in their eyes and called the whole thing an accident. He didn't feel vindicated. He didn't feel cleansed.

He'd killed Shawn as well. Oh, there was still this living, breathing woman who looked like Shawn, but she was clearly an impostor. He was afraid of her. She had weapons in the form of words, which she sharpened to lethal points to throw in his direction.

He lay awake at night in his empty house, trying to think of ways to reach her without being damaged too much in the process. He was very, very fragile. The real Shawn would have known that, but her impostor had no idea he could break so easily, that it wouldn't take much.

When she had been gone three nights, he decided he had to do something. This was crazy. All the years they'd had together, all the incredibly fine years, had to count for something. They had forgotten how to talk. That was his fault. He'd shut down. Why did he do that? What was he afraid of? He might fall apart. Most likely he would. So what? It wouldn't be the end of the earth if he cried in her arms. That's what he'd wanted to do that first night when she came back from Peru, but the weight of his guilt caught up with him then, and he couldn't speak at all.

Now she was so quick with her barbs that it was easier to say nothing, but this could not continue. He had to try. He would tell her it was hard for him. He would beg her to listen to him. He needed her back so badly.

He got out of bed and dressed. He would go now, in the

middle of the night, when she would be soft with sleep and her guard would be down. The thought of holding her filled him with longing. Didn't she miss that closeness? Didn't she miss *him*?

He had his own code card to let him in the main gate of the Conservation Center. The grounds were eerily lit by a round, white moon, and he drove the long road past the maned wolves and zebras, thinking that Shawn was very brave to stay out here by herself.

He parked his car next to her Bronco in the lot and walked down the hill past the Pentagon. There were no lights on in there, and he couldn't tell if the tiny Copper Elves were inside or out tonight. He ran his fingers across the rough stucco of the building. He was happy just to be here, to feel close to Shawn, to have his hand on this building she loved.

He neared the long, one-story building where Shawn had her office. The windows were dark, and there was no answer when he knocked on her door, but he wasn't surprised. Most likely she was staying in Evan's office, where the sofa converted into a bed.

He tapped lightly on the door to Evan's office. There was no answer, and he tried the knob. It turned under his hand, and he shook his head. He wished she would be more careful. Anyone could walk in on her while she slept.

He opened the door. The room was lit only by the moon, but he needed no other light to clarify what he saw. Shawn was in the bed, asleep, curled up in Evan's protective arms. The moon outlined their bare shoulders in gold; their bodies gave off heat he could feel from the doorway.

He stepped back outside, closing the door softly behind him. He forced his legs to move a few steps to the right before lowering himself to the ground. He leaned his back against the cool stucco of the building and tried to steady his breathing. The hills around the Center were bathed with moonlight, and everything was still. The only sound he heard was the blood pumping in his head.

He deserved this. He wanted to be punished, right? This was a fitting punishment for what he had done. He felt no betrayal. Certainly not by Shawn—she was hardly responsible for her actions, and it was clever of her to come up with the most excruciating punishment possible. And Evan? Evan was only lending himself to the cause.

Evan had called him the night before last, after he got back from Peru. He was stunned when David told him about Heather. He said he would speak to Shawn, try to talk her into coming home. But he never said he would spend the night with her. He never said he would be her lover.

David sat there for most of the night, watching the moon work its way across the sky, noticing how the blanket of light slowly shifted from one side of the rolling, chaparral-covered hills to the other. Occasionally he heard coyotes calling from Elephant Ridge and felt the stucco turn cold against his back.

At four-thirty he made himself get up and walk to his car. His legs belonged to someone else, someone returning from a long sea voyage, perhaps. He had to get to the airport. For the first time since Heather's death, he wondered if he could work. He had managed every day so far, and it was his salvation. It gave him a few hours each day when he could think about nothing other than the traffic below him and keeping the plane aloft.

Louise took one look at him when he walked into the airport and called him into her office. "You're sick," she said, staring into his eyes.

"No, I'm not. I'm fine."

He felt drugged as Louise took his arm and led him to a chair. "You're not fine," she said. "Sit down."

He smiled. "I didn't sleep well last night, that's all." He heard the smooth silk of his voice. He could fool anyone.

Louise sat behind her desk and brushed a strand of gray hair off her forehead. "You've done an extraordinary job, David," she said softly. "But enough is enough. I don't want you up there today. You go home, get some sleep. Take a few days off."

The image of the plane sinking into the bay slipped into his mind, and he let it stay there. It would look like an accident. *Popular airborne traffic reporter David Ryder dies in freak plane crash two weeks after daughter's tragic death.* He was well insured. The boys would be taken care of.

"David? Are you listening to me?" Louise's green eyes were narrowed at him. "Go home. Bob can do the traffic from the ground."

"I don't want to go home." The last word caught in his throat. *God, no tears please, not here.* He knew he sounded like a child. He felt like one too, afraid of the emptiness waiting for him at home.

"Let me call Shawn to come get you."

"*No.*" He stood up. "I'll go. I'll be in tomorrow."

* * *

It was six-thirty by the time he got home, and he found Shawn sitting at the kitchen table, drinking coffee. She looked surprised when he walked in. "Why are you home?" she asked.

"Louise thought I looked sick." He couldn't meet her eyes.

"You don't look very well," she said.

He walked stiffly to the counter to pour himself a cup of coffee. "What are you doing home?" he asked.

"Tika's better."

"That's good." He sat down at the table.

"Plus Lynn called this morning. Keith got sick again last night. That's the fifth time. I'm taking him to the doctor."

"I can take him."

"No." She reddened, lifted one shaky hand to her forehead.

He reached over and took her hand. It was cold, and the bones trembled under his fingers. "Are you ever going to trust me with them again?"

"I've made the arrangements." She pulled her hand away. "I'll pick them up at eight-thirty. You can go back to bed."

"Shawn . . ." He stared at his distorted reflection in the coffee cup. He wasn't sure how to word the question he wanted to ask her, and he was afraid of her answer. "Do you . . . have you stopped loving me?"

She stood up and carried her cup to the sink. "I'm pretty confused, David."

She left the room, and he wrapped his hands tightly around the mug. At least she was home, talking to him. It was as much as he could ask for right now.

He was not able to sleep, and when she left to pick up the boys, he got out of bed. He walked to the closet near the bathroom. He rummaged through the shelves looking for Shawn's diaphragm. She had used it for a few months after Heather was born, before he had the vasectomy, but she never threw it away. She still used it sometimes, when the flow was heavy early in her period, and she wanted to make love without a mess.

The diaphragm wasn't there. He didn't know why he felt the need to have tangible proof of her infidelity. Certainly he could ask for no better proof than seeing them together in the same bed.

He found her briefcase in the kitchen. He unzipped the top and slipped his hand first on one side, then the other. His fingers touched the plastic case, and he pulled it out along with a dented tube of spermicidal jelly. He put them back where he found them and returned to bed.

* * *

Evan met him at the health club at ten on Saturday, as he had for the last four years. David was quiet as they walked onto the racquetball court. He couldn't look Evan in the eye, but every chance he got he found himself staring at his old friend as if he had never seen him before. He stared at the muscular dark legs, the tight, powerful arms. He wondered how he made love to Shawn, how his hands touched her, his mouth.

He beat Evan, both games. A true rarity. Evan put a sweaty arm around him as they walked toward the locker room. "Shit, David," he laughed. "You played like you wanted to kill me."

David smiled. The muscles in his arms felt loose and smooth. But for the first time, he felt awkward in the locker room with Evan. He dressed quickly and kept his eyes from Evan's body.

"You up for a burger and beer?" Evan asked.

"Sure."

They drove separately to the restaurant as they did every Saturday in the past and met at a table in the bar.

"Shawn's done a terrific job with that little tamarin," Evan said as he took a swallow of beer. He was trying to make small talk. David felt a little sorry for him.

"She threw herself into taking care of it," David said.

Evan set down the beer and folded his hands on the table in front of him. He stared down at his fingers. When he looked up, his eyes shone in the dim light of the bar, and David felt the muscles in his chest tighten.

"I was so shocked when you told me about Heather on the phone the other night that I didn't have a chance to tell you how sorry I am," Evan said.

"Thanks. It's been rough."

Evan nodded. "I can tell that from talking to Shawn. She's not like herself."

David shook his head. "No."

"And she said the boys haven't taken it too well." He leaned back while their hamburgers were set in front of them.

"Keith's better. He was sick for a while."

Evan nodded. Obviously he knew. "Yeah, Shawn said the doctor gave him something."

Keith took a pill now before he went to bed, and it seemed to settle his stomach. But Jamie still had nightmares; there was no pill for that.

"Poor kids," said Evan. "I guess they saw the whole thing with Heather, huh?"

"Yes."

Evan set his hamburger back on the plate. "If there's any way I can help, please tell me. I asked Shawn to let me take Keith and Jamie for the weekend, so you two could get away or just have some time for yourselves."

"You did?" David was stunned.

"Yeah. I'd love it. You know I'm crazy about your kids. But she said no. Not now, anyway."

"Thanks for trying."

"David, if this isn't any of my business, tell me, okay? But, I love you two. I can't sit back and watch while the two of you . . . I mean, I know things aren't good between you right now."

David watched Evan trying to pick his words, thinking, *this man is not my enemy.*

"She's hurting," Evan continued. "I don't think you know how much."

"She doesn't talk to me."

Evan nodded. "She's angry. You're getting it all, but she's angry at herself and at God and Heather and everyone. You're the only convenient target she has."

"She's angry with everyone except you."

A guarded look came into Evan's eyes. "What do you mean?"

"I mean apparently she's talking to you."

"Yeah, well. Maybe you could try harder, draw her out a little. I know you've got your own shit to carry around with you, but she needs more than she's getting right now."

She needs more than you can give her. Jude Mandell's words. Had they finally come true, in a way he never anticipated? "I guess I don't have it to give right now," David said.

He felt a bizarre rush of gratitude toward Evan for filling the gap. If this was what Shawn needed, fine. He owed Evan.

He picked up the tab for lunch.

• Twenty-Seven •

DAVID LOOKED OVER the meager offerings for breakfast—two tablespoonfuls of oatmeal apiece, one banana appropriated from the tamarin supply, tea—and his stomach growled. He looked across the table at Meg. Her face looked thinner than it did a week ago, her cheeks drawn. How long could she manage on so little to eat?

He had caught no fish the day before. They would literally run out of food in a day or two. They'd been very dependent on Tess's fish, very dependent on *Tess*. Where was she? Evan and Shawn had taken the small canoe out on the stream yesterday to look for her. They went several miles downstream and back but saw no sign of her. David wasn't surprised. Tess was too clever to be found if she didn't want to be. He pictured her nearby, frying fresh catfish over a fire, checking out the flora in a new location. But no, she left her botany books here and her cigarettes. That worried him. She left in a hurry, unprepared to stay away for long. She had the fishing gear only because it was stored in the dugout. She *could* be hurt. She could be dead. Still, in his imagination he saw her waiting a mile or two downstream until Tuesday. She would make them suffer until the last minute.

He decided to take a swim after breakfast. He started out next to the clearing and worked against the current. The water was warm and silky, the current easy to battle. That disappointed him. It gave him too much time to think, and he wanted no more of that.

"David?"

He stopped stroking and looked up. Evan stood in the water a few yards north of him, his hair white with lather. David had reached their bathing pool.

He set his feet on the soft bottom of the stream and walked into the pool. "I didn't realize I'd come this far," he said. He was winded. He was not in his usual good shape.

Evan worked the lather into his scalp. The white suds changed his appearance, made him look softer, a little cherubic despite the beard. "Don't work up an appetite," he said.

"Nothing could make me hungrier than I am already." David boosted himself onto one of the flat rocks. He was wearing a navy blue striped bathing suit. He could see that Evan wore nothing under the water.

David ran his fingers through his wet hair. "I guess Shawn told you about her plans," he said, feeling awkward. It seemed like a long time since he and Evan had really talked.

"What plans?"

"The divorce."

"Oh. Yes, she told me." Evan dipped his hand into the pool and watched the water trickle out from between his fingers. "I was sorry to hear that."

David waited for him to say something more, to ask him how he felt, or to ask if he should try to talk some sense into her. Evan was dependable for that; he was not one to let a difficult topic slip by unconfronted. But he seemed to have no more to say. He lowered himself into the water, rinsing the shampoo from his hair. When he stood up again, his hair sparkled like black jewels and the water glistened on his skin. He started walking toward the bank, and a brittle silence filled the air between them.

"I know you'll still be working with her every day . . ." David said quickly, ". . . but I'd like it if you and I could stay friends."

Evan nodded as though it was not a matter of much consequence, and maybe to him it wasn't. He had his family now, and he would still have Shawn. He would actually see far more of Shawn than David would. Didn't Evan remember what it was like to have no one?

"I think I'll really need . . ." David wanted to say *your friendship* but was afraid of sounding melodramatic. "I'll need those racquetball games. I mean, I'll be living alone then." Living alone. His voice was casual. Ah yes, emotions in hiding.

Evan nodded again. "I hope we can work it out."

David felt alarmed. "Why couldn't we?" he asked.

"No reason. I just meant, we'll have to take things one step at a time." He finally looked David directly in the eye. "Listen, don't worry about this. Of course we'll stay friends."

David rubbed his palms over the smooth surface of the rock. "Do you think she's doing the right thing?" he asked.

"I think she's a fool," Evan said, but then he caught himself. David saw it—Evan didn't want to betray Shawn. "But it's her life and her decision."

"It's my life too," David said.

"And mine." Evan turned away quickly as if he'd said two words too many. David was quiet. He wouldn't ask him what he meant. It could have been any number of things, couldn't it? But the thought that ran through his mind was disquieting. He saw them working on the tamarin again, heads bowed and touching. Could there be something new between them?

He knew exactly when Shawn's affair with Evan ended because he fell into the habit of checking her briefcase for the diaphragm. He watched the tube of spermicidal jelly develop new dents, be replaced, and shrink again. At least she was careful.

At first he thought it would not be an affair at all, not in the true sense. He could understand their making love once or twice, or perhaps several times. He could accept that. But it continued, and he submitted to it powerlessly. He would let Shawn determine the length of his penance.

That year was the hardest of his life. In the evenings, while Shawn was at one of her "meetings," he would feed the twins, take them out for ice cream or a movie, all the while picturing Shawn in Evan's office, Evan unbuttoning her blouse, slipping it off her shoulders. Or worse, he pictured Shawn's long fingers skimming over Evan's skin, her thick black hair grazing his stomach as she leaned down to take him in her mouth. It hurt to imagine Shawn in an active role. At home she was totally passive, her body like so much cold tissue she was obliged to carry around with her. But what hurt most to think about was not the consummation of the act, not their lovemaking at all, but the conversations he imagined preceded and followed, the conversations where Shawn told Evan how she felt, how heavy her heart was with the loss of her daughter, with the lifeless marriage she was forced to live out, and Evan's warm words in return. The thought of that intimacy between them when he was so thoroughly left out hurt him more brutally than the image of their interlocking bodies possibly could.

It ended when Evan got engaged to Robin. The diaphragm disappeared from the briefcase, reappeared on the closet shelf. Suddenly there were fewer meetings Shawn needed to attend, and for a few weeks David felt optimistic. He wanted to give

Evan and Robin something spectacular as a wedding gift, something to solidify that union, an expression of his gratitude that
this miserable year had come to a close. He and Shawn finally
agreed to give the newlyweds a trip to Hawaii. They could easily
afford it. After all, they weren't going anywhere themselves.

He hoped that would change once the affair was over, but
Shawn remained as unreachable as ever. Perhaps she was even
a little worse, embittered at finding herself cut off from Evan
and in a marriage that had crumbled to dust in her absence.

He sat in Meg's tent after dinner that night, skimming through
one of Tess's botany books. He thought the book might tell them
what plants were edible, but the authors apparently saw no need
for that information. He held in his hand a sprig of small, fern-
like leaves and bloodred berries. He could not locate them in
the book at all. Meg sat across from him, turning the pages of
a second book, having no more luck herself.

"Let me see them." She reached for the berries, and he set
them in her fingers. He felt the affection build in him as he
watched her study the book. Her long blond hair was splayed
like a sea creature over her shoulders and across her arms. Her
tan shirt was open to the third button, and she sat with her legs
wide apart, knees bent, left elbow on left knee, right hand turning pages. Her posture was relaxed and open, a human half-
circle, a tempting crescent for him to slip into. If he were to
kiss her now, she wouldn't turn her head away. It would be so
easy. He could ease forward, take the book from under her hand,
lay it next to them on the tent floor, and gently set his lips against
hers. He was certain she wouldn't resist tonight, and so he
mustn't kiss her. It would feel too much like revenge, as angry
as he was with Shawn right now. And there was always a chance
Shawn would change her mind. Then how would he feel if he'd
made love to Meg? Did Meg know how she tempted him tonight? She lifted her head, and he felt a disconcerting crack in
his resolve as she looked out at him from beneath her gold bangs.

"The books are no help." She rolled one of the berries between her fingers. "I'm willing to try them, though. Are you?"

In the shadowy light from the lantern, her lips and the berries
were the same color, as though she had squeezed a berry between her fingers and painted her lips with its juice.

He shook his head. "No, Meg. We can't."

She looked down at the tent floor. "I need more to eat, more
calories. I can't figure out how much insulin to take." She pulled

a folded piece of paper from her spiral notebook and smoothed
it out on the tent floor in front of him. It was a chart of some
sort, full of lines and numbers. "I test my blood sugar and then
factor in what I'm eating and how much exercise I'm getting,
and this chart tells me how much insulin to take. I've done this
for ten years and suddenly I feel as though I've forgotten how."

"How do you test your blood sugar?"

She pulled a small, black plastic device from her camera case.
She set her middle finger along the flat bottom and pressed a
button. A little hammerlike arm shot down and pierced the tip
of her finger with a needle.

He winced. "How often do you have to do that?" he asked
as she squeezed the drop of blood from her finger onto a strip
of plastic.

She held up the four fingers of her left hand while she inserted
the strip into the side of a plastic box. Numbers appeared in a
screen on the top of the box, and she wrote them on her chart.

"You have to stab your finger four times a day in addition to
taking insulin?" He thought that added insult to injury.

Meg shrugged. "It doesn't hurt."

He lifted her hand to his face, but in the dim orange light he
could see nothing other than the shape of her fingers. He drew
the tips of her fingers to his mouth and set them against his lips.

She turned her hand to cup his chin with her palm. "I love
you, David," she said, then quickly pressed a finger to his lips.
"Don't say anything back. I mean, you don't have to. There are
no demands attached to my loving you." She smiled. "I'm gay,
remember? I just wanted to let you know how I feel."

He moved forward, into the nest she had created for him with
her legs. He took her in his arms and held her there, his cheek
resting against her hair. He wouldn't tell her he loved her. He
couldn't use that word with her, not yet. She was young. Only
a person this young could think they loved someone they'd known
for two weeks. He knew a different kind of love, the kind that
grew out of years of living with someone, of sharing thousands
of nights in the same bed, of creating a child together.

"What I feel for you," he said into her hair, "is gratitude,
and admiration, and affection. And desire." He wasn't afraid to
add that word; speaking it aloud didn't mean he had to act on
it.

She leaned away from him, smiling. "Thanks. That took more
effort than saying you love me too."

He wound a strand of her hair around his finger. "Why don't

we move your tent closer to Shawn's and mine? I don't like to think of you way out here by yourself.''

She shook her head. "I'm fine. And I'm the one with the gun.'' The shotgun lay long and black next to her bedroll.

He always had been attracted to brave women. He kissed her forehead, but she lifted her head until her lips met his. He kissed her softly, then pulled away, his hands on her arms.

"I have to go," he said.

She nodded her understanding, and he left the tent, taking the berries with him. He tossed them into the forest. He was afraid that in her desperation she might try to eat them.

He could love Meg, given the chance and the time to nurture the feelings growing inside him. But if there was truth to her theory that homosexuality was inborn, that nothing external could change it, she was the wrong woman to fall in love with.

Shawn was asleep and that was fine with him. He didn't want to talk to her or feel the silence between them. He lay awake for a long time, listening to the buzz of the cicadas, the discordant birdcalls. He thought back to his talk with Evan that afternoon.

Evan knew that deep kind of love with Shawn too, he thought, that love borne of their years together. But Evan had something with Shawn David couldn't lay claim to. He loved her through the hard times after Heather died, he shared her anguish, he was there for her while David hung back along the sidelines. David had thought his marriage to Shawn was one of the best. They knew how to keep the passion alive, turning life into an adventure that took them to the brink of danger but never over the edge. But the truth was they were only good together when life was easy and smooth. What kind of marriage was that, a marriage that disintegrated when the going got rough?

· Twenty-Eight ·

SHE WAS AFRAID to reach for David's note. She couldn't afford to get caught at it again; it would be impossible to plead ignorance a second time. She lay still under the sheet, watching him extract it from his shoe. He chuckled as he read it, and he still smiled as he slipped it into the pocket of his pants.

It was Sunday. They had two days left to capture two more Elves. That was if Tess got them out of here as she was supposed to on Tuesday. They *had* to leave Tuesday—she wouldn't let herself think of the alternative. They would be out of food by then. The insect repellent might last another week, but she had only a few feet of toilet paper left.

"How's your toilet paper supply holding out?" she asked David. It was an insipid question with all that was going on between them, but she wanted to talk to him and toilet paper seemed a safe topic. It was not.

"What?" he asked. His face lost the amused look it had worn since reading Meg's note, and now he looked distracted.

"I'll be out of toilet paper this morning. I was wondering if you'd share yours."

"I'm low too." He turned his back to her and pulled on his socks.

"Does that mean no?" she asked.

He sighed, turned to face her. "Take it," he said. "Take my goddamned toilet paper. Take the house, take the kids, take the cars, take the animals. They're all yours."

She sat up, hurt. "I haven't said anything like that."

"It's in the cards, isn't it? Your lawyer will see to it."

"You're talking about *things*, David. They're not important."

He tied his shoes and then leaned toward her. "The boys aren't *things*, although I'm not surprised you think so. You think people are objects you can shove around to fit your plans."

In all the years she'd known him, she had never heard this

cutting edge to his voice. She didn't know how to respond, what to say. She'd never needed to cope with his anger before.

He pulled a thin, flattened roll of toilet paper from his day pack and threw it at her as he left the tent. "You treat your goddamned tamarins with more compassion than you do me," he called behind him.

The toilet paper caught her in the chest, and she held it there for a moment before setting it on his side of the bed. She would use leaves.

David and Meg were loading film in their cameras when she reached the clearing. She nodded hello to Meg who smiled back at her. What did Meg know of David's marriage? How much had he told her? Did she know a divorce was pending?

She mixed water with the last of the dried egg and fed it to the tamarins along with a banana from the dwindling bunch hanging in a crook of the tree. They would have to gather insects for the Elves soon. They had little left to feed them.

The injured baby was alert and hungry this morning, and her back was healing well. But her mother still showed no interest in her father. Shawn watched the adult female snatch a chunk of banana from the male's hand to give to the babies. Maybe they could separate this pair when they got back to San Diego. Surely there was a male at the Center who would be more to her liking.

She plucked another banana from the bunch and headed toward the Lost Troop to bait the trap for the day. She barely noticed the jungle this morning. She couldn't get her mind off her conversation with David in the tent.

She would not allow her lawyer to be mercenary.

She didn't like to think about the divorce from David's point of view. It hurt to imagine what it would be like for him. But it made no difference. She wouldn't change her mind. There would be pain, yes, but the relief she would feel when it was over would outweigh the pain by far.

She was just past the turnoff to the cathedral and the Howlers' fig tree when she spotted something white on the ground. She leaned over for a closer look. It was a long string of bones, tiny, fragile looking. She knew what they were even before she noticed the leather collar in the brush nearby. A perfect skeleton of a Copper Elf, ChoCho, picked absolutely clean by the scavengers of the jungle.

She knelt down and pulled a T-shirt from her day pack. She

wrapped it around the skeleton and slipped it gently into her pack. Sweet ChoCho. She hoped her end had come swiftly.

Robin and Evan were just finishing breakfast when she got back to the clearing. Shawn sat across from them at the table and pulled the T-shirt from her pack. She unwrapped it carefully and laid the skeleton on the table top. The bones stood out against the grain of the saplings like bleached shells on a beach.

Robin turned her head. "Oh, Shawn, not while we're eating."

Evan lifted the skeleton to his side of the table. "Whew. Frightening, isn't it? She's been missing just a few days, and there's nothing left but bone."

"That will be us if Tess isn't back soon," Robin said.

They found a beautiful female in their trap that afternoon. She was no more than a year and a half old with a full glossy coat and curious eyes. One more to go, Shawn thought. They baited the trap again and carried the new tamarin to the cathedral where they would eat lunch—warm slices of cheese and water from their canteens. They set up their campstools, and Evan pulled the plastic bag containing the cheese from his pack.

After an initial halfhearted series of roars, the Howlers settled down and allowed Shawn and Evan to share the peace of the cathedral. Shawn took tiny bites of the cheese, savoring the flavor, making it last.

"Do you still think Tess is staying away intentionally?" Evan asked.

She scraped a circle of mold from her cheese and shook her head. It was too vicious a thing to do, even for Tess. And too irresponsible. "Something must have happened to the boat." She felt unexpected sympathy for Tess.

"Let Robin think Tess is just being a bitch, okay?" Evan asked. "She doesn't need to think we're stuck here."

"What if we are?"

"The Center will send someone to look for us eventually."

She thought of how long it would take the Center to realize there was a problem and arrange for a search party, how long it would take the rescuers to find them. Even under the best of circumstances, they would be stranded for several weeks.

Evan chatted a little with the new tamarin; then he cleared his throat. "David asked me if he and I would still be friends after you two are divorced." He didn't look at her. He seemed engrossed by the wire mesh on top of the trap.

"Of course you'll still be friends." She thought of how David looked forward to his Saturday mornings with Evan. He told her once that he'd never had a real male friend before, someone to confide in. Evan made it easy, he said. Yes, she knew that firsthand; there was no one in the world easier to talk to. "I don't see why the divorce would make any difference."

Evan shook his head. "I think it will," he said, looking at her now. "I think it will make a big difference to all of us."

"What do you mean?"

"I've been doing a lot of thinking the last few days, so when I tell you what I'm going to tell you, I don't want you to think I'm talking lightly." He set his piece of cheese carefully on the plastic bag and took her hand. "I love you. That's no surprise, is it?"

She shook her head.

"If you're divorced, if you're unattached, I'll go out of my mind. I can't imagine working with you, seeing you every day . . . and wanting you . . . and knowing there's no one waiting for you at home when the day is over. And then," he shook his head, "if you found someone else, someone new, and I had to start thinking about you with him . . . Do you see?"

She shook her head stubbornly. She didn't trust her voice to answer him because she felt close to tears. Was he about to tell her they could no longer work together, that it was impossible for him emotionally? Would he leave the Center? Would he ask her to leave?

"I want to marry you," he said.

She started to laugh; then realized he wasn't joking. He looked down at her hand, obviously disturbed by her reaction.

"You're serious," she said.

"I know it would be a mess at first . . . believe me, I've thought about it. But last night I pictured myself when I'm sixty years old, with Robin and a couple of grown kids, still wanting you. I don't want to feel that way when I'm sixty. I don't want to feel that way next year."

She had an odd feeling of unreality, as if she'd imagined this moment many times before. She thought of being with Evan, sleeping with him, loving him openly . . .

"I'm ungrateful, I know," he continued. "I mean, Robin is a good person. I could be content with her if I had never met you. I can't be around you and not touch you. I don't want to go back to the clandestine stuff, but I don't know if I could stop myself."

"You've managed pretty well since Melissa was born."

She saw the shadow cross his face at the mention of Melissa and knew he had not thought this through, not completely. The fantasy she was creating in her own mind crumbled. She had to play devil's advocate for his sake. She couldn't let him make a decision he would regret. "It wouldn't be just Robin you'd be leaving," she said quietly. *And not just Melissa either.* If he knew about the baby, he would not be speaking to her this way.

He was quiet a moment. "We'd have to work something out about Melissa." His voice was thick, and she reached up to stroke the back of her fingers across his beard.

"This is the wrong time for making major decisions, Evan. Robin's not herself out here. None of us is thinking clearly. All I know right now is that I'm going to hurt David and my children, and I don't want to add Robin and Melissa to that list."

"Promise me you'll think about it."

She nodded. She would not be able to help herself.

· Twenty-Nine ·

BY TEN THE next morning they had another young female in the trap. They weighed and measured her, smiling all the while, because this was the last one. Shawn felt Evan's relief, a reflection of her own.

"Let's go back to the clearing," Evan said as he snapped the door closed on the trap. "I brought champagne just for this occasion."

"Champagne at ten in the morning?" She was delighted by the idea, although she woke up this morning with an uncertain stomach and little sleep behind her. She'd spent the night thinking about Evan. Imagining. She knew her fantasy lacked the disarray of real life. It neatly omitted anyone who might be hurt by it and focused only on Evan and herself.

He'd surprised her yesterday. Since Melissa's birth, he kept his distance from her so carefully that she'd grown to think of the attraction as one-sided. It had changed out here. He could no longer keep up the front. She was relieved, but she felt sorry for him. His effort to keep his feelings hidden from her had truly been herculean. It was easier in San Diego, where their work together was clinical and structured, where they went home each night to Robin and David, where the pact *worked*. It was different in the jungle. You couldn't hide much out here. Everything was raw and near the surface.

She could not let an intimate relationship with Evan become anything more than a fantasy. It would affect too many people. But how would she resist him? If he wanted her, if he no longer hid those feelings, could she work with him without giving in? She couldn't imagine it. God, she was weak. She could see it now. He'd give her one sideways look across the Pentagon, and she'd start pulling off her clothes.

He put his arm around her now as they walked back to the clearing. "We did it, Shawn," he said.

"I only wish we'd gotten that one female's preferred male."

He hugged her closer. "You're too much."

Robin met them in the clearing. "I'm *sorry*," she said, holding up the cage that had held yesterday's captured tamarin.

The cage was empty. Robin nervously fingered the thick gold chain at her neck. "It was an accident," she said. "I was feeding it a piece of banana and it jumped on my hand and I panicked and pulled my hand out and the Elf came with it."

Evan grabbed the cage and peered into the bottom as though he expected to find the tamarin crouching in a corner, the product of a bad joke. He looked up at his wife.

"I can't believe you did this." His cheeks were flushed above his beard. Shawn knew the look. He was furious, trying to hold it in. He would succeed only for another second or two.

"I'm sorry, Evan," said Robin, "I . . ."

"Which way did she go?" Evan asked.

Robin pointed toward the path leading to the Lost Troop. She grabbed his arm. "Evan, I'm *sorry*."

He pulled his arm free of her, and Shawn cringed at the look of disgust he gave her. "Let's go, Shawn," he said as he huffed off toward the trail, the trap swinging from his hand.

She held back for a moment, put her hands on Robin's arms. "We'll get her back," she said.

"What if you don't?" She looked toward the spot where Evan had disappeared into the forest.

"You know Evan," Shawn said. "He blows up fast, then settles down."

Robin looked at her blankly. Perhaps she didn't know Evan.

She caught up with him near the entrance to the cathedral. He was winded, breathing hard and fast as he scanned the trees around him. "I apologize for my wife," he said.

"You were cruel to her."

He looked at her, eyebrows raised. "I'd say there's a 95 percent chance we've lost this Elf for good."

"Robin's feelings are more important."

He narrowed his eyes. "I don't think you're qualified to give advice on forgiveness."

She nodded silently. He was right.

"There she is!" He pointed to a tree off to the left. She was relieved to see the Elf watching them smugly from above. It was obvious who had the power here. Evan bent over to bait the trap with a piece of banana, but the Elf took off. They raced after her, Shawn in the lead, Evan behind her carrying the trap. The

Elf ran past the nesting tree of the Lost Troop, as Shawn guessed she would. She was not about to make it easy for them. She leaped from tree to tree, screeching with what sounded like childish pleasure, while Shawn and Evan panted below her. By the time the Elf stopped to look down at them again, Shawn was drenched with sweat.

Evan looked up at the monkey. "Little bitch," he muttered, but he was smiling. He set the trap and they moved downwind ten yards or so and waited.

Their campstools were back at the clearing, so they stood, awkwardly, arms folded. Evan reached over and smoothed the short damp hair off her cheek, and she saw droplets of her own perspiration on his fingers when he took them away.

"Sorry about before," he said. "I lost it."

"Tell that to Robin."

"I plan to."

They heard the sudden *clack* as the door dropped shut on the trap. It was followed by a long screech of dismay. The Elf had been fooled again.

Evan laughed. "The Elves may be beautiful, but they're not too bright."

They were walking back to the clearing when they heard the sound of a waterfall. They pushed through the undergrowth at the side of the trail, and their faces were struck by a spray of fresh water. The waterfall was tall and narrow, and the canopy opened to the sky above it.

Evan set down the cage and wiped his arm across his sweaty forehead. He took a step forward onto the flat rocks surrounding the pool and began to unbutton his shirt.

Shawn hung back, fingering the top button of her own damp shirt while she watched him undress. The muscles of his back were tight, the hair on his chest dark and symmetrical as it worked its way down to his stomach. Her mouth watered as if she were staring at a piece of rich chocolate. She missed that body.

Evan leaped into the pool. He surfaced and swung the water out of his hair with a toss of his head. "It's *wonderful*," he said. He swam toward the waterfall with choppy strokes, and Shawn smiled to herself. When it came to swimming, Evan would give David no contest. He stood up under the waterfall, the hair on his body plastered black and shining to his skin. "You're missing out, Shawn."

She took a step onto the rocks and bent down to untie her shoes. She took them off along with her socks and stood to unbutton her shirt. Evan waited under the waterfall with his hands on his hips, grinning at her, making no attempt to give her privacy. And she didn't want it. She undressed slowly, folding her damp clothes into a neat pile, feeling freer with each piece of clothing she discarded. She liked the feeling of his eyes on her, although she knew the game she was playing was dangerous. Did he look at her body the way she looked at his? Wistfully? With a desire that must be tamed? This would be a test of both their wills.

She sat down on the rock and lowered herself carefully into the pool. The cool water slipped over the skin of her arms and legs.

"Come over here," he said.

Her feet caught the firm rock bottom, and she joined him on the ledge under the waterfall. The water spiked into the tight muscles of her shoulders. She put her arms over her head and let the water pour down the length of her body, leaned her head back for a drink. And then she felt what she knew was coming, what she wanted to come. Evan's arms were around her, he pressed his body against hers, and she let out her breath in one long stream against the damp warmth of his neck. Her arms dropped to his shoulders, and she held his head in her hands as he kissed her. The flow of water forced its way between their lips, bubbled into their mouths.

"It's a challenge," he said in her ear, "kissing in a waterfall."

He guided her to the side of the pool and lifted her onto a flat rock that just broke the surface of the water. He kissed her again, a kiss that started gently enough but within seconds burned her lips. His hands ran over her water-slick skin. Just for a moment she would allow herself to savor the feeling, the familiar warmth of his palms, the delicate scratching of his beard. She remembered all at once what it was like to make love to him, electric and intense.

She pulled her mouth from his just long enough to say, "No," but he knew better, he knew the word was no more than token resistance. His hands slipped up her sides to her breasts, his thumbs grazing her nipples. When was she going to issue it— the real "No"? She wished there were a way to separate her body from her mind. She could let her body do as it pleased without any guilt, any loss to her self-respect.

She forced herself to think of Robin, to imagine her a few months from now in maternity clothes, to imagine Evan's elation at the birth of another child. She saw him with Robin in the hospital room, proudly showing off their new son or daughter while Shawn stood in the doorway, holding nothing more than a gift in her arms.

"No, Evan, I'm serious." She slipped off the rock and folded her arms across her chest. Her legs shook, and she felt the same nausea inching up on her that she'd felt the first time they made love.

For a moment neither of them spoke. He pried her arms away from her chest and put his own arms around her. She felt his heart beating against her breast.

"We'd regret it," she said. "You know we would."

"I don't think you believe I'm serious about wanting to marry you."

"I believe you mean it now, when things are bad between you and Robin and we're not sure where we'll be tomorrow. But I don't think you'll feel that way in a month or . . ."

"Christ, Shawn, I've felt this way for seven fucking years!"

She set her forehead against his chest, fighting the urge to tell him that she wanted exactly what he wanted. "Let's wait, Evan. Please?" She looked into his eyes. "Let's not do anything we can't undo."

David was already thinking about visiting Meg in San Francisco. If he was living alone, he would owe explanations to no one. He could do as he pleased. The thought was appealing.

He needed to see Meg on her turf. Once she was back among her own friends, would she care anything about him? What would it be like, seeing her outside this jungle, seeing her with women who might be critical of her attachment to a man? Would he wonder what had attracted him to her, or would he find her even more appealing in the chill salt air of Fisherman's Wharf?

And just how crazy was it for him to entertain fantasies about a woman who was gay, who considered her gayness immutable?

"Do you think we should pack everything so we're ready to go tomorrow morning?" Meg asked him now. They were dragging the small canoe along the trail leading upstream. They planned to take it as far as the waterfall. They would return to it tonight and drift back to camp in the darkness, just the two of them.

"I'd hate to do all that if she's not going to show up," he

said. Tomorrow they would know for certain if Tess was playing
games with them or if she had truly met with some misfortune.
They still clung to the hope that she would miraculously appear
in the morning, chuckling in that cold way she had over their
discomfort. She *had* to show up. The alternative was unthink-
able. Except for the thought of separating from Meg, he was
ready to leave this place. His clothes smelled of sweat and repellent and mold. His feet itched; there was a rash in his arm-
pits. The jungle invaded his dreams, and now the darkness of
night seemed preferable to this constant greenness. What he
wouldn't give for a peek at San Diego's dry golden hills and
leathery brown chaparral.

He looked over at Meg. The lines of her body were long and
spare, the muscles in her arms firm as she pulled the rope tied
to the canoe. It was difficult to believe that beneath that efficient
exterior her body did not work as it should.

"You're getting a lot of exercise, dragging this canoe," he
said. "Did you figure that into the amount of insulin you took
this morning?"

She turned her head to flash him a pretty smile. "You learn
quickly," she said. "I reduced the insulin. By enough, I hope."

He heard the sound of the waterfall up ahead. "This is far
enough." He dropped the rope. "Let's leave the canoe here."

"Look." Meg pointed into the canopy.

High above them a pair of toucans basked in a spotlight of
sunshine. Meg quietly set up her tripod and screwed her camera
onto it.

"I'll meet you at the waterfall," he said, picking up her day
pack. They planned to eat their precious chunks of cheese on
the flat rocks; then go for a swim.

He saw their clothes before he saw them, Evan's in a damp,
crumpled pile next to the trap with the tamarin in it, Shawn's
neatly folded a few feet away. He watched them from behind his
veil of ferns and liana, his body filling with venom. He felt the
sheath of his machete down the length of his thigh. If he were
a violent man . . . He wanted to hurt them, both of them. He
felt conspired against, used. *"Of course we'll stay friends."*
Wasn't that what Evan said? *Evan, you bastard.*

He turned on his heel and walked away from the waterfall.
Meg was taking down the tripod when he reached her. He
grabbed her arm to steer her back toward the trail. She nearly
tripped trying to keep up with him, the tripod banging into her
legs.

"I thought we were going to eat by the waterfall," she said.

"No. Come on."

She stopped. "But you said you wanted to swim."

"No." He took her arm again and swung her along with him.

"David."

"I changed my mind, all right?"

She looked hurt.

"Don't make me explain." Let her think it was another one of his irrational fears. He pulled his machete from its sheath and slapped at the branches and vines along the trail.

Meg stopped again and when he turned to look at her he saw fear in her eyes.

"What's wrong with you?" she asked.

"I want to be alone for a while."

"Did I do something?"

He shook his head, angry at her now too. "You think all the world's problems are your creation, Meg. This has nothing to do with you."

He left her behind as he stalked up the trail, slicing vines along the route, feeling with pleasure the cold steel cut.

Shawn threw up once on the walk back to the clearing. She knelt at the edge of the trail while Evan sat next to her and the tamarin chattered nervously in its trap.

She sat back on her heels, wiping the tears from her eyes.

"I always make things worse for you." Evan rubbed her shoulder.

She shook her head. "I wouldn't have survived the year after Heather died if it hadn't been for you."

"Yes, you would have," he said sullenly, dropping his hand. "And your marriage would have survived as well."

She went to bed when they reached the clearing and slept until dinner, having one single dream that went on and on. Her children—all three of them—searched the house in San Diego for her and David. They searched closets and under beds, the way David used to search Heather's room at night to prove there were no monsters. She could see the anxiety growing in the boys' faces, the fear they tried to control for Heather's sake.

She woke up alone, wishing David were there. She wanted to tell him the dream and listen to him reassure her that Tess would show up tomorrow and they would get out of here. She wanted him to hold her. She wanted to go home.

* * *

Her nerves were taut during dinner. David had cooked rice and canned green beans and seasoned it all with a lot of garlic, and while it tasted as delicious as gourmet food, it felt like broken glass in her stomach. She complimented him on it; he didn't respond.

Robin made stickbread with cheese, like Tess had made for them a week or so before.

"You shouldn't have used so much of the flour," Evan snapped at her. "We hardly have any left."

Robin laid down her fork and stared at her plate. "I guess I can't do anything right," she said quietly.

Evan sighed. He set down his own fork and reached across the table to take both Robin's hands in his. "I'm sorry, Robin. It's fine. It tastes good. I'm really sorry, babe."

After dinner Shawn went into the darkening woods, her stomach burning. She found leaves to use as toilet paper. She either had a touch of Montezuma's Revenge or a case of nerves over the afternoon with Evan. As she lowered her shorts, her hand grazed a lump on her hip, just above the place where it met her thigh. She knew what it was, nearly vomited again at the thought.

She found David in the tent, digging extra batteries out of his duffel bag.

"I have a botfly larva," she said, setting her hand on the seat of her shorts. "Right here. Could you help me get it out?"

"Sorry. I'm going out."

She drew back from the glacial tonc. She knew where he was going tonight. He and Meg spent most of dinner talking about their plans to creek-drift. They'd portaged the canoe upstream and would now sail it back down, by themselves, in the seductive darkness of the forest.

"David, please," she asked. "I can't go to sleep knowing this thing is crawling around inside me." She started to unzip her shorts, but he touched her hand to stop her.

"I said I'm going *out*," he repeated. He swung his camera case to his shoulder and slipped out of the tent. He turned around to face her once he was outside and spoke to her through the netting. "Why don't you ask Evan to do it? It won't be the first time he's seen that part of your body." He turned and disappeared into the night.

She sat still for a long time after he left. What did he mean? What was happening to David? She'd never seen him like this before, so angry and hostile.

She followed the beam of her flashlight to Evan's tent. She saw the lantern in front of the entrance and the shadows inside.

"Evan?" she called.

He looked out through the netting. "We have a caller," he said to Robin.

"I have a botfly larva." She made a face.

Evan grinned. "Oh, good. I thought my tobacco was going to turn out to be a waste of space." He unzipped the netting and she ducked inside. She felt as though she'd stepped into a quaint little suburban home. Clothes were neatly stacked along one wall of the tent, next to a row of wilted novels. She wondered if the books were in alphabetical order. Robin set down her magazine.

"You have one of those maggoty things?" she asked.

Shawn nodded. "Disgusting, isn't it?"

Evan dug the tobacco out of his first-aid kit. 'Where is it?"

She put her hand on the seat of her shorts and he laughed.

"What do you bet we all have them there? Yours is probably just the first to grow big enough to notice." He wet the tobacco in the palm of his hand with water from his canteen. "Well, drop your drawers and lie down." He motioned to the side of the bed nearest the wall.

Shawn gave Robin a look of apology for intruding this way as she lowered her shorts and lay down on her stomach. But Robin seemed unabashed by her presence. In fact, the tension between her and Evan at dinner was gone. She wondered if they'd made up by making love. Evan had certainly been in the mood.

"I can see it." Evan peered inside with his flashlight. "He's an ugly little cuss. I wish I had some film left."

"Oh, Evan." Robin made a face.

"You weren't so excited the time you had one of these in your own body," Shawn said.

The tobacco felt cool as Evan taped it in place. "Have to let it sit there for a while," he said.

"Shawn, you have a tattoo!" Robin got to her knees for a closer look.

"It looks like a peace sign," Evan said, as if he had never seen it before, never stroked it with his fingers or licked it with his tongue. "Pretty bizarre, Shawn."

"I'm not responsible for the things I did when I was nineteen," she said.

For half an hour they chatted as if they were neighbors visiting over a cup of coffee. They talked about Melissa and the twins. Day care and soccer camp. They talked as though they were actually going to leave the next day. Shawn was glad for the conversation, for the way it kept her mind off David.

"I think Tess has been up with Charlie, drinking rum and making love, and now she's on her way back to us," said Evan. He removed the tobacco and peered inside. "He's stopped squirming. I'm about to get you back for those stitches without anesthetic, Shawn. You want to hold Robin's hand?"

It hardly seemed necessary, but she took the hand Robin offered. Its manicure was still perfect; it smelled reassuringly of hand lotion. That was the smell Melissa was growing up with and missed right now. God, she didn't want to hurt this woman.

She grit her teeth as he squeezed out the larva.

"Want to see him?" Evan asked.

"Not now." Her stomach wasn't up to it tonight.

"I'll put him in alcohol so you'll have a souvenir." He swabbed alcohol on the empty larva nest and pronounced her cured.

She kissed them both on the cheek and went back to her own disorderly, lonely tent.

David came in around midnight. She hadn't slept. With every minute that passed, she felt the bruise grow bigger and blacker on her hip. She would be sore for quite a while.

"Did you see much?" she asked.

"A few things." He lit the lantern and began to undress.

She raised herself up on her elbows and took a deep breath. "What did you mean before?" she asked. "About Evan seeing that part of my body?"

David pulled off one sock; then the other. He studied a hole in the toe of one, and she felt perspiration form under her arms. He turned to her. "I saw you today," he said. "You and Evan in the waterfall. Making love."

Her heart gave a great, audible *thud*. "We didn't make love." Her voice was a whisper.

"Give me a break." David looked away from her and began unbuttoning his shirt.

"David, we didn't." She felt wronged, oddly indignant. So much effort went into her decision not to make love that she wanted credit for it. But she could imagine how it looked to David. How much had he seen? "If you'd watched from start to finish, you'd know that we didn't."

"I wasn't about to stand there and watch my wife screw another man, from start to finish. I didn't *need* to. What I saw was enough to qualify."

"*No.*"

David leaned toward her, his face so close to hers that she had to pull away. "You were kissing, you had no clothes on, his hand was . . . Damn it, Shawn, do I have to spell it out to you?"

"He wanted to, but I said no." Her cheeks went hot with shame. How could she do that to Evan, pin the blame on him as though she had nothing to do with it?

David's eyes narrowed to lines of disgust. "You're a bitch."

She pulled the sheet from her body. The heat had risen in the tent, and the air was too thick to breathe. She felt the dampness of her T-shirt against her back. "I guess we both wanted to," she said, wondering how deeply she would dig herself into this hole. "We both considered it. But the point is, we didn't."

He got under the sheet, but didn't lie down. "You know," he said, "it really doesn't matter how far it went between you and Evan today. I've known about you two for a long time."

A drop of perspiration rolled from her hair onto her cheek. She forced herself to keep her eyes on his. "What do you mean?"

"What do you think I mean?" He looked cool; no trace of the dizzying heat she felt. She thought there was the tiniest smile on his lips. He was enjoying his power. She looked down into her lap where she gripped the limp sheet in her hands.

"I don't know," she said.

"I know about the affair. I know when it started and when it ended. To the day."

Her stomach lurched and she felt the rice and beans at the back of her throat. She fumbled with the mosquito netting and managed to get out of the tent before she vomited. Her feet were bare; she felt the rough carpet of the forest beneath them. She leaned breathless against a tree. How could he know?

She was shaking when she got back to the tent. David slipped a flannel shirt over her shoulders, but she brushed it away. "Too hot," she said. She sat for a few minutes with her head in her hands, trying to get her breath back, trying to think of something to say. She felt the tips of his fingers on her knee. Finally she lifted her head.

"How did you know?" she asked.

"That doesn't matter."

"Did you know at the time?"

"Yes."

He knew and never let on. What had he felt back then, while she thought only of herself, acted only in her own interest? "David, I'm sorry," she said.

"I don't think so, Shawn." He took his fingers from her knee and folded his hands in his lap. "I think if you could have figured out a more excruciating way to hurt me, short of murder, you would have done it." He lay down and rolled away from her. "You'll get no contest from me on the divorce," he added. "I'm ready. I'm tired of being shit on."

She turned out the lantern and lay down too, careful not to invade his space. She stared at the dark tent ceiling. "David?" she asked. "Are you and Meg lovers?" She felt her voice catch in her throat and hoped it was not that obvious to him.

"No. But that's Meg's decision, not mine."

She felt selfish in her relief. Thank God Meg was not attracted to men. "David?"

"What?" He sounded a little annoyed now.

"Back then, when I was . . . with Evan. It was my doing. My fault. Don't blame him."

"Go to sleep, Shawn."

She heard his breathing grow deep and even while she lay awake and thought back to that year. All those nights Evan came to dinner; all those Saturday racquetball games he and David played together. How did David do it? It would be like him to suffer in silence. But he was suffering in silence no longer.

· *Thirty* ·

IT WAS TUESDAY night and Tess had not returned.

Shawn poured the last of the rice into the boiling water, covered the pot, and set it back on the fire. She wanted to save some of the rice for another meal, but there was so little that she finally turned the bag upside down and shook out every grain. Even so, they would leave the table hungry again tonight.

Robin knelt next to her, silently opening the last can of green beans. Her eyes were red, and she stopped her hands after every few turns of the can opener to brush tears from her cheeks.

They had a little cheese left, eight ounces or so. There was enough oatmeal for each of them to have a tablespoon or two at breakfast the next morning, and about a cup of buggy flour. The coffee was gone, but they had plenty of tea bags and a few packages of grape flavoring for the water, some *Pisco*, and a bottle of rum. That was the sum total of their larder.

They had still been clinging to hope that afternoon at lunch as they ate the thin oat cakes Robin made. That seemed like a lifetime ago. Now each of them was quiet, their reactions dulled by the realization that they were stranded, without food for themselves or the tamarins. Shawn and Evan spent the day plucking grasshoppers and beetles from the underside of leaves for the Elves, but it hadn't been enough. They had to become more skillful at it. She wouldn't let the tamarins die.

"We'll build a raft," Evan said now as Shawn set the rice on the table. She measured out a spoonful for each of them, then another, then a third while Robin did the same with the beans.

"I think we should just stay put," said David. If Evan said *black* today, David would say *white*. Evan was starting to notice. He looked to Shawn for some clue to David's new demeanor, and she quickly looked away. She didn't want David to see her share a look with Evan, or a smile, or a word.

"I think we'll get out of here faster if we work at it ourselves," Evan said carefully, trying not to raise David's ire. "We'll need balsa wood. I've seen some trees out there that will do. The logs will have to dry out for a few days after we cut them, and then we can . . ."

"*A few days,*" Robin said. "We can't survive out here a few days. There's nothing left to eat."

"We'll find food," Shawn said. Her plate was clean, but Robin ate her rice grain by grain, trying to make it last. "Some of these plants must be edible."

"David and I looked through Tess's botany books," Meg said. "They don't say what's edible and what's not."

Evan shook his head. "I don't think we can risk it."

"We can use the traps to catch Spiny Rats," Shawn suggested.

"I couldn't eat a rat," said Robin.

"I'd rather not eat a mammal either," Shawn said, "but I don't think we have much choice."

"What would we use as bait?" Evan asked.

"I don't know . . . frogs?" She had no idea what would work. "We'll have to catch the frogs first."

"Tess left her gun." Meg spoke quietly.

They were silent for a moment. They'd forgotten. They had a gun.

"No guns," Shawn said. "No shooting."

"What's the difference between trapping and eating an animal or shooting and eating an animal?" David asked.

She tried to meet his eyes and found she couldn't. "Shooting's not fair," she said.

"I agree," said Evan. "The gun should be a last resort."

"Especially since there are other things we can eat," said Shawn.

"Like what?" Robin asked.

"Bugs. Remember Tess telling us the natives ate . . ."

"Forget it," Robin interrupted. She picked up the last grain of rice in her bowl and slipped it between her lips.

"We have to forage for the tamarins," Evan said. "We might as well do it for ourselves at the same time."

Shawn wasn't certain she could eat an insect herself, but they had to try. "We'll start early in the day, when the insects are most abundant. If we all did it, we could . . ."

"You're serious about this." David frowned at her.

She nodded. She suddenly remembered the Howlers fig tree in the cathedral. "The fig tree!"

"Ah, yes," said Evan. He looked relieved. "Figs and bugs. We'll be fine."

"I wish Tess were here," Robin said. "She'd know what plants we could eat."

Meg shut her eyes. "She must be dead."

It was the first time anyone had said those words out loud, and no one bothered to disagree with her. Shawn couldn't get the image of ChoCho's picked-clean skeleton out of her mind.

Meg looked at David. "I feel like this is all my fault," she said.

"It's Tess's fault," said David. "No one else's."

Meg *was* attracted to David. Shawn saw it all at once. It was new; so apparent that she couldn't have missed it had it existed before. Meg looked to him for approval, her body leaned into the table to get closer to him. When he said he would do the dishes, she rushed to help him. She took the rice pot from his hands, her own hands touching his in a planned accident. She wanted to be close to him. She wanted him to touch her.

"Do you think you could eat bugs?" she asked David in bed that night. She wished he would talk to her.

"No." He reached through the netting to turn out the lantern. She watched him settle onto his side of the bed.

"What if you were starving?"

"I'll eat the figs."

"You'll get diarrhea if you eat only figs."

"Bugs would give me worse than diarrhea."

"I just don't think the figs will be . . ."

"I don't want to argue over this, Shawn. Good night."

Is there anything you'd be willing to talk to me about? she thought. *Anything at all? You name the topic; I'll talk.* It would be better if he'd yell at her again, accuse her of something. Do anything other than treat her like a piece of the tent.

But he was already asleep.

She shut her eyes and lay still. They were supposed to be sleeping on Charlie's boat tonight. Tomorrow evening Manuel was to pick them up to take them to Iquitos. How many more nights would they be lying here, wondering what went wrong, what happened to Tess? How many more nights could they survive?

She rolled onto her side and looked at David's back in the darkness. She remembered how he liked to talk when he made love. He'd talk about anything—the events of the day, an article

he'd read in the paper, the traffic backups that morning. It was
a game to him, to see how long they could keep a conversation
going. Who would give in first, who would lose the ability to
concentrate on anything other than physical sensation?

She listened to his quiet breathing. Sometimes when they made
love, David talked about what he was doing to her body, what
he planned to do next. He was graphic, and her body reacted to
his words as if they were his hands on her.

She pulled the sheet tighter around her shoulders. There was
a stirring in her body, a gentle but insistent ache. She wished
she could wake him, ask him to make love to her. But if he had
a shred of pride, he would reject her. Or worse, he might agree
to make love and then fantasize she was Meg the entire time.

Oh, yes. The tables had turned.

She thought of the house in San Diego. Could she live there
without thinking of him constantly? The house was his. He put
the new roof on; he tended the garden. He laid the tile floor in
the foyer and fixed the leaky plumbing. She could see his "reading" sign on the hall closet. She thought of the times she set her
forehead to the cool wood of the door to listen to the soothing
sound of his voice.

He had ruined it all. Maybe if he'd been remorseful . . . She
understood he was human; people make mistakes. But he acted
as though it was nothing. Win some, lose some. One down, two
to go. He never stopped working, never even considered it.

The memory of their meeting with the coroner slipped unin-
vited into her mind. The coroner's office was ice cold, the air
conditioning malfunctioning, and she blew on her hands to warm
them while David sat relaxed and tan in a short-sleeved shirt.
The coroner described how Heather died; how she was conscious at the time of death, fully aware of everything happening
to her. Shawn asked questions. She wanted to hear; she wanted
to know what Heather felt during those last few seconds. She
wanted *David* to know. David said nothing. He stared at the edge
of the coroner's gray metal desk as if in a trance.

As they walked across the parking lot to the car after the
meeting, Shawn felt a pressure in her lungs she thought might
kill her. She walked ahead of David, trying to pull in enough
air to rid her lungs of the pain. And finally, David spoke. She
heard him draw in his breath behind her and she turned to listen,
to hear what he would say. An apology, perhaps. A word of
regret.

He ran his fingers through his hair. "Let's go to McDonald's for a quick lunch before you go back to work," he said.

She was so filled with hatred for him at that moment that she could easily have killed him. But she lacked the means; so instead she cut him with her words, calling him names, swearing at him like a madwoman in the middle of the parking lot while he hurriedly stuck the key in the car door to escape her. She let him have his escape. She took a taxi home. That night he slept in Heather's room again, as he did with more and more frequency. She was certain he slept well. She was certain he was asleep by the time his head hit the pillow.

And now he slept next to her, his breathing easy, unburdened. She felt her hands ball into fists, her own breathing coarse with anger. She almost slipped, remembering the good things about David. Loving David meant betraying Heather. That was what she had to remember.

He would find a new woman, Meg or some other, who knew nothing of his past. No woman could love him if she knew. He would live out the life of an impostor, a fugitive from the truth. He could melt his new woman with his eyes and touch her hand so that she hungered for more, and she would never know the devastation he had left behind him in a previous life.

• *Thirty-One* •

SHE WANTED TO read Meg's note. She felt driven, and David was so deep in sleep that she was certain she would be safe. She quietly unzipped the mosquito netting and slipped her fingers into his shoe.

I'm nearly out of film [*Meg wrote*] but I'm still up early. I'm addicted to the mist, I guess.

I wish we knew what happened to Tess. I realize now how superficial my relationship with her was. If she knew the real Meg, the "imperfect" Meg you've accepted so easily, she wouldn't have wanted anything to do with her. I feel far closer to you than I ever did to her, in spite of the fact that you and I are not lovers. I know you want that now, but I'm still afraid. Last night, when you told me I looked beautiful, I thought about it. And I'm thinking about it this morning—actually, there's little else on my mind. Funny how your mind works when you think you're going to die.

Love, Meg

Shawn put the note back in David's shoe and lay down again. So he told her she was beautiful. *God, David, how soppy.* The divorce must be setting off a midlife crisis in him. At thirty-eight. Pathetic.

She felt a tick on her neck and dug to the bottom of her duffel bag for a hand mirror. In the beam of her flashlight, she could see that the tick was just settling in. She plucked it from her throat and tossed it outside the netting. Then she raised the mirror to her face and let out her breath in a near wail. She hadn't seen herself since leaving San Diego. Her skin had paled after two weeks under the canopy. It was a floury, unhealthy white. There were lines around her eyes, dark circles beneath the lower lashes. Her hair was growing in at bizarre spiky angles. She thought of Meg, light and young and beautiful, as David had seen fit to tell her, and felt shrewish and bitter. How had this happened? How had she become the type of woman who spent her time rooting through her husband's private correspondence? She stared at her face again, illuminated by the unkind beam of the flashlight. There was not one appealing thing left in this face. Not one good, honorable thing.

She grabbed her toiletries bag and left the tent. She wanted to leave before David woke up and got a look at her, then read the note and thought of Meg. She walked to the pool and undressed on the bank. A quiet mist rose around her shoulders as she lowered herself into the water. She scrubbed her skin until it stung, washed her hair, shaved her legs. She dressed in a pair of shorts and a shirt she'd washed out the day before, and walked with a determined stride to Evan and Robin's tent.

Evan was sitting on the bed in a pair of running shorts. He was bare-chested; his hair, uncombed. Robin sat next to him in a blue nightshirt, a pair of scissors in her hand, and Shawn knew she had just trimmed Evan's beard.

Shawn sat down, feeling the tent fill with her own clean scent. "May I talk to Robin, please?" she asked. "In private?"

Evan looked alarmed for a second, but he knew she was nothing if not discreet. He picked up his shirt and stepped out of the tent. "I'll start the fire," he said.

Robin looked at her expectantly.

"Can I borrow some makeup?" Shawn asked.

Robin laughed. "Do you have a date or something?" She reached for a red paisley bag in the corner of the tent.

"I feel so pale."

"We're going to starve to death, and you're worried about the color in your cheeks." Robin set the bulging makeup case between them on the bedroll, unzipped it, and laid it flat. Plastic bottles and compacts sprang free of the paisley.

"Robin, you've got half of Merle Norman in here!"

Robin shrugged. "I'm vain."

Shawn shook her head happily. "No, you're wonderful. Make me up." She leaned forward, chin up, eyes closed, offering Robin her face. This would be good therapy for both of them, she thought. But Robin didn't move.

"You don't need it," she said. "If I had eyes like yours, I'd never bother with all this stuff. Just a little color on your cheeks, maybe." She opened a compact and brushed the mauvey powder across Shawn's cheeks.

Shawn looked at herself in the compact mirror and shook her head. It was not enough. "These dark circles." She touched her eyes, then dove into the paisley bag with desperation. "Don't you have anything in here for the circles under my eyes?"

"Shawn, *stop it*," Robin frowned. "You're *scaring* me. You're not yourself."

Shawn set her hands in her lap. "Yes, I am myself," she said quietly. "And I don't like myself much right now."

Robin touched the back of her hand. "Is it David?" she asked.

Shawn stared into her lap, embarrassed that Robin felt sorry for her. She was relieved to hear Evan's footsteps outside the tent.

"Are you two done yet?" he called.

"In a minute, Evan." Robin slipped the blush, a tube of concealing cream, and a gray pencil into Shawn's hand. "Go easy with them," she said. "You really don't need them."

Evan caught a frog near the stream. It was dull-eyed and yellow. He killed it and set it in a trap in the hope of catching a Spiny Rat.

The five of them spent the rest of the morning foraging insects for the Elves. They split up, and Shawn was glad to see David and Meg walk into the forest in opposite directions. They filled clear plastic bags with crickets and beetles, ants, termites, and an occasional grasshopper. It wasn't long before they had enough.

The trap was still empty at noon. The Spiny Rats that dominated the forest only two weeks earlier had disappeared. No one could recall seeing any in days.

They sat at the sapling table and divided the last of the cheese as reality set in. They'd had no breakfast, and only this little sliver of rubbery, molding cheese for lunch. There was nothing left.

Shawn maneuvered to sit across the table from David. She had covered the circles under her eyes, reapplied the blush, combed the spikes of her hair into place. She felt herself posing, trying to get him to notice her. She remembered this feeling from junior high school. Wanting the attention of some boy who didn't know she existed, wishing she could pull his eyes to her but not certain what she would do if she succeeded.

Once David's eyes met hers, just darted over her on their way to Meg, who sat at her left. And there they rested, smiled, flirted. How did David feel, now that Meg told him there was little or her mind other than the possibility of making love to him? How would any man feel, especially a man who had received nothing in the way of loving for three years?

After lunch, they walked along the trail by the stream until they reached the cathedral. They stood quietly in the brush, looking at the tree they hoped would nourish them.

"Let me go in," Shawn said. She wanted to be the one to climb this tree, to feel herself a part of the Howlers' troop.

She walked slowly toward the tree, a plastic bag folded in the pocket of her shorts. The Howlers roared at her. They were so loud that she was tempted to put her hands over her ears, but they threw nothing at her. They were accustomed to having people around now. Their howling was more from habit than alarm.

She circled the tree, her footsteps soft on the ground. She counted twenty-three monkeys and thousands of figs. She made her circles smaller and smaller, as close to the massive trunk as she could get with the curtains of aerial roots blocking her path. The sound was deafening and beautiful.

She looked up. The first available branch for climbing was a couple of feet above her head. But then it would be easy. A network of stout branches radiated from the center. She would have to climb up and out only a short distance to reach the figs.

She walked back to the others. "It looks easy, but I'll need a boost." She took David's arm and gave him a tug toward the clearing. "Come with me. You're a little taller than Evan." Her voice shook. She was nervous talking to her own husband.

He lifted her up, his arms wrapped around her legs, ignoring her admonition not to hurt his back. In a second she was face to face with the branch. She wrapped her arms around it and swung her left leg up and over, bringing a few of the snakelike aerial roots with it. She felt the bark scrape at her skin.

"How is it up there?" David shouted to be heard over the Howlers.

"Great!" she shouted back, although she felt vulnerable, alone in the world of the Howlers without their advantage of knowing the territory, without their mobility. She stood up carefully, climbed to another branch, and slid herself outward along it. The Howlers were suddenly quiet, watching her. A huge cluster of purple figs hung a yard or so in front of her.

A Howler moved himself to within a few feet of the clump. His face was leathery and dark, his fur a rich cinnamon. On his shoulder were two white botfly larva nests. Poor thing, she thought. The Howler opened his mouth into a perfect, pink-lined O and let out one halfhearted roar. Then he sat back to watch her, following the movement of her hands with his gentle brown eyes.

She leaned forward along the branch and began to pluck the figs from the tree and drop them into her bag. Her mouth watered at the soft ripe feel of them in her fingers. When the bag was full, she slipped off the branch to the one below it. She straddled it and was working her way toward the trunk when she spotted a snake, no more than two yards in front of her, coiled, angry, tongue flashing, waiting for her next move. She froze. It was beautiful, banded with red, yellow, and black, and it was poisonous. She sat still for several minutes, afraid to move, afraid to call out to the others. She knew David was just below her waiting to help her down, but she was afraid to speak at all.

"Shawn?" he asked.

She said nothing. Her heart pulsed in her thighs where they clutched the branch.

"Oh my God," David said. "Evan!"

She heard Evan's footsteps as he ran across the cathedral, but she didn't look down. She couldn't take her eyes off the snake.

"Hold still, Shawn," Evan said, as if she could possibly do anything else. "It looks like a coral from down here."

She nodded her head, slowly, eyes riveted on the round black eyes of her enemy.

"You can back up," Evan said. "Very slowly. The branch will hold you, and when you're a safe distance from the snake you can let yourself down and we'll catch you. Okay?"

She nodded. The snake issued an ominous *hiss* as she inched her way backward. Its bejeweled body remained coiled over the branch, deceptively languorous except for its erect, alert head.

"A little further, babe," Evan said. From the corner of her eye, she saw him below the branch, following her progress.

The bark scraped without mercy at the inside of her thighs. "I think this is far enough," she said softly, hoping he could hear her. She was no longer close enough to see the snake's forked tongue darting from its mouth and that gave her a sense of security.

"Drop the bag," Evan said.

She did as she was told. The bag took a long time reaching the ground. Evan seemed far below her.

"Lower yourself slowly," he said.

She leaned forward to wrap her arms around the branch and

slid her right leg over it. She expected the snake to slip toward her at any second. She would jump if that happened. She would rather risk a broken back than a poisonous snakebite.

"You're doing great," Evan reassured her.

She lowered her body from the branch. The bark chewed at her arms. She couldn't see the snake now. She had no idea if it was still coiled over the branch or ready to strike at her hands.

"Let yourself fall," Evan said. "David and I are right here to catch you."

She looked down. David's arms formed a circle with Evan's for her to fall into; the tips of his fingers touched her heel.

She let go, and in a second the three of them were on the ground, tangled in the aerial roots. She laughed, giddy with relief, while the men wiped the sweat from their foreheads, and Evan chastised her for wearing shorts.

"Next time I'll go up," Evan said. All five of them sat on the flat rocks near the pool, gorging themselves on figs.

Shawn shook her head. "I've got the feel for it now. My only concern is meeting another snake."

"Where there's one, there are more," said Evan.

For a moment no one spoke as they focused on the meal. The figs were heavy with seeds and very juicy, nearly overripe.

Evan shifted on his rock. "I think we should take the gun next time," he said quietly. "I could have blown that coral's head off."

Shawn cupped a fig in her palm. "The tree is full of Howlers," she said. "What if you hit one of them at the same time?"

There were a few seconds of silence before Evan spoke again. "Then we'd have meat for dinner."

She looked at him sharply. His eyes were apologetic but determined. He had the look of a traitor.

"You're joking," she said.

"I hate the idea too, Shawn," said Evan. "But they're just sitting there. It's like they were put there for us."

She couldn't believe she was hearing these words from Evan. "I never realized you were that egocentric," she said.

Robin looked thoughtful. "I might be able to eat meat from a larger animal like that," she said. "More easily than I could eat a rat."

"If we were going to use the gun on monkeys, we could use it on other game as well," said David. He sounded delighted with the idea.

"There's plenty of ammunition," Meg joined in. "It does seem as though they're just sitting there for us."

Shawn stood up and looked Meg in the eye. "And the jaguar could be saying the same thing about *you*," she snapped. "*No guns*. You've only been hungry for one day, and you already want to start killing."

"As a last resort," Evan said calmly.

"We're far from needing a last resort," she said.

She turned away and began walking back to the clearing. She couldn't explain to them the grief she felt at the thought of gunning down an animal. Only Evan stood a chance of understanding, and he had already betrayed her.

• *Thirty-Two* •

HE DISCOVERED A flood of caterpillars under a log. Gooseflesh rose on the skin of his arms as he watched them squirm over one another. There were hundreds of them, fat, lime green, certainly enough for Shawn to make some sort of meal from. He hesitated. He could leave them here, say nothing about finding them. But that wouldn't be fair to the others. Just because he couldn't bring himself to eat bugs didn't give him the right to deprive everyone else.

And Meg needed food. She told him earlier that morning that the figs were passing right through her. Even if they were not, she wasn't certain of their exchange value in figuring the amount of insulin she should take. He saw in her eyes her fear of dying out here, and for the first time he realized it was a possibility. The rest of them could survive for a while without eating, but Meg needed food in a way they did not.

He scooped the caterpillars by the handful into his plastic bag. They filled it to the brim, a writhing green mass speckled with hundreds of black eyes. He headed back to the clearing, wondering if Shawn could do something with these repulsive creatures to disguise them. How would they taste? He was truly hungry to be thinking seriously about this. The figs he had eaten at breakfast had barely touched the gnawing pit in his stomach.

Those figs. He could see Shawn straddling that branch, the bark rough against the skin of her legs, the snake rearing up in front of her. A crudely sexual portrait that left him with mixed feelings of arousal, admiration, and fear, as well as that familiar helpless feeling as he watched Evan coax her down. David had stood paralyzed in a near panic, just as he had in the past anytime something challenged his nerves. He could hardly blame Shawn for turning to Evan when she needed someone to lean on.

He handed the caterpillars to Shawn when he reached the clearing and watched her cheeks flush. She held the bulging, living bag softly between her palms, and he fought a smile. He didn't want to give her that. Maybe that was the reason he'd been reluctant to bring the caterpillars in at all: He didn't want to give her anything. She was selfish. She'd taken enough for herself already.

"This one's no good," Evan said, rapping his knuckles against the trunk of a balsa tree. "Too full of sap."

The two men had walked a half-mile from the clearing, hunting balsa trees for a raft. They finally came across a grove of them. The trees were young and the right size, but Evan said that only the female trees would be buoyant enough. David wondered where he'd gotten this information, and how he would know a female from a male, but he didn't ask.

"Perfect." The tree Evan rapped on this time gave a hollow sound. "You work on this one with the saw; I'll find another and use the machete."

David obeyed without speaking. He had said very little to Evan over the last couple of days, and he hadn't spoken to him at all on the walk out here. He had plenty to say to him, but now was not the right time. Not when they needed to spend the rest of the afternoon working side by side.

Evan found a tree nearby and began working at its base with the machete while David sawed. The wood was soft, but the thin saw Tess left behind was dull and the work went slowly. In minutes David's shirt was soaked, and he peeled it from his body. Evan did the same, and in another minute they had both stripped to their shorts. Gnats landed on the damp skin of David's chest and arms, and ticks settled on his legs. He scratched at a few, but it was futile. He would have to pick them off later.

His tree fell first. He watched the branches twist and snap as they caught on the trees around them, watched the white, bell-shaped blossoms float to the ground. Then he moved on to the next tree. After a couple of hours, they had felled five trees and began cutting them into long logs. Evan said they needed ten, maybe twelve. When they were nearly finished, David rolled the logs next to each other while Evan continued cutting. The bark still needed to be stripped from the wood, but David could already see the raft taking shape in front of him.

He picked up the saw again and sat down on a log to work at the last cut. He was close to Evan now, so close he could see the thick ropy veins in Evan's arms as he worked the machete, the sweat at the tips of his black eyelashes. David was finally ready to say what he'd been wanting to say to Evan for days.

He slipped the saw into the wood and looked over at Evan.

"Is Shawn leaving me because of you?" he asked, casually, as if he were asking a question about the weather.

"What?" Evan looked up. *"No."*

He liked the look of terror in Evan's eyes.

"I know you were lovers after Heather died." David turned his attention back to the log, working the saw back and forth.

"Did she tell you that?" Evan set his machete across the top of the log he was straddling.

"No. I walked in on you one night, right after you got back from Peru. You were both asleep in your office." The saw was going through this piece of wood like a steak knife through butter. "I kept track after that. She'd lie to me, tell me she was going to meetings. I knew she was with you. *You* lied to me, too. Sometimes I'd ask you where you were Friday night, and you'd say you had a date with some new woman. But it was Shawn. You were screwing my wife."

"David . . ." Evan stood up.

"You know I felt *grateful* to you back then?" David looked up at Evan. "I thought you were helping her somehow, in a way I couldn't. And I loved her so much . . ." He heard his voice crack; he looked down at the logs. He wouldn't give Evan the satisfaction of seeing him break down. He took a deep breath. "I loved her so much and felt so shitty for what I'd done that I didn't care what it took to make her happy. I was a fool." He leaned back and fixed his eyes on Evan's. "You're still lovers, aren't you? You and Shawn?"

"No." Evan ran a hand through his hair. "I wish you'd told me back then that you knew. I wish you'd tried to stop it."

"Oh, I see. It was my fault."

"That's not what I'm saying. Look, you're right that we were lovers then, but not now. The truth is, I wish we were, but she doesn't want that. She doesn't want to hurt you more than she already has. And she doesn't want to hurt Robin."

He believed Evan. He felt a crazy rush of relief, but he was not through with his anger. "Our friendship must have meant nothing to you back then."

"That's not true," Evan said. "You two were all I had, remember? I wasn't proud of what I was doing. I carried this shitload of guilt around with me."

David laughed. "It must have been terrible for you. You have my deepest sympathy." He stood up and stretched, suddenly very tired. "We're done for today, right?"

Evan took a step toward him. "David, please. Let's talk this out."

"I've said all I want to say." David picked up his clothes and headed back to the clearing.

"It doesn't look good, so close your eyes while you eat it." Shawn set the pot on the table. It smelled vaguely like chili.

"I can't do it," said Robin. "I can't eat caterpillars."

"You'll never even know they're caterpillars," Shawn said.

David watched Meg bite her lower lip as Shawn ladled the thick green concoction into her bowl. He wondered what had happened to all the shiny black eyeballs.

Evan sat across from him. He looked drained; his face white above the beard. His hand shook as he lifted the spoon to his mouth. David's muscles shook as well, from the saw and hunger, from anger and release. He regretted nothing of his conversation with Evan. It was a relief. Bit by bit he was ridding himself of the pain and guilt of the last three years.

The chili powder couldn't mask the decaying fish flavor of the caterpillars. Each spoonful burst and expanded in David's mouth before slipping jellylike down his throat. He ate more than anyone. Shawn had worked hard on it. Evan and Meg made an appreciable dent in theirs, while Robin nibbled on a fig left over from Shawn's second journey into the tree. Shawn herself ate no more than a mouthful or two of the green chili before setting her spoon on the table.

Suddenly, Meg gagged. She covered her mouth with her hand, slid off the bench, and ran into the forest. David followed close behind, not to provide comfort but because he was going to be sick himself. Within a few minutes all of them, including Robin who had only watched them eat the gooey green mass, had emptied their stomachs in the woods.

They returned to the table, drawn but still hungry. Shawn looked terrible, her face white, eyes red. David reached across the table and surprised her with his touch on her hand.

"Someday we'll look back on this scene and laugh," he said.

"I wanted us to be able to live on insects."

Robin was crying. "What are we going to do for food? I don't think I can get down another fig."

"We have to use the gun," Meg said quietly.

Shawn shook her head. "We can get more figs, and we haven't even tried to catch fish yet. I'll work on it tomorrow."

* * *

David did the dishes alone and then went to Meg's tent. She had excused herself from the others after dinner, and he could see she was crumbling. He was afraid she would give up.

She was dressed the way she'd been the night he saw her with Tess, in that long blue shirt—buttoned this time—and bare legs. When he stepped into the tent, she was holding one hand in front of her, a drop of blood on the tip of her index finger.

"How are you?" he asked, sitting on her bed.

Her eyes were wet. "The batteries are dead in my meter. They were new, but I guess the heat or something . . ." She transferred the drop of blood from her fingertip to the plastic strip. "I'll have to use the color chart to read it." She showed him a chart on the back of the box of plastic strips. "I'm nearly out of strips too. Then I won't know what my blood sugar's doing. I'm already so confused about how much insulin to take. I thought the caterpillars would help, but I just couldn't . . ."

"Neither could I." He smiled and took her hand. Her fingers were the coldest thing in the jungle, and he set his other hand on top of them. "I'm going to tell Shawn why we have to use the gun. She'll understand."

"No, please don't tell her about me. She already hates me."

"No, she doesn't. She's not the hating type." He had never known Shawn to hate anyone, with the exception of himself.

"Let her try to catch some fish first. Fish would be fine."

"Are you sure you can wait?"

"Yes." She studied the numbers on her chart, shaking her head. "Eight units, I guess," she said, adjusting the syringe.

"Meg."

She looked up.

"Figure some exertion into that, okay?"

She frowned. "Why? I'm just going to bed . . . Oh." She smiled, blushed deeply. "I want to, David, but I . . ."

He moved in front of her and unbuttoned the top button of her shirt, then the next, and the next, while she sat perfectly still, one hand on her knee, the other holding the syringe. He heard her swallow, felt her breath against his cheek. When he had unbuttoned her shirt from top to bottom, he slid the back of his fingers across the skin above her waist.

"Which side do you want?"

"What?"

"For the insulin."

"Oh." She looked at the syringe in her hand as though she had no idea how it got there. "I forgot about it. Left, I guess."

He opened the left side of her shirt and watched the gold strands of her hair curve over her breast as she injected the insulin into the silky skin at her waist. She set the syringe back in its case, her hands trembling.

"Don't be nervous," he said. "We don't have to."

"I *want* to. I was going to ask you tonight if we could . . . but I *am* nervous." She pulled her shirt closed over her breast. "And if I survive this trip, I don't want to be pregnant."

He laughed. "I had a vasectomy years ago."

"Really?"

He nodded.

She touched his shoulder, tentatively. "You understand this won't change anything, don't you? I mean, I'll still be gay."

He shrugged. "You're the expert on that subject."

She raised herself to her knees in front of him. She took his face in her hands and very softly, very tenderly, kissed him. She leaned back, biting her lip. "I wish you were a woman," she said. "I wouldn't be such a nervous wreck."

"What can I do to make you less nervous?"

"Just put up with my . . . awkwardness, I guess."

He smiled. She was lovely. He pulled her to him and kissed her slowly as she unbuttoned his shirt. He asked her what she'd like. Gentleness was her only request, and he worried that his fingers were too hard and eager as he tugged her shirt from her shoulders, his mouth too hungry on her breasts. She grew shy when he slipped his hand between her legs, and he concentrated on slowing down. He knelt between her legs and looked down at her body, every inch of it golden in the light from the lantern. Her pillow was on fire with gold strands of her hair.

"You are exquisite," he said.

"And you are enormous," she laughed. "In my imagination, you were about half that size."

"It won't be a problem." He touched his fingers to her again and watched the shiver run through her body. How long had it been since he touched a woman so ready for him? He rolled onto his back and pulled her on top of him, and he saw the relief in her eyes. She needed to feel as though she had some control.

She lowered herself onto him as if he were made of delicate china. "Are you sure I'm not hurting you?" she asked.

He managed a laugh. "Trust me; it doesn't hurt a bit. How about you?"

But her eyes were shut in concentration, and she moved her body in time with his. She didn't need to answer.

* * *

It was eleven o'clock and David was still with Meg. Shawn lay in the dark, fingering the gold tamarin chain at her throat. They were supposed to be getting off the plane in San Diego right now. It was due to arrive at 8:05, California time. The boys were waiting for them at the airport with Lynn. She could picture them in the long hallway where people stood on tiptoe waiting for that first glimpse of someone they loved. And they would wait, Keith and Jamie and Lynn, and Lynn would be the first to wonder what was wrong. She would check the itinerary and see that it was the right plane. Perhaps she'd think they missed it, that they would be on the next plane from Miami. And she and the boys would wait, but Shawn and David wouldn't be on that one either. Then finally it would sink in. David and Shawn were missing.

David came into the tent at eleven-thirty, filling it with the odor of alcohol and Meg. He undressed quietly and collapsed into the bed. She felt the hair on his legs brush past her, felt his skin, hot and damp. She imagined Meg's body had left its mark on all of him.

She swallowed the lump forming in her throat. "We were supposed to arrive in San Diego a half-hour ago," she said.

He rolled onto his back and looked up at the roof of the tent. "I'd forgotten," he said. "I lost track of the days."

"Right now Keith and Jamie are wondering where we are."

He was quiet a moment; then he slipped his arm around her shoulders, and as if he'd touched a trigger in her, the tears came. She wept against his chest, so warm and familiar. He held her close to him with both arms and kissed the top of her head, and he kept her with him until she fell asleep.

She watched him in the morning, struggling to get Meg's note from his shoe. It was wedged into the toe. He read it and put it in his shirt pocket.

"Did she say you were good?" she asked. She couldn't help herself, yet there was no bitterness in her voice.

He turned to look at her, and in the pale light that passed through the netting she saw sympathy in his eyes. He knew how she felt. He knew all too well what it was like to imagine your lover in someone else's arms.

He cupped her hand with his own. "Meg's diabetic," he said. "She needs food to be able to use her insulin properly, and the figs aren't enough. If we don't catch any fish today, we have no choice but to use the gun."

• *Thirty-Three* •

THE BLADE OF his machete slipped neatly between the bark and the wood, and he worked it back and forth until the bark peeled smoothly from the log. There was pleasure in this work, despite the heat and his ever-present hunger, despite the tension that filled the air between him and Evan. He wondered if they would work together the entire day without speaking to each other. It was an idle curiosity, something to ponder as he slid his machete along the log; he didn't really care. The discomfort was Evan's now; it was David's no longer. He liked having things out in the open. Let everyone else grapple with them for a change.

He finished the log and stood back to look at it, satisfied. The bark lay empty and discarded, and the smooth white wood gleamed. He settled onto another, as Evan did the same behind him.

His arms shook as he worked the machete again. He had eaten two paltry figs for breakfast, and there would be no time to gather more this morning. He and Evan were stuck here in the balsa grove, Meg and Robin were foraging for the tamarins, and Shawn was trying to fish. He hoped she was successful, not just because he was hungry. He knew how she felt about using the gun. He would hate to see her have to give in to that.

She found turtle eggs this morning. She'd gotten up early and carved a fishhook from a piece of wood, and while the rest of them nibbled figs for breakfast, she went down to the stream. He saw the optimism in her gait as she walked away from them. She thought she would find a vine to use as line, a bug to use as bait. She came back within a few minutes and held out her hands to Meg. Four leathery eggs, the size of Ping-Pong balls, rested on her palms. His mouth watered at the sight of them.

"These are for you," she said to Meg.

He tried to read Meg's eyes. He'd persuaded her to tell all of them about her diabetes that morning, what it meant if she didn't eat. How must she feel, being offered food from the wife of the man she'd made love to the night before?

"Not just for me," she said.

"Yes," said Shawn, a familiar maternal firmness in her voice.

The relief in Meg's face was palpable. "I'm sorry, everyone," she said as she took the eggs from Shawn's hands.

Shawn. He hadn't meant to hurt her last night. He got it into his head that she was rock hard and unfeeling. He didn't think of her at all when he was with Meg. He hadn't felt married, hadn't felt a particle of guilt. Your thinking fell apart out here. You shaped your thoughts to suit yourself, to justify your actions. In the light of day he could not believe he had made love to another woman while his wife lay a few hundred yards away from him, weeping about his sons.

He *had* hurt her. No matter how much she wanted to end their marriage, she was not ready to see him with someone else. He wouldn't do it again.

He finished the second log, the wood on this one marbled with the sweat pouring steadily from his hair and face. He stood up, reaching for the canteen he'd hung on the knob of a tree, and felt a sudden sharp sting on his shoulder.

"Damn!" He swatted at his shoulder just as a spider scrambled down his arm and into the brush. Evan leaped to his feet and tried to follow the spider's path, but he was too late.

"What did it look like?" Evan asked.

David shrugged. "Black. Dark brown. I only got a glimpse."

Evan ran his fingers over the bite. It was already swollen. "You'd better take it easy. Maybe we should head back."

"I'm all right." He sat down on the third log and knew within minutes he was *not* all right. He couldn't bring the log into focus, and the floor of the jungle rose and fell around him in waves. He turned to look back at Evan, to tell him something was wrong, but Evan was already walking toward him.

"Can you walk?" he asked, his hand on David's elbow.

David stood up. He was cold. His teeth chattered. He veered to one side and Evan caught him. The burning wet skin of Evan's arm loomed in front of him, taking up his entire field of vision.

"*Jesus*, David." Evan's voice rang loudly in his ears. There was fear in it. David wanted to laugh, to tell Evan he was all right, but his tongue swam thickly in his mouth and no words came out. He managed a smile, though. He touched his lips with his fingers to be sure they curved upward.

"Lie down," Evan commanded.

David frowned. He wasn't certain what Evan was asking him to do. He stared hard at Evan's blue eyes, trying to remember what *down* meant. He leaned against Evan like a lover, his breathing hot and shallow. Then he felt himself floating to the ground, in slow motion. Evan's voice was miles away, saying something to him about trust and friendship.

Shawn and Evan carried David back to her tent. He was unconscious, a dead weight. Evan injected him with adrenaline, and his breathing gradually smoothed out.

She stayed with David while Evan took her place at the stream. She had caught nothing that morning. She'd attached the wooden hook to a vine that seemed flexible and strong. She baited it with a grasshopper and within minutes had a bite. But the hook snapped like a toothpick, and the fish swam away with a free meal. Maybe Evan would have better luck.

David's skin was ash dry and pale, except where the spider had left a round, red welt on his shoulder. She watched his chest rise and fall, too rapidly. She left her fingers on his wrist for minutes at a time, counting the beat of his heart. She covered him with the sheet and lay next to him, leaning on her elbow so she could watch him for any change.

She was afraid that he might stop breathing, that his pulse would vanish from beneath her fingers. She wished he would wake up. Once she thought he made a sound, and she set her ear close to his lips, holding her breath, listening, but the cicada's were all she could hear. She turned her head and gently set her lips against his. Warm. Soft. They felt forbidden to her.

Evan came in around three in the afternoon. "I caught a fish," he said. "Smallest in the stream, but we'll have dinner."

"What did you use for a hook?"

"I carved one out of bone."

"Where did you ever find a piece of bone?"

He said nothing and she knew.

"ChoCho?" she whispered.

"Bone was the only thing that would work."

She nodded. "Do you think he'll be all right?" she asked as Evan sat down at the foot of the bed.

"God, I hope so," Evan said. "He and I have some unfinished business. I wish you'd told me he knew about us."

"Did he tell you?"

Evan nodded. "Can you imagine what that was like for him, knowing all that time?"

She felt her eyes fill. "You were right, Evan, when you said I was still in love with him. I think I am."

Evan smiled at her, the smile of a man who was losing something he knew was never his to begin with. "Of course you are," he said.

She was bathing David with a washcloth in the light from the lantern when she heard footsteps on the trail.

"I have some fish for you." Meg stood outside the tent.

Shawn parted the netting to let her in. Meg knelt at the end of the bed and handed Shawn a bowl. In the bottom was a thin white piece of fish, two inches square. Shawn lifted it to her mouth with her fingers and ate it slowly, lovingly, eyes closed.

"Has there been any change?" Meg's eyes were on David.

Shawn shook her head. She wet the cloth with water from the canteen, wishing Meg would leave. She felt on display and unprotected. What had David told her? How much of their marriage had been exposed to this woman?

"He's rare," Meg said.

Shawn looked at her in surprise. Then she nodded, smiling to herself. Meg had known him two and a half weeks. She could have no idea how rare David was. She folded the washcloth and set it on his forehead, feeling the heat of his skin beneath her fingers.

"He told me about your daughter. About Heather."

She started at the sound of Heather's name. He didn't say it out loud to people he'd known for years. Not even to her.

"I'm sorry, Shawn. That must have been terrible for you."

"What did he tell you?"

"How she died. How much he loved her."

She was suddenly angry with David all over again. He exploited his daughter for his own gain. "He played on your emotions," she said.

Meg frowned. "I don't think so. I think he just needed to get it all out."

"Why didn't he get it all out to me then? He's had three years to do it."

"I'm sorry." Meg shrank. "I shouldn't have said anything."

Shawn was glad it was dark in the tent. She hoped Meg couldn't see the array of emotions in her face. "How did he say she died?" she asked quietly. She had to know what he told her.

She heard Meg take a breath, heard the reluctance in it. "He said she drowned. That it was his fault; he wasn't watching her so carefully as he should have."

Shawn shut her eyes. He'd told Meg the truth. She looked over at her. "How could you look him in the eye after he told you that? How could you make love to him?"

Meg's eyes flew open, so wide that Shawn could see the lantern light flicker in the pale irises, but she said nothing.

"I suppose the whole story was a great sympathy catcher." Shawn couldn't mask the acid in her voice.

Meg shook her head. "You are so unbelievably unforgiving."

Shawn threw the cloth into the corner of the tent. "Shut up, Meg!" she said. "It wasn't your daughter who died."

"No." Meg opened the netting, preparing for her retreat. "But she was David's daughter as well as yours. I think you've forgotten that."

She lay awake that night, listening to his breathing, striking bargains with God. *Let him live and I'll never think of Evan again.*

Meg was right. She had forgotten that Heather was David's child as well as hers. It was easier that way, far easier to feel anger than to feel his grief on top of her own, to feel that grief compounded by his guilt. Anger had been the easy way out.

His fever broke in the middle of the night, and he regained consciousness. She gave him sips of water from her hand. She slept very little, holding him close to her as he had held her the night before. He soaked the sleeping bag through with his sweat. He didn't speak, except once as he drew his knees up and moaned the word *bellyache* in her ear.

He was better in the morning, though weak, his muscles slack, his face pale. He was hungry, and he spoke to her in whispers. "Is there any food?" he asked. "Is Meg all right?"

She went to the clearing to see what she could find for him to eat. Evan was there alone. He handed her a few figs; then took her arm. "Listen, Shawn. Meg's not doing well, and David's going to need something more than figs and an occasional ounce of fish to get his strength back. We *all* need something more."

She knew he was telling her they had to use the gun, and she knew he was right. "A Howler?" she asked.

"They're right there. It would be the quickest way."

She pictured the cathedral in the morning light, the Howlers scattered in the branches of the fig tree. "They trust us now," she said quietly. "They don't even object when we take the figs."

"Don't make me feel worse about this than I already do."

* * *

She was cleaning the tamarins' cages when she heard the shot. It reverberated under the canopy, and for a moment the cicadas stopped, her own breathing stopped, and then all began again, joined by the mournful wailing of the Howlers.

She slipped some termites into one of the cages hanging from the tamarin tree. There was a second shot, and Shawn turned to look in the direction of the cathedral. Either he'd missed the first time or the shot hadn't been clean.

She was feeding the last tamarin when Evan returned to the clearing, carrying the rifle limply at his side.

"I won't ever do that again," he said, his cheeks red. "I swear I'll starve first."

She took the gun from him and leaned it carefully against the table.

"I left her down by the stream. I couldn't carry her any longer. She was like a big stuffed toy. All arms and . . . sweet eyes."

"I heard two shots."

He sat down at the table. "I aimed for her heart. I pulled the trigger and then I saw this look on her face . . . it was the same look you or I would have if someone we trusted hurt us." He looked down at his hands. He was twisting his wedding band around on his finger. "Tell me she was just an animal, Shawn."

"She was just an animal."

He sighed. "Then she fell to the ground and the other Howlers started calling, but even with all that noise I could hear her struggling for breath. *Rasping*." He squeezed his eyes shut. "I'm going to have nightmares about that sound. I'd gotten her in the lung. I walked over to her. She looked up at me, and I put the gun right to her heart and pulled the trigger again."

She winced. She had seen Evan hurt before; she had seen his tears often enough because he never thought to hide them. But this was different.

"I can't look at her again," he said.

"I'll take care of it."

She saw his relief. "I'm sorry," he said.

"Robin's in the tent. Why don't you lie down for a while?"

He shook his head. "I want to be alone."

He reached into his pocket and drew out the brown carved rosary beads and her heart snapped.

"You did what you had to do, Evan." She kissed his cheek. "I love you."

The Howler was smaller than she imagined. Harmless. Defenseless. Her huge brown eyes were still open, glazed over. Shawn forced the lids shut with her fingertips. She envied Evan his rosary and his faith. He had a means for getting comfort that was closed to her.

She didn't know how to butcher an animal for meat. She followed logic, removing the entrails and cleaning the cavity with water from the stream. She saved the liver and kidneys but buried the other organs. She buried the head as well, although she had intended to save all of her. If you killed an animal for your use, it was wrong to waste any of it. But she couldn't even look at the head, with its human features. She cut it from the body with her eyes half-closed.

She found a single fetus inside, a whimsical, fragile little thing. She added it to the hole in the earth. She wouldn't tell Evan about that.

She skinned the Howler and cut it into pieces in an attempt to make it unrecognizable as a monkey. She piled it all into a large white plastic bag and stood up, satisfied with what she'd done. Then she stripped down to her underwear and added her bloodstained clothes to the hole before filling it in with dirt.

There was soup by late afternoon. The broth was thin, but full of stringy pieces of meat. She propped David up with their duffel bags and fed him. He ate hungrily, and by the end of his second bowlful, he could hold the spoon himself without spilling.

"Thank Evan for me," he said. "This couldn't have been easy for him."

Evan had been the only one not to eat. She took him aside, tried to tell him that unless they used the Howler for their nourishment and survival, her death would be wasted.

"Not yet," he said. "I can't do it yet."

A light drizzle started after dinner, and she decided not to return to the clearing. She was exhausted—she'd had so little sleep the night before. She settled into the bed, her arm across David's stomach. She hadn't slept in that position in years.

Just before she fell asleep, the Howlers started their evening calls and she pulled herself closer to David. Perhaps it was just the rain, but she thought their voices sounded thinner, more distant, reduced by one.

The next day was clear, but the rain left everything damp, and a bright green fungus sprouted everywhere. One side of their tent was covered by it; it coated the rims of their shoes.

Evan spent the morning dragging the logs from the balsa grove to the clearing so David could work on them. David wasn't strong enough to walk that far into the woods yet, but he could strip the bark from them in the clearing.

Meg was weak and shaky. She spent most of the day sitting at the table, fashioning fishhooks from the Howler's skeleton, talking with David. Shawn foraged for insects, and each time she passed through the clearing she tried to listen to Meg and David's conversation. Their words were soft, muted. The bantering over the opera was gone. Sometimes they didn't speak at all, and on one occasion Meg was asleep, her head resting on her arms on top of the table. Shawn felt disturbed by her stillness. She sat down on the log David was stripping.

"Is there anything we should do for her?" she asked.

David shook his head. "She's not certain if her diabetes is out of control or if she's just worn out. I think the only thing we can do is make sure she has enough to eat."

She lay next to him in bed that night, her arm once again across his stomach. "Maybe I can make a net out of vines," she said. "We might be able to catch the fish in the bathing pool."

David wasn't listening. "Do you remember the night we went creek-drifting?" he asked. "Didn't Tess say something about another group of researchers out here?"

"The ornithologists!" Shawn sprang up. "They probably have a radio we could use to call for help."

"It was a couple of miles upstream, wasn't it?"

"There were boulders in the stream. I remember. I can go."

He shook his head. "No. Let me. In the morning."

She didn't want him to go alone. He was still too weak.

"I'll take Evan with me," he said. "You stay here and work on a net. Just in case we can't find them."

She lay down again. They were quiet for a few minutes while she steeled herself for what she wanted to say next.

"Meg said you told her about Heather," she said finally. She sounded casual, she thought, ridiculously so.

"Yes."

"Would you tell me?"

"What do you want to know?"

"Everything."

He sat up and moved to the other side of the bed. She felt alone. The arm she'd had across his stomach lay limp on the sleeping bag. The light from the lantern cast eerie shadows across his face, and she saw the uneasiness in his eyes.

"I felt as though Heather was more my child than yours," he said.

She was stunned. She felt the anger again, the anger she had nursed over the past three years. "I gave birth to her alone, David," she said. "I don't see how you can say that."

"I know." He reached over and touched her cheek lightly with the side of one finger; then set his hand in his lap. "I know you were alone. But you started work right away, and then she was mine. I had her practically to myself for the first couple of months. I'm the one who fed her and changed her and rocked her to sleep."

She'd forgotten. She'd forgotten how she depended on him during those months in San Diego before he got a job. When he finally did start working, Heather was his first stop in the house in the evening. She'd forgotten how Heather lit up when she saw him; how she could never fall asleep until David sang to her in her room.

"She was needier than the boys," David continued. "And certainly needier than you. And I enjoyed that, taking care of her. Ultimately, I guess I did a shitty job of it."

He told her about the day Heather died, and for the first time she saw that day unfold from David's perspective. She stiffened in panic when he spoke of realizing Heather was missing; her eyes welled up as he described his anguish over hitting Keith.

"I couldn't wait for you to get back," he said. "I thought somehow you could make things better, make me feel better. But of course you couldn't."

"I made things harder for you."

"I thought I deserved it. I wanted to be punished."

"I went overboard, though."

His hand gripped her wrist. "You shut me out, Shawn."

"I couldn't see what you were going through."

"You never *tried*."

"I know. I'm sorry." She sat up, hugging her knees to her chest. "David, I don't want a divorce."

He laughed. "Is that supposed to be my reward for spilling my guts here? I did a good job of it, so no divorce?"

She was frightened by his bitterness. "No, I'd already decided I was making a mistake. I know we have problems. But I want to try to work them out."

"What brought on this change of heart?"

She shrugged uncomfortably. She missed the relationship they used to have, when she didn't have to speak to him so cautiously, when she was safe in anything she said. "I realized when you were sick that I still love you. I got scared. I thought you might die. I don't want to be without you.''

''But I'm no longer certain I want to be with *you*.''

''Oh.'' She pressed her hands together in her lap until they hurt. ''Meg?'' she asked.

He shrugged. ''I don't know. I don't know if there's a future with Meg. I'm not even sure that's what I want. The point is she's made me feel as though I've got some worth as a human being. For three years I've felt like a criminal. You avoided me, you looked repulsed if I wanted sex, all the while you were making love to someone else . . .''

''Not all the while,'' she said weakly.

''. . . You've made me feel like some kind of monster for what happened to Heather. And I put up with it because you convinced me that I deserved it. But I don't.''

''No,'' she said. ''You don't.''

He leaned forward and dug his fingers into her wrist. ''God, it makes me furious to hear you say that! Look what you put me through.''

''I'm so sorry, David. I wish I could turn back the clock.''

''Well, I don't. The last thing I want is to relive the past three years. I want a new start on my life.''

''David, please . . . I want to be in it.''

''You're a constant reminder to me of something I want to forget. I look at you now and I feel guilt and anger and distrust. Don't you see that I can't let myself love you again? I don't even trust you *now*. You might mean what you're saying right this minute, but I think as soon as we get out of this jungle, as soon as we get back in that house with memories of Heather all over it, you'll remember whatever it was you found so despicable about me. And there I'll be, loving you again, and you'll turn around and spit in my face.'' He had moved to the door of the tent. He unzipped the netting and reached for his shoes.

''David, no.'' She grabbed his arm. ''Please don't go. Please don't leave me here alone again tonight.''

But he was gone. The darkness swallowed all of him except for the beam from his flashlight, and she watched until it too disappeared into the forest. Then she followed him in her imagination. She saw him reach the clearing, make a right onto the trail that led to Meg's tent. And there he would turn out the flashlight and rest for the night, with the woman who made him feel safe in the darkness.

• *Thirty-Four* •

DAVID COULDN'T SLEEP. He lay in the curved, splintery bottom of the yellow canoe where it rested on the bank of the stream, breathing the acrid smoke from the mosquito repellent coils he'd lit on the ground. He stared at the dark canopy above him and thought of the two tents he was welcome in, knowing he could go to neither. He would feel guilty turning to Meg, using her for his comfort tonight. And Shawn. He rolled onto his side and winced as a splinter slid into his thigh. He was too vulnerable with Shawn. He meant every word he said to her, but already his anger was fading and there was nothing he wanted more than to crawl back into that tent and spend the rest of the night in her arms. He couldn't do that though, not until he was sure of her.

He went to Evan's tent before the sun was up and told him about his plan to look for the ornithologists. Evan was excited. He was dressed by the time David finished talking.

It felt good to be out on the stream, good to be moving. He was in the stern; Evan, in the bow. The current was not strong, but as he pulled the oar through the water, he knew he could not have managed this trip alone.

"Today's my mother's birthday," Evan said after a while.

"Sorry, Evan. I know you wanted to be there."

Evan shrugged. "She won't know the difference. But I will. She doesn't have anyone else. The staff at the nursing home will treat it like any other day. They don't care."

David studied Evan's back, indistinct in the misty half-light, and felt a softness toward him, an inability to stay angry with him. "You know," he said, "you are one of the most generous, good-hearted people I know. How could you do it?"

Evan dug the oar into the inky water a few times before answering. "I asked myself that question plenty of times," he said quietly. "The answer I always came up with was that I was in love with her."

"Are you still?"

"I think I always will be." He turned to look at David. "What am I supposed to do? Move away? Find a new partner? I've thought of the options, believe me. I don't like any of them."

David nodded and suddenly it was very clear to him. The solution lay in his marriage to Shawn, Evan's marriage to Robin. The stronger those relationships were, the less need Evan and Shawn would have for each other.

He opened his mouth to tell Evan his thoughts, but then he spotted the boulders, huge and gray, jutting from the stream into the early morning fog. They were familiar, although it seemed like months rather than two weeks since he'd last seen them.

They banked the canoe at the side of the stream. The brush was flattened as though a large dugout, or a couple of them, had been pulled up and down this bank many times. But there was no sign of a boat now.

Tess said the group was inland about a mile. David and Evan found a wide trail cut into the forest and set out to follow it. Neither of them spoke, saving their words and their energy for the meeting they hoped lay ahead of them.

They were soaked with sweat by the time they reached the ornithologists' clearing. It was deserted. The firepit was cold; green fungus coated the long sapling table.

"How long ago do you think they left?" David asked. He sat down on a bench by the table. His muscles felt heavy.

Evan poked a stick into the firepit. "Days," he said in a tired voice. "Maybe a week." He dropped the stick and sat down next to David. He scraped some of the slimy green fungus from the tabletop onto the back of his thumbnail and held it up in front of him. "I wonder how this stuff tastes," he mused.

"I'd rather eat caterpillars."

Evan sighed and leaned back from the table to look at him. "It doesn't matter how I feel about Shawn, David," he said. "It's you she wants, not me."

Shawn found a note from David in her shoe. It was just one line, a few words to let her know that he and Evan were on their way to the ornithologists' camp. She dressed slowly and walked to the clearing where Robin greeted her with a bag of insects.

"You collected these by yourself?" Shawn asked, astounded.

"I'm getting good at it." Robin shrugged. "Too bad there's no market back home for this skill."

Shawn carried the bag to the tamarin tree and started feeding the Elves. She was about to open the cage door of the breeding pair when she noticed the female was grooming the male, running her fingers through his fur, her dark little eyes full of concentration. The male basked in the attention.

You were smart, Shawn thought as she set a few beetles in front of the female. *You didn't wait until it was too late.*

"Is David still in the tent?" It was Meg's voice. Shawn turned to see her rush into the clearing.

"No," she answered, annoyed. "Didn't you get enough of him last night?"

Meg frowned. "What do you mean?"

Shawn turned back to the Elves without answering.

"Where is he?" Meg asked.

"With Evan. They've gone upstream to look for the ornithologists Tess told us about."

"Is his camera case still in your tent?" Meg asked.

Shawn shook her head. "He took it with him."

"Oh *no*." Meg pressed her hands to the sides of her head. "He's got *my* case. They must have gotten mixed up yesterday."

Shawn looked at her. The skin of her face was as gray as the morning mist. "Are you sick?" she asked.

"I took too much insulin this morning. I barely took any, but it was still too much. I need the glucose tablets in my camera case. I looked for them and found David's camera instead."

"Can you wait a few hours?"

Meg shook her head and sat down on the bench by the table. Her hands trembled as she smoothed her hair from her damp cheek, and Shawn couldn't help but feel compassion for her. She wished Meg were easier to dislike.

Shawn opened the cage of the last tamarin, trying to sort out her options. What should she do? How long would David and Evan stay at the ornithologists' camp before coming back? She pictured them receiving a warm welcome, taking in a hearty meal, using the radio. It could be a long time before they returned.

Meg suddenly stood up. Shawn followed her gaze to a fig on the ground. It must have fallen from one of the cages. It was half-eaten, dusty and crawling with maggots. Meg fell on it and raised it to her mouth.

Shawn dove for her and pulled the fig from her hand. "You can't eat *that*."

"Please, Shawn, I need it."

The maggots squirmed onto Shawn's fingers and she tossed the fig into the woods.

"Shawn!" Robin pointed to the cage. Shawn had left the door open in her rush to get to Meg, and now the Elf scampered onto a branch of the tree. Shawn stood up and tried to grab it, but the Elf bit her, as viciously as an animal that tiny could bite, plunging its teeth into the flesh between her thumb and fingers. She held her hand to her chest while the little Elf taunted her from the tree. She looked back at Meg who sat glassy-eyed on the ground, dust around her mouth from the fig.

Shawn set the bag of insects on the table and turned to Robin. "I'm going to try to find David and Evan," she said. "I want you to get some figs for Meg."

Robin stared at her. "Shawn, I can't . . ."

"You don't have to climb. Take a stick and try to knock some down." She looked at Meg. "Figs would help, wouldn't they?"

Meg looked up at her. "I think . . . yes."

Shawn grabbed Robin's arm and started for the trail. She left Robin at the entrance to the cathedral and continued running next to the stream. She would have to cross it at some point, but once she crossed there would be no trail to follow and that would slow her down. She waited until she reached the fork in the stream and then jumped into the water. She walked across, the water to her chin, her bleeding hand held high above her head.

The brush was thick next to the stream on the other side, too thick to get through even with her machete, and she had to move inland a bit. She climbed over fallen trees and skirted clumps of razor grass. She tried to keep her mind off the tamarin she had surely lost that morning. Evan would be angry. But what choice did she have? She could hardly leave Meg to die while she chased a monkey.

She saw the boulders rising from the stream and spotted the canoe pulled up on the bank. She turned to follow the trail, not certain she could make it another mile. She slowed to a walk, panting, her lungs balking at the thick jungle air.

A few yards into the forest, she heard voices.

"David?" she called.

David and Evan appeared around a bend in the trail. David stared at her, openmouthed.

"What are you doing here?" Evan asked.

"Meg is sick and . . ." she had to catch her breath before she could finish the sentence, ". . . you have her camera case, David, with the glucose in it."

David unzipped his case and looked inside. He ran for the canoe, and she and Evan followed. She sat between them in the boat, head on her knees, trying to get her breath back.

The men paddled feverishly with the current, and the canoe slipped quickly downstream. She raised her head. "Did you find the ornithologists?" she asked, cradling her hand in her lap. The blood was drying. She wouldn't tell Evan about the tamarin yet.

"They're gone," David said from behind her. "What's wrong with your hand?"

"Tamarin bite." Shawn put her head back on her knees. *The ornithologists were gone.* Would they ever get out of here?

Meg was unconscious when they reached the clearing. She lay on the ground next to the table. Robin sat on the bench above her, two bruised purple figs in her hand. "She was lying here when I got back with the figs," she said.

David dropped to the ground next to Meg and opened the camera case again.

"She can't take glucose if she's unconscious," said Evan.

"There's a syringe in here," David said. He found it, tore off the paper wrapping, and injected the liquid it contained into a vial filled with powder, then drew the mixture back into the syringe. He seemed to know what he was doing. Shawn thought of taking the syringe from him. She'd given hundreds of injections to animals; it would be easier for her. But she held back. He needed to do this himself. She watched his careful eyes, his hands that shook ever so slightly as he lifted Meg's shirt and smoothed his fingers across the skin above her stomach, searching for the right spot. Shawn turned away. She couldn't watch him touch Meg, not that way, not with that familiarity and concern.

It seemed like a long time before Meg's eyes opened and she began to stir. When she was alert enough to talk with them, David carried her back to her tent. Shawn watched him walk down the trail until the green curtain of leaves closed behind him.

Evan sat down next to her at the table and lifted her hand. "Nasty," he said, looking at the bite.

"It's nothing." She wanted to cry, wanted to lie on the ground and pound the earth with her fists. But she didn't have the luxury of time. "One of the females is gone," she said.

Evan looked over at the tamarin tree. The muscles tightened in his cheeks.

"I'm sorry," she said. "I was feeding her and Meg started acting crazy and . . . we'd better go look for her." She started to her feet, but Evan held her down by the shoulder.

"Robin and I will go," he said. "You've done enough. Put some alcohol on that hand and take it easy."

She looked up at him without argument. She was hungry; her body shook with exhaustion.

After Evan and Robin left, she wrapped a bandage around her hand and walked slowly to the pool. The muscles in her calves contracted into painful knots with each step. She undressed and lowered her body into the water, careful to keep her bandaged hand dry. She toweled herself off, dressed again, and sat on a rock, staring into the dark water. She had no strength to go back. What was there to go back to? Her empty tent, the empty clearing. She pictured Meg's tent, pictured David comforting Meg, taking care of her.

She remembered a spring day near the end of her junior year in college. She was studying with David at his apartment, but he was having trouble concentrating. The championship swim meet was the next day, and his coach called him every hour, telling him to stretch, to eat, to sleep, to relax. The team was relying on him, the coach said, his peak performance was critical.

David worked at his desk while she studied on his bed. As the afternoon wore on, she watched his shoulders hunch up and his fingers tighten into a claw around his pencil.

Finally she closed her biology book. "Lie down, David." She patted the bed next to her. "Let me rub your back."

He needed no encouragement. He took off his shirt and lay down on his stomach. His muscles were rigid under her fingers as she kneaded his shoulders. He had nearly fallen asleep beneath her hands when the phone rang again. He jumped.

"Let it ring," she said.

"Can't," he said as he reached for the phone.

It was his mother. His father had fallen down the back steps, she said. The ambulance just took him to the hospital.

Shawn watched from the bed while David stuffed clothes into a suitcase. Then he called his coach. She hugged her knees as she listened to David's terse side of the conversation. "No . . . sorry . . . there's no way." His voice was calm, but his fingers anxiously worked the cord to the phone. He hung up, kissed her distractedly on the forehead, and asked her to lock the apartment when she left. She knew better than to try to talk him out of going. She understood his priorities.

He called her the next day to report that his father's hip was broken and to ask her to go to the meet so she could tell him how his team fared. She went to the meet and watched his team lose by a few points. The worst possible outcome.

Afterward, she took Jude out to dinner. He seemed pleasantly surprised by the invitation; it had been a while.

"They would have won if David had been there," she said, nervously playing with her spaghetti. She was putting off telling Jude the real reason for this date.

Jude narrowed his eyes at her. "Do you really care about a swim team winning or losing? Has that honestly become important to you?"

She shrugged and looked down at her plate. Yes, it was important to her because it was important to David.

"Why are you so uptight tonight?" he asked. "You haven't looked me straight in the eye since we sat down."

She looked at him now. His eyes were nickel-colored. Cold. His hair hung Christlike around his shoulders. But he was not God, only Jude Mandell. She felt her courage rise. She pushed her plate away from her and took a deep breath.

"I don't want to see you anymore," she said.

Jude's face registered a flash of surprise. Then he took a swallow of wine and shrugged. "Hey, whatever you want. Have I ever tried to run your life? Just please tell me it's not because of Ryder."

"It *is* because of David." She thought of David, at the hospital with his father when he should be with his team. "He's a caring person. I can't hurt him any more."

"A caring person on a small scale," said Jude. "He can be sweet as honey to you, woman, but what good will it do you if you're living in a country at war?"

"Jude." She shook her head with a smile. "I know how important your work is. But it's not enough for me anymore."

"Tell me this," Jude continued. "If he cares about you so much, why hasn't he tried to stop you from seeing me?"

She didn't have to think through her answer. "He loves me enough to let me make my own decisions," she said.

* * *

Shawn started at the rustle of leaves behind her. She felt David's hand on her shoulder. He sat in front of her and pulled her against him, and she gritted her teeth to keep back tears.

"How is she?" she asked.

"All right for now."

"You saved her life."

He pulled away from her, looked into her eyes. "No, *you* did. She told me you lost one of the Elves in the process."

"I was clumsy."

"You were incredible." He took her bandaged hand and held it in his palm. She wanted to clutch his fingers, to make him work at getting free, but instead let her hand rest softly in his.

He stroked his thumb across the bandage. "Meg said you think I slept with her last night."

"Didn't you?"

He shook his head. "That wasn't what I wanted. I wanted to be with you, but I was afraid that you'd wake up this morning and wonder what the hell you were doing with me."

"David . . ."

He bent his head to kiss her palm. She smelled the clean soap smell of his hair as the top of his head brushed through the valley between her breasts.

"Where did you sleep last night?" she whispered.

"The little canoe." He smiled. "I have the splinters to prove it." His eyes were soft and loving. Somehow that love had stayed alive in him despite all she'd done to kill it.

He kissed her, tentatively at first, then more surely as he discovered he was welcome. His tongue was warm against hers. He undressed her slowly, making a pillow for her head from her shirt and shorts. The rock was warm beneath her, and she felt the texture of his clothes against her skin—his belt buckle cool on her stomach, the fabric of his shirt soft on her breasts.

He gently touched her cheek. "I love you," he said.

She felt a sliver of ice pass through her. He must have sensed it. He held his breath above her, waiting to see if he had stumbled into quicksand and was about to be pulled under by her once again. *I love you too, David.* She wished she could get those words out, but she couldn't. Not yet.

She slipped her hands between them until they cupped the buckle to his belt. "Let me see those splinters now," she said.

David caught her hand and sat up suddenly. "Listen!" he said, looking up at the canopy.

She heard it too. The thrumming whir of a helicopter was

directly above them. The trees blocked their view, but the leaves of the canopy danced furiously, like whitecaps in a rough green sea.

"Hey!" David yelled. He jumped up and waved his arms, although he couldn't possibly be seen, while Shawn hurriedly pulled on her clothes.

They met Evan and Robin in the clearing and sat with them at the table, eyes focused on the canopy. They could still hear the beautiful purr of the helicopter. And then it stopped. Shawn looked at David. He reached across the table to take her hand.

They waited, listening. No one spoke.

"It's hell trying to park a helicopter around here!"

They turned at the sound of Charlie's voice. She'd slipped into the clearing from the west, looking beautiful and familiar with her crazy black hair and homespun smile. "I'm so glad to see you're all right," she said as she hugged each of them. Then she turned around in a circle, searching the clearing with her eyes. "Where's Meg?"

"We need to get her to a hospital," David said. He told Charlie about Meg's diabetes.

"You lost your *food*?" Charlie asked. "Tess will die when she hears that. She's so worried about all of you." She told them Tess was in a hospital in Iquitos. She'd wrecked the dugout in some rocks the night she left and broke her leg. "A terrible break," Charlie shuddered. "Three places. But she managed to fix the canoe—though the engine was demolished—and yesterday she floated up to the side door of my boat."

The helicopter pilot was waiting, Charlie said, but the helicopter could hold all five of them only if they were willing to leave their gear and the tamarins behind. Shawn and Evan shook their heads.

"The gear, yes," said Evan. "The tamarins, no."

"A couple of you could stay behind and we'll come back for you tomorrow," Charlie suggested.

Evan looked at Shawn, eyebrow raised. She felt David's hand touch the back of her neck.

"David and I can stay one more night," she said.

Evan and David carried Meg on a litter made from her tent, while the rest of them carried the Elves. The helicopter sat like a beached white whale in a circle of trees. Shawn looked up. The break in the canopy seemed hardly big enough for the helicopter to fit through.

Meg asked the men to stop before they reached the helicopter so she could take a picture of it. She sat up on the litter, her hair falling over David's arm. She snapped the shutter and then lay back again, closing her eyes, looking as though that small effort had exhausted her.

Evan left a trap behind in case Shawn found the missing tamarin, but she knew she wouldn't look for it. The pilot gave David his fishing tackle, along with a beautiful overripe mango.

They watched the helicopter lift into the trees and disappear behind the canopy. David turned her toward him and kissed her, holding the cool skin of the mango against the side of her throat. "Let's go to the tent," he said.

Shawn shook her head. "The cathedral."

They stopped by the tent to pick up their sleeping bag, then walked slowly along the trail to the cathedral. Shawn was tempted to rush; her body still burned with anticipation from an hour earlier. She forced herself to stand calmly outside the entrance to the cathedral as they pulled the mango apart with their fingers and ate the sticky, spicy orange flesh inside.

"This is only an appetizer," David said.

They slipped through the brush into the cathedral. The Howlers set up a slow-paced, gentle roar as David spread the sleeping bag on the ground under the fig tree. He sat down, but Shawn stood a moment longer, watching the Howlers, listening to them. There was no malice in their song; they bore no grudge. Their voices echoed softly, tempered with forgiveness.

David ran his hand up her calf. "Sit down, Shawn," he said.

She took one last look at the Howlers and then lowered herself to the sleeping bag. It was time to do some forgiving of her own.

• Thirty-Five •

DAVID TURNED THE Jeep off Blue Snake Road and drove through the open Conservation Center gates. They didn't need a code card tonight. Shawn saw a car on the curved road ahead of them, another behind them. There would probably be a few hundred people here. It was the bimonthly buffet dinner for the members of the Conservation Center. "Armchair naturalists," David called them, people who wanted to hear more about Shawn and Evan's mission in Peru.

Jamie and Keith sat stiffly in the backseat of the car, dressed in summer suits bought in June and nearly outgrown already. They didn't want to come tonight, but they'd been easy to persuade. They no longer seemed so argumentative, no longer sour and irritable. Shawn wasn't certain if that was the result of the scare they had, thinking Shawn and David might be gone forever, or if they were reacting to having two parents who liked one another again. They didn't seem to know what to make of Shawn and David these days. The first time David kissed her in front of them—just a quick, warming kiss in the kitchen—they blushed and nearly fell over each other trying to back out of the room.

"They haven't seen any affection between us since they were ten," David said. "They thought we were dried-out adults. It's going to take them a while to adjust."

It took Shawn a while to adjust as well. The house depressed her, as David had predicted. The memories were everywhere, not so much of Heather, but of the anger she'd felt toward David. She'd despised him from the rocking chair in the living room, she'd plotted to divorce him over the sink in the kitchen. But it was the king-size bed that held the worst memories for her. How many nights had she cried in that bed while David ignored her tears?

But that was the past. David didn't let her nurture those old feelings, and she no longer wanted to. They courted each other again. They went sailing and water-skiing, and at night they sat in the hot tub and talked. Shawn watched the wall that had stood for so long between them crumble under the touch of their words.

The morning of August twenty-sixth, the third anniversary of Heather's death, she went up in the plane with David. When his report was over, they stayed in the air, talking about Heather, gently chiding themselves for falling away from each other when they needed each other the most.

After work that evening, she met David at a furniture store where they bought a double bed. They carted it home, set it up in their bedroom, and stood back to look at it. Shawn smiled and put her arm around David's waist. The bed was perfect, no bigger than the air mattress in their tent. The king-size bed had become too vast a plain.

That night, her first in the new bed, she had a canopy dream. She flew under the lacework of green leaves, her body light as mist. She still felt airborne the next morning as she made waffles for breakfast.

"You don't need to go up with me this morning." David smiled while she poured the batter into the waffle iron. "I can tell you spent most of the night flying."

After he left for work she tied the old *I LOVE YOU* sign to her roof rack again. She drove to the Center, listening to his traffic report, hands tense on the steering wheel.

"I'm over by Poway road," he said, "and it looks like we've got an accident in the number three lane of . . ." and then he spotted it. She heard the break in his concentration. "Oh, damn, Shawn," he said, "I love you, too."

"Look at the cars," David said now as they turned around a curve in the road, and a string of red tail lights stretched out in front of them. "You're going to have a full house tonight."

Shawn could recall only one other time the road to the Center had been this congested. The zoological awards dinner, years ago. "Do you remember that awards dinner when Heather announced to the audience and the TV cameras that she had to go potty?" she asked.

David laughed, and reached for her hand. There was silence in the backseat, as though the boys had disappeared. They didn't know what to make of Shawn mentioning Heather, of David laughing in response.

David looked in the rearview mirror. "I guess you guys are too young to remember that," he said.

"We remember," said Keith. "It was embarrassing."

"She embarrassed us all the time," said Jamie. "She was always doing stupid things in front of our friends."

David pulled into the parking lot and parked the Jeep in Shawn's spot, next to Evan's car. There was silence again from the backseat. She pictured the boys looking at each other, biting their lips, worried they had gone too far.

"Like the time she told Kevin's sister her front teeth made her look like a beaver?" Shawn encouraged them.

Keith laughed. "It wouldn't have been so bad only she wouldn't shut up about it. Everytime somebody new came over she'd say 'Don't you think Patty looks like a beaver?' in that little voice she had."

"No, she stuttered sometimes, remember? Like this." Jamie raised his voice an octave. " 'D-don't you think Patty looks like a b-beaver?' "

He did a passable imitation. David squeezed her hand.

"She would be seven now," said Jamie.

"Did you just figure that out?" Shawn asked, surprised.

"No. We talk about her sometimes," Jamie said as though admitting to a guilty little secret.

Evan appeared at her window. "Aren't you folks coming in?"

They climbed out of the Jeep, and Shawn watched Evan walk ahead of them with her sons, an arm around each of them. She heard Keith ask him: "Do you remember that time Heather said she had to pee on television?"

Tess wouldn't be here tonight. She had to wear a toe-to-hip cast for another few months, and flying was a chore for her. But Meg was here, setting up her projector. For a second Shawn didn't recognize her. Her hair was up in a French braid, all the different shades of blond twisting and merging at the back of her head. She wore a white knit dress that sloped over her breasts and clung to her hips in a way that made her look both sensual and sweet. She smiled when they walked into the little auditorium. Obviously she had been watching the door for David. He hugged her; then held her at arm's length.

"It's so good to see you," he said.

"I've missed you," said Meg. "I have no one to sing duets with." She turned to Shawn and took her hand. "It seems like a year ago instead of a month, doesn't it?"

"You look wonderful, Meg," she said. She knew David had spoken to Meg a few times by phone. He reported that her diabetes was once again under control, and added with a smile that she thought she was in love with a flight attendant she met on her flight back to San Francisco.

"Female?" Shawn asked.

"Of course."

"I can't understand it," she said. "I'd think that having you as a lover would be enough to make any woman go straight."

They sat together—Shawn, David, the twins, Meg, Evan, and Robin—at a table near the front of the crowded auditorium. The Center was serving Peruvian food—ceviche, grilled fish, rice, and beans.

"Is this what they think we ate down there?" David asked.

"Shawn and I suggested they serve caterpillars, but the idea didn't go over too well," said Evan. He fed Robin a piece of fish from his fork. Shawn knew he was worried about the toll the weeks in the jungle might have taken on the baby she carried.

Meg showed her slides after dinner. The projector was in the back of the room, but she sat up front, next to David, the remote control in her hand and a microphone attached to the neckline of her white dress. Evan and Shawn wore microphones as well, but as the slides slipped onto the screen one by one in the darkness, there was very little to say.

There were a few pictures that required clarification—Shawn stitching the wound on Evan's arm, Tess readying the dugout for creek-drifting—but words would only get in the way of Meg's portraits of tamarins in the mist, the cathedral pierced with slivers of early morning sunlight, a single toucan in a fog-shrouded tree. The forest looked different through Meg's lens, possibly benevolent, possibly not, mist-filled and holding secrets.

The audience was hushed throughout most of the show, uttering an occasional gasp at the beauty on the screen. But finally Meg came to the slide of the helicopter waiting for them.

"I was sick and we were all hungry and more than ready to get out of there," she said. "But it could only fit three of us and the tamarins. So Shawn and David volunteered to stay behind and wait for the helicopter to return the next day."

She showed her final slide, a picture taken from inside the helicopter. David and Shawn stood together against the green backdrop of the forest. They were not waving good-bye, just standing, waiting. Shawn remembered wanting the helicopter to disappear so that she and David could be alone.

But the audience murmured words of admiration and sympathy, and she realized with a smile that they thought she and David had made a great sacrifice. An easy mistake to make. It was impossible to tell from the picture whether this couple was ending an adventure or just beginning one.

They said good-bye to the others in the parking lot. David told Meg to keep in touch while Evan hugged Shawn and whispered in her ear that he would still want her when he was sixty. She got into the Jeep and let her head rest against the back of the seat.

"They were great pictures," said Jamie. His tone was so adult, so genteel, that she and David both turned around to look at him. He shrugged sheepishly. "I liked them."

"By the way," Keith said. "We're gonna stay up all night tonight."

"Oh, you are?" Shawn asked. She didn't miss the apprehension in his voice.

"Yeah, Mom," said Jamie. "See, MTV's having this all-night special and *everybody's* watching it. I mean, everybody's parents said it's okay."

"Interesting how you waited until the last minute to tell us about it." David looked over at Shawn. She shrugged. The boys would have all weekend to recuperate.

"Watch it from your sleeping bags in the family room," David said.

"All *right*."

David looked at Shawn again and smiled. "Maybe you and I should stay up all night too."

She knew what David had in mind, and it wasn't watching television. She kicked off her shoes, unbuckled her seat belt, and turned in her seat to put her feet in his lap. "Sounds good to me," she said as he circled her ankle with his hand.

She would be too excited to sleep tonight anyhow. Tomorrow they were going skydiving.